CW01502230

Chapter One

Eliana

I had to break every traffic law in the state, and I was still going to be late to dinner. Mom was going to kill me. I drifted into the driveway and ran out of my car almost forgetting to turn the engine off.

"Shit. Shit. Shit. Shit. Shit." I mumbled as I ran up the front steps. Frankie was waiting for me at the front door.

"You're late." He smiled, as he followed behind me.

I ignored his teasing and headed to the kitchen. I found Mom getting the dinner plates ready. Nora was in the kitchen looking for the wine glasses. Isabella and Thomas ran around the kitchen fighting with each other. From a stranger's perspective, all that could be seen was one big happy family, getting ready to enjoy each other's company. But to those that knew us, they saw the Mariani's all gathering for their obligatory Sunday supper.

Standing in the doorway of the kitchen I considered letting

Frankie shoot me in the arm like he always offers every time I show up to something late. I run the risk of Mom being upset about blood on her carpets, but then at least she wouldn't be complaining about my tardiness. I'd always declined his kind offer, but I'd missed the last two-family dinners and I knew Mom was mad. Ask anyone, there's nothing more terrifying than pissing off Milena Mariani. The only reason I survived her constant disapproval is because she is a woman of God. My mother was many things, but a Catholic first and foremost. Lucky for me the bible has my mother convinced her children are a gift and are always deserving of forgiveness.

"Isabella and Thomas, I swear to God if you break a dish because you were running around in here you'll be grounded for the rest of your life. Go find Uncle Raff and tell him dinner is ready." Nora yelled as her kids ran down the hallway.

As soon as Mom and Nora saw me they gave me the same disappointed glance. I hated how similar they were. The older Nora got and the more kids she had the more she turned into Mom.

"I know, I'm sorry. Traffic was bad." I lied.

"Sure." They both sighed at the same time.

"Take this to the table and find your father." Mom said, handing me a salad.

I set the bowl down and walked to Dad's office. On my way, I found Frankie.

"Be careful he's in a bad mood today."

"Why? What happened?"

"He lost a lot of money last weekend because of one of his clients down south, and now he has distributors trying to back out of contracts. Raff says he hasn't stopped working since

An Italian Mafia Series

Lilac and Honey

Ada Taylor

Lilac and Honey

ISBN: 9798840778227

Lilac and Honey

Dedication

To all the masochists that enjoy the slow burn

Lilac and Honey

CONTENTS

Lilac and Honey

ACKNOWLEDGMENTS

To Mallory, for always pretending to care about my crazy ideas for this book. Even when I called in the middle of the night you never failed to show excitement. Cheers.

Lilac and Honey

Monday."

"Great." I complained, knocking on Dad's door.

"Come in."

I slowly opened his office door and walked closer to his desk.

"It's time for dinner. Mom asked me to come get you."

He nodded his head not even bothering to look up at me. He waved his hand signaling me to leave. He didn't have to ask twice. Just when I thought I made it out of the office unscathed he called my name.

"Eliana, I need to talk with you after dinner. It's important. Do not leave without seeing me first."

He took my silence as a yes and went back to work. The last time Dad asked to see me in his office after dinner I threw a bottle of 1937 Cognac at his head. Neither of us said a word to each other after that fight until we were forced to make amends at Thomas' birthday party. Mom told us we could apologize to each other before presents, or she was taking the two of us to church so we could apologize in front of God. We both accepted her first offer, and never mentioned the fight again in front of her.

I took my time walking back to the table. I knew once I sat down I was trapped for the next hour. As soon as Mom said grace hands went flying across the table. Bowls were passed, drinks were poured. It was madness for the next ten minutes. It didn't quiet down until everyone was too busy eating to shout and yell. This was the only part of Sunday dinner that I liked. The part where no one was forcing me to play twenty questions. I knew today would be one of those days because of the last two dinners I missed while traveling for work.

"El, Isabella has a dance recital coming up. She'd love it if you could make it. If you're not too busy with work of course." Nora said.

"Please Auntie El? I'm in the Ballet performance, and I have a solo at the end of the show!" Isabella shared, with a wide toothless smile.

"Of course I'll be there Isabella. I wouldn't miss it for the world. When is it?"

"It's in a couple of months at the end of December. It's at that old theater you used to practice at." Nora said.

"Make sure to get that day off from work dear." Mom added.

Here we go.

"I can't keep up with that schedule of yours Eliana. I don't know how you do it. One minute you're here in the city and then next thing I know you're in Texas. I had no idea this job had you traveling so much. Is that safe?" She asked.

"I don't travel that much Mom. I was only traveling with one of our clients and her family. We were trying to get them out of their house, and to Texas to stay with relatives. They have a court hearing coming up, and we thought it would be safer to create some distance with her ex-husband." I tried to explain.

They didn't understand. They thought I was wasting my time working for the Women's Work. They hear the words "non-profit" and suddenly it's not a real job. They don't see the families I help. I might as well be like Frankie running around and wasting my twenties.

"That doesn't sound safe at all Eliana." Mom said.

"It's not as bad as it sounds. It was a one-time situation. A few case workers were out sick, and I stepped in for a week, no big deal."

"When you said you wanted to become a lawyer, your father and I thought you would work for Uncle Joseph after you graduated. He says he has a spot for you at his firm, and all you need to do is call and set up an interview." Mom said eagerly.

"I'm not going to work for the family firm Mom. I told you I have a strict 'no defending drug lords, and mob bosses' policy."

The room went quiet. Everyone looked up from their plate and stared at me.

"Oh, I'm sorry. Are we still pretending Dad and Raff run a shipping company? I always get that confused."

"Eliana, that's enough." My dad shouted, slamming his fork on his table. "You will not come into my home, eat my food, sit at my table and disrespect your family like that. The same family that raised you and supported you your whole life. The family that always made sure you were taken care of. I'm sick of your constant disrespect. It ends today."

The room went quiet. Everyone looked down at their plate while my dad and I stared at each other. He gave me a tired, irritated look that told me to quit it with the attitude. Lucky for him I was tired of arguing. After a few minutes of silence, Mom did her best to change the subject.

"I ran into Mrs. Carson this morning at Pilates Frankie. She says Madison just graduated and moved back from California. I know you two were close in high school. Maybe you want to reach out."

"Yeah, maybe." He mumbled, still focused on eating.

"Nora, where's Mikey tonight?" Raffael asked.

"He had to work late." She said shortly.

Yeah, right... working late. I'm sure that's where he was.

The rest of dinner was forced. Raffael did his best to mediate the tension, like always, and Nora continued to interrogate me about work. The longer dinner went on the more I worried about my conversation with Dad. I had already pissed him off, and I knew whatever he had to tell me I wasn't going to like.

After stalling by helping to clear the table and wash the dishes I went to look for Dad in his office. I found him looking over the same papers he was looking at before dinner.

"Have a seat." He said when he heard me open his office doors.

I sat in front of his desk as he stood up and walked closer to me.

"Do you remember when you left for college and I asked you to come to work for me?"

No, please no.

"Dad, please. I still have more time."

"I'm afraid it's me that's running out of time. I've done my best to protect this family, but I'm struggling. I reached out to Cristiano a few weeks ago. We both agree it's now or never. He's feeling pressure from some smaller families in Italy, and I can't keep things running smoothly here without his support." He said, avoiding my stares.

"Dad, don't do this." I begged.

"I let you leave to get your degree, and I didn't argue when you asked to go to law school. You knew what the deal was when you left. For four years I said nothing, and let you avoid your family responsibilities. You promised me that you would come back to support this family Eliana and now I'm cashing in my favor. It's time you live up to your end of the deal. You knew this was always how it was going to end. I wish I could give you more time, but I can't."

I was going to be sick.

"I met with Cristiano last week. His son, Apollo, has agreed to the arrangement as well. He says under the circumstances this is the best way to unite the families. He knows that we're stronger together than apart."

If I wasn't already sitting I think I would have passed out.

"Cristiano thinks it'd be best if we had the wedding before the spring and I agree. I can't keep this family safe without Cristiano's resources and support."

"Jesus Christ, Dad." I scoffed, "You can't be serious. Have you lost your mind?"

"If you care about your siblings or your mother at all, you'll agree to marry Apollo. Without Cristiano, this family won't survive another year. Your mother and I have sacrificed so much in this lifetime to give you a good life, and we asked for little in return. The business I built from nothing will crumble without this deal."

"I'm not marrying Apollo, Dad. I'll do anything else I can to support this family, but I won't spend the rest of my life married to a Costa!"

"This isn't negotiable Eliana. I'm not asking for your opinion. I'm giving you an order."

I couldn't breathe. My lungs felt heavy, and my head felt like exploding. I had to get out of Dad's office before I had a breakdown. Without saying another word, I stormed out into the living room, and looked for my keys. I could hear Raff yelling my name and trying to run after me as I ran out the front door, but I didn't look back.

When I finally got back to my car I let out a deep breath and tried to hold back the tears that threatened to fall. I started my car, but I had no idea where I was heading. My mind was blank. All I could think about was my conversation with Dad. This family was completely mental if they thought I would ever agree to this. I expected this from Dad, but there was no way Raff would agree to this. He was in line to take over for Dad, and Dad trusted him with all the big decisions. He knew how much I hated being a part of this family. What would possess him to think I would survive becoming a Costa?

Just when I thought I was finally free, Dad does something like this and pulls me back into a world I want nothing to do with. As I drove back to my apartment only one thought bounced around in my mind.

There's no way in hell I'm marrying Apollo fucking Costa.

I called in sick on Monday and haven't left my apartment since. I was too afraid of leaving and one of Dad's men coming to find me, or worse Dad stopping by at work to talk. I was safe in my apartment at least for a little while. I was sending everyone that called me to voicemail, even Raff. I knew he just wanted to talk, but I was too mad at the whole family to pick up the phone.

I thought back to the last time I saw Apollo. We always ran into each other at different family events and parties over the years. When we were younger Dad made the whole family travel to Italy for the summer. He would spend the summer working and taking care of business in Europe. I was heading into my senior year and Apollo was working as his dad's right-hand man. The only thing I knew about Apollo was that he wasn't much of a talker. A man as intimidating as Apollo didn't need to use words to get what he wanted. I was afraid of the teenage version of

Apollo, so I can't even imagine him all grown up. He was an absolute sadist. His father made him the family's enforcer. Everyone says that if you make him mad you should pray the Devil takes you before Apollo gets to you.

The last I heard anything about him he was in a really bad car accident. No one knew exactly what happened, but there were rumors it was a hit on Apollo. No one had seen or heard from Apollo in months. His dad had him hiding out in Italy until he was healed. I guess him agreeing to marry me meant he was out of hiding.

I was lucky to go a whole week before being bothered by anyone. Friday morning, I heard a knock on my door.

"Eliana, I know you're in there. Your car is in the garage. If you don't open the door I'll let myself in." I heard Raff say.

Damn it. I forgot I gave him a key. I attempted to tidy up the place as I walked to the door before letting him in. I opened the door and waved him in. He followed me to the kitchen.

"Why haven't you been picking up your phone?"

"My phone died. I didn't notice."

"Bullshit Eliana. We're all worried about you. It wouldn't kill you to call back." He argued.

"I have nothing to say to any of you."

"And what's that supposed to mean?"

"Don't act like you don't know what's going on. How hard did you pretend to fight this before agreeing with Dad? I bet you two can't wait to marry me off. Then you'd have one less person to worry about." I spat.

"Don't do that Eliana. You have no idea the pressure I'm under right now. You've never cared about the family, so don't be mad at me for trying to do what's best for all of us. If I thought there was any other way we could get out of this alive and safe I would have suggested it."

Before I threw a plate at his head I stormed out of the kitchen into the living room. I sat down on the couch and wrapped myself in a blanket.

Raff sat down next to me and sat in silence.

"Please don't make me do this." I said, trying not to cry. I had to clench my jaw to keep it from shaking.

"He told me you two made a deal. What did you do Eliana?"

"You know how bad I wanted to leave here after high school, so I made a deal with him. He gave me freedom to go to school, and in return I had to eventually come home. Then I wanted to go to law school and we got into a big fight. He told me I was stalling, and after law school I would find something else to do to avoid coming home. He said I couldn't keep running forever, so like an idiot I promised I would do anything he wanted if he let me have a few more years."

"Why would you do that?"

"I don't know. After graduating I was in a really bad place. I needed to do something to give me more time. I think Dad knew how vulnerable and desperate I was and that's why he made that deal. I was sick and he took advantage of that. I just thought he would never bring it up again. Years went by and he said nothing to me. A part of me thought he forgot."

"He didn't forget. This was his plan all along, from the very beginning." Raff said. "That son of a bitch."

"I trust you Raff, and I always will, so if you tell me this is the only way to keep everyone safe I'll do it."

Raff dropped his head and shook his head, "If you don't do this I don't know how I'm going to keep this family running. We have a target on our backs. I couldn't live with myself if something happened to you. Don't do this for Dad. Do this for me and everyone else."

I stood up from the couch and walked to the front door. Raff took it as his cue to leave. I appreciated him stopping by, but I wanted to be alone. There was nothing he could say that would make this better. Grabbing his keys from his pocket and walking to the door he stopped to give me a hug.

"If you make your decision there's a dinner tonight at the house. I hope I see you there."

He walked out of my apartment and into the hallway.

"Raff wait." I shouted after him. He turned back to face me.

"Do you remember when I graduated high school? I snuck out to go to a house party, and you had to come pick me up?" I asked.

"Yeah."

"Do you remember what you said to me on the drive back?"

"No."

"You told me to run and never look back. You said if I stayed that I would get stuck like you did."

Raff nodded his head remembering that night.

"I should have run."

Apollo

"Is it true?" Juliette shouted, storming into my office.

"Juliette, what the hell are you doing here? You're supposed to be in school."

"I ditched with Emily, but then we overheard Dad say you're getting married, so we ran over here!"

"Juliette I'm really bus-"

"Oh my god you didn't deny it! Who the hell would ever agree to marry you? You're a nightmare. Does this mean I'm finally getting a sister? Can I be a bridesmaid, wait no, can I be the flower girl?"

"Juliette."

"What if she doesn't like me? How did you propose? I didn't even know you were dating. This is crazy, I have to tell Emily."

"Juliette." I shouted a little louder to get her attention.

She asked one more question, "Who is she?"

"It's Eliana. Marco's daughter."

"Why didn't you tell me you were planning on getting married?"

"Because I wasn't planning on getting married. Look, it's complicated. There's a lot of moving parts to this. Don't get your hopes up. Dad says she's close to backing out."

"What if she says no? Do you love her?"

"I don't even know her. This isn't like one of your novels. This is a business partnership. I'm doing it for Dad."

"I would back out too if I found out I had to marry someone

like you." She scoffed. "Wait, Eliana? As in Frankie's sister? Not the one you were always mean to when they came to visit. There's no way she says yes to marrying you!"

"She doesn't really have a choice. Dad needs Marco to help him with some things back home, and we agreed to help them here in the States. She'll agree if she wants to keep her family safe." I explained.

Juliette moved to my couch setting down her bag and getting comfortable.

I coughed hoping she would take a hint. She scoffed and rolled her eyes, but eventually stood up grabbing her bag.

"Fine I'll leave, but it's gonna cost you." She grinned.

"Okay, you leave right now, and I won't tell Dad you snuck out of Saint Katherine's again.

She thought about my offer as if she had a choice, gave me a nod, and ran out of the office as mysteriously as she arrived. With Juliette gone I could get back to work.

After working for a few hours with no interruptions, Dane entered my office after a quick knock on my door. The knock was more of a habit than him asking for permission to come in. It had me wishing I'd locked the door after Juliette left.

"This is everything I could find on her. Eliana likes to keep her personal information private. It's not easy trying to climb the ladder as an attorney when your dad runs New York."

"What did you find out?" I asked.

"After high school, she went to Boston University and double majored in Criminology and Sociology. After college, just like her dad said, she went to Columbia for law school, passed the Bar earlier than most and started working around town. None of the big firms wanted her so she found a couple of small

15

nonprofits to work for to build her resume. Where she's at now has her working a number of jobs. Legal aid, counseling, helping women escape domestic abuse situations around the East Coast. She's also spent quite a lot of time in court representing these women. That takes up most of her time. If she's not in court she's busy doing something else for work. We tracked her travel over the past few months. She's been flying with families all over the U.S."

"What else did you find?"

"Well, you know Raffael, and Frankie too. They have been busy with the family business. Nora has two kids now. One just started the second grade. The other one just turned six. Her husband Mikey works as an accountant in the city and has been working a lot of *overtime* lately. From what I can tell he's spending more time at work than with Nora and the kids."

"Keep your tail on Eliana until dinner. I don't want her going anywhere without me knowing." I ordered.

"I'll keep a couple guys on it, but she hasn't left her apartment all week. I doubt she's going anywhere anytime soon." Dane said leaving the folder on my desk and walking back out to reception to make a call.

I looked over Eliana's files. If you didn't know who Eliana's father was you would think of her as a normal girl. She had worked really hard to hide she was a Mariani. Only someone who is afraid of the truth tries this hard to hide it. She knows who she is and what she wants, but she can't admit to herself mafia and murder runs in her blood.

Four hours later, I was waiting in Marco's office with Dad and Dane. Every minute that ticked by had Marco more and more nervous. He must have thought his daughter wasn't going to show. It would be trouble for him if she didn't. He had already signed the contract and agreed to the engagement.

"She's not going to show." Dane whispered in my ear as we waited for Eliana.

Dad was losing his patience, but I knew it was only a matter of time before she arrived. She was hot-tempered, but she was smart. She knew the risks of saying no. The sooner Eliana showed up the sooner we could all leave. I wanted tonight to be a quick social appearance. As soon as I didn't need to be here I was leaving. I would make an appearance like Dad asked, but then I needed to get back to work. If Eliana didn't get here soon I would be leaving before Dad had a chance to announce the engagement.

I was pulled from my thoughts when I heard the office doors open. In walked Eliana.

She looked tired and angry. She walked in perfectly dressed for a funeral. Black dress, black heels, black jewelry. Even when we were younger she always had to make a statement. She looked around the room and locked eyes with me.

Chapter Two

Eliana

I debated showing up all morning and when I did it left me little time to get ready. I settled for a black velvet dress with long sleeves and a square collar. The fabric fell just below my knees. I settled on black heels to really tie the outfit together. I struggled to hide how tired I looked with make-up, but in a way, it matched the outfit.

The driveway had turned into a valet, and the noise of people poured out of the house. I didn't want to walk through the main entrance, so I walked around to the side. In the kitchen, I found Nora bossing everyone around. A few people were working on refilling champagne, others were focused on plating desserts and appetizers.

The last person I wanted to talk to was Nora, so I snuck past her and went looking for Raff and Dad. I could hear Dad talking to someone in his office. I wasted no time opening the office doors. I silenced the room with my sudden arrival. All eyes were on me. In the corner leaned up against the back of a chair stood Apollo. He stared at me with cold eyes. He gave me no emotion as I walked into the room.

"I'd like everyone to leave please. I need to talk to Apollo alone." I ordered.

Dad and Cristiano looked at each other then back at me. They nodded their heads and led their men out of the room. The last one to leave the room was Raff. He squeezed my hand as I gave him a reassuring nod letting him know I'd be okay.

Apollo stayed silent once it was just the two of us. When I entered the room earlier, he was the only one who hadn't looked surprised to see me. It was like he knew. He knew I had to agree to this wedding. He looked like he wanted to say something. Maybe to make a joke about how predictable I've always been. How he knew all along I'd show up to protect my family. His eyes glared at me, mocking me as I walked over to him.

"I wrote up a contract." I said not being able to stand the silence anymore.

"A what?"

"A contract for the both of us. Marrying you comes with a lot of risk. I'll marry you, but I won't endanger my future, or put myself in a vulnerable position. I have a few things written already."

I paused waiting for a response.

"By all means. Let's hear them." He said, giving me a teasing grin. Almost as if he found this humorous.

"I will legally marry you, but we'll keep our finances separate. If in a year things are working out I will agree to creating a joint bank account for the benefit of our living situation. I do not want your *business* jeopardizing my safety and future. I see it all the time with the women I help. The reason they stayed with their abusers was because they felt financially trapped. I won't risk that type of dependency."

He said nothing, only giving me a small nod to continue.

"Two, I don't plan on quitting my job. Despite what I'm sure my dad has told you about me, I did not get my law degree to avoid my family responsibilities. I'm asking you to keep your work separate from mine. There should be no overlap. You're not worth losing my license over. I have a five-year plan that involves me opening up my own firm. Don't ruin that for me."

I turned to the next page of the contract.

"Three, no dating. It's bad enough I'm becoming a Costa. I will not be talked and gossiped about by the other wives because you got caught sneaking around behind my back. As far as the public is concerned this is a real marriage."

That caused Apollo to shift on his feet. I already knew rule three was going to be a tough one for him not to break.

"Four, no secrets. This isn't going to work if I'm left in the dark about your business. Raff has always been honest with me about issues within the family, and I expect the same from you. I'm not asking you to share every event of your life, but when something important happens that affects me I'd like to know. If you're honest with me I'll support any decision you need to make about the family."

"Anything else?"

I looked up from the paper I was reading to see that he had stood up from leaning on the back of the chair. He was taller than I remember. Teenager Apollo was a charmer. His smile sent girls tripping over their own feet. Looking at him now I could see how his line of work had aged him. His smile was gone, and his eyes were laced with a few small wrinkles. He kept his jaw tight, defining its fine lined structure. His dark wavy hair matched his black suit. His broad shoulders tensed as I walked closer to him. His eyes that used to look like a golden autumn day now lacked any warmth.

"That's it for now. I'll give you a few days to add anything you want to the contract. Send it over to my office when you're finished."

I tried to hand him the contract, but he pushed it back towards me.

"I don't have anything to add, just stay out of my way." He said before walking out of the office.

I left the contract on Dad's desk and went looking for Raff in the hallway. I was stopped by a few of Cristiano's men before I found Raff. At least six of them had me conveniently cornered. I understood why when Cristiano turned the corner and started walking over to me.

"Ms. Mariani It's a pleasure to see you." He said, reaching out his hand.

"I'm sure it is." I spoke dryly.

"I wanted to be the first to welcome you to the family. If there's anything you need, and I mean anything, please let me know."

"That's very kind of you Cristiano. Thank you." I said, trying to get past him.

He stopped me, stepping to his left and blocking my path.

"You're a smart girl Eliana. I do not need to remind you of the risks, do I? You'll be on your best behavior?" He threatened.

"You have nothing to worry about. I would never do anything to ruin the family name. Sir." I smiled.

"In that case let me escort you to the party. Everyone is dying to meet you."

What a fucking nightmare.

The party was dragging on, so I spent the majority of the night hiding at the bar. Just when I thought the night couldn't get any worse I heard Dad and Cristiano mess with the band's microphone. They were quieting the crowd. Once they were sure they had everyone's attention Dad started talking.

"We are always overjoyed to share these nights with all of you. It means so much to both families that you all could make it." Dad cheered through the microphone. "We called you all here to celebrate some exciting news!"

Cristiano interrupted Dad, "If Apollo and Eliana would join us up here please." He grinned.

I was pulled from the back of the room and escorted by Frankie to the front of the stage. Apollo was close behind me. Once we were both on stage Apollo put an arm around my waist and pulled me close.

I froze at the sudden connection. His hand rested low on my hip, and his grip tightened until he had me in his grasp. I looked up at him, giving him a warning look, which was enough for him to let go. Of course, before letting go he gave me one of his devilishly annoying smirks.

"My Eliana and Apollo shared with the family over the weekend that they are engaged, and we couldn't be happier for the two of them!" Dad announced.

The room erupted both with cheers, and people shocked by the news. Most people hid their confusion with congratulations and cheers, but some couldn't hide the concern on their face.

Dad announced the engagement here for a reason. He wanted everyone from New York and Italy to know the two families were working together. I did my best to give a fake smile, as I looked around the room. I caught Mom and Nora in the corner being congratulated by friends. Looking up at Apollo he stood there like a statue waiting for Cristiano to say something. I couldn't tell if he was angry, sad, happy, or nervous. His eyes scanned the room as he watched the men he worked with panic.

The longer I stood next to Apollo the faster my heart pounded in my chest. I'd always avoided him when we spent time together. Even wearing heels, I barely came up to his shoulders. Standing next to Apollo was all I could think about. His strong cologne clouded my judgment and had me forgetting where I was. He smelled like rich tobacco, and fresh citrus. I zoned out the rest of Dad and Cristiano's congratulations. As soon as Dad finished his long speech I tried to get away. If I didn't get some fresh air I was going to pass out.

Before I could leave the party, I was stopped by dozens of people. Apollo was taller than me and better at getting away from the crowd, but I was stuck. A small part of me thought he would help me and get me out of there, but he left without looking back. I was trapped. I had no way of getting away from these strangers. Not wanting to anger Dad I was patient with the guests and thanked them for their congratulations. I couldn't give a shit if I never had to see any of these people again, but if they were here it meant they were important to the family, so I faked my way through the evening.

"How does Dad even know this many people? I could have sworn like half of these people were dead." Nora joked, handing me a glass of wine.

"If one more person comes up and pinches my cheeks telling me how grown up I am I'm going to snap."

We both laughed and looked for an empty table to sit at. Nora stayed by my side for the rest of the night. She took care of everything. Relatives I didn't know existed, Apollo's family members who wanted to know everything about me, and some of Dad's men who were there to warn me about Apollo. Mom stopped by only to remind me to smile and fix my posture.

The night was winding down, and I was busy planning my escape. I needed to get out the front doors without Dad seeing. I looked around the room and saw Apollo alone with a man I hadn't met yet. Although a few inches shorter than Apollo, he made up the difference in height with pure muscle. His shoulders barely fit in his suit, and the glass in his hand looked like it belonged in a doll house. He was the only one Apollo had talked to all night. No one approached him or tried to engage him in conversation. Apollo caught me looking at him, which caused me to panic and look away. When I looked out of the corner of my eye I could see him still staring. I could feel my cheeks turn red.

Why was I blushing?

Not being able to stay another minute I left the table and made my way to the door. Just a few feet from the exit I was stopped by a few of Dad's men. They raised their arms and blocked the door. I looked behind me and saw Dad shaking his head.

Damn, so close.

I walked back to the table and found Dad waiting for me.

"Would it kill you to at least pretend you are enjoying yourself? You and Apollo are acting like strangers. You're embarrassing me!" He yelled at me in a low whisper.

I rolled my eyes, "We are strangers."

"Enough."

I wasn't the only one who was getting yelled at. Cristiano was arguing with Apollo in the corner. The two of them looked over at Dad and me. Apollo yelled one more thing to his Dad before walking over to me.

He towered over me and stuck out his hand.

"Would you like to dance?" He asked.

"I'd rather eat glass." I smiled, taking his hand, and letting him lead me to the dance floor.

Apollo

Eliana gave me her hand and followed behind me. She let me know I was walking too fast by squeezing my hand and doing her best to run to keep up. I slowed down, giving her a chance to catch up. I was impatient to get this dance over with. Dad promised if I spent a few minutes with her I could leave. I had an important client I was meeting at the bar tonight, and I couldn't risk being late.

I stopped and turned to face Eliana once we were in the middle of the dance floor. I grabbed her hand and waited for her to grab my shoulder as I lowered my hand on her waist. I could feel her hitch her breathing as I came close to her. Was she really that frightened to be near me? I hadn't given her a reason to hate me yet. I tried to brush off the disgust in her eyes as the music started. She waited for me to start dancing and followed my lead for half of the song.

25

"You can relax Eliana. I won't hurt you. We're just dancing." I whispered in her ear.

That made her shiver as she tried to create some space between us. She failed in her attempt as I continued to keep her close to me. I moved my hand to her lower back, and I kept her close to my chest as we danced.

"I thought of something I want to add to the contract." I spoke.

She looked up at me, "What is it?"

"I need you to move in with me. I can't keep track of you if you're an hour away in your apartment. It will be easier on your security if you move into the house."

"Security?"

"I have a few guys who will drive you to work and keep an eye on you throughout the week. Everywhere you go they go. It's nothing personal. Everyone in the family gets protection."

"I don't need protection. I'm fine on my own." She complained.

"You said it yourself; you're putting yourself in danger becoming a Costa. It would be a headache for me if something happened to you. I'll agree to all of your demands if you agree to this one. It makes my life easier. I'm busy enough as it is."

"Fine." She agreed.

We went back to dancing in silence. The silence was eventually broken when Eliana let out a quiet laugh. I looked down at her and saw her doing her best to hide a smile.

"What's wrong?" I asked.

"Nothing." She said.

"Tell me."

"No."

"Eliana..." I warned.

"You were counting the steps."

"No, I wasn't."

"Yes, you were. Your lips move with the tempo to keep you in time with the music."

"I think I would know if I was counting." I lied.

Maybe I was counting. I wasn't paying much attention to myself, rather Eliana dancing in my arms.

"Sure." She teased.

I ignored her, but when I looked at her for a second time she went into another laughing fit. This time she leaned into me to hide her laughing. Her head rested on my chest as she tried to calm down. I was uncomfortable with how close she leaned against me, but it was the first time all night I had seen her smile, and I didn't want to ruin her fun. She continued to lean into my chest and hide for what felt like an eternity. When she finally leaned back my chest felt cold. A small part of my brain wished she had stayed relaxed like that, using me to guard her.

I was so caught up in the moment I didn't realize the reason she leaned away from me was because the song was over. Eliana pulling away from me quickly sent me back to reality. I was back in the ballroom surrounded by family. The dance was over, and I could finally get back to work. Eliana and I walked our separate ways and lost each other in the crowd.

This was my chance. I could leave before Dad asked me to stay longer. I nodded to Dane letting him know it was time to go. He sat the drink in his hand down onto a random table and followed me outside. While waiting for the valet to bring the car around, Dane lit a cigarette. The valet driver was taking forever, and I was starting to get impatient. Out of the corner of my eye I saw a woman running down the stairs. Now only a few steps away I could see it was Eliana.

Heels in one hand, the end of her dress in the other she ran like she was being chased. She stopped right next to me and looked behind her. Out of breath, she did her best to speak.

"You didn't see me." She panted.

She didn't give me a chance to respond before running to the right of me and jumping over the side of the stairs. Startled, Dane and I looked over the ledge. She had jumped a good fifteen feet and was leaned up against the wall.

Shortly after her jump two men came running down the stairs.

"Sir, have you seen Eliana? Mr. Mariani is looking for her."

Dane and I gave each other a look before responding.

"No. Haven't seen her since we came out here." I responded. Dane nodded in agreement.

"Thank you, Sir. Enjoy the rest of your evening." One of the men said before running back up the stairs.

We waited for them to walk back into the house before looking behind the stairs again. This time when we looked Eliana was gone.

"Where did she go?" I asked.

"Um Apollo," Dane paused, pointing behind me. "I found her."

I turned just in time to see Eliana hop into my car and start the engine.

"Hey! That's my fucking car!" I shouted after her.

That small fact didn't seem to bother Eliana. She rolled down the window, gave me a wave and drove out the front gates disappearing into the night. I looked at Dane who was still on the stairs trying to hold back his laughter.

Eliana

It was a beautiful, peaceful ride back into the city. I made a mental note to look into getting a car like this and rolled down my window to enjoy the breeze. My flawless escape was interrupted with a phone call coming through the car's system. Is he really calling his own car right now? How is that even possible?

Wanting the ringing to stop I answered his call.

"It's dangerous calling someone when they're driving."

"Bring my car back right now." An angry Apollo shouted through the phone.

"Apollo I'll have to call you back! You're cutting out. I didn't hear a thing you said. I must be driving through a dead spot."

"I swear to god Eliana if you don't bring my car back in ten minutes I'll fu-"

beep

Oops. I must have accidentally hung up. He continued to call, but each time I sent him to voicemail. He gave up calling his own car and started calling my phone. I could hear it vibrate in the seat next to me. His calls were starting to give me a headache, so I turned up the radio and enjoyed the rest of the drive.

On my way back to my apartment I stopped by Tony's for a pizza. While waiting for my food I pulled my phone out of my purse. Nine missed calls and voicemails.

First message, "I'm going to give you the benefit of the doubt Eliana and trust you're driving back to the house right now. I'm sure I don't have to tell you I have little patience. You have five minutes."

Second message, "Time's up Eliana, and I still don't see you pulling into the driveway. I will find you, and when I do I won't be happy. I'm not big on forgiveness."

Third message, "I know you think this is funny, but I paid over half a million for that car, and if I find a single scratch or dent on it you're buying me another one."

Fourth message, "Hey Eliana, Dane here. Apollo has this thing about other people driving his cars. Some might say he has control issues. Anyways, he's starting to give me a bit of a headache, so if you'd return the car that'd be great. Also, I'm sure he didn't mean it when he said he'd kill you. Give me a call back when you get this. Thanks, bye."

"Order for El?" The man behind the counter shouted. I turned off my phone after that last voicemail, grabbed my pizza, and walked back to the car.

Well I wasn't going home that's for sure. I needed to find someone who'd let me crash for the night. I wanted Apollo to panic at least for tonight. There was only one person I knew that Apollo didn't know about. Emma's was down the block, and had a nice parking garage I could keep the car safe in.

A few turns later and I was at Emma's. I couldn't turn my phone on and risk Apollo tracking me, so I had to use the old doorbell system.

"Hello?"

"Em, it's me. I'm in the garage. Can you ring me in? I don't have the spare key on me."

"Eliana? What the hell? It's past twelve."

"Please. I'll explain everything when I get up there."

I heard silence for a few seconds and then a click unlocking the main door. I rested the pizza box on my hip and reached for the front door. Once I was in I made my way up to Emma's floor.

She was waiting for me in the hallway. Already in her pajamas she looked confused to see me in a dress and my good heels.

"That better be Tony's." She said holding the door open for me.

"Half pepperoni, half extra cheese. Just like you like it." I grinned.

I sat my stuff down on her kitchen counter and walked to her closet looking for clothes to change into.

"So, tell me everything." She said already helping herself to the pizza.

"Well, for starters I'm engaged."

I had been at Emma's for a couple of hours updating her on everything. Apollo, the engagement, Dad's party, and of course the car.

"Wait, show me again, how did he hold you when you two danced?" She asked.

"Like this. He wrapped his arm around my waist, and he held me so tight I pressed up against his chest." I explained giving her a walk-through of the dance. "He only let go of me when he heard the band stop playing. As soon as it stopped he stormed off the dance floor. The way he looks at me Emma, it's dreadful. It makes me sick to my stomach. Why did he agree to marry me?"

"He must have had his reasons just like you did."

"I don't think I can do this, Em. I can't spend the rest of my life with him. What am I going to do?"

"All you can do is take it one day at a time. One day you'll wake up and you won't feel as miserable as you do now. It will just be a normal day, and you'll find comfort in knowing you did this to keep your family safe."

I nodded my head. Emma was right.

"And maybe tomorrow you can start day one by giving him his car back before he murders you and then me for letting you hide out here." She joked.

"Yeah." I laughed. "God, he's going to be so pissed. Maybe it would be better if you just kept the car and we pretend this never happened."

"Hell no! I like my boring life and I want to live it for a very long time. You better go to bed before you come up with another dumb ass plan."

Chapter Three

Eliana

I was woken up by Emma cleaning early in the morning. It was nice knowing some things never change. In college Emma would black out on a Friday night and wake up at seven the next day to go to work. I tried sleeping through the vacuum, but I knew I had to get up and return the car back to Apollo. I didn't want him hating me for the rest of our lives. I said a quick goodbye to Emma and drove home.

Parking the car, I took the elevator up to my apartment. Turning in the hallway I could see my door was messed with. I know I locked it last night which meant only one thing. Apollo was here. *Shit.* Don't tell me he spent the whole night waiting. I considered leaving, but I knew he was angry and I didn't want to push it. He's not actually going to kill me, right?

Slowly pushing my door open I quietly dropped my heels to the floor. I had left my dress at Emma's and was still wearing her clothes. The lights were off, but I could hear something, or someone in the living room. I left the lights off and walked carefully through the entrance into my living room. Sitting on my couch facing away from me was Apollo. I'm sure Dane was around here somewhere, but I didn't see him.

"Good morning." I spoke not knowing what else to say.

He stood up, turning around to face me. He was in the same suit as last night, only now his sleeves were rolled up and a couple of the buttons on his shirt were undone. He obviously hadn't slept. I can't believe he stayed here the whole night.

"Where is it?"

"Where's what?" I asked.

"My car. The one that you stole."

"Stole is a bit harsh don't you think? I like the term borrowed. Without your assistance, I wouldn't have been able to get away from the party."

"Where did you stay last night?" He asked, walking closer to me.

"I stayed at a friend's."

"And this friend, where does he live?" He asked, annoyed.

"She, and I'm not telling you."

He continued to walk closer to me. I was running out of room to step back. I ended up in the kitchen pressed against the counter. I hid my hands behind my back.

He walked up close to me and wrapped an arm around my waist. He searched for my hands and found the key I was holding. He was quick to pull it out of my grasp and start to walk away.

"This won't happen again Eliana. The last person that stole from me was forced to cut off his own hand before earning

35

himself a trip to the bottom of the Atlantic." He threatened.

"I'm not afraid of you." I spoke up. "You may have gotten away with bossing people around your entire life and them being too afraid to talk back, but you don't scare me. And just so we're clear I didn't steal from you. I took good care of your car, and I only did it to get away from my dad. I'm sure you can understand what that's like."

He walked back into the kitchen.

He leaned down, grabbing the counter on either side of me. We were eye level. I could see my reflection in his dark brown eyes as they stared back at me. His eyebrows were furrowed, and he wore a tired expression. I saw a small scar on the right side of his jaw under his ear. I didn't notice that before when we were dancing. Last night his hair was pulled out of his eyes and gelled back, but now a few strands fell out onto his forehead. He looked me up and down, trapping me in his arms. I could see a few tattoos on his forearms that were hidden the night before by his suit. I looked back at Apollo, starting to feel my heartbeat get faster. If he could hear my breathing rising I was screwed.

"You're not afraid of me?" He smiled.

I nodded my head no.

He looked me up and down before speaking. "You should be."

He let go of the counter and walked back to the living room. I followed him out of the kitchen. I watched him pick up his jacket and a gun he had resting on the arm chair. He put his jacket back on and tucked the gun away in his chest pocket.

He walked out of my apartment without saying another word. When the door closed I ran to lock it, not that it mattered. That wasn't so bad I thought. I headed to the bathroom to take a shower. I needed to wash off all of the memories of last night and this morning.

After Apollo left on Saturday I spent my whole weekend sleeping. I planned on getting some work done, but Apollo was proving to be a bit of a distraction. Who does he think he is coming into my house, threatening me like that? I don't know how I was going to survive living with him if I couldn't even handle him in my apartment for five minutes.

Late Sunday night I got a call from a number I didn't recognize.

"Eliana speaking." I answered.

"It's me." Apollo replied. "A few of my men are waiting outside your apartment. I had them send over some information about the house, and codes you'll need to get in."

I looked out my window and down on the street one of Apollo's men sat waiting in his car.

"I had one of our cleaners get a room ready for you. Bring whatever you need. The folder gives details about the house. You're allowed anywhere in the house, except my room and office. I need you completely moved in by Wednesday."

"That's not possible. I'm busy with work all week. I need more time to pack and get ready."

"Make it work." He ordered, hanging up.

There was no way I could pack up my entire apartment and get it moved to his place by Wednesday. I walked over to my closet, grabbed some sneakers to slip on and walked down to the lobby to meet Apollo's men.

A man met me halfway, folder in hand. Before he walked away I asked him to let Apollo know it was going to take me longer than Wednesday to move in, and he would have to wait.

Back in my room I took a look at the folder. I had the gate

code, garage code, and a couple of keys for the house. My room looked like it was on the second floor across from what I assumed was Apollo's room. Both rooms were down a long hallway towards the back of the house. The kitchen, a dining room and a lounge room were just past the main entrance. The second floor looked like smaller guest rooms and a small library. I could see there was a basement, but until I saw it for myself I wouldn't know what was down there.

Throwing the folder onto my coffee table I went to get ready for bed. I locked the front door, turned off the kitchen lights and headed to my room.

Work was dragging on. Monday's were my long days, and it didn't help that I was getting calls and texts from Apollo every ten minutes. He was upset I hadn't started moving in yet. After a few meetings in the morning with clients and my boss, I had an hour to catch up on work and eat some lunch before court in the afternoon.

I used that time to see what I could find on Apollo. Should I be using work's database on him? Probably not, but I needed answers.

I found a few family records, different leases under his name, different property assets, but what surprised me was a clean record. I knew it wasn't clean, so who was he paying off to give him such a spotless record? Not even a parking ticket. I didn't want to admit it, but it was almost impressive. After finding nothing in the database I continued my search. I couldn't find anything about his personal life. He was a ghost.

Not finding any current photos of him I thought back to the party, and when he broke into my apartment. I remembered how it felt when we danced. I could feel his fingers trace over mine as he spun me, and his back muscles tightening when I held onto him. That night when Dad announced the engagement he stood tall and straight next to me, but that night at my apartment he hovered over me trying to intimidate me. He stared at me like he knew all of my secrets. It was like-

"Eliana..." Someone interrupted, knocking on my door. I snapped out of my thoughts and looked down at my computer. Crap, it was past one. I was late.

Mal opened my office door and started grabbing some case files from my desk.

"You're going to be late if you don't leave right now. I have a cab waiting for you downstairs." Mal said.

"Thank you!" I yelled back at her as I ran to the elevator. I had to put Apollo on the back burner. I was too busy with work to be worrying about the engagement.

Apollo

I waited in Eliana's apartment all night. By three I knew she probably wasn't coming home, but I still waited. Where was she? Who was she with? More importantly, what did she do to my car? While I waited for her I took a look through her apartment. I scanned the photos all neatly framed on the walls. She had dozens of photos, and memories of her friends, but I didn't see a single photo of her family anywhere. I already knew how hard she tried to distance herself from the family, but it surprised me to see no sign of them in her apartment. I went through a few work files on her desk and found nothing important.

In her room, I did find one old photo of her and her siblings. It was at least 15 years old. Raff looked like he was in high school, and Eliana looked young. That was the Eliana I remember. The one who stayed with us over the summer. Even back then she was stubborn. Always got her way.

I sent Dane back to the house. No point in making him wait around with me. Around seven I heard the front door open. I heard her quietly set her things down and walk into the living room.

"Good morning."

I turned and saw Eliana walking into the living room. She wasn't wearing her dress from last night. She was in an old t-shirt, her hair tangled in a bun. I could see my keys in her hand. All I cared about was getting my car back, she had wasted enough of my time. I cornered her in the kitchen and grabbed my keys from behind her back.

I had my keys back and was ready to leave.

"I'm not afraid of you." I heard her shout.

That made me laugh. Not afraid of me? She sure didn't act like she wasn't afraid of me. I walked back to her, trapping her against the counter. The closer I was to her the more nervous she became. I could see it in her face how she really felt about me. She couldn't stand to be anywhere near me. She wasn't fooling anybody. She did her best to hide it, but she was terrified of me. She hated everything about me. Who I was, what I did, and how she had to spend the rest of her life with me. I could see her chest rise and fall as she tried to steady her breathing.

"You should be." I replied.

Walking away, I grabbed my things and left Eliana's apartment before she tried to stop me again.

Before I knew it, it was Wednesday morning, and Eliana

had been avoiding my calls all week. I was going away for a few days, and I needed her moved in before I left. I wanted her settled into the house, so she wouldn't cause problems while I was away. I thought I made myself clear, but apparently, she thought moving in by Wednesday was optional.

"No sign of Eliana yet. I tried stopping by her office, but they told me she was downtown." Dane said, walking into the kitchen.

"What do you want me to do?" He asked.

"Go to her apartment, pack everything up, and bring it over."

"I don't know Apollo. She's not going to like that."

"I don't care. It's what she gets for ignoring me all week. Maybe this time she'll learn her lesson."

Eliana

I sat in my car trying to gain enough strength to get out and walk up to my apartment. I rested my head on the steering wheel. I was exhausted. Maybe I'll just sleep in my car tonight. That could work. No, come on El, get inside. Inside has food and vodka, and your bed. I let out a groan grabbing a few boxes, and my work bag from the back seat. Margaret had me staying a few hours late today, and she needed me in early tomorrow. The only good thing about today was that Apollo finally stopped bothering me.

In the elevator, I leaned the boxes on my hip, and waited for the doors to open. Setting down the boxes on the floor in front of my door I messed with my key unlocking it. I entered my apartment turning on the light and dropping my keys into the bowl near the door. I was confused to hear my keys fall onto the floor. When I looked to my left to see how I could have missed the bowl I found not only the bowl, but my shelf gone.

Finally finding the light switch and turning the lights on, I scanned the room. It was gone. Everything was fucking gone. My furniture, my television, everything from work I left sitting on my table. I opened the closet door next to me and found it empty with only a few hangers left. Running to my room I found it even more empty than the living room. My bed was gone, clothes, shoes, bags, everything, it was all gone. Someone had taken everything I owned from my apartment. That son of a bitch.

Running back out to the elevator I grabbed my keys and my work boxes. I threw the boxes into the trunk of my car, not even caring how they fell in, and I drove to Apollo's. I pulled up to the front gate and punched in the security code. Driving towards the house I parked right in front of the garage. I pulled up the second code I needed for the front doors. I wasted no time letting myself in as I searched the house for Apollo.

The house was quiet, too quiet. I couldn't find a single living person in any of the rooms. Failing to find anybody who could help me I started yelling.

"Apollo!" I yelled, walking through the hallways. After screaming for a few seconds, a few of Apollo's men found me. They tried calming me down as I continued to search for Apollo.

"Miss, please, Mr. Costa is on a work call, keep your voice down. Why don't you wait in the lounge and we'll have Mr. Costa come out and talk to you when he's free?"

"I don't give a damn if he's busy. I need to speak to him

right now. Tell him his fiancé's here to visit him."

A few of Apollo's men tried holding me back from going towards the hallway where I knew his office was. One tried to grab my elbow, so I knocked him in the stomach, and used my free hand to punch the other one.

"Get your fucking hands off me!" I screamed.

More men came and tried to hold me back, but that only pissed me off more. Where the hell was Apollo?

"Enough." I heard someone yell from down the hall.

Looking up I saw Apollo walking out of his office.

"Let go. She's not a threat." He ordered.

They all hesitantly let go of me, as I fixed my shirt that had bunched up during the struggle. Apollo waited for me near his office. I walked towards him standing directly in front of him.

"Eliana, welcome-"

He didn't get to finish his sentence. I slapped him across the face as hard as I could. Apollo rubbed his cheek letting out an annoyed laugh and turned back to face me. He raised a hand stopping his men who were running towards me again. I took a step back. He gave them a look, and just like that they were gone. It was just the two of us, alone in the hallway.

"What the fuck Apollo! You have no right breaking into my apartment again and taking all of my things. Is this some game to you?"

"I gave you a chance to move in on your own Eliana. It's not my fault you didn't take my orders seriously. I needed you moved in here by tonight. I didn't have a choice."

"I told you I was busy, and let's get one thing straight. I don't take orders from you. I'm not some little bitch you can boss around like your boys over there. They may think you're a god and would jump off a cliff if you told them to, but that doesn't mean you can treat me the same way you treat them."

"I warned you Eliana. I won't hesitate-"

"You won't hesitate to what? Silence me? Punish me? Go ahead. I fucking dare you." I said, trying to calm down.

Apollo clenched his jaw. Before he could say anything a phone in his office rang. He turned his head back to his office. He took a deep breath like he wanted to say something, but he changed his mind and walked away. Before closing the door, he shouted out to one of his men to take me to my room. One of the men who tried holding me back earlier waited for me at the end of the hall. He tried leading me to my room.

"I know where my room is." I told him, storming off down the hallway across from the stairs. I stood in front of my new room. Opening the doors, I found everything that had been taken from my apartment. It was thrown on the ground like trash. Nothing was in boxes. It looked like Apollo had his men grab a few items, and then just dropped them by the house one by one. It would take me days to unpack and go through everything. I should have been sleeping, but instead I would be trying to organize some of this mess.

The first thing I needed to do was find where all of my work files and documents had been tossed. I needed those for tomorrow. Changing out of my work clothes and into something a bit more comfortable, I started filing through everything. It was close to two, and I hadn't made a dent. I needed to be up in four hours for work. I was so upset when I got here I forgot to eat. I hadn't had anything since breakfast yesterday. I left my room for the first time that night and walked down to the kitchen. I stopped right outside of the kitchen in the hallway when I heard a few of Apollo's men talking.

44

"And then she just slapped him. Like it was nothing. I thought he was gonna cut her hand off." A younger boy explained to the men in the kitchen.

"What did he do?" The man asked.

"Nothing. He walked away when he heard his phone ringing. It was insane."

"Damn. I can't believe I wasn't here to see that. The one day I get sent out to work the gate. I wonder what he's going to do to her. I hear she's a total bitch." He joked. "She's a nightmare. I feel bad for Apollo. He's the one that has to marry her. He needs to show her who's boss. How are we supposed to take him seriously if he can't even keep his girl under control?"

I stood there with my ear leaned up against the door frame trying not to cry. They act like I wanted this to happen. I was about to leave and go back to my room when I heard another person enter the kitchen.

"Sir, you're still up, we thought you were asleep." One of the men said, stepping out of his chair.

I could hear Apollo walking towards the table where the men were sitting. I peeked around the door frame and watched as Apollo pulled one of his men from the table. He dragged him to the wall and wrapped his hand around his throat.

"What did you just say about Eliana?" He asked.

"Sir I can explain-" The man choked.

"I pay you a lot of money to guard this house, and instead I find you talking shit. Give me one reason I shouldn't snap your neck for being negligent."

Apollo pressed harder into the man's throat until he couldn't breathe. His head started to drop.

"You only have one job, and you can't even do that right."

45

Apollo let the man drop to the floor and watched him squirm. Then he turned to the other men at the table.

"Get back to work before I fire all of you."

They all ran out of the kitchen as soon as Apollo turned around. I continued to hide in the hallway for a few minutes. After calming down, I walked in. I found Apollo sitting at the counter eating what looked like leftovers.

Without saying a word, I walked to the fridge, and pulled it open. Apollo pretended I wasn't there and continued to eat his food. I grabbed some snacks I could take back to my room, and a bottle of water. Walking back to my room I heard Apollo behind me.

"I'll be gone for a few days. If you need anything while I'm away just ask Kim. She'll take care of you."

Back in my room I locked the door and dropped to the floor. I couldn't get the image of Apollo choking that man out of my head. It played on a loop, over and over again. I took my snacks over to the small table in my room and tried to relax. After eating I was ready for bed. I pushed some stuff off of my bed, crawled under the covers, and did my best to forget about Apollo before falling asleep.

After barely getting any sleep, I woke up to my alarm blaring. Maybe I should call in. No, I can't. I have that briefing with Margaret today. I kicked and threw around the comforter a few times before I gave in and woke up.

I walked still half asleep to the shower. When I turned on the shower I had to do a double take. On the shelf of the shower were all of my products. Apollo must have had them moved. Taking a look around the bathroom I found more of my stuff. My make-up, robe, curlers and new towels all organized neatly in the bathroom. Great, if he found someone to organize my bathroom maybe he could find someone to fix the mess in my room.

I waited until the shower was enough to burn me and steam up the whole bathroom, and then I stepped in. I tried forgetting about last night, so I could focus on work this morning. Out of the shower and trying to find clothes to wear I heard a knock on my door. A small woman was waiting for me in the hallway.

"Good morning, Ms. Mariani, I'm Kim. Mr. Costa asked me to bring you to his office. He has a few things he'd like to discuss with you."

"Please tell Apollo I'm late for work, and if he has something he'd like to talk with me about he can come find me himself."

"Of course, I'll let him know. Please let me know if there's anything I can do for you." She said leaving.

I rushed to finish getting ready. My hair was pulled into a low bun, and I looked for the belt that matched my navy-blue suit. Rummaging through the piles of clothes I looked for my button up. Hiding under a pile of bags I found it and threw it around my shoulders. I was on the first button when my door swung open. In stormed Apollo in his workout clothes.

"Jesus Christ Apollo knock! I'm getting dressed." I shouted at him.

He paused seeing me struggle to button the rest of my shirt up.

"Good morning." He smiled, looking me up and down.

I threw a towel at him, annoyed he felt he could enter my room whenever he wanted.

"What do you want?"

"You already know I'm leaving for a few days, but I wanted

47

to give you a heads up that my sister will be staying here. She usually stays here when our parents are out of town. She hates staying at the house all alone. If that's a problem for you I can tell her not to come over."

"No, no it's fine. Of course, she can stay here. How long are you going to be gone?" I asked.

Apollo walked around my room taking a look at my mess. Now it was me who was staring. While he had his head turned I watched him move. His work out shirt was clung to his chest, and I could see his muscles stick out of the fabric. His arms were exposed, and his muscles tensed when he walked. When I looked back at him I realized he had turned back around to face me and was giving me a smart look.

"I don't know. Less than a week if everything goes to plan. I'll call you if I'm gone longer. Text me if anything happens at the house or if Juliette needs me." He said before giving me one more look and leaving my room.

With Apollo gone I finished getting dressed, ran to the kitchen to grab some coffee, and ran to my car. Margaret was going to be so pissed if I was late again.

Chapter Four

Eliana

Sitting in Margaret's office I thought of ways I could fake a medical emergency to leave. I loved Margaret to death, but she just didn't know when to quit. Maybe if I walked out really slowly she wouldn't notice. Like an angel sent from heaven Mal walked into Margaret's office with dinner. She whispered for me to get out of here while she distracted Margaret with food.

While Margaret was happy and distracted by Mal I took my chance to leave, and I didn't look back. Stopping by my office first to grab a few things I headed out. I was also hungry, but I was too tired to stop and pick something up. Maybe there would be food at the house.

Back at the house I smelt something amazing coming from the kitchen. It made my stomach growl. I walked into the kitchen and found Juliette cooking at the stove. I coughed so she knew I had entered the kitchen. She turned around, and her face lit up.

"Oh my God! You're finally here. I thought you weren't going to come back home or something. Hi, it's so good to see you again!"

Juliette grabbed me into a big hug and spun me around. After crushing all of my bones, she finally let me out of her bear hug, and did her best to calm down.

"Sorry, Apollo told me to not get too excited, but I just can't help it. I've always wanted a sister. Wait, sorry is that too forward? I promised him I wouldn't make you feel uncomfortable. Ah, I can't believe it. You're marrying Apollo. I have a sister, and someone to go to all those tragic family events with." Juliette rambled on while I listened. I felt guilty that I couldn't match her energy. She was so excited for me. I did my best to smile and give her a minute to get her excitement out.

"Have you had anything to eat yet?" She asked.

"No, I got out of work late, and was hoping I could make something up really quick once I got home."

"Well, perfect timing. I took a study break, and I'm making some pasta. Why don't you go change, and settle in and we can have some dinner?" She offered.

"Sounds great." I smiled. "I'll be right back."

After changing and walking back into the kitchen I started to get a little nervous. I knew I probably didn't have a reason to be nervous, but I honestly didn't think I'd be spending time with Apollo's family so soon. Juliette had finished setting the table and was waiting for me.

She sat at the table with a big smile on her face. I took a seat across from her and filled my plate with pasta and salad. We ate in silence for a few minutes, and that only made me more nervous.

"I think the last time I saw you; you were in middle school?" I asked.

"Hmhmm, but I'm a Junior at St. Katherine's now." She answered.

"Ugh, junior year is the worst. Everyone always asks if you've committed to a university yet. And on top of all those classes you have to worry about the SAT and testing into different programs."

"Yes, exactly! It's awful. My best friend Emily, she already got a scholarship to Penn, and now Dad is putting all this pressure on me to make a decision, but he doesn't like any of the schools I want to go to."

"What do you want to study?"

"Dad wants me to stay here in the States and become a doctor or something, but I want to move back to Italy and study art history. He's convinced that's not a real major. Last time I tried bringing it up he exploded. I can't even talk to him about it anymore." She complained.

"And what does Apollo think?"

"He wants me to stay here too so I'm closer in case anything happens, but Dad let him live in Italy by himself for a few years, and I'm just as smart as him! I wouldn't get myself in danger, and we have family over there still. It would be perfect."

"Have you looked into any schools?" I asked biting into my salad.

"Yes, but Dad won't even consider looking at them with me, or touring, and Apollo's too busy."

"Well maybe over your winter break we could take a trip. I'll fly you out, you introduce me to some of your family, and we secretly tour some schools?" I offered.

"Are you serious? You would do that for me?"

"Of course. I mean pretty soon we'll be family, and when I was your age Raff went with me on some trips out to the West Coast. It could be fun. We'll make it a holiday."

Juliette's face lit up again. She was nothing like her brother. Juliette was kind and warm, and sweet. Juliette told me all about school, and we talked about the summer trips when my family would visit. It was nice finally having someone to talk to about the two families without being afraid you'd spill any secrets.

Juliette finished her dinner and helped me bring the dirty dishes to the kitchen. I cleaned while she dried. I knew she was dying to ask about the engagement all night, and towards the end of cleaning she finally found the courage to ask.

"So," she paused, "have you talked to Apollo about the wedding at all?"

I set down the bowl I was scrubbing. I hadn't thought about the wedding yet. I could barely get past the idea of being engaged to Apollo.

"Oh shit, sorry. I didn't mean to upset you. I was only curious. Apollo won't talk about it with me."

"It's fine. You're just the first person to ask about it. I didn't even realize eventually there'd be a wedding. I guess I thought I would stay engaged for as long as Dad needed me to."

"Well whenever you do end up planning the wedding I'd love to help. I have it all figured out. I know a couple shops in the city where we can look for dresses. I know everything Apollo likes and hates, so we don't have to bother him for anything which will make things easier. And I am really good at dealing with the crazy Costa side of the family, so don't worry about a thing. I got you. Also, if you wanted to make me a bridesmaid that'd be cool, but no pressure."

I let out a small laugh.

"You'll be the first person I ask for wedding advice. But right now, we need to go to bed. It's late, I'm tired, and you have school in the morning."

"Yeah... about that. It's Friday. Emily and I don't usually go to school on Friday." She tried to convince me.

"Well good for Emily, but one of my bridesmaids isn't going to be caught skipping school. So, you choose. I'll take you to school tomorrow or you can hang out with Emily."

Juliette dropped the dry towel was holding and surprised me with another hug.

"Really?! You'll let me be a bridesmaid?"

I gave her a nod and smile as she danced around the kitchen. Juliette danced her way up to her room with no more complaints of going to school tomorrow.

Once I was back in my room I thought about the wedding. In a couple of months, I'd be married to Apollo, and there'd be no turning back. I hadn't thought much about who I'd end up marrying or what I wanted my wedding to be like. I didn't see me getting married like Nora and immediately having kids. I was afraid of marrying Apollo and living a life of regret.

Apollo

I didn't want to leave Eliana alone at the house to meet Juliette for the first time alone, but I didn't have a choice. A few of my contractors who were supposed to be running a bar for me in North Carolina were causing problems. Their job was simple. Launder some money for me and keep a low profile. Keeping a low profile was the last thing they did. Dane told me they'd been giving a couple of townie drug dealers a booth to sell and were making a little on the side.

They didn't know I was paying them a visit, and they had no idea I'd caught onto their side gig. It had drawn in some unwanted attention from the local cops. It would have taken them less than a year to pay back their debt, but they couldn't even manage that.

A couple hours of driving and we finally pulled up to the restaurant. We didn't see any customers inside, so I grabbed my bag from the car and walked in.

Jackson was behind the counter and when he saw me he ran out the back. Carson was working at the host table and didn't have a chance to run. Dane had him tied down to a chair in the kitchen in under a minute. Carlos ran out to find Jackson, but he'd already jumped into his truck, and was long gone. That's okay. I'll worry about Jackson later.

Dane took the bag from me and pulled out my knife for me. Before I killed Carson, I needed some information about the drug dealers who had been working there.

"Apollo please, there's been a misunderstanding. We've been running the bar just like you asked." Carson cried.

"I gave you a second chance. Something I don't do often,

and you still thought you'd play me." I said taking a step closer and drawing a long cut down his forearm.

"You promised me you two could run this place with no problems, and then two months in you get greedy. You hate seeing me take all the money, so you decide a small partnership with a couple of dealers from town won't hurt anybody. Only problem is you got caught. The police are days from making an arrest here, and now you've compromised my family's entire business." I explain.

Carson tried to break out of the chair, but he wasn't going anywhere.

"I need the names of the guys you let work out of the bar." I said cutting deeper into the cut I'd just made.

"Sawyer! One of them is named Sawyer. They all live in a house together on Cherry Street. It's the one with the blue mailbox."

I looked back at Dane. He gave me a nod and took two guys with him to go find Sawyer, and his friends.

I was left alone with Carson. I had already wasted too much of my time with this idiot, and his brother. I pulled a rifle out from behind the counter and shot him in the chest a couple of times. I staged the place to look like a robbery gone bad. I threw Carson behind the cash register and took what was in the drawer. Taking my bag, and the gun with me I drove back up the driveway to go find Dane.

By the time I arrived at Sawyer's house I found Dane had already taken care of the problem. He had a few guys wrapping the bodies up and getting them to the car. I waited to hear anything back from Carlos. I needed Jackson found as soon as possible. I didn't need him running to the police or causing issues now that his brother was dead. I had already trashed his place, and I didn't know where else he would go. Until he found him, Carlos would stay down here.

A couple hours later, Dane and I were ready to drive back to the city. He took his men to one of the warehouses, and I started the seven-hour drive back to the house. I drove straight through not wanting to stop. I had meetings Monday, and I couldn't reschedule. I hadn't heard anything from Juliette or Eliana, so I'm assuming things were fine. I missed the days when I could drive back home knowing the house was empty of people. Now when I came home Eliana would be there too.

I pulled into the garage and walked through to the kitchen. The house was quiet. I wasn't sure where anyone was. I found Juliette asleep in her room, but Eliana's room was undisturbed. The bed was made, and her things were finally put away. I searched the whole house and found her asleep on the couch. The TV was on, and she was covered in paperwork. I went to turn the light off, so she could sleep, but that woke her up. I must have startled her because she nearly jumped off the couch.

"You're back. That was quick."

"I took care of things faster than I thought. Decided to drive back tonight in time for work tomorrow."

Eliana nodded in response as she organized the papers on the coffee table.

"Aren't you going to ask me about my trip?" I asked.

"Does it affect me? Am I in danger?"

"No, it was a small management problem."

"Then I don't care." She said, picking up her blanket and leaving the room.

It was late, so following Eliana I went to bed. I took a quick shower and got a few things ready for tomorrow. Laying down I thought about Eliana. That night when she came home, I'd really pissed her off. I didn't care much for Eliana. After all we both knew what the situation was, but when I heard Jackie talk about her like that I lost it. I shouldn't have let go of his neck. I should have squeezed until he turned blue, then he would have learned his lesson. She drove me crazy, and liked to steal my shit, but she didn't deserve the things they said about her. Tomorrow I'd pay Jackie a visit and remind him of the rules in case he forgot who he worked for.

I hadn't seen Eliana all week. She was gone for work before I woke up, and I was gone at night before she came home. It was nice. Neither of us had to see the other. The few times I had seen her she was busy with work. That's all she ever did. She would come home, prep a few cases, fall asleep and do it all over again the next day. She had surprisingly been behaving when it came to her security. She always let me know where she was going, and she made sure to communicate with Alex if her plans changed. It gave me one less thing to worry about. When I first agreed to her moving in I was nervous how it would go. We don't have compatible living situations or personalities, but if we continued to give each other space things might just work out.

I still doubted she was actually Marco's daughter. She acted nothing like the girl I spent my summers with. She reminded me every time we met that she didn't belong in this world. With her actions, or snide comments she reminded us that we had nothing in common besides wanting to protect our families. That's what doesn't make sense to me. If she truly hated this life, and her family, she should have had no problem turning down my offer. But she said yes, and that meant she saw a small part of me in her. I spent the whole week asking myself if this engagement was worth it. Should I have agreed to marry her? What if there was something I could have done to help the family without needing

Eliana's family? I was afraid I'd spend the rest of my life doubting my decisions.

It was Friday, and I had little planned for the day. Dane had taken over the search for Jackson, and some other guys were taking care of things at the warehouse. I spent the morning with Dad and had time in the afternoon to work on things at the house.

I was in the office working when Dane called.

"We might have a small problem."

"What now?" I asked.

"I think Jackson is on his way to New York. I tracked some payments he made. I'm pretty sure he's here looking for you. He made a few stops in North Carolina, and then one of his cards pinged in New Jersey a few days ago."

"Have you been able to track him any closer?"

"Not yet. I haven't seen any movement since Tuesday. I can drive over to Jersey, and take a couple of guys with me, but that would leave the warehouse under protected."

"Just take who you need to take, and I'll have Alex and a couple of guys from the house move over to the warehouse until you get back. I don't want Jackson making it to New York. Do you understand?"

"Yes, Sir. I'll call you when I know more."

I called Alex and told him he could take a few guys over to the warehouse with him. With Alex gone I needed coverage on Eliana. The warehouse and Jackson issue meant I was low on protection. Not having anybody I could call, I grabbed my keys and left for the courthouse.

Eliana

"That whole situation is a nightmare." I complained. "Did you have any idea they were going to bring in Adam's mom to testify as a character witness? And the things she said about Theresa, all lies! I mean who would buy that?"

"Well the jury might. I need you working on this over the weekend. Find anything you can that proves Adam's mom is lying for him. We know he's a terrible person, but we need the jury to believe it too. Theresa kept a log of everything over the last year. Use that to prove Adam hasn't supported Theresa or the kids financially in months." Margaret said.

Margaret held the door for me as we walked onto the steps of the courthouse. It was almost five, and I had no plans on going back to the office. I looked around for Alex but couldn't find him. Pausing on the steps wondering if maybe he was walking around I found a familiar face. *Oh no.*

Before I could grab Margaret's hand and run, Apollo made his way over to us.

"Good evening ladies." He smiled.

Margaret, obviously confused, looked at me. I gave Apollo a fake smile and turned to Margaret.

"Margaret I'd like you to meet Apollo, my- "

"Fiancé. I'm Eliana's fiancé. You must be Margaret. Eliana's told me some incredible things about you."

Shocked, and speechless Margaret shook his hand, "Eliana! You didn't tell me you were engaged! When did this happen? I don't even see a ring. You know it's not official until there's a ring."

"I've been so busy lately I forgot to mention it! Between work, and family stuff it's been crazy." I gave a small laugh hoping to make things less awkward.

"We have to celebrate!" Margaret cheered. I looked at Apollo and shook my head no, begging him to get me out of this.

"I'm afraid tonight won't work. I promised Eliana I'd take her out to dinner. We promised each other no matter how busy work got we would always make time for each other." Apollo grabbed me into a side hug and leaned into me. There's no way Margaret is buying this little act of his.

"Oh of course! I don't want to keep you any longer. Have fun tonight Eliana. Just make sure you're ready for Monday."

Margaret waved goodbye to us and got into a cab. Once she was gone I elbowed Apollo off of me.

"What the hell? Where's Alex?"

"He's taking care of a few things, so I came down to get you."

Apollo walked back to the car not waiting for me. I can't believe he showed up in front of Margaret. Now everyone at work would know about us.

"I told you I wanted to keep this and work separate." I complained. "And then you show up and introduce yourself to my boss? And don't get me started on how terrible of a performance that was. No one is going to buy our engagement if you act like that."

"You were going to have to tell them eventually, besides it's not like I told her anything about me. For all she knows I work in finance, or marketing."

"Still, you should have called me first. I could have gotten home on my own. I don't even need this level of protection. I'm only doing this because you asked for it."

"Actually, you do. We may have a small problem."

I looked over at Apollo. He was hiding something. He gave his full attention to the road and twitched his thumbs.

"What happened?"

"Nothing." He lied.

"Apollo..."

"A few days ago, I made a trip to North Carolina, and took care of a small issue with two brothers I had running a restaurant for me. I solved the problem, but one of the brothers escaped. Until we find him I can't have you going anywhere alone."

"What happened to the other brother?"

Apollo went silent again. He was really good at pretending I didn't exist. I leaned over the middle console waiting for an answer.

"Nothing important."

"Tell me."

Apollo said nothing.

"Are you really not going to tell me?"

"It's nothing serious. I'm handling it."

"Obviously not very well."

Apollo ignored me for the rest of the drive.

I was annoyed, irritated even at how easily Apollo ignored me. I had been honest with Apollo about my life, and work. I even let his men follow me around everywhere, but when I wanted to know anything about him he shut down.

Back at home I slammed the car door and walked through the kitchen.

"Next time just tell me when you're mad. Don't go and break my car."

"Oh, fuck off Apollo."

"Excuse me?" He asked, his voice raising.

"I asked you about North Carolina, and you completely ignored me. You said you would be honest about things happening with the family. Whatever happened on your trip obviously affects me, but you make no attempt to share information with me about anything!"

"I don't want to talk about it. End of story."

"Why not? What is so wrong about me that I can't handle this North Carolina problem? Is it because I'm a Mariani or because of the attorney thing? You think I'll hear about what you did and get sick to my stomach, or faint from terror? Is that it? You're never going to take me seriously are you?"

"I never said that." He tried to argue.

"But it's what you're thinking isn't it? You don't think I'll be able to handle whatever it is you've got going on with the family. I'm not an idiot Apollo. I hear things, and I see things. I know there's something going on with you. Am I really that intolerable? What more do you want from me? I let your men follow me around. I've given up my life, my friends, everything. And still when you see me you act like I've stabbed you in the chest. "

Without saying a word Apollo left me and started walking towards his room.

"I'm not done talking to you!" I yelled after him.

"You want the truth Eliana? Is that what will make you happy? Fine. I hired two brothers to run a restaurant for me. I found out they were dealing on the side. I killed one of them, but Jackson is on his way here to kill me, or you for all I know. And I didn't tell you about it because I didn't want to get lectured about the justice system or how I'm a sociopath with anger issues. I wasn't in the mood to be interrogated by my attorney fiancé. Forgive me if I'm a little too busy to sit around, and make sure your feelings aren't hurt all the time."

I stood there trying to process what he had just said to me.

Apollo turned around, "If you really want to be a part of this family then start acting like it. I see the way you look at me, and my men. You walk around my house like you're better than me. You go to work every day and live this- this fucking lie! You may have everyone around you fooled, but I know why you work so hard, why you do what you do. It's because the guilt is eating you alive."

Apollo paused, leaning against the counter. "When are you going to stop lying to yourself Eliana? Look around you, look at the house you're standing in and the money that paid for it. You can't admit to yourself there's just as much blood on your hands as there is on mine."

"I'll stop pretending my 'hands are clean' when you stop pretending to enjoy this Apollo. I can't look at myself in the mirror without seeing the sin my family's committed, but you revel in it. You feel no shame for the things you have done. Forgive me for wanting to distance myself from a life I didn't ask to be a part of. I remember you when you were little. How young were you when he first made you kill for him? Thirteen? Fourteen? The difference between you and me, Apollo, is that I stopped pretending to enjoy it. I stood up for myself, and I got out. But you were stuck, weren't you? Couldn't disappoint your dad. You were his only son, and I'm sure you couldn't force Juliette into this life, right? I can't imagine how hard it is for you every day, but you have no right taking that anger out on me. You're angry at me because I had the guts to stand up to my dad, but you, you're still chasing yours around for his approval. You think I'm a liar, that's fine, I probably am. But you... you're a fucking coward."

Leaving Apollo, I walked back to my room. I locked the door and threw my bag against the wall. I wanted to scream until my lungs bled. I wanted to do something, anything, but I didn't want Apollo to hear me lose it. I thought running a shower would do something to calm my nerves. Waiting for the water to turn warm I thought about the fight between the two of us. I knew I struck a nerve, and I was afraid to leave my room for the rest of the night. Hopefully, he was gone in the morning.

I stayed in my room for the rest of the night. Occasionally I could hear Apollo walking around and based on the pace of his walking he was still angry. I ignored his temper tantrum and did my best to fall asleep. I was woken up by my phone ringing in the middle of the night. I looked over at the clock on the nightstand, three a.m. Who thought they could call me at three in the morning? I ignored the ringing and tried to fall back asleep. It was quiet again for a minute, but the ringing started again. Rolling over I grabbed my phone and brought it back to the bed. My eyes adjusted and I could see Frankie's name pop up on the screen.

"Frankie?" I answered.

"No, it's Eric. I'm sorry to bother you, but Frankie wouldn't let me call Raff."

I sat up in my bed now fully awake.

"What happened? Where's Frankie?"

"He's fine. Everything's okay, but if I sent you an address do you think you could come pick him up?"

"Yeah sure, I'll be there as soon as I can." I answered.

Eric thanked me, hung up the phone then sent me a message. I changed into some clothes and looked for my keys. I must have been loud when getting ready because Apollo was standing in the hallway when I walked out. I walked past him down the hallway.

"Where are you going?" He shouted after me.

"It's Frankie. Something happened, and he needs me to pick him up."

"Wait."

I stopped in my tracks. When I looked back Apollo was gone. He returned a minute later putting on a sweatshirt.

"What are you doing?"

"I'm coming with you."

I rolled my eyes and waited for him to grab his keys from the kitchen. The ride to the address Eric sent was awkward. We both sat there not saying a word. I didn't want him coming, but I also didn't want to fight with him again.

"Turn left here." I spoke, pointing to his side of the car.

He sighed and pulled into a driveway of a house I had never been to before. I could see a group of people in the living room through the window. Apollo parked and waited for me to get out of the car. I wanted him to stay in the car, but he followed close behind me.

I rang the doorbell and waited on the porch. Frankie's friend Eric opened the door and grabbed me inside.

"I didn't know who else to call. Raff doesn't know he's here, and I knew not to call your dad. We weren't supposed to go out tonight."

"Eric, calm down. Where's Frankie?" I asked, trying to

refocus Eric.

He led me to a room where I found an almost passed out Frankie lying on a bed. His face was covered in blood, and you couldn't see his eyes. His hands were cut up, and there was a gash on his forehead.

"What the hell happened?" I asked, grabbing Eric and keeping him from trying to sneak out of the room.

"Raff and Frankie got in a fight last week about this client of his, Teddy. Frankie was sleeping with Teddy's girlfriend, and Raff found out. Raff told him he had to lay low until the deal was over, but Frankie snuck out to see her again. We ran into Raff's client at the club tonight. He brought like ten of his guys with him. I had to call security, just to get them off of him, and then I brought him here. Please you can't tell Raff, he's going to be so pissed. If Teddy backs out of the deal he's going to lose a shit ton of money."

I looked over at Apollo who was now taking care of Frankie. He looked back at me, and then at Eric. I walked over to Frankie to see if he was still conscious. I don't think Frankie even knew where he was, let alone who was with him.

"I can take him to our place tonight, but you're going to have to tell Raff eventually. He's not going to be able to hide these bruises, or what happened to Teddy for long."

Eric nodded his head and left to grab some of Frankie's things. Apollo helped me carry Frankie to the car. I grabbed Frankie's wallet and phone from Eric, and then drove back home with Apollo.

On the drive home, I sat in the back with Frankie, and kept his head from falling. He couldn't even sit up straight. Apollo helped me get Frankie from the garage to one of the guest rooms.

He laid him down on the bed and brought a few towels over

from the bathroom. After that he started to leave, but I stopped him.

"I need your first aid kit, some bottles of water and a bowl."

Apollo quickly left to get me everything I needed from down in the kitchen.

Apollo

I stood a few feet behind Eliana and watched her take care of Frankie. She started with cleaning off the dried blood on his face and taking care of the cut on his forehead. Every few minutes she had to splash water in his face to keep him from passing out. His hands weren't as bad as the rest of them, but they looked like they'd been cut by glass. It took her over an hour to stop the bleeding and bandage the cuts. When she was done she let him rest. Frankie couldn't answer any questions. He mumbled sentences that made no sense. Eliana cleaned up the night stand she had all her trash on and left the room.

I found her in the kitchen cleaning her hands. She wrung out the rags and rinsed them. Then she grabbed a few pieces of gauze and bandages from the first aid kit bag and set them aside on the counter.

"I'm sure he has a concussion, so I'll stay up with him tonight, and keep an eye on him. In the morning, I'll call Raff and have him come pick him up."

She finished drying her hands, and then looked up at me.

"Can you do me a favor and find out what you can about

this Teddy person, and what he was doing with Raff? I want to try and fix the problem before Raff finds out about Frankie. See what he wanted from Teddy, and anything you can about his girlfriend."

She walked back to Frankie's room and left me in the kitchen. I threw the rags in the laundry room and put away the kit. I left the bandages out for her because I knew she was going to need them in a few hours.

I didn't find much on Teddy or his girlfriend. There was little record of the girlfriend, and I didn't find anything on Frankie's phone. We had barely started working together with Raff and the Mariani's. I didn't know about anything they were working on, and I bet they knew little about what we did.

I wish I was more helpful to Eliana, but I had no information to give her. I started to feel bad about our fight. I don't regret what I said, but it was terrible timing. I wouldn't have upset her if I knew she'd be dealing with all this. She was right. She didn't belong here, but like always when her family needed her she was the first person they called. I wonder what her life would have been like if there wasn't her family, or me, to hold her back.

I was going to stay up with Eliana, and watch Frankie with her, but I knew she wouldn't want that. I went back to bed for a few hours and woke up around six to check in on the two of them. Frankie was finally asleep, but Eliana was still awake in the chair next to him.

Eliana heard me walk into the room and sat up. She pointed to the water and some pills on the dresser. I brought them over to her, and unscrewed the cap. She took the water and splashed it on Frankie's face. He sat up in shock. He shook the water off of his face and looked around.

"El?" He asked, confused.

She handed him three painkillers, and the rest of the water.

"Drink and tell me what the fuck happened last night."

Sitting up the rest of the way Frankie sunk his head into his hands.

"How much do you know already?"

"I know that you've been sleeping with another man's girlfriend, a man who Raff is working with, and I also know you got the shit beat out of you last night."

"Okay yes, I was sleeping with Angela, but she played me. She was using me. I found out after my fight with Raff that she knew who I was, and she was trying to scam Teddy. I swear on my life El that I broke things off with her! But then I got this text from her saying she would tell Raff we were still hooking up, so I went to talk to her but it was a set up. She had Teddy over, and he saw me. You have to believe me; this bitch isn't who she says she is! I bet you she's also tricking Teddy. She said she makes a lot of money working with him."

Eliana looked back at me, "What did you find out about Teddy?"

"I couldn't find anything aside from what we already know, and I don't know anything about his girlfriend."

Eliana looked back at Frankie, and pulled her phone out of her pocket, "Call him."

Frankie sighed, and tried tossing the phone back to her, but she threw it right back.

"Apollo stay here, and deal with Raff when he gets here. Frankie, don't do anything until I get back, and please don't get in a fight with Raff."

Eliana grabbed Frankie's phone from the dresser and left. I ran after Eliana and followed her to her room.

"Where are you going?"

"Please, Apollo, trust me on this one. I don't want you getting involved in my family problems. It's not safe for you or your business. Don't worry, I'll be safe. I'll watch out for Jackson, and I'll be back in a couple of hours."

I didn't know who to look after. Eliana was running out the front door, and Frankie was half conscious in my guest room. I went back up to the room with Frankie and waited for Raff to show up. When he did he was pissed. I had to hold him off of Frankie. If Frankie wasn't already beaten up I knew Raff would have hurt him.

"I asked you to stop seeing her! I told you how important this was." He shouted.

"And I'm telling you I did. She's crazy, Raff. She told me all this stuff about me, and you, and things about Teddy. You can't trust her!"

"And what should I tell Teddy? Hey, my douchebag brother thinks your girlfriend is crazy, and is setting you up. Do you know how dumb that makes me look? And the worst part is you didn't call me last night. Your friends called Eliana because you all knew she would take care of it for you."

Raff turned and looked back at me, "Where is Eliana, and why didn't you two call me last night?"

"She was too focused on Frankie last night to call. I don't know where she is now, she wouldn't tell me."

"You and Eliana better hope things don't go south with Teddy before I can fix this mess you two made."

I stood in front of Raff, "Eliana had nothing to do with this. This is your problem, not Eliana's. If she was here right now I hope that you'd be thanking her. She stayed up with Frankie all

70

night making sure he woke up this morning."

Raff tried calling Eliana a few times before giving up. A few hours went by and she still wasn't back. Frankie was in the kitchen trying to have some breakfast, and Raff was pacing the hallways making calls to everyone he knew. I needed Eliana to come home soon because I was going crazy being stuck alone with Raff and Frankie. Finally, I heard the front door open. Eliana walked to the kitchen with Raff right behind. She ignored his yelling and went to check on Frankie.

"Fuck, calm down Raff I handled it. Stop your bitching." She complained.

"What do you mean you handled it?" Frankie asked, mouth full.

"I paid Angela a visit, and we worked it out. She won't be bothering Frankie anymore, and she also wants to send her apologies to you, Raff, for causing problems. After I had a chat with Angela she explained the situation to Teddy. He said he'd call you tomorrow to work out the rest of your agreement."

The room was quiet. Raff and Frankie looked at each other before looking back at Eliana.

"What did you do Eliana?" Raff asked, nervous to hear her answer.

"We had a heart to heart, just us girls. Don't worry about it." Eliana said, pouring herself some coffee.

I watched Eliana pour cream into her coffee. Her hands were cut, and red. They weren't like that when she left. The clean jacket she was wearing when she left was stained too. Her two brothers weren't phased at all with what Eliana left to do. No one but me seemed to care what happened to Angela. Raff and Frankie started fighting again. The two of them bickered over Eliana cleaning up Frankie's mess.

"Enough. I'm tired and haven't slept all week. I'm going to bed."

Eliana took her coffee and breakfast back to her room.

"You better hope Angela's still alive." Raff said, slapping Frankie over the head.

"You knew exactly what would happen when you had your friends call Eliana instead of me. Now your problem with Angela is fixed, and she magically fixed things with Teddy. You promised me you'd stop using Eliana like that. You know she'd do anything for you, asshole."

"Enough!" I yelled. "You two, get out of my house. Grab your shit, and leave. And don't bother Eliana for the rest of the weekend. She has a case on Monday. She doesn't need to be worrying about you two right now."

Frankie and Raff left, and the house was finally quiet again. Back in my room trying to get some sleep, I thought about what Raff said to Frankie. How far would Eliana go to protect her family?

Chapter Five

Eliana

I shouldn't have gone back to bed in the morning because I slept all day. I woke up in a panic around seven. I got up and tried getting some work done afraid I wouldn't be able to fall asleep again tonight. I was getting ready to take a break and get some dinner when Apollo knocked on my door.

I opened the door for him and gave him some room to step into the room.

"I have to work tonight at the bar. Dane set up a few meetings for me, and I don't know when I'll be back. Until I get back please don't leave. I have protection at the gate, but I don't want you going anywhere alone. I probably won't have my phone on me, so try not to need anything."

"Okay." I said, sitting down and getting back to work.

Apollo lingered for another minute but left when he realized I had nothing left to say to him. I don't care where he was going, all that mattered was that I got the house to myself for a few hours. Almost an hour later I heard Apollo leave the house. I grabbed all of my work and went out to the living room. Spreading out my stuff I ran to the kitchen to get some food. Apollo would be gone for hours. I could finally relax.

I prepped for Monday and even had enough time to catch up on some work for Margaret. I had things ready for every meeting this week and had a few minutes to myself before I went back to bed. I was looking for something on TV to watch when my phone rang in the other room. I threw off my blanket and walked to the kitchen. I considered not picking up the phone when I saw it was Mom, but I had been avoiding her all week.

"Thank goodness, I was ready to call the police and file a missing person's report."

I rolled my eyes, and tried to not snap a mean comment back, "Hello to you too Mom."

"I heard you finally found some time to move in with Apollo. I think that's going to be so good for you Eliana."

"Yeah, it's going great. Never been happier."

"I'm sure you're busy, so I don't want to keep you, but I was calling to ask if you two decided on a date for your engagement party. Apollo's mother wants a Friday, but I don't love that idea. I was hoping you could convince her to move it to a Saturday."

"Wait, hold on." I stopped her, "What engagement party?"

"Apollo didn't tell you yet? Catalina asked Apollo if we could throw you a party to celebrate the engagement, and he said you were fine with it. He thinks it's a good idea for the two families to get together."

"Apollo didn't bother telling me anything. I had no idea you wanted to throw us a party. I don't want one. Call Catalina and let her know that's not necessary."

"Eliana, I'm not going to tell her she can't host the party. That would be so rude! And besides, the food and drinks have already been paid for. I can't get the catering deposit back. Why don't you figure out a time that works best for the two of you and call me back when you've figured it out."

"Fine, I'll call you in the morning."

"Promise?"

"Yes, I promise. Goodnight."

I hung up, sliding my phone onto the counter. I couldn't catch a break.

Apollo never mentioned anything to me about a party. If I had known I would have told him not to say yes to his mom. He knew if he asked I would have said no, and that's exactly why he didn't bother telling me. He knew little about me, but at the very least he should have known a party with my family was not how I wanted to spend my weekend. I was ready for bed, but I didn't want to be asleep when Apollo came home. I cleaned up the living room and went back to my room to wait for him.

I was forcing myself not to fall asleep and keep my eyes open when I heard Apollo come home. I found him walking into his room. I followed behind him, stopping his door from closing. I don't think he knew I was behind him because he jumped when I stopped the door.

"How was work?" I asked.

"It was fine, but I'm tired." He said, trying to close his door, and get me to leave.

"I had a fun conversation with my mom earlier. She mentioned our engagement party. When were you going to tell me about it?"

He sighed, unbuttoning his shirt, "I didn't keep it from you on purpose. I was a little busy this week."

"I don't want our mom's throwing us a party. We already announced it at my dad's party."

"They're doing it for extended family. There are a couple of people from Italy that are flying in, and my parents want to celebrate. Also, your dad and mine have some work to take care of, and Raff wants to get to know some of the men he'll be working with."

"And what about me? What am I getting out of this? Am I just supposed to follow you around to different staged events every time you need me to? "

"This is what you agreed to. You told me to treat this like a real relationship. How does it look if you don't show up to these things? I have important people in my life that would like to meet you. In the future, I'm going to need your support at events like this."

I hated to admit it, but he was right. We were a team, and probably a threat to a lot of people in Apollo's circle. It was important for me to be at any event he went to.

"Okay" I said.

Apollo looked up at me in shock. He couldn't believe I wasn't arguing.

"Okay?"

"Yeah, I'll go, but you have to tell your mom we're doing it on a Saturday. It will save me some drama with my mom. If you say you need me I'll be there to support you."

Apollo processed what I said and gave me a nod.

"Okay, I'll call my mom tomorrow then." He started to walk away but looked back at me one more time. He was checking to see if he really heard me agree to the dinner party.

I stepped back, letting go of Apollo's door, and walked back to my room. I was tired, and the week hadn't even started yet. I packed a few things for work in the morning and went to bed.

For almost a week my life felt like it was back to normal. I only saw Apollo when he drove me to work, or back home again. I was busy working in the office, and I was starting to feel like my normal self again. Apollo had built a routine around the house. I knew when he left to work out, he knew when I liked to eat dinner, and neither of us had to spend time with the other. The week got even better when Alex and Dane returned on Friday. Alex was waiting for me Friday night to take me back to the house.

"You're back!" I shouted at him as I climbed into the back seat of the SUV. I was almost excited to see him. Maybe because it meant Apollo was done following me around.

"Yes Ma'am. A few guys came back to the warehouse, so I'm back working at the house."

"Alex, what did I tell you? Please stop calling me Ma'am, it's too weird. Eliana is fine."

"I'm sorry I can't do that Ma'am. Mr. Costa has asked me to call you Ma'am or Mrs. Costa. If you have an issue, take it up with him."

"Why would Apollo care?"

"He's ordered us to look after you like his family. You'll be treated the same as him from now on."

His family. We aren't family.

Alex drove back to the house and disappeared until I needed him again. I found Apollo on the phone in the living room. When I entered he said a quick goodbye and put his phone in his jacket pocket.

"Who was that?"

"Nobody."

"It had to be somebody Apollo. Don't lie to me."

"It was Dane. He's taking care of some things for me." Apollo looked uncomfortable, and I could tell he wanted to change the subject. Instead of getting angry at him for keeping things from me I walked to my room to change before going to get dinner. Apollo was back in his office when I left my room to find Alex.

I wondered why Apollo was still keeping things from me. He had been a part of the Frankie situation, and I was always open with him about my issues. Why was he holding back?

I found Alex eating in the kitchen alone.

"Alex, can I ask you something?"

"Of course." He answered.

"Promise you'll give me an honest answer?"

"Cross my heart Ma'am."

"What's Apollo's problem with me? I know he's hiding something from me, and this past week he's been distant."

"If I had to guess I'd say it's because he doesn't trust you. No disrespect to you, but you're an outsider. All of us that work for him had to prove our loyalty, and it wasn't easy. I can count on one hand the people he truly trusts. How do you expect a Costa to trust a Mariani?"

"But I'm not a stranger, I know our families haven't always gotten along, but we have a history. That should be worth something, right? What do the rest of you think about me?

Alex was quiet. He pretended not to hear my last question.

"Alex, please."

"They think Apollo would be better off without you. Not me, but others think you don't belong here, and they think you put the whole family at risk."

"And does Apollo agree with them?"

"I don't know. He doesn't really let us talk about you, but if I had to guess I would say he has a hard time picturing you running the business with him. That's all Apollo cares about, protecting the family. If he doesn't think you can be trusted then he won't ever let you be a part of his close circle. You have to ask yourself if you're ready to change who you are just to fit in. Is it worth changing yourself just to be accepted by Apollo and the rest of us?"

I didn't know the answers to Alex's question. It was getting harder and harder to separate myself from my past. Some days I couldn't look in a mirror without being reminded of all the terrible things I'd done. I was haunted by those I'd hurt. It took me months to feel normal again once I moved away to college. If I opened that door up would I be able to find a balance between the old me, and who I am now?

The plan for Saturday was to sleep in, and relax before going to Apollo's parent's house, but Mom had other plans. She called me for the first time at seven asking me if I was on any diets, so she knew what I could have for dinner. The second call ten minutes later was to suggest I start a diet, and her letting me know I'd be having the chicken. A dozen more calls were made throughout the day. Some letting me know Nora and the kids were coming, some asking about what I was wearing, and the rest were about Apollo.

It was four in the afternoon, and the calls finally stopped. I could get ready in peace. It was made very clear to me by Mom that I had to wear off white to the party. I missed the days when the only event you had to go to when someone was getting married was the wedding. Mom explained to me that the engagement party came first, then the bridal shower, then the rehearsal dinner, and then the wedding. If I had known that I would have drugged Apollo to Vegas and eloped.

I looked through my closet and found a blush tulle dress. Thin straps crossed each other across my back and connected to the thin straps of the dress. The dress hung low on my chest and gave focus to my diamond tennis necklace. It was a gift from Mom when I graduated, and I hadn't had an occasion to wear it since. I knew it would make her happy to see me wearing it. I let my hair fall to my back, pinned up against the sides showing the set of diamonds that scattered my ears. I usually left my ears empty, but the sparkle of the diamonds complimented the necklace.

I could hear Apollo calling for Alex to bring the car around, so I grabbed a small purse, and left for the living room. Apollo was waiting, wearing one of his black suits with a black tie. Half of his hair was pushed back, while a few strands fell onto his forehead. I could tell by the way he was pacing that he was upset. He was yelling on the phone again, not noticing I'd entered the room. He didn't notice I was right next to him until he heard my heels on the marble. He looked over, ending his phone call. He looked me up and down, pausing before walking to the door. Saying a quick prayer, I followed behind him to the car.

On the drive over I could see Apollo still staring from the

corner of my eye. When I would look towards his direction I could feel him shift in his seat. I tried to focus on Alex's driving and forget about Apollo sitting next to me. It was distracting sitting this close to him. I could sense he was still upset with the person he was on the phone with before I walked into the living room. I wanted to ask what was wrong, but I didn't want us fighting before the party.

Alex had pulled into the driveway and waited at the front of the house for Dane. I could see Dane pulling up, so I opened the door and started to get out. Apollo grabbed my arm.

"Wait."

I sat back into the car, confused.

"Here." He said, pulling something out of his pocket. Apollo put a small box in my hands. Not waiting for me to ask what it was he got out of the car. I sat in the car looking at the small velvet box. Inside the box sat a pear diamond ring. It sat on a beautiful gold band and was surrounded by a few smaller diamonds. I looked out the window for Apollo, but he was already walking up the stairs to the house.

I took the ring out of the box and held it up to the light. I could feel my chest get heavy, and tears start to form. I had been given a ring by a man who didn't love me and couldn't even be bothered to propose. I tried putting the ring on, but my hands were shaking. I looked back and saw Apollo waiting at the door looking back at the car. I took a deep breath, slipping the ring on. I got out of the car and walked up to Apollo. There were worse things to cry over than a diamond. Apollo wasn't worth the tears that threatened to fall, so I held them back.

Apollo held the door open for me as I walked in. My spine shivered when he rested his hand on my back as we walked into the party. It looked like we were the last to arrive. The house was full of guests. I could see Catalina, and Mom talking to a group of friends in the middle of the room. Dad was hidden behind a group of his men with Raff. The room went quiet when they noticed Apollo and I had arrived. Apollo whispered something to Dane, sending his men off down a hallway. Apollo led me to a table at the front of the room. It was a small table for the two of us next to a few tables for family. Leaving me alone at the table Apollo went to say hello to his mom.

Saving me from the stares of strangers, Raff came to say hello.

"How are you doing?" He asked.

"I need a drink."

Raff left to grab me some champagne and came back with Frankie. The two of them were putting their fight aside to be with me tonight. They almost had me convinced they weren't mad at each other still.

"Who are all of these people?" I asked.

"Do you see those men in the back, by the kitchen?" Raff asked.

I nodded my head looking over at them.

"They're Apollo's extended family. They're the ones who have been causing issues back in Italy. It's obvious by the way they're acting that they're not happy about the wedding. They came just to see if Cristiano was telling the truth. The men talking with Dad right now are people who have agreed to help us with our shortage here in the States. They are going to make a lot of money working with us. No one is more excited for the two of you than those men. And of course, you recognize Dad's men and cousins. They showed up for free booze."

I hung out with Raff and Frankie for most of the night. Nora finally found someone to take care of the kids and had some free time to hang out with the three of us. Back when we were all younger the four of us would suffer through parties like these together. Mom and Dad would insist on staying out all night long, and the four of us were left to fend for ourselves. Most of the time we managed to sneak out, but tonight we were stuck.

Mom and Dad ended up coming to steal Nora and Frankie from me, and Raff had a few people he needed to meet with. I was back to being alone with no one to talk to. While looking around the room a man approached me. He looked like a younger Apollo. His features were not as defined as Apollo's, but there was an eerie similarity between the two of them. He took my empty drink and offered me another. I cautiously accepted taking a sip.

"So, you're the famous Eliana."

"And you are?"

"Giovanni, I'm Apollo's cousin on the Costa side."

"That's odd, he's never mentioned you."

"Well I'm not surprised. He did keep you a secret from all of us. We were all so surprised when we heard the two of you were engaged. It couldn't have happened at a more convenient time for the two of you."

"Excuse me?"

"Oh, no offense, it's just he's not really the settle down type of guy. You're either madly in love or he's paying you enough to not care."

I was thrown off by Giovanni's words. Before I could respond an arm wrapped around my shoulders pulling me close. I looked up and saw an angry Apollo.

"Giovanni, glad you could make it. You're not bothering

Eliana, are you?"

"Of course not. I was just telling her how excited I am for the two of you. I'm sure it will be a beautiful wedding. Isn't that right Eliana?"

Giovanni looked down at me, intentionally ignoring Apollo right beside me.

Apollo shifted his body putting distance between Giovanni and me. I was starting to get uncomfortable. I gave a small nod and looked to the ground. Apollo's grip on me only tightened. Giovanni said goodbye to Apollo, finished his drink and left back to the bar.

"Are you okay?" Apollo asked, letting go of me.

"I'm fine." I answered, still feeling embarrassed. The whole room was watching me as Apollo put his hands on my shoulders, making sure I was okay. He rubbed my arms, in an almost comforting manner. He looked back to see Giovanni was gone.

"Who was that?"

"That's Giovanni. His dad, my uncle, has spent his whole life trying to take over for my dad. If he comes up to you again you need to run and find me. I don't want you alone with him. He's top of the list of people who don't want this wedding to happen. Do you understand?"

"Yes." I answered. Raff warned me there were people who didn't want us getting married, but I didn't think they'd bother showing up to the party. I looked around the room with a different lens. How many of these people felt the same way about Apollo and me?

Apollo stayed with me for the rest of the night. The less he trusted a person who came to talk to me, the closer he held me. He held my hand or wrapped his arm around my waist when it was someone he didn't want near me. He only relaxed when someone like Nora came to talk to me. It made me wonder what Apollo knew about these people that I didn't know. Why were they here if Apollo couldn't trust them?

I had finally gotten used to being by Apollo's side all night when Dane came over to us. I hadn't seen him all night, but as soon as he whispered something to Apollo the two of them took off. I looked around the room and noticed every single one of Apollo's men had disappeared. Alex, Julien, I couldn't find anyone. I looked near the kitchen where I last saw Apollo. He wasn't there, so I took a walk around the house. I walked through the kitchen into a small hallway. There were a few rooms down the thin, long hallway. I could hear Apollo's yelling coming through one of the rooms. I stopped at each door trying to find him.

When I got to the last room I heard Apollo giving orders to his men. Opening the door to see into the room I found a man tied to a chair, and Apollo standing in front of him. Dane and a few other men stood around the room watching. The man in the chair was half dead. He had cuts on his chest, and his face was swollen.

Julien was the first to see me behind the door. The rest of the room turned to see me walk into the room. Alex tried dragging me out, but I shoved him off of me before he could.

"Eliana-"

"Who the fuck is this?"

85

Chapter Six

Apollo

"Eliana, why don't you go back out to the party?" I asked, trying to get her to leave.

Instead she walked around the tarp in the middle of the room that Jackson sat on.

"Dane? Who is this?" She asked.

I shook my head telling Dane not to say anything.

"It's Jackson, the brother from North Carolina. We found him in New Jersey and brought him back here late last night."

"You couldn't wait one day to deal with this? You had to bring him here, to our engagement party? A party I didn't even want to have in the first place?"

"I told Dane not to bring him back to our house, so he

brought him here. He didn't know there was going to be a party tonight. I had no idea Jackson was even here until the drive over." I explained.

"He must be pretty important for you to leave the party and deal with him. Is he valuable to you Apollo? Does he have information you need, or maybe he's got something on you?"

"He's a nobody."

"So, the only reason he's here is to kill him?" She asked.

"Yes."

"And once you've taken care of him you can come back to the party?"

"Yes."

She walked right up to me with anger in her eyes.

"Promise?"

"I promise."

Eliana slid her hand under my jacket. Her hand snaked around my torso, and ribs. Before I could even register what she was doing she'd pulled out my gun from my holster. I tried grabbing the gun out of her hands, but she aimed it right at me. I took a step back from her raising my hand. She turned and pointed it to the rest of the guys. They all took a step back trying to shield their bodies from the gun she had pointed at them.

"Eliana, please, don't-"

"Shut up." She said pointing the gun back at me.

She walked up to Jackson and leaned down so they were eye level. She held her dress up to her knees to keep it from getting stained.

"It's time, Jackson. Are you ready?"

Jackson had little energy left in his body, but he made one more attempt to escape the chair.

She stood up, cocked the gun and pulled the trigger. Jackson's head dropped as blood dripped from his forehead. She turned to me, shoving the gun back into my chest. Then she walked over to Julien and Levi.

"You two are going to clean this up so Apollo and I can get back to our party. You won't bother us for the rest of the night. Understood?"

They both nodded their heads and started to untie Jackson. Turning around, Eliana walked over to Dane, "Make sure they don't fuck it up."

Careful to avoid the blood that began to spill onto the floor, Eliana walked over to me.

"You have five minutes to get cleaned up. I'll be out there waiting for you."

Eliana took one more look around the room and went back to the party like nothing had happened. I went to the restroom cleaning blood off of my hands, and then found Eliana talking to my mom.

A minute ago, Eliana held a gun to a man's head, and now she was making small talk with my mother. First the Angela issue, and now this. It scared me knowing so little about Eliana.

I was back to enjoying the party and staying close to her to keep her safe. She was still mad at me, but that didn't change all the people in this room who wanted to hurt her, or me. She understood because even though she was irritated she stayed close to me. As soon as the doors closed for the last time Eliana dropped her arm from mine.

"I want to go home."

"I'll go get Alex."

She was waiting for me at the doors when Alex brought the car around. I tried helping her into her side of the car, but she ignored my help. She avoided my hand, climbing into the car on her own. In the car, she looked out of her window not making eye contact with me.

"Are we not going to talk about what just happened?" I asked.

"Talk about what? Me giving you space, and trying to make things easier for us by going to this stupid party, or you bringing one of your hitman projects to our party without telling me?"

"I want to talk about the man you just killed in my parents' guest room."

"There's nothing to talk about. Jackson is dead, and you don't have to worry about him anymore. You should be thanking me." She continued to look out her window pretending I wasn't sitting right next to her.

"Eliana look at me."

Her shoulders didn't move. She stayed facing the street.

"Damn it, look at me when I'm talking to you! That shit was reckless. You shouldn't have done that." I shouted, losing my temper.

I finally got a reaction out of her. She turned, irritated.

"I'm the reckless one? Jackson was your problem! I'm not the one who messed up the first time you went to take care of him."

"You're right, Jackson was *my* problem. I'm warning you not to get in the way of my work. Pull something like that again, and you'll regret it."

Eliana scoffed and rolled her eyes.

I hated when she did that. I lifted her chin so she was facing me again.

"You won't roll your eyes at me again. Do you understand?"

"Yes, Sir." She teased.

Alex pulled into the driveway. The car was parked, but neither of us moved. She stared me down, not blinking. Alex let out an awkward cough, and Eliana opened her door behind her. I let go of her and watched her walk up to the house.

She was halfway to her room when I caught up to her.

"We aren't done talking."

"Yes, we are." She answered.

"No, we're not. Why did you do it?"

Her back still facing me, she spoke.

"I know everything Apollo. I know I don't belong here. You hate having me around, and I hear what your men say about me when they think I can't hear them. I'm really trying here, but I don't know how much longer I can put up with it. When I saw all of you in that room tonight all I saw were a bunch of hypocrites. The way they laugh and sneer when I walk into a room, I'm sick of it. I shouldn't have killed Jackson, and I'm sorry, but I'm tired of being ignored. You act like I don't exist, and that gives your men an excuse to treat me like shit. You've gotten good at masking how you feel about me, but the rest of them... they don't even try to hide it anymore."

"Eliana, I didn't know-"

"I'm tired." She said, cutting me off. "I'll head to bed first." I tried to walk up to her, but she locked her door before I could get close enough.

I had no idea they were still treating her like that. I told them not to cause any problems for her. I still couldn't believe Eliana had shot Jackson. I could still hear the ringing of the gun in my ear. I took a quick shower before going to bed, hoping it would relax me. The water dripped down my face as I thought about Eliana. The way her dress bounced when she entered into the room, the fabric light and flowing with her steps. The goosebumps she got when I rested my hand on her back, her skin exposed because of her dress. Her hand wrapping around my arm, digging her nails into me. I tried to forget the look she gave me as she held my own gun to my chest. I ran my hands over my face trying to think of something else. Turning off the shower I grabbed my towel and got ready for bed.

I tossed around for an hour. Sleep wasn't coming. I threw the blankets off of me and walked to the kitchen.

Walking to the kitchen I found the lights already on. Opening the door, I saw Eliana reaching for a bowl from the cabinet. She set down the bowl and grabbed a spoon.

"I was trying to be quiet; did I wake you up?"

"No, it's fine. I couldn't sleep. I was coming to get a snack."

"I made brownies. They should be done soon. I was getting the ice cream ready. You can stay and have some if you want."

I nodded my head and grabbed a bowl. The silence between us was torture. We both sat there not saying a word to each other. The smell of chocolate filled the kitchen, and soon the oven beeped. Eliana stood up grabbing an oven mitt pulling out the brownies. She took a knife out of the drawer and started cutting squares.

"Aren't you supposed to let brownies cool before you cut them?" I asked.

"I don't have the patience for that. They're better with ice cream when they're still warm."

She placed a few on a plate and brought it over to the small kitchen table. I brought the bowls, spoons and ice cream. Eliana sat across from me filling up her bowl with ice cream, then with the warm brownies. We sat at the table together and ate our dessert. I think this is the longest we've gone without fighting and yelling at each other.

"Can I ask you a question?"

"I have a feeling even if I say no you're still going to ask." She said.

"Have you ever done that before?" I asked.

"Make brownies?"

"No, kill someone."

Eliana put her spoon down, "No, it wasn't my first."

"How many more before Jackson?"

"I don't know. I try not to keep track. What about you? Everyone's told me stories about you and your list. Is it true what they say?"

"What do they say?" I asked.

"They say you enjoy it."

"I don't enjoy it. They only say that because I'm constantly having to clean up other people's messes. Why do you do it?"

"I worked for Raff before I went to school."

Eliana took another bite. A drop of ice cream fell off of her spoon. My eyes trailed to her lips as she licked them clean. When I looked back up at her she was staring at me. I lowered my head and swirled my spoon around in my melting ice cream. Very few people had the nerve to look me in the eyes. It was weird for her to do it so casually.

I was so distracted by Eliana I didn't notice she was already finished. She pushed her chair back and took her bowl to the sink. She wrapped up the brownies and put the ice cream back. She had almost left the kitchen without saying goodnight before I stopped her.

"I'm sorry about the way my men have been treating you. It won't happen again, I promise. And if it does you need to tell me, so I can take care of it."

"Thank you." She answered walking away into the dark hallway.

Eliana

Apollo could promise he would take care of his men all he wanted, but I knew it wasn't going to change anything. It wouldn't change the looks of dread they tried to hide when they got assigned to work with me or their whispers when I left the room. The only person who wasn't awful to me was Alex. He kept his distance, and always tried to make me feel comfortable at the house.

I wasted Sunday sleeping and lying around the house. I had to go into work early on Monday, so right after dinner I went to bed. I didn't see Apollo at all after our talk Saturday night. On Monday morning when I woke up things were different. A group of workers were waiting for me in the kitchen to cook me breakfast. All of Apollo's men who saw me around the house treated me like royalty. Some of them didn't even raise their heads. Apollo must have talked to them.

When I left a room I didn't hear anything, and no one at the front gate said anything to me as we drove through. Alex drove me to work, anxiously looking back at me as he drove. After work, I was greeted by a handful of staff around the house. They couldn't have been nicer. It felt like the mean girls from high school were being nice to me as a joke.

Around six I went looking for dinner. I found food in the dining room attached to the kitchen. Apollo didn't show even though there was a plate set out for him. His food sat there getting cold. It was another quiet dinner alone. I didn't mind it, in fact, it gave me some time to work through my week. Margaret had asked me to go to Texas with her to check on a family, and I quickly offered to go with. I was eager to go and get away from the house, and Apollo, but I didn't know how I was going to tell him. I was afraid he wouldn't let me go. Not that it would stop me from going, but I didn't want to fight again. Before I went to my room to pack I thought it best to tell Apollo I was leaving.

I knocked on his door and waited for a response. I didn't hear anything, but I knew he was in there. I knocked again.

"Apollo it's me. I need to talk to you."

"What?" He shouted through the doors.

Great, he was in a bad mood.

"Can I come in?"

The room went quiet again, and then I heard footsteps. The door opened and Apollo popped his head out.

"What do you want?"

"I'm going to Texas for a few days. I wanted to give you a heads up. I'll be back on Friday at the latest."

"Why?"

"It's a work thing. It's only me and Margaret, and if you want I'll even bring Alex as protection."

"Fine. I don't care." He said slamming the office door closed.

Four days away from this place was not long enough.

I found Alex at the front gates and let him know we'd be going to Texas, and then I went to my room to pack. I wasn't thrilled about spending the week with Margaret, but it was better than being stuck at the house. After packing I went to bed. I didn't want to be walking around the house when Apollo left his office. He was in a bad mood, and I couldn't risk him changing his mind about Texas. In the morning, I left a quick note for Apollo letting him know when I'd be back.

Alex dropped me off in front of the airport, and then drove off. I thought maybe he wasn't coming with me, but when I boarded my plane I saw him a few rows behind me. He was a ghost. I only ever saw Alex when he wanted to be seen. I slept through most of the flight, and only woke when the plane landed.

I didn't have time to go to a hotel first and drop off my things. Margaret wanted to start working as soon as I landed. Alex got a rental car and held onto our luggage while I worked with Margaret. We spent all afternoon driving around neighborhoods trying to find family members of our client. Margaret was concerned about a family going missing for a while, and then last week they stopped replying to messages. Something had happened to them, and we needed to make sure they were safe. Every few blocks I could see Alex right behind us while we worked. We drove to every known connection to the family and found nothing. After hours of walking and driving Margaret and I were exhausted. We decided to call it a night.

Margaret had offered to let me stay with her at her hotel, but I needed my own room. She agreed to let me stay at my own hotel if I was ready to work early the next morning. I watched her leave for her hotel and went looking for Alex. He was on the phone with someone and waiting for me in a parking lot down the street.

"Did you find who you were looking for?" Alex asked.

"No, we called it a night, but we'll continue tomorrow. Can you take me back to my hotel please?"

"Sure thing." He said opening my door for me.

I was tired and struggling to stay awake on the drive back to the hotel. I barely noticed Alex wasn't driving the right way. We missed a turn a few minutes ago.

"Alex?"

"Yes Ma'am?"

"My hotel is behind us. I think you're going the wrong way."

"Mr. Costa didn't tell you?"

"Tell me what?"

"He changed your reservation. He didn't want you staying at your old hotel. He upgraded your room at a hotel a client owns."

"No, Alex, I don't want to bother anyone. Can you take me back to my hotel?"

"I'm afraid it's too late for that."

It was irritating of Apollo to change my hotel reservations like that. I would have called and argued with him, but I was too tired. At the end of the day a bed was a bed, and I needed sleep. I slept in the car until Alex woke me up. I let Alex take care of checking in as I waited by the elevators.

Alex stepped into the elevator behind me handing me my bags.

"Alex, you accidentally pushed the penthouse. You need a special key for that."

"I meant to hit it." Alex answered, holding up a swipe card.

I looked at Alex in shock as the elevator started to rise faster and faster. A ding signaled the opening of a door that led into another small hallway. I dropped my bags in the hallway opening the doors into the main room. The suite was beautiful. Inside was a bed that stretched across the entire room, and a balcony that overlooked the city. The best part about the room was how quiet it was. The noise from the busy streets was gone.

I looked at Alex in disbelief, "Why did he do this? This is too much."

"I told him you had a rough day, and he wanted to do something to help. But if you tell him I told you he did something nice I'll deny it!" Alex said, setting my bags down near my bed.

"If you need anything I'll be a few floors down. If you leave the building let me know."

Alex went back to the elevator as I continued to walk about the room. After walking around a few times, I grabbed some champagne from the mini bar and went to the bathroom to turn the bathtub on. While I waited for it to fill I called Apollo.

"Is everything okay?"

"Yeah, everything's fine. I just wanted to say thank you."

"For what?"

"The room. Really, it's great. Thank you."

"It's no big deal, I know a guy." He answered, trying to

brush it off.

"Apollo, stop being modest, have you seen this room? The bed is like four times the size of mine!"

I heard a small laugh from Apollo's end of the phone making me smile. Apollo was trying to play it cool, but I could tell he was excited for me.

"Get some rest tonight so you can focus on work tomorrow."

"Okay." I answered, waiting for one of us to hang up.

"Eliana? You still there?"

"I'm still here." I answered, walking around the room.

"I'm going to hang up now. I have a meeting to get to."

"Okay, goodnight Apollo."

"Goodnight El."

Apollo

I was fully prepared to answer the phone, and get yelled at by Eliana, but I was pleasantly surprised. Alex told me all about driving around with Margaret. I knew she was glad to get away for a few days, and I wanted to do something to help relieve her stress. If she came back relaxed it would make my life easier. Eliana sounded really happy. I could almost see her smile through the phone. Hanging up, I slid my phone back into my pocket. I had a meeting with a friend of Raff's. They were trying to take advantage of our new arrangement. I didn't want to be responsible when things went south. Oscar was asking for my men to push products out, and I didn't trust their system. I wasn't looking forward to telling Raff no, but I didn't want to be working with them. Raff was trying to push it, but he could tell I didn't like Oscar.

All I had to do was get through drinks with the two of them. I wasn't going to let them get me drunk enough to agree to any deals. Heading back to the table I found an already drunk Oscar. I called the waiter over for a beer and watched the two of them take shot after shot.

A few hours in I got a text. I would have left it alone, but it could have been Dane with updates. I unlocked my phone and saw a photo from Eliana. She was in a big t-shirt, her hair in a towel and she was doing her best to jump on the bed. Her legs and arms stretched out, and she had the biggest smile on her face that I'd ever seen. The photo was blurry like she ran and jumped just in time for the camera timer. I let a small laugh escape as I looked at the photo. After the picture came a text.

Eliana: I wasn't kidding about the size of this bed.

"What's got you smiling?" Oscar asked, leaning onto my shoulder.

"Nothing, get off of me."

"Sure." He slurred.

"Raffael, I really need to go now. I have meetings in the morning."

"You can't leave now; we're just getting started!" A drunk Raff complained.

"I think all of us should leave before it gets any later. If you want, I have some free time on Friday. We can set up another meeting at my office, but I need to go."

"Don't be like that!" Oscar shouted.

I pried Oscar off of me and watched him fall back to his chair.

"I'm leaving. Call the office if you'd like to meet with me."

On the ride home, stuck at a red light I opened up my text from Eliana. I hadn't had a chance to text her back because of Oscar. I wanted to text her, but I knew she was sleeping. I looked at her text a little longer and decided to text her in the morning.

I worked until the sun came up in New York. I didn't know what time it was in Texas, but I sent a message to Eliana anyway.

Did you get some sleep?

I turned my phone's sound off, nervous to not get a response. I distracted myself with another hour of work before getting ready. After a shower, I saw a new message from Eliana.

Eliana: Slept so well I woke up and almost forgot I was stuck in Texas with Margaret.

It was Friday, and Eliana was flying back. Alex said they'd get home around noon. That would have been fine, if Raff and

Oscar hadn't decided to pay me a surprise visit.

"Apollo, good morning! Your men told us you were busy. I'm glad we found you."

"You actually caught me as I was leaving. I have to go down to the warehouse with Dane."

"This will only take a minute. We want to work out a schedule with you."

"I already told you; I'm not interested."

Raff walked into my office behind Oscar.

"You know how much money you could make from this deal. Why would you not want to partner with Oscar?"

"There's nothing about this deal I like. I know how Oscar runs his operations. He's impulsive, and he doesn't care about his men. I'm not putting mine in danger just to work with Oscar."

"That's bullshit. You don't care about your men. You don't want to have to split any profit with me." Oscar said.

"Trust me. It has nothing to do with that." I laughed. "I think you should leave now while I'm being nice."

"I'm not going anywhere! Rafael promised me a fucking deal, and I'm not leaving until I get it."

I was too busy for this bullshit today. I was ready to grab Oscar by his collar and drag him out of my office when I heard a familiar voice.

"Shit." I sighed, leaving my office. When I looked into the living room I saw Eliana and Alex bringing in their luggage.

I went back to my office to get rid of Oscar.

"Go, now. Eliana just got home and I don't want her a part of this."

101

"No, I think we should ask Eliana how she feels. Let her have a say in the partnership. After all, you two are a team, right?" Raff asked.

"Eliana!" Raff shouted leaving the office. I didn't want her and Oscar to meet. She was going to take her brother's side, and I would look like the bad guy for saying no.

I sat on the couch waiting for the inevitable.

Eliana walked into the office with Raff right next to her trying to explain the situation.

"Eliana, Oscar. Oscar, Eliana."

She gave Oscar a polite smile and handshake, but I could tell she didn't want to be here. She looked for me in the room to try and figure out what was going on.

"Please tell Apollo he'd be an idiot not to work with Oscar."

"Eliana, it's a pleasure I've heard so much about you." Oscar smiled.

"I really think the three of you should work this out on your own. I don't know anything about Oscar or his business, and I don't want to know the details." She suggested.

"We tried, but Apollo is causing some problems. After a week of planning he's backing out of an agreement we made."

"I never agreed to anything." I chimed in.

Eliana looked back at me, and then at Raff.

"Oscar, would you mind stepping out for a minute. I'd like to talk with Raff and Apollo alone. Alex is right outside in the hallway. He could get you something from the kitchen while you wait."

"Sure thing, beautiful." He flirted.

God, I hated him. Once the doors were closed Eliana turned back to Raff.

"Why do you want this deal so bad? That guy's a creep."

"You know how long I've waited to expand distribution. Oscar can give me that. I know he's not great, but I can't expand without him. I need Apollo's men to help us get past Chicago."

"And you don't trust him?" She asked me.

"No, I know people he's burned before, and I don't want to risk my men. I can help Raff expand without Oscar."

"But it would take too long! Oscar already has a system, and workers. We speed up the process by a few months if we work with Oscar. He knows the territory better than anyone." Raff argued.

Eliana looked at me, unsure what to do.

"Eliana, please. Do it for the family." Raff begged.

I lowered my head knowing I'd lost. There's no way she wouldn't give Raff what he wanted.

"No."

I shot my head up. Did I hear that right?

"No?" Raff asked.

"If Apollo doesn't trust him, I don't trust him."

I stood up, still trying to process her words.

"El, come on. Do you have any idea how much money I'm losing?"

"I don't care. I'd like you and Oscar to leave my house now."

Raff stood there in disbelief. Eliana crossed her arms waiting for him to leave. When he didn't move she opened the office doors and went looking for Oscar.

"There's my girl! How did it go? Did you and Raff work everything out?"

"Raff and I did talk, but I'm afraid I agree with Apollo this time. I've had a long flight and I'm tired, so I'd like you to leave now."

"You've got to be kidding me! Raff are you really going to sit back and let your bitch of a sister kick me out?"

Alright, that's it. This son of a bitch is getting his ass kicked. I walked up behind Eliana ready to beat the shit out of Oscar when Eliana stopped me, putting a hand on my chest.

"Alex." She ordered.

In one movement Alex had Oscar curled over with his shoulder dislocated up to the sky. Oscar shrieked in pain as Alex dragged him out of the house while Eliana held the door open for Alex. Alex threw out Oscar and waited for Raff to follow.

"I'll call you later when I'm free. Don't do anything without talking to us first."

"Eliana, wait-"

The door slammed shut and Eliana walked back to her bags.

"Why did you do that?" I asked still in disbelief.

"I could tell you didn't trust Oscar."

Eliana grabbed her bags and left the living room.

"I'm tired. Don't bother me unless the house is on fire or someone's dead."

I watched her walk back to her room. I stood there in the living room trying to process what just happened. I can't believe it.

She chose me.

Chapter Seven

"Eliana, you have a call on three."

"Thanks Mal."

To my surprise the world stopped when Margaret and I went to Texas. Everyone in the office forgot how to function without us babysitting them and I was drowning in paperwork. It would take weeks to get caught up. I was hoping for little distractions, but I was getting calls every ten minutes.

"Eliana speaking." I answered.

"Ms. Mariani, you have a few guests down at the front desk. We think they might be clients of yours. They are causing a bit of a scene. We wanted to give you a call before we called the police."

"They asked to see me?"

"Yes, they said they have something important to talk to you about. We can ask them to leave if you want."

"No, it's fine. I'll be down in a minute."

I hung up the phone and left my office. I wasn't expecting anyone to stop by the office today. Most of my clients called first. I had no idea who could be downstairs waiting for me.

The elevator doors opened and I stepped into the hallway.

Oh my God.

Two of Apollo 's men were arguing with the receptionist. The security guard right behind them. They did little to hide who they were. When they swung their arms, you could see their guns under their jackets, and their neck tattoos helped them stand out in the crowd. What the hell were they doing here?

"We're not leaving until we see Eliana." The shorter one shouted. I hadn't worked with these two yet, but I think the lean tall one was Ricky and the short one was Mateo.

I hurried over to the front desk putting myself in front of the two idiots and the receptionist.

"I'm so sorry Talia. I'll take care of it. They are here to see me. We're leaving. Again, I'm so sorry. They won't be back."

I grabbed the two by their jacket sleeves and dragged them out to the parking lot. I let go of them when we turned behind the building.

"What are you two doing here?"

"Apollo sent us. We have something we need you to take a look at."

"Apollo sent you?"

"Yes Ma'am." The taller one handed me a folder.

"We were hoping you could find out some information on

106

this person. We are having some difficulty tracking them down."

I grabbed the folder looking through it.

"You interrupted me at work and caused a disturbance at my office, so I could look up an MIA for you? Are you two fucking kidding me?"

"We only came because-"

"No. You're done talking. Let me make this very clear because apparently Apollo thinks he can do whatever he wants. You will leave here today, and never come back. When you leave and get back to the office, tell Apollo I'm pissed. Tell him if he pulls shit like this again he'll regret it."

The two men tried to speak, but I cut them off.

"I don't want to hear anything you have to say. Leave now and tell Apollo I'll deal with him later."

That was so embarrassing. I don't want to walk back into the building. One of my rules was that Apollo didn't get involved with my work. He knew that from the very beginning. It was obvious he didn't respect me. I walked back to the elevator with my head down. Maybe if I bought Talia an apology gift she would forgive me. I was screwed if I got on her bad side.

It was obvious all of my coworkers heard about what happened because when I walked back to my office I could hear the whispers. Margaret was waiting for me when I opened my door.

Shit.

"Who were those people?"

"They were a few want-to-be clients. They heard about the work we do, and they thought I would take a case for them."

"Don't lie to me Eliana."

"I'm not lying. I had no idea they were coming."

"I know it's not a coincidence you keep your personal life private. Don't think I haven't caught on. I know the kinds of people you choose to spend your time with, and even marry. I can't run this company if you're causing issues as my number one attorney. I ignored your family connections because you're a good worker, but if something like that happens again you're gone. Do you understand?"

"Yes, I am so sorry. It won't happen again."

"Good." Margaret said leaving my office.

I walked to my desk and sat down. I can't believe him. We had a deal. He knew he wasn't allowed to interfere with my work.

I didn't leave my office for the rest of the day. I tried leaving for lunch, but everyone's head turned when I opened my door. I was so upset and distracted by Apollo 's men and Margaret yelling at me, that I didn't get as much work done as I should have.

I had to wait until six when the office was almost empty to leave. I could have handled the stares and whispers, but I couldn't have handled someone coming up to me and asking questions. I didn't have answers for them. I couldn't tell them why I was marrying Apollo, and I couldn't tell them his men stopped by so I could illegally search a missing persons case.

Alex was surprised to see me coming back to the car so late, but he didn't say anything. I'm sure he knew all about Ricky and Mateo.

Back at the house, I went looking for Apollo. I found him working in his office. I would have knocked, but if he doesn't care about my rules I don't give a fuck about his.

"Eliana, I'm busy plea-"

"I don't care."

I waited for him to put his phone down and give me his full attention.

"Did you give Ricky and Mateo permission to stop by my office today?"

"Yes. I sent them to get information on a person."

"I told you not to get in the way of my career. You are the biggest fucking idiot I know."

"Don't say another word Eliana." He said standing up. "I have put up with your attitude for a while because I didn't want us fighting more than we already do, but I'm done being disrespected by you. If you want to barge into my office, and interrupt my work, the least you can do is act with a little bit of decency."

"You want respect? After everything you've done to me? I had to grab your men out of my office today by their coats before the police did. I almost got fired by Margaret, and I was talked about in my own office by all of my coworkers. I have been treated like shit since the day we met, and *you* want a little bit of respect?"

I spoke so fast I didn't process the words coming out of my mouth. I had pissed off Apollo, and I was starting to regret it.

"We made a deal. You promised you wouldn't get in the way of my work."

"You didn't really think I wouldn't need your help on certain cases, did you? You asked to be kept in the loop about family stuff. This is family related. I needed help finding someone. There are worse things I could have done. Maybe next time I'll personally pay a visit to your office." He teased.

"Do you think this is a joke? Is this funny to you?"

"I'd be lying if I didn't find your little outbursts entertaining.

Everyday it's something new with you. If you're done yelling at me, get out of my office. I have a lot of work."

"I'm not leaving until you apologize."

"Apologize, are you serious? It's not that big of a deal. So what, I had a few of my men stop by your work. Next time I'll have them bring the work to the house. I'm not apologizing."

I stood there thinking about my next move.

"You're right. I was being dramatic. I mean it's okay for the two of us to help each other with work, right?"

"Exactly. Now, doors that way. I have a few phone calls to make."

I left the office and closed the doors. Walking back to my room I thought about what to do next. All I knew is that Apollo was going to regret pissing me off. He hadn't seen me angry yet, and he was about to regret it.

Apollo

Eliana was mad about my surprise visit to her office, but she was fine helping me take care of Jackson. She didn't get to pick and choose when she helped and when she didn't. I was hoping she would calm down later in the night, but when I left for the bar she was still pissed. I was meeting an old friend tonight, and didn't have time to deal with her, so I left her at the house. When I was younger, I was Dad's main guy for fixing problems. Now that I was busier and had less time to travel I hired Gomez to work for me. He was helping me with one of my warehouse guys who disappeared. A few months ago, when Jason got frustrated he wasn't moving up in ranks he threatened to tell on the family. I didn't consider it a real threat until Jason went missing. Even though I doubt Jason was stupid enough to talk I needed him found. I wanted Gomez to take care of him before it became a bigger issue.

I hated doing work at the bar, but it made the most sense when I was meeting with clients, or people like Gomez. They weren't willing to come to my office to meet. They needed security and anonymity. It was the easiest place to sneak out if something happened.

I was in a booth in the far corner of the club with Dane on my left and Gomez on my right. I could see a few of my men sitting at the bar, and the rest making rounds around the dance floor.

"I don't think I'll be able to help Apollo. He's a ghost. I haven't found anything. There's a good chance the state is hiding him." Gomez said.

"If they do have him I don't know what he would be telling them. He's a nobody. I know he doesn't have anything on me."

"You don't know that." Dane replied. "People talk. We can't be sure we're safe."

I took a sip of my drink. I didn't have any leads on Jason, and I was running out of time to find him. An hour later Gomez and I were still trying to make a plan. I was tired and running out of ideas. I was about to call it a night when one of my men approached the table.

"Sir, we have a small problem."

I turned, "What now?"

"She's here." One of them answered.

"Who?" Dane asked.

One of my men nodded his head to the bar. Sitting next to a man I didn't know was Eliana. Jesus, what the fuck was she doing here? She laughed and threw her head back, enjoying the company. I watched her take another sip of her drink and waited for her to look my way. When she finally looked over we made eye contact. She grabbed her drink and started making her way through the crowd.

It was cruel really, being engaged to a woman like Eliana and only ever being able to look. She was killing me, slowly. Her long legs shimmered in the club lights, and her breasts teased me as they bounced out of her dress. I'm sure she dug around in her closet for a long time looking for the tiniest dress she could find. It hugged her hips and left everyone around her turning their heads for a second look. I wanted nothing more than to untie those little pieces of string that held her dress together. I wanted to rip that goddamn dress up and watch it fall to the floor. Of course, now that only had me imagining what she wore underneath. *Fuck.* I was no longer living in purgatory; this was my own personal hell.

I wasn't the only one who noticed Eliana's bold fashion statements. My men thought they did a good job of hiding the stares, and the way they whispered about her, but I wasn't an idiot. It was starting to become tiresome. Real or fake, Eliana was mine. I wanted to be the only one who got to look at her and admire all that she was. I made a mental note to take care of the bartender that made her laugh so much as I watched her walk closer to my table.

I turned to my right and saw Gomez and half of my men eyeing Eliana like one of the whores they usually brought home. It was infuriating. I wanted to smash every single one of their heads into the table, but I had to try and find a way to stay calm in public. I bit my tongue trying not to say the wrong thing in front of all these people.

"Eliana, what brings you here?"

"Oh, was I not invited? I'm sorry, it's just that last time I checked I was a part of the family. I thought you needed me, or was I mistaken?"

I knew why she was doing this. I invaded her work space, and now she was paying mine a visit. I looked over to Gomez. He had a big smile on his face as he looked Eliana up and down. He reached out an arm.

"The more the merrier. Eliana, why don't you join us?"

Eliana shook his hand with a cheeky smile.

"Gomez, give us a minute please. I need to talk to Eliana."

I grabbed Eliana and led her to the back of the bar, down a quiet hallway.

"What are you doing here?"

"Earlier you said I was being dramatic, and I agree. If you come to my work I should be helpful and stop by your meetings."

"You know that's not what I meant. It's not safe for you to come here alone."

"Why not? I'm a Costa now, right? I should be able to visit my own bars."

"I'm too busy to deal with this right now Eliana, go home."

"No."

I had run out of patience. Turning around I pressed Eliana up against the wall. I held her arms at her side.

"I'm telling you to leave."

"And I'm telling you I think I'll stay for a while. It took me forever to get ready, and it would be a shame to waste a dress like this."

I continued to press her against the wall. She wasn't afraid, she wasn't intimidated. She didn't try to fight me off. Instead she gave me a sinister smile as she held still. Slowly, she leaned in and whispered in my ear.

"Do you think you're the first guy to trap me against a wall Apollo? I kind of like it. Grab my wrists a little tighter. Will that make you feel like you're in control? Do you like it too? Pressing into me against the cold brick, your knee just above my dress?"

Frustrated, I let go. Hoping Eliana would leave, I went back to the table. I unbuttoned my jacket and tried to calm down. Unfortunately, Eliana followed me back out to the main floor. She walked past the table and went looking for another drink. While Eliana flirted her way to the front of the bar and ordered, I looked around at all of my men.

I grabbed one of my men by his neck, gaining the attention of everyone around me.

"Look at my fiancé's ass again Johnny and I will carve your eyes out with a fucking butter knife and send them to your mother. Do you understand?" I asked.

Releasing him from my grip, Johnny shook his head, unable to spit out any words. The rest of my men shifted in their seats.

"So much as look at Eliana wrong and I will make your life a living hell. You will beg for the devil himself to take you down to hell with him. I don't care if the next time she walks into this club she's wearing a god damn bikini, you will treat her with more respect than the fucking dogs you are." I threatened.

I watched Eliana and made sure she got back to the table safely. I knew I had nothing to worry about, and that Alex was around here somewhere, but I couldn't concentrate on anything but her. She was distracting to say the least. I didn't care about anyone in this club, or why Gomez was here tonight. All I could focus on was where Eliana traveled to.

Finally making it back to the table Eliana handed me a drink. She had ordered me another whiskey, and what looked like a double shot of vodka for herself. She wasted no time throwing back her drink. She carelessly let a few drops of her drink spill down her chin and onto her neck. If alone I would have grabbed her by the nape of her neck and licked off everything she spilt, but I was thankfully snapped back to reality by the coughs of a few of my men.

Either she had no idea what she was doing and she was a fool, or she knew exactly the effect she had on me and she was playing me like a fucking fiddle.

"Don't worry, I'm not staying." She said, standing up. "I just came to say goodbye and good luck."

Before leaving the table, she leaned into me. Resting her hand on my shoulder, and stopping only an inch away from my ear, she spoke.

"By the way, I know where Jason is."

I snapped my head turning to her. That evil smile was back as she grabbed my drink and took a sip. She slid out of the booth, grabbed her purse and started to walk away. I tried to follow after her but was slowed down by the heavy crowd.

"Eliana, wait!"

She turned around right before she got to the exit. She held up both hands and flipped me off. I had no chance of getting to her before she reached the door. Knowing I was too far behind her to stop her, she blew me a kiss and shouted a classy 'fuck you' across the bar before turning on her heels and leaving.

Eliana

As I drove away from the bar I watched a pathetic Apollo run after the car. I heard my phone buzzing in my purse but chose to ignore it. In a few hours, I would have Alex drop off the information I found, but right now I wanted him to suffer a little.

I didn't plan on giving him any information on Jason, but I got curious at work and dug into the case a little bit. Apollo was wrong. The police weren't helping him hide. He ran on his own. Jason is a paranoid thief with a lot of people looking for him. Apollo isn't even his biggest concern. Jason is running from a few guys that loaned him a lot of money. I sort of feel bad for him. I don't know what's worse, Apollo finding him first or the loan sharks.

I would have stayed at the bar longer just to piss off Apollo, but I had work in the morning. I was asleep before Apollo came home. Just in case he came home angry I locked my doors and turned off my notifications. On my drive to work in the morning I got a call from Apollo.

"Hello?"

"Did Alex tell you? I left with Gomez. We're going to take care of Jason. I won't be home for a few days."

"Are you actually going to take care of Jason or am I going

to find him tied to a chair at our wedding?" I asked.

"You're hilarious Eliana. Always making me smile. Remember the rules. Don't leave the house without Alex, and don't cause any problems."

"Be safe. I'll try not to miss you too much."

Annoyed, he hung up first.

Apollo was gone, and I had a few nights of freedom. I thought about Emma. She had been asking me to have dinner for a while now. Because of Apollo I had been avoiding her invites, but if he was going to be gone for a few days maybe I'll invite her over. She's been dying to see the house. Plus, it would be nice having someone at the house who didn't completely hate me.

It was Thursday night and I hadn't heard anything from Apollo. He hadn't even reached out to Alex. I assumed he was still busy, so I invited Emma and Kelsey over for drinks and dinner. It was usually Apollo's chef who made dinner, but I gave everyone the night off so it would just be us girls. Emma and Kelsey showed up right at seven as I was taking the chicken parmesan out of the oven.

I could hear Emma's voice echoing down the hallway as Alex brought them to the kitchen.

"This is bigger than most museums! You could let a hundred people live here, and you'd still have extra rooms. El, where are you? We're lost!"

I stuck my head out into the hallway and saw an already tipsy Emma run towards me. She jumped onto me in a big hug almost crashing us to the ground.

Kelsey helped her stay on her feet and grabbed the wine bottle from her hand.

"Sorry, she had a rough day at work. She had a drink on the

ride over." She explained.

"That sounds about right." I laughed.

Emma helped herself to the kitchen and set her stuff down. Kelsey followed behind me.

"So how have you been? The last few times you and Emma hung out I was working. It feels like years since I've seen you. Emma's told me everything. Tell me honestly, are you doing okay?"

"I've been doing the best I can. It's not easy living here, but it's getting easier."

"I'll trade you spots if you want. This house is amazing." Emma said.

"But..." Kelsey corrected.

"But I'm sure it's hard living here with Apollo." She continued.

"Ugh I don't want to even think about him. Emma go pour me a glass of that wine, and Kelsey help me set the table."

Halfway through dinner I was starting to relax a little. It was nice having Emma and Kelsey over. It made the house feel less empty. For maybe the first time since I moved in I was having fun.

I was quiet for most of the dinner as Emma and Kelsey caught me up on everything I missed. Kelsey was still working at the hospital, and Emma was spending more time with her mom who wasn't doing great. I was so distracted with everything going on with me I had no idea Emma was struggling. I wanted to blame Apollo, but I knew it was nobody's fault but my own.

"Enough about us. We want to know everything. How's work? What's Apollo like?"

"Work is work. Margaret threatened to fire me a few days ago. Because of Apollo and his idiot men. I'm not surprised. I knew she'd only be able to tolerate me for so long. As for Apollo," I sighed. "He's intolerable. Living here with him is suffocating. The only person he cares about is himself. Every night before I go to bed I try to picture marrying him and it makes me break down. I don't think I can do it."

Emma and Kelsey listened while I vented.

"When we're in public we have to be in love, and celebrate our engagement, but when it's just the two of us it's cold and lonely. He's so charming when we're around family, but to me he acts like I don't exist. Some days he makes me feel like a part of the family, and we can make it work, and then he does something stupid to drive me crazy."

"Is he really as awful as everyone says he is?" Emma asked.

"Worse."

"Oh, babe I'm sorry. Has it gotten any easier since the night of the engagement?" Emma asked.

"No." I took a sip of my wine. "And Mom keeps calling me to ask about wedding details and I don't know what to tell her. I mean, I see you two and you're so happy. In my head, I thought I wouldn't ever get married if I couldn't find someone that made me as happy as you two make each other."

"Well it hasn't always been easy. You remember us in college. We thought the only way we'd keep the passion alive is if we were fighting. It took us a really long time for us to get to where we are now. We even almost took a break that first year Kelsey was working nights. I told her I couldn't do it, and Kelsey told me she wasn't going to quit being a nurse just because I didn't like her schedule."

"You guys never told me that."

"We had to really work at our relationship to get where we are now. Sure, we weren't forced into an engagement, but it hasn't always been easy."

"Then what am I going to do?"

"Maybe you're struggling with Apollo because you swore you'd never get married. You always made it very clear you had no plans on settling down. Of course, it's hard getting engaged and moving in with a stranger. I mean, we both know what happened after that fight with your dad. After everything that happened freshman year of course you hold resentment towards the idea of your dad picking your husband." Emma said.

"This doesn't have anything to do with that." I answered.

"El, come on it's okay to admit this is hard for you, not just because it's Apollo."

"I said it's not that." I raised my voice a little higher than anticipated.

Emma paused, not saying anything more. She knew I didn't like to talk about what happened my freshman year at Boston. What was going on with Apollo had nothing to do with that.

"Alright, fine. I'm sorry, I won't bring it up again."

I set my fork down on my plate and stood up walking to the kitchen. I started to rinse off my plates as the two of them followed behind me.

"El we didn't mean to upset you. Why don't you give us a house tour?" Kelsey suggested.

"Here, take this and show us around this insane mansion." Emma said, handing me another drink.

I took them all around the house. The basement movie room, the guest rooms upstairs, my room, and even the backyard.

"Are you kidding? You have a pool?" Emma shouted from far away.

Kelsey and I followed after her. We found her near the pool house.

"Yeah, but I haven't used it yet. I've been so busy."

"Then let's try it out right now."

"What? No, we don't have suits, Em."

"Who cares!" She said, jumping into the pool with all of her clothes on. It took her a minute to stick her head out of the water. Kelsey looked nervous until we saw her swimming back up.

"Jump in!" She yelled at us. Kelsey gave me a look that said why not and jumped in leaving her phone on a table.

The two of them swam around waiting for me to get in.

"Let's go Eliana! The water is perfect."

"I don't know guys." I said looking around for anyone. I didn't see any of Apollo's men, and the water did look amazing, so without thinking anymore I jumped in.

God, it felt amazing. My cheeks that felt warm from all the wine cooled down in the ice-cold water. It was refreshing.

Kelsey and Emma held onto each other as they swam around the side of the pool. I laid on my back and floated around the pool holding my dress in my hand. I could see a million stars out here. I never noticed how beautiful it was outside at night. It was quiet, no people, no Apollo. It was perfect.

I would have fallen asleep drifting away but Emma splashed me. Lifting my head out of the water I yelled over to her.

"What the hell?"

She said nothing, only looking behind me. I knew what, or who, she was looking at. I turned around and saw an angry Apollo standing at the edge of the pool. His hands were in his suit pockets as he looked down at me.

"You didn't tell me you were having guests over." He shouted over to us.

"And you didn't tell me when you were coming home."

Apollo was silent. He crouched down to the edge of the pool and waited for me to swim over. He towered over me as I leaned against the edge. There was little lighting aside from the lights coming from the back patio. I tried to pull my hair out of my face so I could see him better.

"Who did you invite over?"

"Emma and her girlfriend Kelsey. She's the friend I was with the night I borrowed your car."

He looked past me at the two of them still in the pool, then looked back at me.

"Don't stay up all night, please." He sighed, standing up and walking away.

As Apollo walked back to the house, I climbed out of the pool and ran after him.

"Hey!" I shouted.

He turned rubbing his forehead like he had a headache.

"I'm not done talking to you."

I got closer to him and stopped just before the back door. Now in the light I could see I made a mistake. Apollo's eyes wandered down my dress. He gave a pleased smile when he saw the dress I was wearing was soaked. You could see everything underneath my dress as the water dripped off of me onto the concrete.

"Apollo." I mumbled. He finally looked up at me and waited for me to continue. I awkwardly tried to shift, so I wasn't in the light.

"How was your trip?"

"It was fine. No problems this time. You were right. The police didn't have him. We got lucky."

"Good." I answered not knowing what else to say. I wanted to ask more questions, but I could tell he was tired, and wanted to go inside.

"Then, goodnight Apollo."

"Goodnight." He replied, walking away and looking back one more time before closing the door.

Chapter Eight

Apollo

I heard Eliana's friends leave around twelve. They tried their best not to bother me. I wasn't excited about the idea of Eliana bringing strangers over, but I did a background check on Emma and had nothing to worry about. She was a family friend who grew up with Eliana. There was probably little she didn't already know.

I fell asleep right away after I got home. I was exhausted after the trip. We tracked Jason down out west. He was hiding with his brother. If it weren't for Gomez I would have been looking for him for a lot longer. Now that he was taken care of I could get back to my regular schedule. We had a lot of work to do before the end of the month. Dad wanted to expand our resources out to new families. We were struggling trying to balance distribution in Italy and New York. I needed to get New York figured out before I went back to deal with things in Italy.

I was sitting in a meeting right now with Dane, and a few other men I didn't care about. They were arguing over territory, and I was struggling to pay attention. Every time I tried to focus Eliana popped up in my head. I could see her standing there, dress stuck to her body in the shadows last night. I could still picture the way she tried to cover her chest when she realized. Her hair clinging to her shoulders dripping wet. It was distracting, and because of her I wasn't getting any work done. On top of my Eliana distraction I felt like shit. I woke up in the morning wishing I could have stayed in bed all day. I still needed time to recover from the trip.

"Apollo." Dane called out.

"What?"

"Kyle said he thinks he can get the Dunne's to commit to a distribution center up in Chicago."

"Fine, that works for me. Whatever they need to get it started we can supply. Take a few men up with Kyle and try to work something out." I said standing up.

"Where are you going? We aren't finished." Dane asked.

"I'm going home. You can take care of everything else. Only call me if it's an emergency."

I should have stayed, but I wasn't getting any work done at the office. I wanted to go home and sleep it off. It was rare for me to leave Dane like that, but I wasn't helpful to the guys like this.

Back at the house I walked through the front door and didn't even make it past the living room. I found myself laying down on the sofa. Falling asleep I looked across the living room. It was covered in Eliana's things. So, this is how she lived when I was gone.

She had folders and files of work stuff spread out across the coffee table, clothes hanging from the back of chairs, and even a few take out boxes. This was the first time it's ever felt like someone else lived here. When I'm home she never spends any time out here. She only runs from the kitchen to her room when I'm at the house. I tried to force the images of Eliana relaxed in my living room out of my head, so that I could fall asleep.

The slamming of the garage door woke me up. I must have been asleep for a long time because when I looked out the window it was dark outside. I could hear someone walking past the living room and stopping right by the couch. Based on the quiet steps it had to be Eliana. Propping myself up on my elbows I found her watching me from behind the couch. I looked up at her as she walked into the living room.

"I'm sorry I didn't know you were home. I would have come in more quietly."

"It's okay." I yawned, trying to sit up.

"What's wrong with you? Are you getting sick?" She asked.

Eliana sat down on the edge of the couch and leaned over to me. She took the back of her hand and pressed it against my forehead. Her hand was cold as she checked my temperature.

She sat back looking at me concerned, "You don't have a fever. Does your head still hurt?"

"I think I'm just tired from the trip. I'll be okay. Don't worry about it." I got up from the couch and grabbed my jacket.

"And Eliana, it's fine if you use this space when I'm here. I know you like it. I won't bother you if you want to come out here and work." I said pointing to the living room she'd taken over.

She looked around and smiled a little embarrassed to see her things thrown about.

126

"Thank you." She said, picking up her clothes.

I thought about stopping in the kitchen for something to eat, but I needed more sleep. I couldn't miss another day of work.

Eliana

That night was the last time I saw Apollo for a while. I started spending more time in the living room like Apollo suggested. I stopped hiding afraid I would run into him. Apollo was busy, but I was busier. He didn't have to put up with the moms like I did. They had been calling me for a week asking me to go to lunch so we could finalize a venue. Now that Apollo was back, and things were back to normal I finally agreed.

I met Mom and Catalina at a small restaurant for brunch on Wednesday. It was going to take a couple Xanax and bottomless mimosas to survive.

"Eliana, over here." Mom called from across the restaurant as I walked in.

We were one of the only tables in the whole restaurant. Mom had this thing about restaurants being too crowded and noisy when we went out. She was always bribing and renting out reservations anywhere she went. Catalina and Mom had their drinks at the table already and were looking through a big binder. When I got to the table I saw it was the venue catalog Mom used when Nora got married.

"You're right on time. Catalina was just telling me about a

beautiful vineyard she threw her twenty-fifth wedding anniversary at. It sounds incredible."

"It would be perfect for you and Apollo sweetie. It's got a beautiful reception space that overlooks the whole vineyard. And don't even get me started on how beautiful the pictures would be."

"It sounds amazing." I said sitting down and grabbing a menu.

"Have you considered your color scheme yet? Flowers? Guests?" Mom asked. "I've been sending over a bunch of stuff to you, but you haven't been responding."

"I think Apollo and I would prefer a small ceremony. I don't want to make a big deal out of the vows either." I suggested.

"Eliana, let's be realistic. We can't do small. Do you know how many people are dying to get an invite to this wedding? I just don't see how we can do anything less than three hundred, and even that would be a miracle."

"Mom, three hundred? Come on, that's too much. It would be overwhelming." I complained.

"Your mother's right Eliana. This is an important event for the families. Why don't you and Apollo send over a list of people you want to invite, and we'll take care of the rest?"

I sat there internally screaming for the rest of lunch. I was seconds away from bashing my head against the white linen tablecloth. I just had to sit there and listen as Mom planned my whole wedding. The dress, my bridesmaids, dinner, and everything in between. This wasn't what I wanted. I always pictured a small wedding. I couldn't see myself walking down the aisle past hundreds of people with Apollo waiting for me at the end.

After picking at a cobb salad and having all of my ideas shot down by Mom it was time to leave. Mal scheduled a meeting at two, and I'd never been more grateful for her.

"Mom I know, I'm sorry, but I have to go. You can send me everything we talked about today, and I'll talk about it with Apollo tonight." I lied.

"In the morning, I'll have him call you Catalina, and then you two can finalize the venue. Please."

"Okay, but if you don't call us tomorrow I swear to god I'm going to show up at your work and drag you out of there."

I knew she was serious. One time I didn't call her back about her Easter party and she showed up at my dorm room with a gun in her purse, and she was ready to use it.

"I promise Mama, I'll call in the morning."

I spent most of work looking through the emails Mom had sent over. I really hoped she found a wedding planner soon, so she could work with her and not me.

I brought everything she sent me back to the house. I found Apollo working in the dining room.

"Here." I said walking in. "This is for you."

I poured all of the wedding stuff out of my bag and onto the table.

"What is this?"

"I had lunch with both our moms today. They have our entire wedding planned out, and they need us to send them some details."

"And why do they need the details from us? Can't they do it?"

"I don't know. I sat with them for two hours and watched

129

them veto every suggestion I made. It was overwhelming, so I told your mom you would call her in the morning."

"What do they even need us to do? This is ridiculous."

"Well, they said our dads will take care of the guest list. Your mom has a venue already, and my mom is taking care of the food. You need to figure out who your groomsmen are, and your vows. I need to figure out who I'm inviting, and who my bridesmaids will be."

Apollo looked around the pile of papers and magazines.

"I can't do this right now."

"And you think I can? Do you think I wanted to spend my lunch planning our wedding by myself? Hearing my mom tell me I'll have to lose ten pounds before we even think about going dress shopping? Or your mom telling me I'm not doing enough to make you happy, and if I can't change my attitude you're going to want to leave me before the wedding even happens? This is the least you can do."

He threw the papers back down on the table.

"Alright, I'll call my mom in the morning and work some things out with her."

"Thank you. Now, I feel like I got hit by a car, so I'm going to take a bath, and order in some dinner." I said walking back to my room.

"And you better not forget to call your mom tomorrow or I'll suffocate you when you're sleeping." I shouted back to him as I walked away.

Apollo kept his promise. He called Catalina in the morning and bought us some more time to figure out the wedding details. I spent a few hours yesterday trying to decide on bridesmaids. I had a short list to pick from. There were few people Mom would say yes to. Nora would be one of course. I was in her wedding, and I already promised Juliette. The only other people I could imagine asking were Emma and Kelsey. Hopefully Mom would be fine with only four girls. I didn't want her adding on random cousins I hadn't seen in years.

I put the wedding plans on the back burner and tried to refocus. I was working through lunch to get ready for a meeting with Margaret. I had a few cases coming up, and I needed her help prepping. We hadn't talked since Apollo's men caused a scene, but I knew she was keeping a close eye on me.

I took one more big bite of my salad and started to get ready for the meeting when Mal ran into my office.

"Eliana-" She called. She looked like she had bad news.

"What's wrong?"

"It's Apollo. He's at the police station. He got picked up with a few of his men at his office. Everyone's talking about it. One of the detectives called here asking to talk to you."

"What do you mean he got picked up? Picked up for what?"

"I don't know. There's someone on line two for you."

I nodded for Mal to leave as I answered the phone.

"Hello?"

"Ms. Mariani, glad you finally picked up. It's Sterling. I heard rumors you were engaged to Apollo, but I didn't think it was true. I didn't believe it myself until Junior told me when we brought him in. He said Apollo was getting married to a big shot attorney. He must not know you very well."

"What do you want Sterling?"

"I just wanted to give you a heads up before we booked Apollo and his men. He's not talking, not even for an attorney, so it will be a pretty easy one for us."

I could hear Sterling smile through the phone. He was living for this.

"Nobody does anything until I get down there. And you better start praying you have enough evidence bringing them in." I threatened.

"See you soon Eliana."

I slammed the phone down, "Fuck!" I cursed.

I grabbed my things and threw them in my bag as fast as I could. I ran out of my office and found everyone staring at me. In front of the elevator was Margaret.

"Where do you think you're going?"

"A family emergency came up. I'm taking the rest of the day off."

"Mal told me who was on the phone. If you leave here you're done." She threatened.

I stood to the left of her deciding whether or not to leave. I didn't have a choice. If Apollo went down, I went down too. I was just as involved as him now. Even if I stayed, my life was over. If I left now I still had a chance to save my own ass.

I pressed the down button and stepped into the elevator.

All eyes were on me as I pressed the button to the lobby.

"Eliana, did you hear me? Done!" Margaret shouted.

"I know." I replied as the elevator doors closed.

Apollo

"I don't care how big the shipment is. I ordered a crate from Italy weeks ago. It should be here by now!" I yelled into the phone. Some of my men had messed up an order of guns, and clients were waiting on them. They were making me look bad here in the states. I hung up the call and went to see how Dane was doing. Before I made it to his office I heard something going on in the front.

"We're looking for Apollo Costa." A loud voice shouted.

"Sir, you can't go back there!"

I stepped into the room and saw a dozen police officers holding empty boxes.

"Ah, there he is. Just the man I was looking for."

The short detective grabbed my wrist and turned me around. I tried to resist, but he had handcuffs on me before I could react.

"Get the fuck off me!" I yelled.

"We have a warrant for anything on Jason Stevens. We know he was an employee of yours. Get that girl over there to help us."

Dane came running out of his office and was grabbed by a few other men. The harder he resisted the tighter the cops held him.

"We're also looking for Junior Ramirez. Go, find him." He ordered.

I was pulled out of the office as cops destroyed our filing system. They threw papers all over the office and the front desk. They knocked over a few plants and computers. I tried to kick out of the arms of the detective, but he led me to a cop car.

133

"What the hell do you think you're doing? Do you have any idea who I am?"

"Oh, trust me, I know exactly who you are." The detective grinned.

The three of us were taken in separate cars to the station. Then Dane, Junior and I were thrown into different rooms. It was a long time before the tall detective from the office came back into the room.

"Do you know who I am, Mr. Costa?"

I stayed silent.

"I'm detective Sterling. I'm the lead on the missing persons case concerning Jason Stevens. We have reason to believe you're involved in his disappearance."

I gave him nothing. I knew his type. He wanted to get a reaction out of me. This wasn't my first time in a holding cell, and it wouldn't be the last. I leaned back, crossing my arms. Trying to relax.

"It doesn't matter if you stay silent Mr. Costa. We have enough evidence to send you to trial." Sterling said, standing up and grabbing his files.

He left me alone in the room, so I looked to my right at the double mirror. I gave a smile to whoever was watching me. Sterling returned pretty quickly. This time with another detective.

"That Junior boy sure likes to talk. Doesn't it make you nervous?" He asked.

Again, I pretended to hear nothing. I knew Junior was young, but he wouldn't be rattled by someone like Sterling. He was a good kid. Sterling went to say something else, but an argument outside of the door caused him to turn around. The door to the interrogation room swung open.

Eliana.

"He's my client. I'll let myself into the room anytime I please." She shouted, walking into the room.

Eliana walked over to the chair next to me and sat down.

"Did you say anything?" She asked me.

"No." I smiled.

Eliana turned to Sterling.

"This is low. Even for someone like you Sterling." Eliana took out a few stacks of papers and threw them at Sterling.

"This is the lawsuit I'll be filing as soon as we leave here today. I wonder how your boss is going to react when he hears you're causing problems again."

"This is different. We have evidence connecting Mr. Costa to Mr. Stevens. We have enough to hold him."

"You and I both know you have nothing on my client Sterling. Do I need to remind you what happened last time you went after my family?"

Sterling shifted in his seat.

"You were on desk duty for months, right? The chief was drowned in paperwork after your witch hunt last year. I'm surprised you still have your badge. If I were your boss you wouldn't see another interrogation room again."

"We have witnesses who saw Dane and Jason together."

"That's it? That's all you have? Mr. Stevens was an employee for three years at my client's warehouse, and you want to take us to court over an eye witness seeing a boss and an employee working together?"

"We know Mr. Costa is responsible for Jason's disappearance."

"The disappearance we reported. You see, when Mr. Stevens didn't show up for work a few weeks ago, my client reported him missing. Mr. Costa is nothing but a concerned boss. Is reporting someone missing a crime now? Because last time I checked it wasn't. Apollo was trying to help your department by reporting Jason, and now he's in here being interrogated by an incompetent detective who can't read a file properly."

Eliana took out a file on Jason. A file I didn't even know she had.

"This is everything Mr. Costa has on Jason Stevens. His employment history, his family relations and his work schedule. On the last page, you will find all three of my client's schedule's and alibi's over the past week. If you had done your job you would know my clients have no connection to Jason Stevens other than a professional one."

"Listen, whether you like it or not we will be holding your fiancé for questioning. All of this proves nothing. We've been watching him for a while now, and we know there's more you're not telling us. We have a right to detain Mr. Costa for seventy-two hours."

Eliana laughed, looking over at Sterling's partner.

I had never seen this side of Eliana. She was terrifying.

"You are going to release Mr. Costa right now, and if you don't I will be filing a defamation lawsuit against your precinct for the second time. I also heard about the unlawful search and seizure at the office. In addition to a lawsuit we'll be filing charges for any damages caused by the New York City Police Department. I spoke with your boss on my drive over here. He knows what you did Sterling, and he's not happy. Harass my client again about this case, and I will take your ass to court so fast you'll be begging for early retirement."

"You got lucky last time Eliana, but I'm-"

"No, Sterling. I *won* last time. It wasn't luck. You tried to frame my brother for murder, and you got your ass handed to you on a silver platter. You're upset, I get that. You think this is your chance to prove to everyone you were right, but it's not. You're just a washed-up detective, who is losing his grasp on reality. I have internal affairs on speed dial Sterling. Go tell your men to let Dane and Junior go before you're back on desk duty by Monday."

Sterling looked at his partner, and then back at me. His jaw was clenched, and his fights tightened.

"Go." He said to his partner.

He grabbed his keys and unlocked my handcuffs. I grabbed my wrists rubbing the bruises. Eliana nodded for me to leave the room as she grabbed her bag.

When I walked out into the hallway I saw Dane and Junior being handed back their stuff by a couple of cops. Eliana went over to the two of them and walked over to me. She grabbed my arm and led me down the hallway. Looking back at Sterling I gave him a smile and a wave.

Eliana didn't say a word to either of us until we were in her car. She sped out of the parking garage, and onto the highway. I would have told her to slow down, but I could tell how pissed she was.

"Eliana-" Dane finally spoke.

"Shut the fuck up. All three of you. Not another word until we're back at the house."

Chapter Nine

Eliana

I sat in Apollo's office waiting for an explanation. I was absolutely furious that Apollo and Dane were reckless enough to cause issues with Sterling.

"So, who did it? Which one of you killed Jason?"

Junior and Apollo looked over at Dane.

"And who was there helping?"

Slowly, Junior raised his hand.

"Jesus Apollo, he's just a kid!" I shouted.

"Junior turned eighteen a few months ago, and you have him working with Dane?"

"How I run things is none of your business." He snapped back.

"None of my business? Who just saved your ass back there?

You have no idea how bad Sterling wanted to throw all three of you in jail. Not to mention the heat this is going to bring the family for the next couple of months! You can't expand distribution with the police trailing your every move."

"I'll figure it out."

"Until I get more information about what they have on the three of you, you need to be extra careful. Dane, start giving your work to other people. They're probably going to be watching you the closest. And Junior please be safe. I don't want to have to tell your mom you got arrested because of these two dumbasses."

"Hey, this isn't my fault. We were careful." Apollo argued. "It's obvious Sterling has something against you. He clearly doesn't have anything on us or we would still be at the police station."

"Until I know for sure he doesn't have any evidence please don't go anywhere." I said, grabbing my phone off the table and leaving.

"Where are you going?" Apollo shouted after me.

"I'm going to meet with a friend and see what Sterling knows. While I'm gone go get someone to assess damages at your office. I am planning on suing them for the search. Take pictures, videos, and document anything missing."

I waited for Alex to pull up with the car. The adrenaline of today was starting to fade. Everything that had happened was finally hitting me. I climbed into the car quickly so no one could see me start to break down. My lungs felt heavy, and my heart beat like someone was playing the drums on my chest. It took everything in me not to throw up. I had to pinch my thigh to try and refocus. Alex watched through the mirror as I tried to calm down. I pulled my phone out to show Alex an address. I needed him to go to the district attorney's office. He understood what I was asking him to do and drove off.

Christian, an old college friend, was waiting for me in his office. He always helped me out when Raff or Dad got in trouble.

"I promise he has nothing on you Eliana. He's fishing because there's pressure from the court to pin anything on the Costa's. He had to beg a judge to sign the warrant. No one with any credibility was willing to sign it for him. Everyone knows Apollo was Jason's employer, and this is a dead end." Christian explained.

"So now what? What if Sterling keeps digging?"

"I doubt he has any power to do anything after Ortega hears what he did today. They gave him an inch of freedom and he took a mile. Everyone knows he's on borrowed time. I wouldn't worry about it. Until someone else gets involved you have nothing to worry about."

I took a deep breath, "Thank you. I'm going to go home and get started on some paperwork. If you hear anything let me know. I owe you one Christian." I said starting to leave his office.

"Eliana wait." He stood up, hands on his desk, "Is it true?"

"Is what true?"

"That you and Apollo are getting married. Everyone here has been talking."

"It's true." I answered.

"And you're happy... with him?"

"Never been happier." I lied, turning to the door.

Leaving the office and walking back to the car I stopped before the parking lot. I wasn't ready to go home. I pulled out my phone and sent Alex a text.

Going out for a drink. Don't worry, I'll be safe.

Turning off my phone I walked down the street. That was my last time at the courthouse, and the last time any DA would ever agree to work with me again. In one day my dreams, my career, were over.

I don't know how long I had been walking. I left the bar and meant to call Alex. I remember turning on my phone, but now that I was walking I wasn't sure if I had called him. I walked far enough to find a small creek. I looked down over the bridge. The water flowing underneath me gave the air a cool breeze. I couldn't see anything down below. Was the water deep? Were there rocks? A small part of me wanted to find out. I gripped the railing of the bridge trying to snap back to reality.

I felt a heavy anger in my heart. I wanted to lash out and yell and scream, but I had no one to scream at. Everything that's happened to me was nobody's fault but my own. I stayed when I should have left. I agreed to Dad's law school deal, I said yes to Apollo, and it was me who left Margaret today.

I had no one to blame but me, and that's what hurt the most. I opened my eyes and saw my hands still clutching the railing. I watched my ring glisten in the street light. I let out a laugh. Maybe this was a good thing. It was time to say goodbye to the past. Now that I was free of Margaret and the firm I could focus on becoming a Costa. This was a fresh start. I didn't have to hide anymore.

Bright car lights forced me to turn my head. I stepped off of the bridge railing, and saw Alex get out of the car.

"I tracked your phone." He yelled over to me. "Let's go home."

I walked to the car and slid into the back seat. I rested my head on the cold window, and let Alex drive me home. I tried closing my eyes, but I could see Alex staring. When I sat up and looked at him he got nervous.

"I won't tell anyone." He blurted out.

"What are you talking about?"

"I saw what you were doing. You were leaning over the ledge Ma'am. I'll keep it a secret, just don't run away like that again. Mr. Costa would kill me if something happened to you."

"Thank you, Alex." I replied, closing my eyes and falling asleep.

Apollo

I left early in the morning to go check on the office with Dane. I canceled a few meetings I had with clients just in case Eliana was right and we were being watched. Until things cooled down I was going to play it safe. I didn't hear Eliana come home last night, and she must have gone to work early in the morning because I didn't see her when I left with Dane.

The office was destroyed. File cabinets and desks were thrown and knocked over with documents pouring out of them. I did what Eliana asked and had Dane film some stuff. They took Jason's employment records, but that wouldn't be helpful to them. We kept our books clean in case something like this happened.

I also asked Dane to call Gomez. He was with us when we killed Jason, so he needed to be careful. I asked everyone who works in the office to take a few days off. I didn't want anyone working here until things settled.

"They ruined the conference room. I'll call someone next week to come and do repairs." Dane said, walking into the lobby.

"I want to go home and make sure Sterling can't connect us to Jason. Eliana says he's harmless, but if another cop takes over the case I want to make sure there's no issues with our alibi's."

"I'll bring over a few things and meet you at your office. I need to stop at the other warehouse for a few things. I doubt they will try anything now, but I don't want Sterling finding information there." Dane said.

"Meet me back at the house in an hour."

When I walked into the house there were voices coming from the kitchen. Nobody should be in there. They should all be working. I found Alex eating a sandwich and talking with a few of my men. Why was Alex here in my kitchen, and not with Eliana?

"What are you doing here? You're supposed to be with Eliana."

Everyone looked at Alex. He looked confused by my words.

"What?" I asked.

"Sir, Eliana is at home today." He answered in a quiet voice.

"Why didn't she go to work?"

Again, Alex paused before answering.

"Margaret fired her yesterday. Told her not to come back if she left to go bail you out. She didn't tell you?"

Of course she didn't tell me. Did she really get fired because of me?

"So, she's been here all day?" I asked, walking towards her room.

Everyone that was in the kitchen ran after me. Alex stopped me in the hallway.

"I wouldn't bother her if I were you. She's been sleeping all day. She asked me to not let anyone in."

My men waited behind Alex to see what my next move was.

"Get out of my way. I need to talk to her."

One more time Alex got between me and the door.

"I can't let you. You asked me to keep her safe. This isn't what she needs right now. Give her some space."

A few more guys stood with Alex. It wasn't worth my energy trying to get past all of them. They weren't letting me through. I was annoyed and had other things to worry about.

"Call me when she's up."

Leaving Alex and the boys I went to my office to get some work done. I needed to distract myself from Eliana. It was my fault she was fired. She was going to kill me. I promised I wouldn't do anything to jeopardize her work. Every day I broke another promise I had made to Eliana.

Three days. She hadn't left her room in three days. She wasn't eating and she wasn't letting anyone in. If she did need something she told Alex to deal with it.

Someone knocked on my door, and walked in.

"She sent back her dinner again, and she won't touch the water we sent in." Kim said.

"When was the last time she ate?"

"Since before the incident. She won't even talk to Alex anymore. What do you want me to do?"

"Leave her alone for now. I'll handle it."

Kim left, and I was stuck trying to figure out what to do. I didn't care much for her job in the past, but I knew that it was the only thing that made her happy. I didn't know what else to do for her, so I called Raff. Maybe he would be able to help.

"Hello?"

"Raff, something happened to Eliana I need your help."

"What's wrong? Is she hurt? I swear Apollo-"

"No, physically she's fine. Some shit went down with the cops, and she lost her job covering for me. She's locked herself in her room. She's not eating and I'm starting to get worried."

"How long has she been in there?"

"Almost four days." I said.

"If she's been in there that long it probably won't last for much longer. She does this sometimes. Just give her some space and wait for her."

"I can't just wait Raff she's torturing herself in that room. Can't you come and talk to her? I know she doesn't want anything to do with me right now. It's all my fault."

"I'm working out of town right now, and Frankie is on a trip. I know it's hard to watch but give her some time. When something like this happens to her she grieves like she's lost something, and then gets back to the real world in a couple of days. It's normal for her."

Raff hung up and left me to figure this shit out on my own. I can't just let her do this to herself. I don't care how pissed she was at me. It's time I paid her a visit.

I knocked on her door and received no answer. I was running out of patience, so I broke down her bedroom door and let myself in. As soon as I walked in I could see her turning in her comforter so that her back was facing me.

"Eliana, get up. I know you're angry, but you can't keep doing this. Do anything else. Beat me up, yell at me, throw something, just stop doing whatever this is."

She remained silent.

"Eliana." I called out again, this time walking around the bed trying to find her hidden in her covers.

"I had Kim make you a couple different things. Come out and eat at least one of them. Then I'll let you come back to bed. I don't care if you hate me right now. I promised I would take care of you, so let's go."

I tried pulling off her covers, but for someone who hadn't eaten in four days she had a lot of grip strength.

"Fuck off, Apollo." I heard her mumble.

I was running out of options. I didn't want to do this, but I knew it would work.

"Go eat something or I'm inviting your mom over to come take care of you."

After a few seconds, the blanket started to rustle. Eliana threw the covers off and sat up.

"I hate you."

"I don't care. Let's go, now."

Eliana took my hand as I helped her get out of bed. She walked with me to the kitchen and ate a sandwich Kim made. While she was eating I had Charlotte change her bed sheets and find her some clean clothes.

I waited for Eliana back in her room.

"Charlotte cleaned the space up for you. I know you don't have the energy for a shower, so she pulled out some clean clothes. Go back to sleep if you want, but I'll be back in a few hours to take you to dinner."

Eliana grabbed the clean shirt I was holding and nodded her head. I left so she could get dressed. I felt a little better knowing she had some food in her stomach.

Back in my office I couldn't stop thinking about Eliana. She looked terrible. She hadn't been sleeping, and her cheekbones were hollow. I tried to distract myself with work to avoid thinking about how terrible I felt about her. I was busy with an email when Dane walked in.

"I told you not to bother me for the rest of the day."

"I know, and I'm sorry, but I just got a call from Rio." Dane said, sitting down in front of my desk.

"Why did he call?"

"He's invited you and Eliana to Italy."

Rio was the only man in all of Italy who had more power than the Costa family. If you didn't have his support you had nothing.

"I can't leave right now. There's too much going on."

"I don't think you have a choice. If you don't get his blessing for the wedding we're screwed. We can't run business in Italy without him. Plus, it might be good for you to get away for a few days. I'll keep an eye on things here, and you can come back when things aren't so hot with the cops."

"Eliana won't agree to this. I can't even get her to leave her room. She's not going to fly with me to Italy. I can't ask her to do that."

"You don't have a choice. He's expecting you by the weekend."

"Go call him back and let him know we'll be leaving tomorrow. Have Charlotte pack a few bags for Eliana. Tell her to wait until after dinner when I tell her about Italy."

Damn it. This is terrible timing. How was I going to get Eliana to agree to this?

Eliana

I tried to go back to sleep after lunch, but Apollo pacing in the hallway kept me awake. I could hear him coming to check on me every few minutes. He had been doing that all week. I tried eating every time someone brought me food, but I couldn't force myself to eat it. It was like my throat closed up. I had nowhere to go, and no one to help. Without the firm, I was useless. Forget opening up my own firm, and after what happened with Margaret no one was going to hire me.

All the sacrifices I made to become an attorney were over. I'm sure everyone knew by now. I could picture the stares and the phone calls I would get if I left my room.

Just like he promised Apollo was back to bring me to dinner. He'd never been so kind to me. The guilt must be eating him alive. He must think it's all his fault.

"It's time for dinner Eliana, let's go." He ordered, hovering over me.

I didn't argue with him this time. I got out of bed on my own and walked to the kitchen. At lunch, I sat at the counter, but tonight dinner was set up in the dining room. He had Kim using the nice silverware and dishes. I watched him nervously sit down. He grabbed his napkin and motioned for me to sit. Apollo was hiding something. He's never once willingly sat down to have dinner with me. He usually goes out of his way to avoid meals with me.

I held my spoon in my hand watching him. He finally looked up at me.

"What's wrong?" He asked.

"You. You're hiding something."

"Eat first, and then we'll talk."

"No. Tell me or I'm leaving."

Apollo sighed, shifting in his seat.

"We're leaving for Italy tomorrow."

"We?"

"Yes, we've been invited by Rio. I think he's trying to figure out how legit this engagement is."

"I don't want to go."

"I already told him the two of us would be there late Sunday. Charlotte is going to help you pack."

Apollo knew I had to go. It was Rio. I would never hear the end of it from Raff and Dad if I declined an invitation.

When I got back to my room Charlotte was already packing for me. It looks like everyone in the house except for me knew

149

we were leaving for Italy. Apollo had avoided telling me about Italy for as long as he could. He was stalling because he knew we had to go. Even if I wanted to stay here we couldn't decline an invitation from Rio. Rio Castello was a terrifying man, one who'd worked hard to build an empire for himself. He was a powerful man, and there were a lot of reasons he might have wanted us to visit, but I had a feeling this invitation was coming from his wife. Maria wanted to meet me before the wedding. If Maria didn't like me it would cause problems for Apollo and me. Apollo had no power without Castello's support.

I couldn't sit and watch Charlotte pack for me, so I finished the rest of the bags. I packed more than I thought I would need. Charlotte came back right before I fell asleep again to take all of my luggage away. After she left I was finally alone. No one was bothering me, pacing around my door, or dragging me out to eat. The next week was going to be exhausting, so I went to bed early to get as much sleep as I could.

Apollo wasted no time waking me up in the morning and rushing me to get ready. I barely had time for a shower.

"We're late." Apollo told me when I finally made it to the living room.

"You own the plane. Just tell the pilot to wait."

"That's not the point. We're on a schedule." He complained.

Alex had finished packing the car and was waiting for the two of us in the driveway.

"Where is everybody else?" I asked.

"Alex is taking us to the airport, but I have men waiting in Italy who will travel with us. I need Dane working here in the States with the others."

Apollo was not happy to be going back to Italy. He had been on edge all morning. I couldn't even take a short nap on the ride to the airport because he was on the phone with Dane the whole time. The drive to the airport was quick, and it gave me little time to process I was even leaving. I had a heavy feeling of dread weighing me down as we pulled up to the landing strip. The pilot and a few flight attendants were waiting for us, giving us big smiles and waves. Apollo pretended they didn't exist as he opened the door with a big sigh. Apollo handed me my day bag and left me at the car while he walked up the stairs.

"Always a gentleman." I mumbled.

Apollo's plane was bigger than I imagined. There were a few chairs that were styled to look like a living room, and a few private rooms in the back. Apollo had his computer out and was already working when I sat across from him.

The jet took off and a flight attendant came up to Apollo.

"Can I get you anything, Sir?"

"Two coffees, eggs, toast and any fruit you have."

The woman gave Apollo a big smile and went back to the small kitchen. Apollo got right back to work, but I had nothing to do. A week ago, I was drowning in case work. All of the women I'd helped, all of the cases I worked on with Margaret meant nothing. I would never get to help anyone like that again.

The turbulence of the plane reminded me how tired I was. I could feel my body trying to fall asleep again. My eyes were drifting shut.

"You should try and stay awake." Apollo suggested.

"Why?"

"When we get to Italy it will be night time. If you sleep now you won't be able to fall asleep tonight."

"I'll be okay." I argued.

I shut my eyes but was woken up by Apollo again. When I sat up I saw breakfast in front of me.

"What's this?"

"Eggs and toast. Eat it."

"I thought you ordered this for you?"

"I ate before we left. I'm fine." He said, taking a sip of his coffee.

"I'm not hungry."

That was a lie. I was hungry when we left the house, but now that the food was in front of me I couldn't stomach it.

"Eat what you can. You'll need your energy for the trip."

Apollo slid the plate over to me. I grabbed the fork and took a bite of the eggs.

"We need to make sure our stories match up." I said. "Everyone is going to want the details about our relationship. It needs to be believable to convince Maria."

"Okay, what do you suggest?"

"We'll tell them we met eight months ago at one of your dad's parties. A week before the announcement you proposed to me at dinner."

"What's your favorite restaurant?" He asked.

"Rosalie's." I answered.

"Okay, I proposed at Rosalie's, and we waited to announce it until the party."

I nodded my head. It was risky going to stay with the Castello's and not knowing anything about each other, but we could make things up as we went.

I didn't want to sit across from Apollo for the whole flight, so I got up and found a few books to read. I must have fallen asleep on the couch because when I woke I was wrapped up in a blanket. I looked out the window and saw nothing but water.

"We're about to land." Apollo said. "You slept for six hours. There's a car waiting for us when we land to take us to the villa."

"Where's my bag?" I asked, looking around.

"I set it down in the other room with the rest of your stuff."

I walked back to the bedroom and found my things. I didn't have the energy to get ready, but I wasn't showing up to the house looking like a wreck. The last hour of the flight flew by. I looked at myself in the mirror, it wasn't great, but it was as good as it was going to get. At the very least I was in a comfortable dress, and my hair was pinned back.

I sat with Apollo as the plane landed and held his hand as we took the stairs off the plane.

A few cars were waiting for us. Apollo put his hand on my back and led me to a car. He opened the door letting me in first. A man went to the car behind us and started packing up our luggage. Someone who only spoke Italian drove Apollo and I to Rio's.

An hour later we pulled up to the estate. Maria and Rio were waiting for us out front. Our driver got out of the car and waited by Apollo's side of the car.

"Here we go." he sighed, taking my hand.

Chapter Ten

Eliana

"Welcome!" Maria smiled. "We're so glad you could make it with our last-minute invite. You must be Eliana!"

Maria pulled me away from Apollo and wrapped her arms around me.

"Apollo, we missed you!" Rio said.

"Come inside, Rueben will bring in your things." Maria said, grabbing my hand and leading me into the house.

"Mrs. Castello, your home is beautiful." I smiled.

"Please dear, call me Maria. By the end of your trip we'll be close friends. Mrs. Castello makes me feel old." She laughed.

Rio and Apollo followed behind the two of us. Their living room was three times the size as Apollo's. The high ceilings went on forever, and a staircase led to a beautiful second floor. Old paintings and art covered the walls and hallways of the house.

Maria walked us through the house and stopped in a small dining room connected to what looked like Rio's lounge.

"We know it's late and I'm sure you're tired, but we had our cooks leave you some food if you're hungry. After you eat we'll show you to your rooms. With the flight and the drive here, you two must be exhausted."

"Thank you." I said having a seat next to Apollo.

I placed a napkin in my lap as Apollo poured me a glass of wine. Maria and Rio sat across from us smiling and watching the two of us. Apollo was quick to fill his plate and eat. I still didn't have much of an appetite so I ate some chicken and garden squash.

"Maria, the food was delicious, thank you." Apollo said, taking a sip of his drink.

Finishing his plate, Apollo looked at me, "Are you ready for bed?"

Apollo had never spoken so kindly to me. His voice was soft and warm.

I gave him a smile, "I didn't think the plane ride was long, but now that I'm here I think I need sleep." I admitted.

"Come with me I'll show you where you two will be staying."

Maria stood up and quickly started walking up the stairs, turning down the left wing.

"Rueben brought everything up here for you already. If you need anything tonight someone will be down the hall on your right. Please try to relax and enjoy your trip. We are so excited the two of you could visit on such short notice. Breakfast is at eight, so come down when you're ready."

Maria nodded her head to one of her maids who opened the door to the guest room. Apollo let me walk in first and waited by

155

the door.

"Good night Eliana, I'll see you in the morning." He said looking towards Maria for directions to his room.

"Oh please, you don't have to pretend with me. You two are engaged, we wouldn't expect you to sleep in separate rooms." Maria said.

Apollo looked back at me unsure what to do.

"It's fine really. We thought you two would be more comfortable sharing a room. Now goodnight, get some rest."

Maria closed the door behind Apollo and left the two of us alone in the dark room.

Apollo looked for the light switch near the door. I walked into the room in search of our things. We found them near the bed. The lights flickered on as Apollo walked in behind me. He grabbed a few of his bags and a blanket from the bed.

"I'll sleep on the floor. You take the bed."

"Apollo, you're not sleeping on the floor. This bed is more than big enough, we're adults we can share a bed for a few nights. Plus, if one of Maria's staff walks in I don't want them to see you asleep on the floor. We would never hear the end of it from Maria or our mother's."

Apollo considered his options. He looked down at the floor, and back up at the king-sized bed. He knew I was right.

He sat his bags down near mine and left for the bathroom. While he was gone I unpacked one of my bags. I found clothes for tomorrow and hung them up on the closet door. After unpacking a few more things I looked for a shirt I could wear to bed. Just as I finished changing out of my dress Apollo came back into the room wearing sweatpants. He threw his suit onto a chair and sat on his side of the bed scrolling through his phone. I took my bag to the bathroom and closed the door. After brushing my teeth and organizing some stuff on the counter I was ready for bed.

Maria was right, I was exhausted. Even with the sleep I had been getting my muscles still felt sore and stiff. If I was going to survive the trip I needed rest. When I walked back into the room Apollo was sitting at a small table with his computer open.

"I'm going to bed, turn the light off when you're done." I said, sliding under the covers.

I rolled onto my side so I didn't have to face Apollo at the table. My body relaxed under the covers and the soft bed, and I could feel my brain start to shut down. I was almost completely asleep when I felt Apollo grab the covers and lay into bed.

I went from relaxed to tense when I felt the bed shift under us. Freezing in my place I listened to him roll onto his side. Both of us leaned as far as we could away from each other.

Any chance I had of getting sleep tonight was gone. I couldn't even think straight knowing Apollo was asleep next to me.

"Eliana." Apollo spoke, pushing my shoulder. "Wake up, it's time for breakfast."

I opened my eyes to see Apollo standing over me. I sat up and took a minute to wake up. The room looked so different during the day. Last night I was so focused on Apollo I didn't even notice the layout or design of the room.

"What time is it?"

"It's almost eight. I tried to let you sleep, but Maria wants us down for breakfast."

I climbed out of the bed stretching my arms. The sun

coming through the windows felt warm. Apollo looked away as my shirt lifted showing I was only in boxers. He went into the closet changing into some real clothes.

I left for the bathroom to shower and get ready. I didn't know what Maria had planned, so I wore an old summer dress that I could match with a sweater.

"Apollo?" I called out looking around the room.

He walked out of the closet finishing up his tie.

"Are you ready?" He asked.

I nodded, walking to the door.

"Remember, we're in love, and excited for the wedding." He spoke.

"I know." I answered, rolling my eyes.

Apollo

Eliana walked to the bathroom with her clothes still half asleep. She tossed and turned all night. Neither of us got any sleep. Every time I was close to passing out I remembered I was a few feet from a sleeping Eliana.

Eliana and I walked down to breakfast together.

"What does Maria have planned for us today?"

"I don't know. I'm sure she'll want to take us sightseeing or take us to visit family." I answered.

"Please just don't leave me alone with her." Eliana asked.

A big breakfast was waiting for us in the dining hall.

"Good morning you two." Maria said when we walked in.

"Did you two sleep alright?" Rio asked.

"Yes, thank you." Eliana lied.

"Eat a lot now while you can. We have a busy day. I want to take the two of you out to the farm and the vineyards. I know you're anxious to get some work done with Rio Apollo, but you two can spare one day."

"It's been a while since I've been in Italy and had some free time. I'd love to go visit the horses." I said.

Eliana was quiet at breakfast. She forced down some food. I knew she didn't want to, but Maria was watching her closely. I tried keeping the conversation focused on me, so she would feel less pressure.

"Are you two ready?" Maria asked, taking a few dishes back to the kitchen.

"Let me go grab my purse and I'll meet you at the car."

Eliana squeezed my arm as she left the table. I gave her a smile knowing Rio was still watching.

Maria had Rio bring around an old mustang convertible. Eliana walked behind me down the driveway. I reached my hand back for her as we walked. She was hesitant to take it but took quicker steps to walk beside me.

Once in the car Maria had a thousand questions for Eliana.

"So, when was the last time you visited Italy Eliana?" She asked.

"It's been a few years. Dad brought me out here as a gift

after I graduated from Boston. Unfortunately, I had no one to go with, but now that I have Apollo I hope to come back and visit family more often."

"Apollo spends a lot of his time here. Is that going to be difficult with your work schedule? It would be hard on newlyweds to constantly be in different cities."

"We'll make it work." I answered for her. "All that matters right now is no matter where work takes us we're together."

"That's true. Besides, you want to travel and enjoy those first few years before you start a family." Maria added.

I could see Eliana tense up beside me. She was trying to hide her disgust for what Maria had just said. I grabbed her hand in mine and squeezed it hard. It was only day one. I couldn't have her losing it yet.

"Oh, we're here." Maria said, turning in her seat.

"After the tour of the vineyard we're having lunch at a little restaurant down the road. I already called ahead."

"Can't wait!" I smiled following Rio to the barn.

Three long hours later, and it was time for lunch. Eliana survived Rio's tour, and Maria was too busy catching up with me to bother her.

"And I told Claire I just didn't have time for a party, but she insisted on celebrating at the end of the summer, so Rio set up the house for the celebration."

Maria was telling us about their busy summer and an even busier winter yet to come. It was hard for Eliana to focus, but she was doing her best to show Maria her excitement.

"Apollo this is where I took your mom when she came to visit with her friends. They stayed with us for a few weeks last summer, and we found this place when we were shopping. It was close to closing, but Rio saved it. It has the best food you're ever going to find in Italy. It reminds me of food my grandmother used to make when I was little."

"It's almost as good as Maria's cooking." Rio added opening the door for Maria.

"Oh Rio, you're too much." Maria smiled.

Eliana followed Maria to the table. I helped her sit and sat her purse along her chair. She opened a menu for me and leaned in to pick something to eat. The table was quiet as we all looked over the menu and ordered drinks.

Eliana had kept her energy up for most of the day. From what I could tell Maria was starting to like her. Everyone loved Eliana the minute they met her. When she was younger she could make friends with anyone.

Eliana

After lunch Apollo and Rio left to get some work done. I had to go back to the house with Maria. I got the tour, and a family history lesson. I had to learn about their kids, their grandkids, and every milestone.

The afternoon was going well until I got a call from Mom. Apollo told Raff about me being fired before I had the chance to tell my own family. She was beyond furious I didn't call to tell her about Margaret firing me. She was mad I didn't call, but she struggled to hide her excitement that I was no longer working for

Margaret. I'm sure in her mind I could put my work behind me and focus entirely on the wedding. As I sat in Rio's library and listened to Mom tell me what a blessing getting fired was, I thought of different ways I could hurt Apollo for telling my family about being fired.

I heard Apollo come back with Rio and found him in the bedroom. I shut the door and ignored him when I saw him.

"Hello to you, too." He teased me.

I wasn't going to start anything with him during the trip, but I couldn't hold it in anymore.

"You told my family I got fired?"

Apollo looked at me, his smile fading.

"I only told Raff because I was worried about you. You locked yourself in your room all week, and I didn't know what to do."

"Well here's an idea. Leave me the fuck alone!"

"I couldn't just let you starve yourself in your room, and spiral into a depression. I promised your family I would take care of you."

"When were you taking care of me? When have you ever done anything to protect me that didn't affect you? You only tried to help me out of pity. You feel guilty for what happened, and you want me to forgive you so you can stop worrying about me."

"Eliana I'm sorry. I know it's my fault Margaret fired you, but I don't know what else to do. I can't sit by and watch you torture yourself because of a job."

"It wasn't just a job Apollo! It was the only thing in my life that made me feel normal. It was the only thing I had that separated me from my family, and you. I can't live like this. I was trying to do some good and make up for all the horrible things our families have done, and now I can't even do that." I said, trying not to cry.

"But you have no idea what other opportunities are waiting for you! This could be just the beginning. Why are you giving up?"

"I'm not giving up! The minute Margaret fired me, was the minute my career ended. I tried for months to get a real job, and Margaret was the only one willing to hire me. I won't find a firm like that ever again. The only chance I have at practicing law is representing you and our family, which is the one thing I promised I would never do!"

"Eliana keep your voice down please."

"Keep my voice down? Are you kidding me? Why? Are you afraid Rio and Maria will hear our little lover's fight and think less of you? Can't have our relationship getting in the way of your image, can we?" I spat.

"You know it's not like that. I want to help you Eliana, I really do. I know you don't believe it or want to hear it, but I am sorry."

"Are you done?" I asked.

"No, I'm not done." Apollo said, raising his voice. "When are you going to realize that you're three times the attorney Margaret is? I'm glad Margaret fired you because now there's nothing holding you back. Whenever you're ready to stop feeling sorry for yourself and get back out there let me know. Because I miss the old Eliana, the one that drives me bat shit crazy."

Apollo left me alone in the bedroom. I'd seen Apollo angry before, but I'd never seen him angry like that. I wished it was as easy as he thought to get over Margaret. I couldn't bounce back from something like that so easily.

I looked at the clock and saw it was almost time for dinner. Maria was probably waiting for me downstairs, so I left the room and went looking for Apollo.

"Eliana, Apollo and Rio have work tomorrow, so I thought I'd show you around town and get dinner with some friends."

"I saw a cute shop when we were driving back last night. I'd love to take a look in it." I suggested.

"Perfect!" Maria said.

The four of us ate quietly for a few minutes until Maria broke the silence.

"So, tell us everything. We want to know about the engagement, and the plans so far! I miss getting to plan weddings."

"It's been fun getting to know Apollo's mom a little better. Before the wedding we didn't get to spend a lot of time just the two of us. I'll never get tired of her embarrassing Apollo stories." I smiled.

"I don't know how Eliana does it. She balances work and planning the wedding, and I can only focus on the business. I owe everything to her." Apollo said, wrapping his arm around my shoulders.

I smiled at Apollo. Rio and Maria smiled at us from across the table. I stayed with my head resting on Apollo's shoulder and started to feel my eyes get heavy.

"Are you ready for bed?" He whispered in my ear.

"Mhmm."

"Let's go." He said standing up and holding out his hand. I took his hand and left the table with him.

"I'll see you in the morning, Rio. Just let me know when you want to leave."

"Sure thing. Goodnight you two."

Apollo took me back to the room. Once the door was closed we dropped each other's hand. I went to the closet to get out of my dress. I struggled with the zipper, unable to reach it. The closet door creaked and I saw Apollo standing there watching me struggle.

"Stop," He said, stepping up behind me.

He pulled my hair across my shoulder. I got the chills when his hands ran over my neck. I held my hair while he pulled the zipper down. As the dress fell, I caught it as it dropped off my shoulders. Apollo stepped back and grabbed a towel from the door. He left for the bathroom leaving me alone in the room.

Apollo's touch left burns on my skin. My spine was warm where his fingertips traced. I tried to push out the thoughts of what else his hands were capable of. I'd seen them kill a man, and strangle one half to death, and there was a small curiosity inside me wondering what else they'd look good doing.

I heard Apollo turn on the shower as I got ready for bed. I read a book as I waited for Apollo to get out of the shower. I think Apollo was expecting me to be asleep when he came out because he walked back into the room wearing only a towel, low on his waist.

I got caught staring when he walked past the bed. I didn't mean to stare, but his leg caught my eye. Apollo's leg was covered in scars starting at his thigh and ending at his ankle. I sat up as he walked to the closet.

"Wait." I said.

Apollo stopped, turning around, holding the towel with one hand.

I looked at his leg, and the scars around his knee.

"Eliana..." He said.

I looked up, not realizing I'd been staring for a while.

"I'm sorry. I just- I didn't know. I mean I heard rumors about an accident, but I didn't think..."

"If you're done staring, I'll go get dressed."

Apollo slammed the closet door behind him. I didn't mean to upset him. I was just thrown off with the scars. Half asleep, I heard Apollo crawl into bed. The lights were off, and the room was dark, but I could still see his outline. I turned towards him and watched to see if he was asleep.

Apollo sighed, "I can feel you staring."

"Sorry." I said shifting back under the covers.

It was quiet again for a few seconds until he spoke.

"They're scars from the surgeries I had after the car accident." He said.

"How many surgeries?"

"Four. I couldn't walk for seven months. I had to do physical therapy for a year before I was ready to start working again."

"What happened?" I asked.

"Someone shot up my car while I was driving back home and hit me until the car flipped. I was alone and had no idea I was going to be ambushed. Rio was the one who helped me. He let me hide here until I recovered. It was the only place I could go and not have to worry about another attack."

"Do you know who planned the accident?"

"No. If I had to guess I'd say my uncle had something to do

with it. It's one of the main reasons I ever agreed to marry you. Giovanni, my cousin, wants my title. He's always thought I took it from him. Something's happening here in Italy, and Dad is losing control."

The room went quiet again. I didn't know what to say. I didn't feel great knowing there were men here in Italy waiting for Apollo's downfall. All I could do was go to bed and hope tomorrow was a better day for us.

I heard Apollo leave early in the morning. He did his best not to wake me. He would be gone most of the day with Rio. They were traveling around Italy working through some plans for after we left. I was stuck spending another day at the house with Maria.

After breakfast Maria took me to see some of her friends and family I vaguely remember from when I used to visit Italy. It had been so long I didn't remember much. I had a chance to get to know Apollo's family a little better. I knew more about Apollo's uncle and how Giovanni was trying to take Apollo's spot. After shopping we went home to get dinner started. Maria insisted on cooking tonight. Apollo did tell me she was the best cook in Italy, so I was excited for whatever she planned on making.

"Eliana, can I ask you something?"

"Of course."

"Do you love him?"

"Apollo?" I asked, surprised by her question.

She nodded her head, taking a break from dicing peppers.

"I see the way you two look at each other, and it doesn't look like love. A marriage won't last if there's anything you love in the world more than him."

"I love him." I lied, hoping to sound convincing.

"I think Apollo is a good man, but I'm struggling to believe you." She said, "I know there's something going on between you two. You tense up when he holds you, and I see how nervous he is when he's around you."

How I answered Maria was incredibly important. If Maria didn't give her blessing the two families wouldn't move forward with the wedding. I had to think of something to say to convince her.

"When we first started dating things were perfect. I thought that the love we had was special, but after we announced the engagement it stopped being enough. I'm trying my best, but it's getting harder every day. I love him, but it feels like the more I love the more I worry." I said. "I don't know how you do it Maria. You and Rio have been together for decades, and you've always stayed by his side. I see how hard he's been working himself lately, and it's overwhelming I guess?"

Maria set her knife down, "It's not going to be easy Eliana. Rio and I didn't wake up one day and have all this. We had to fight for it. I see the same passion in you as I had when I was your age. You and Apollo are a team, and partnerships like that don't work if there's no trust."

"What do I do to build that trust? Did Rio ever shut you out when things got stressful for him?" I asked.

"All the time! But he only did it because he was trying not to worry me. He wanted to fix the problem before I found out about it. Men are idiots like that. Have you talked to Apollo about how you're feeling?"

"I don't know where to even begin. Sometimes I wish we could go back in time when the relationship was still a secret between us."

"Maybe you can. You two get to decide how involved your families are with the relationship. I love Catalina and your mother, but have you and Apollo decided what's best for you?"

"No." I admitted.

"You have to be patient with each other. Try to get back to the relationship you two had in the beginning."

"Thank you." I said grabbing a few bowls for the dinner table.

Maria looked pleased, like she had really helped, but there was no beginning. Apollo and I were doomed from the very start. Apollo and I had everyone tricked, including Maria. I didn't know if I should be proud of myself for the lies, or if I was disgusted. Apollo and I would have to be more convincing during the rest of the trip. It was only the second day, and Maria could already tell there was something wrong.

Maria and I were finishing up dinner when Rio and Apollo came back. I set down the plate I was holding and went up to Apollo. I wrapped my arms around Apollo giving him a kiss on the cheek. While I held him close I whispered in his ear.

"Pretend you missed me."

Chapter Eleven

Eliana

Apollo tried to hide his confusion as he wrapped his arms around me. He gave me a kiss on my cheek and whispered in my ear.

"What are you doing?"

"I'll explain everything later." I whispered back.

Letting go of me, Apollo walked to the fridge and grabbed a water.

"How was your day?" I asked.

"It was fine. Rio took me up north, and I got to connect with a few old friends."

"Apollo, why don't you go help Eliana set the table." Maria suggested.

Apollo followed behind me into the dining room.

"What was that?" He asked.

"Maria knows something is wrong with us. She has doubts about us being able to make it. I lied and said it was because of stress, and how hard you've been working, but she obviously isn't buying it. We have to do better. Just be a little more affectionate until she starts to lay off. She asked me if I loved you today."

"And what did you say?" he teased, slapping his hand over his heart.

"What do you mean what did I say? I told her I was crazy in love with you, and I lose sleep over how much I worry. I can't go another day without being married to you, Apollo." I joked.

"Maybe she knows that you're not good enough for me, and I deserve better."

"Yeah, I'm sure that's exactly what she thinks." I said, rolling my eyes. "Either way it doesn't matter. Until we leave here we need to start being more careful."

"Fine." He said, setting down the last of the napkins. Just in time Maria and Rio walked to the table.

"Let's eat!" Maria said. "I'm starving."

"Maria, that was delicious." I complimented.

"I told you she was the best." Apollo said.

"I ate so much it feels like I'm going to pop." I joked.

Apollo stretched his arm across the back of my chair.

"You can't be full El; we still have dessert."

"Why don't you three head into the piano room, and I'll bring the dessert?" Maria said.

Apollo took my hand and wrapped it over his forearm. He

led me to Rio's lounge. I started to walk over to the couch near the window, but Apollo held onto my hand leading me to a small loveseat. There was no way the two of us would fit, and Apollo knew that. He sat down and pulled me by my waist forcing me to sit on the chair with him. I sat almost completely on his lap with my legs draped over his thighs. I tried to scoot over to the left of me where there was a little bit of room, but he kept his arms wrapped around my waist.

Apollo had a few drinks at dinner, but not enough for him to be drunk. He knew what he was doing. He continued to sip on his whiskey talking to Rio. Maria walked in with cake and a few plates.

"What do you think you're doing?" I asked.

"I'm just doing what you asked me to do." He said.

Apollo lowered his hand on my waist. I slapped his hand off while Maria wasn't looking. Every few minutes or so Apollo would run his hand over my legs, leaving his hand there to rest. I tried focusing on Rio, and his stories, but all I could think about was Apollo. His hands were warm, and they were heating up my body. My stomach had flipped upside down, and I was super aware of my breathing. Every time I breathed in I could also feel Apollo's breath and heartbeat.

"Get your hand off my ass." I whispered only for Apollo to hear.

Maria handed me a plate of her chocolate cake. She started to cut another piece for Apollo, but he declined.

"It looks delicious, but no thank you."

"You never say no to my dessert, are you sick?"

"I'm still too full from dinner. I promise I'm okay."

Maria gave up and went over to sit with Rio. The two of

them got lost in conversation, and almost forgot we were there.

I took a bite of the cake and put another piece on the fork.

"Are you sure you don't want a bite?" I asked.

"I'll have a taste." He said.

Apollo grabbed my hand and pulled me closer to him. He let go of my hand that was holding the fork and put his hand on the back of my neck. With no warning, he leaned in kissing off the chocolate icing on my lips, and then pulled away like nothing happened.

"Delicious." Apollo licked his lips.

I sat there frozen, almost dropping my fork.

What. The. Fuck.

I looked around the room and saw Rio and Maria smiling at the two of us.

"I think we're going to head to bed." Rio said.

"Yes, we're exhausted, we should really be going." Maria said, standing up and taking the cake back to the kitchen. The two of them hid their laughs as they left us.

Apollo and I were left alone in the room.

"Apollo!"

"What?" He asked.

"You can't just get drunk like that and kiss me!"

"I'm not drunk."

"What?"

"I said I'm not drunk. I just wanted to kiss you while Maria was watching, and you were driving me crazy with those little moans you made every time you ate a piece of that cake. I wanted to see if a cake could really be that good."

I punched his shoulder.

"You're an asshole!" I said, storming out of the room.

I went up to the room and locked myself in the bathroom to keep myself from storming back into the living room and beating the shit out of him.

I turned on the shower without getting in. I leaned against the sink replaying everything that had happened tonight. I looked in the mirror, and saw my bottom lip was red and swollen. I ran my fingers over my lips. I could still taste Apollo's whiskey on my tongue. He kissed me, Apollo just fucking kissed me.

Apollo didn't come back to the room after dinner. I hoped he would fall asleep on the couch, so I didn't have to see him, but an hour later, a loud thud woke me up. I looked around the room and saw Apollo's side of the bed was empty. I listened again for the noise. One more time a scratch and a thud came from outside the door.

I opened the door a few inches and looked down. A drunk Apollo was sitting against the door.

"Apollo." I whispered.

"Eliana?" He asked, confused. He lifted his head up trying to see where I was.

"Turn around Apollo."

Apollo slowly stumbled and stood on his feet, "The door was locked."

"The door wasn't locked." I answered.

"I'm pretty sure it was."

I opened the door to let him in. He took one step and started to lean. I started to walk back to bed, but he tripped again.

"Apollo, stand up straight." I said holding him up and walking him to the bed.

Halfway across the room he stopped and let go of me. I turned around and saw a smiling Apollo staring at me.

"That's my shirt." Apollo said, grabbing the hem of my shirt.

"What, no it's not-" I paused and looked down.

Shit, it was his shirt. I grabbed it from my side of the closet, but our laundry must have gotten mixed up.

"You can get yourself to bed." I told him.

"Don't be embarrassed, it's cute on you." He teased.

"Listen-" I said, turning around fast. When I turned around he was closer than I thought. I ran right into his chest, as he grabbed my shoulders. I looked up at him, trying to take a step back.

"If you liked the kiss you should have just told me." He said.

I snapped out of it and stepped back. I took his shirt off and threw it at him. The shirt being thrown at him threw him off a bit. His smile faded as he stared at me. Left standing in my bra and shorts I stormed off to the closet. I wasn't going back out there until he was passed out. I couldn't face him after what just happened. I waited until I couldn't hear him walking around anymore, and then I went back to bed. Clutching the covers over my chest, I pushed out a quiet sigh.

Apollo Costa was going to be the death of me.

175

Apollo

I woke up with a pounding headache. I looked around and found an empty bed. Eliana must have left for breakfast already.

I went to the bathroom to take a shower. I threw my clothes behind the door and started the water. I stood under the water and tried to remember what happened last night. All I can remember was dinner with Maria and arguing with Eliana. I'm sure if we did fight Eliana would remind me as soon as I got to breakfast.

After my shower, I put on some pants and a button up. Walking down the stairs I heard Eliana's voice in the kitchen. When I walked in, Maria, Rio and Eliana stared at me. That means something definitely happened last night.

I walked around the kitchen island closer to Eliana. Eliana rolled her eyes, grabbed a pitcher of lemonade and took it out to the patio. I followed behind her to the table. Eliana grabbed a strawberry from the table and took a bite. She wiped off the juice from her lips, and the events from last night came back. Oh my God, I kissed Eliana.

The rest of the night came flooding back to me making my headache worse. The door being locked, the shirt. Fuck, I'm surprised Eliana didn't kill me in my sleep last night. To be fair she was trying to kill me with the way she rubbed her ass against my lap all night long. I couldn't focus on anything but her sitting with her legs pressed against my thigh, her hair brushing against my face and those fucking moans. It was the first time I'd ever been jealous of a fucking piece of cake.

Eliana tried to rush right past me back into the house.

"Eliana wait." I spoke. I tried to step in front of her, blocking the kitchen off.

"Get out of my way, or I'll cut your throat Apollo. I don't want to hear anything you have to say."

"Eliana please, let me explain."

Eliana looked at me, then pushed me out of her way. I heard her a minute later talking with Maria in the kitchen. I would deal with Eliana later, but right now I needed something for my head.

Breakfast was awkward. Eliana ignored me, and Rio and Maria pretended not to notice there was something wrong with us.

"Well," Maria said, breaking the ice. "I have a few things to do today, and I know Rio is busy, so why don't the two of you spend a day together. You haven't had a minute alone just the two of you since you got here. Go explore and enjoy Italy."

"Oh, I don't know." Eliana said, pausing. "Are you sure it won't take away from anything you have planned?"

"Of course not! It's been awhile since you two were in Italy, go enjoy it!" Rio said.

"I'll go get ready now, and we can leave around nine. Does that work?" Eliana asked me.

"Fine." I said.

Eliana excused herself from the table, as I helped Maria clear plates. I did anything I could to not be in the room alone with Eliana, but too soon the table was clean and I couldn't stall any longer. I had to go back to the room and get ready. I opened the door to the room and found an angry Eliana rushing to get dressed.

I tried to get a word in, but every time I spoke up Eliana left to a different part of the room or dropped something making noise.

"Eliana." I finally spoke, raising my voice a little.

She sat up from looking through her bag and dropped the shoes she was holding.

"Can we talk about last night?"

"No." She replied, taking her dress with her to the bathroom, and locking the door.

It was going to be a long day.

I got dressed in one of my suits and worked until Eliana was ready to go. I looked up from my computer when I heard her heels as she walked out of the bathroom. She had dressed up in a light green summer dress. She grabbed her purse from the table and walked out of the room. She waited for me in the car. Rio was generous enough to let us borrow his old convertible again.

"Have a nice day you two!" Maria shouted from the house, waving goodbye.

Driving off down the road, Eliana and I headed into town.

"We're going to visit Grandma's old shop."

"That's fine." She told me.

I could have used being stuck in the car with me as my chance to explain myself to Eliana, but I knew that would only make things worse. I gave Eliana her space and let her enjoy the drive into town. I wanted to give her at least a few minutes of peace before we were walking through my old neighborhood. It still wasn't safe for us to be so public about our visit to Italy, but Eliana was dying to get out of that house.

Before Eliana opened her door, I stopped her.

"Eliana, please stay close to me while we're here. There aren't a lot of people I trust. Don't go wandering off without me."

"Okay." She said, getting out of the car.

We stepped out of the car, and immediately I was recognized. A few people gave friendly smiles, but I was more concerned about the people who looked upset to see me.

Eliana could tell we weren't welcomed guests and stayed close to me. She followed me to the small cafe my aunt still owned.

"Hello?" I called out, into the empty restaurant.

"Apollo!" Someone shouted from the back. "You're back, it's true!"

"Lizzi, how have you been?" I asked.

"Busy, but I don't mind it." Lizzi said, squeezing me into a hug.

Looking behind me she smiled, "Eliana! You're back, it's so good to see you. We missed you."

"Not as much as I missed you and your crème cake Lizzi." Eliana laughed.

That made Lizzi happy, she opened her arms for Eliana. Although short in height, Lizzi's personality was quite the opposite. She loved everyone, and never passed up an opportunity for a hug. Now that everyone was getting older she got less visitors. Once grandma died she had to take over the shop all by herself.

"Come, have a seat and I'll get you two some cake and drinks."

"Thank you." Eliana said, having a seat near the wall. She looked around the shop admiring all of the art on the walls.

"Do you remember that summer your mom made us work here to help out your grandma?" She asked.

"Oh, I remember. It was horrible. I couldn't make coffee or bake to save my life. I begged her to let me work with Dad, but no, I was stuck here cleaning tables."

"Oh please. Don't act like it was all bad. You loved when the girls would come in and order food just to see you. You were the biggest flirt." Eliana teased.

"If I remember things correctly I wasn't the flirt. Isn't this where you met the love of your life Alejandro? He spent quite some time here as well."

Eliana's cheeks blushed, and an embarrassed smile spread across her face.

"I haven't thought about him in forever. God, he was dreamy, wasn't he?"

"Please, he wasn't that great." I responded. "Whatever happened to him?"

"Raff and Frankie scared him off when they caught us sneaking out." She complained. "I should see if he still lives around here. Maybe it would be good to catch up."

"No, absolutely not."

"Why? Scared Apollo?"

"He's no good for you. Plus, you've got all you need with me. I've been told I can be quite dreamy if that's what you want."

"Yeah dreamy until you ghost the girls on the third date. At least that's what I heard from the girls you 'dated'. Were you ever serious with anyone?"

"I don't know what you heard, but it's all lies. I was always a gentleman. Unlike Alejandro..." I replied under my breath.

Eliana let out a surprised gasp as she hit my arm. She laughed and a big smile spread across her face.

"I loved it here." She said.

"Why did you stop coming back? Your family still visits."

"I don't know. Eventually it just stopped feeling like I belonged. No one wanted anything to do with me after I got into law school. Dad stopped trusting me with jobs, and I got invited to fewer events and trips. It made it easy to want to leave. I stopped coming because I wasn't welcome anymore. Why did you stop?"

"I had to. There's too many people here trying to kill me. You already know my uncle wants to take over for my father, and thinks I'm doing a terrible job."

"If it's not safe for you here, why bother coming back now?" She asked.

"I owe it to Rio. He saved me after my accident. I know he still looks for whoever hurt me. He won't stop until we find who it was. You're in the same amount of danger as I am now. Someone will try to use you to hurt me. I need you to always stay alert. Never assume you're safe."

"I know." She sighed.

"I'm being serious Eliana. I really worry about something happening to you. Don't trust anyone you meet. Even if they tell you they're my family. Stay alert here in Italy, and focus on getting back to the States safely."

Our conversation was interrupted when Lizzi came back with food. We sat and chatted with Lizzi for an hour. I know Eliana wanted to stay here with Lizzi a little while longer, but I had other plans.

"Lizzi, it's been great visiting, but we have a few more places to visit before we drive back to Rio's."

"Please visit more often, Apollo. Don't go this long without coming home." She asked.

"I promise we'll come back soon."

I didn't know if I could keep that promise, but I would try.

Eliana and I started to leave Lizzi's, but we were stopped by a few guys near our car.

I held Eliana's waist as we walked. Eliana looked up at me. I gave her a nod to let her know I wasn't concerned about the men waiting by the car.

"Apollo, we heard you were stopping by and visiting family. We wondered if you'd come say hi to us." Antonio said.

"We're a little short on time Antonio." I answered.

"We all want to meet your new girl." Antonio said, looking over at Eliana. He took her hand and kissed it.

I didn't mind Antonio. He was a good worker, but I didn't want to spend any time with him.

"It was great seeing you, but we have reservations to get to."

"Hold on, Apollo." Antonio said. He stepped in front of my car door.

"Antonio..." I spoke.

He could tell I wasn't in the mood for a reunion, so he stepped to the side. Eliana waited for Antonio's brother to step away from the car, and then walked to her side of the car.

I opened my door, and saw Antonio's hand hold the top open.

"Why don't you two stop by for drinks on Friday?" He offered. "Some drinks, dancing, a break from Rio, come on, it'll be fun."

"Maybe." I said closing the door.

I drove off with Eliana and Antonio faded in the background.

"Are we going to drinks on Friday?" She asked.

"I don't know. We probably have to. Everyone knows I'm here now. We can't hide."

Eliana agreed, as I drove up the coast.

"Why does this place look so familiar?" Eliana asked when we parked.

"It's the museum I own. It's been in the family for years. We've been silent owners ever since I could remember."

"You own a museum and you're just now bringing me to it?" She asked.

"I would have led with that if I knew that's what it took to get you to like me. And for the record, I don't own a museum." I said opening the door. "I own four."

Eliana rolled her eyes, and walked into the front lobby.

Immediately Eliana was in her own world as she walked around the exhibits. Museums were her favorite place to visit back in high school. She had to drag Frankie to go with her whenever she had free time. One night after a dinner party her dad had to send out a search party, and they found her wandering through a local gallery. We were all surprised to find out the owner had given her the key, so she could visit whenever she wanted.

Eliana walked around by herself while I checked in with the management staff. I had a lot to catch them up on. The museum would always be good for my business. After working for a few minutes, I went to go find Eliana.

I found her admiring a painting. She was so mesmerized she didn't hear me walk up behind her. I startled her when she finally heard me.

"It's beautiful, isn't it?" She asked.

"Hmhmm." I said, smiling at her as she admired the painting.

I followed behind her for a little while longer as she walked the halls. When she had walked through every exhibit a few times we decided to leave. It was almost time for dinner, and I had reservations at a restaurant I knew Eliana would like.

Eliana sipped her wine and ate some bread while we waited for our food. I looked around the restaurant admiring the view from the balcony we were sitting on.

"I know what you're doing." She said.

"And what is that?"

"You think if you're extra nice to me, and you get me drunk on expensive wine I'll forget about last night."

"Is that so?" I asked.

"Mhmm, but unfortunately for you I didn't forget, and it's going to take a lot more than this to not be mad about the kiss and coming back to the room drunk."

"If you were really that upset about it you'd still be giving me the silent treatment. Plus, that wasn't even a kiss." I explained.

"Then what was it? Because it was definitely something."

"A peck?" I replied.

"A peck?" Eliana scoffed. "You're kidding, right?"

"No, you asked me to be more affectionate in front of Maria.

I don't see why I'm in trouble for doing what you asked."

"You heard affectionate and immediately assumed I wanted you to kiss me?"

"It was an honest mistake." I answered.

"You're ridiculous."

"I see what's going on." I said, leaning back in my chair.

"And what would that be?"

"You're upset because deep down you didn't hate it."

"You are sick in the head." Eliana said.

"Go ahead, keep lying to yourself, but we both know the truth." I said cutting her off.

Eliana pointed at me, and started to argue back, but I stopped her.

"Wait, be quiet." I said looking around.

"Don't tell me to be quiet. I'm not done talking about this-"

"No, I'm serious. There's something going on outside." I said, seeing something fly past the window.

Eliana stopped her arguing and looked at me.

As soon as I stood up from my chair a loud crash came from the kitchen. I pushed my chair out and grabbed Eliana's hand.

"Run!"

Chapter Twelve

Eliana

Apollo took my hand and ran out of the restaurant. As soon as we got to the door a few men came rushing out of the kitchen. One of them pointed a gun at Apollo. We barely made it out of the restaurant and down the street before the men chasing us caught up to us again.

Apollo didn't have time to get to the car. We continued to run down the street. Apollo's grip on my wrist tightened as he ran. I did my best to keep up with him in heels, but I was struggling.

Turning a corner, I stopped him.

"What are you doing?"

"Just give me a minute!" I shouted, tossing my shoes off.

Now barefoot, Apollo led me down an empty street. We could hear a car turning onto the road we were on. Apollo looked around the closed shops and stores. He found a small alley between two shops that would be hard to spot from the road.

He helped me slide into it, and then followed after me. There was hardly enough room for the two of us. I had to lean my head over Apollo's shoulder while he looked out at the street. I saw car lights drive past our hiding spot.

Things quieted down, and the two of us became super aware of the situation. Apollo's hand rested on my waist, and I was now fully leaned into his chest. Apollo tried giving me more room, but it only made things worse. He tried to shift his weight and ended up pressing into my chest. Pausing, he looked down at me.

"Don't look at me like that." I whispered.

"Why not?"

"Because the last time you looked at me like that you kissed me."

"Oh my god it wasn't a kiss!" He argued.

"Just look to your left please." I asked.

"What if I don't want to? I'm comfortable like this."

"Apollo-" Once again I was cut off. This time by Apollo putting his hand over my mouth.

He got one arm free and wrapped me closer to him, resting my head into his chest, so that all I could see was the dark alleyway to my left. I couldn't see what was going on. He shielded me with his body, looking out towards the sidewalk again. A few voices could be heard. I could feel Apollo stop breathing, and his chest tighten. We stayed quiet until the voices left. The adrenaline of the chase was wearing down, and I was starting to feel the nerves.

After what felt like forever Apollo relaxed and let go of me.

"I think they're gone." He whispered. "Stay here."

Apollo stuck his head out of the alley and looked around. He took my hand again and helped me crawl out between the two walls.

The street was quiet again, and we had a chance to try and get back to the car. We almost made it back, but there were people waiting for us.

"What do we do now?" I asked.

"We have to get out of here and wait for one of Rio's men to pick us up. Let's go." He said, pulling out his phone.

I walked next to Apollo down a small sidewalk in the opposite direction of the car. We only went down streets with little lighting that looked dark enough for us to stay hidden as we walked.

"Apollo?" I asked.

"What?"

"Who were those people?"

"I don't know." He said, looking down at me. "I've never seen them before."

I tried to keep up with Apollo, but the more we walked the more my feet started to hurt. They were cut up from the run. Apollo noticed I was slowing down.

"Eliana, you're bleeding." He said, leaning down to the sidewalk. I tried to hide the cuts, but there wasn't much I could do.

"I'm fine. I'll deal with it when I get home."

Apollo looked up, unsure if we should keep going. I knew we couldn't stop. We had to get back to Rio's. Apollo didn't want me to keep walking, but we had no other choice.

We walked for another mile before Apollo got a call. Shortly after, a car pulled up and a man I recognized from Rio's house rolled his window down.

"Get in."

Apollo grabbed me by the waist and lifted me into the car. He kept his arm wrapped around me as we drove back to Rio's. The longer we drove, the more my feet began to hurt. I tried to hide the pain, but there was no comfortable way to sit. Noticing I was in pain Apollo let go of me, and grabbed my legs. He moved so that I could lay my feet across his lap. It wasn't a perfect solution, but it did help.

Before I could even attempt to step out of the car Apollo swung my arm around his shoulders and carried me in his arms up to the house. He held me tight to his chest as he walked up the steps.

Maria and Rio were waiting for us in the living room when we walked in.

"Are you two okay?"

"We're fine. We lost the group near the restaurant." Apollo answered. Now in the light I saw the state of Apollo and me. We were a mess. Apollo's suit was ruined, and my dress had cuts all down the skirt. My bloody feet were worse than anything else.

"Rio, I need to figure out who did this, and our car is still in town."

"I'll call a few guys. They can meet us here, and work on whoever tried to chase you."

"Why don't you help Eliana to your room, and meet me down here?"

"Bring someone up to help El with her cuts." Apollo ordered.

Rio nodded, and left the room. Apollo and I walked back to the room. I refused to let him carry me this time, so he demanded we walk slowly to the room. He held my waist like I was going to fall over any minute.

"Are you going to be okay until I get back?" Apollo asked.

"I'll be fine. Just go and do what you need to do."

There was something wrong with Apollo. He was avoiding me, and stalling to leave.

He helped me get a few things from the closet, and finally agreed to leave. I needed a few minutes to myself, and I couldn't do that with Apollo hovering over me. I thought I was finally alone, but I was wrong.

"Eliana..." Apollo called out.

"Yes?" I asked, turning around.

When I turned around Apollo grabbed my waist and pulled me close to him. He brushed my hair behind my ear, rested his hand on my cheek and then pulled me into a kiss.

It wasn't anything like last night. His lips crashed into mine, bruising me as he let out a deep sigh. He waited to deepen the kiss until I gave him permission to continue. I hesitated, surprised by Apollo's actions, but eventually I gave in and kissed back. Apollo held me like it was the last chance he'd ever have to kiss me. He softly bit on my lower lip, begging for more. I almost fell backward when he finally let go, and pulled away from me. Opening my eyes, I saw him staring down at me.

He brushed my lips with his fingers, "*That* was a kiss."

Not saying another word Apollo left the room, and closed the door. Leaving me alone in the room.

Shit.

Apollo didn't come back to the room last night, but when I went down for breakfast he was there at the table with Rio. He looked like he hadn't slept all night.

I was glad he didn't come back into the room last night. I was up all night processing the past two days. I decided the only reason I was so vulnerable was because of everything happening in my life. I let my guard down, and let Apollo in. This wouldn't have happened if we were back in New York. Apollo knew we weren't good for each other. He must be feeling the same way. The two of us just got caught up in the moment. Things would go back to normal when we left Italy.

It didn't make sitting next to him any easier even though. It was still hard being so close to him, and acting like a couple. He put his hand on my thigh and looked down at my feet. His hand sent shocks to my brain reminding me of how he held me last night.

"Did someone help you with your cuts?" He asked.

"I cleaned them up last night. Did you figure out what happened last night?"

"No, we're still trying to get some answers. I'll have to be out with Rio today. Are you going to be okay staying at the house?"

"Of course. Maria and I will find something to do." I said.

I wasn't loving the idea of being trapped in the house alone with Maria, but I knew Apollo didn't want me leaving, especially right now.

I had barely been at the table for five minutes before Apollo finished his food, and left in a hurry. In a minute, he was back wearing new clothes. Before leaving again he kissed the top of my head, and left with Rio.

"Be safe." I shouted as he left for the car.

"Always."

Maria kept me busy all day. She didn't want to sit and have time to worry about Rio and Apollo. House project after house project she was finally tired, and wanted to head to bed early after dinner. Maria was asleep, and Apollo wasn't back yet, so I thought it'd be a good time to call Emma and see how things were back home.

"Took you long enough to call!" Emma answered. "I've been dying to know how things are going."

"I've been a little busy."

"How's Italy?"

"It's fine, the weather has been perfect."

"Cut the crap. You didn't call to talk about the weather, what's going on?"

"Apollo kissed me last night." I blurted out, unable to keep it in anymore.

"He kissed you?!" Emma shouted through the phone.

"Mhmm." I told her, "And I might have kissed him back."

"What happened after the kiss? Did he say anything, did you say anything? What happens now? Do you have feelings for him?" Emma asked, unable to get her questions out fast enough.

"I don't know what happens now. He kissed me, and then he just left. I haven't talked to him since it happened. I'm too embarrassed to even look at him, let alone talk to him about it. I don't know how I feel, or what this means for us."

"Well, what was it like? Was it bad?" She asked.

"It was really fucking hot. He grabbed my waist and pulled

me flush to his chest. I almost didn't kiss him back, but there was this voice in my head screaming at me to stop holding back. This is all Maria's fault." I complained.

"How is Apollo kissing you Maria's fault?"

"The only reason we kissed the first time was because Apollo and I decided we needed to be more affectionate around the two of them. Then we got into an argument about the first kiss, and I guess Apollo had been thinking about it just as much as I was."

"What, slow down. There was another kiss, different from this one?"

"Well, I wouldn't call it a kiss. It was more of a peck."

"I can't believe this. I thought you hated everything about this man? I thought you were repulsed by the idea of him and everything he represents."

"I did hate him, maybe I still do, but that doesn't mean he's not the hottest man I've ever met. I mean come on, you've met him. There's something about him that drives me crazy."

"People change, feelings change. Would it really be terrible to lower your guard a little bit and see where things go with him?" She asked.

"What if he's playing me? What if this is just one of his games and when he knows I have feelings for him he can turn it off?"

"I doubt that's what's happening here Eliana. You're being paranoid. I think it's worth talking with him about it, and trying to figure out what's going on between you two."

"Yeah, you might be right." I said.

"I am right. Before you decide anything about Apollo and that kiss you need to talk with him about it. Don't avoid this just because you're scared. And please for the love of everything holy call me as soon as anything exciting happens. Promise you'll call?" She asked.

"I promise if anything happens you'll be the first to know, but right now I need to focus on surviving another day with Maria."

"You'll be back home soon. Enjoy the trip while you still can. Love you El."

"Bye, love you."

There was nothing I could do about Apollo now. Maybe tomorrow I'd have a clearer head.

Apollo

The last few days flew by. I was busy working with Rio, and we weren't anywhere closer to tracking down the men who tried to kill me. It wasn't new to have someone coming after me, but I couldn't put Eliana in danger every time she went out in public with me. I didn't want to go get drinks with Antonio, but he might have some answers for me. He'd be able to help me out, and he knew the people here in town better than anybody.

I sent Eliana a text.

Leaving for drinks with Antonio at seven. Be ready at six-thirty.

I was left on read for a few hours until she texted me back a few photos.

Eliana: Which one of these is more 'getting drinks with your psycho fiancé and his sketchy friends'?

The two photos were of Eliana in a few different outfits. Both of the dresses were something only I wanted to see her in, but I wasn't going to stop her from wearing them. She knew exactly what she was doing to me when she sent me photos like that.

Gold is fine.

I replied, trying to play it cool, like I had no interest in either.

I would have a hard time being out with Eliana tonight. We hadn't talked about what happened a few nights ago when I kissed her. She acted like it didn't bother her. I was expecting an argument or a fight or two, but the fight never came. I don't know what it was, but getting away from New York, and getting some space changed our dynamic. We stopped fighting for once, and being back in Italy helped us connect. It made the future less daunting. We had grown apart over the years, but no one knew me better than Eliana. Even with the distance we created when we were kids, no one else grew up the same way I did.

I didn't know what was going to happen when we left Italy, so I was trying to enjoy it while we were here. I was waiting in the driveway at exactly six-thirty. Eliana was running late. I tried calling, but I was sent to voicemail. Frustrated, I went up to the front door.

"Eliana!" I shouted.

"Jesus Christ, calm down. I'm coming!" She yelled back at me. I held the door open for a running Eliana. She walked in front of me towards the car putting in her earrings. The gold dress looked even more amazing from the back. It was going to be a long night.

I noticed Eliana wearing her heels again. She was barely healed from the attack. She hid her pain as she got into the car.

"You're going to hurt yourself wearing your heels tonight."

"But they make my legs look good." She smiled.

Eliana lifted her legs up, her dress pushing up showing more of her thigh. I shifted in my seat, signaling for the driver to start the engine. I tried to focus on the view during the drive, and not on Eliana sitting a foot away from me.

Eliana

Antonio was a few drinks in when we got to the club. He was drinking with a few guys I remembered from the other day. Antonio worked for Rio, but I didn't know how any of the others were connected.

"I made a bet you two weren't going to show!" Antonio shouted over the music.

"I'd never miss a chance to party with you Antonio."

"Have a seat. I'll get a server to come over and get you two a drink."

Antonio came back a minute later with a girl ready to take our orders. Apollo ordered for the both of us. When the drinks arrived, I took a small sip, and set mine down on the table. I wasn't going to be drinking tonight. After what happened at dinner I didn't want to let my guard down. The club was loud, and busy. Alcohol would only make things worse. The group of men around the table were suspiciously friendly. They were probably only polite to me to piss off Apollo, but if it upset him he wasn't showing it.

"So how long have you two been engaged?" Antonio asked.

"Almost a month." I answered. "We were engaged before we announced it at our dad's party."

"Time flies." Apollo added.

"He keeping you happy?" He crudely asked.

"Alright, Antonio." Apollo said, deflecting the question.

"No, come on, I want to know. If you don't treat her right, and keep her happy she'll leave you Apollo." He said, spilling his drink as he pointed. "I get the feeling she moves on fast." He joked.

"Antonio, enough I'm serious." Apollo said, his voice more serious than before.

"You're no fun!" Antonio said. "I'm going to get another drink, why don't you two come with me, and we can talk about why you really came here tonight?"

I grabbed my drink, and walked with Apollo to a smaller room that muffled the noise of the club. Now that we were around strangers Apollo's guard was up. He stayed close to me, and avoided leaving me alone at the table. Eventually he didn't have a choice.

"Apollo, I know why you're here, and I know who

ambushed you. Why don't we grab a few drinks for the table and I'll tell you about some contractors I used to work with before I started working for Rio."

"Will you be alright for a few minutes? I'll come right back." Apollo asked me.

"I'll wait here, just be quick."

Apollo left with Antonio, and I was left alone in the room with strangers. Things were going fine until a man approached my table. I tried to ignore him, but he wasn't going away.

"I asked you if you were Apollo's fiancé." He said, raising his voice.

One of his friends who was shorter, but older, sat to the left of me, as the man sat near the end of the table to my right. I was hoping they would leave because looking around the table it felt like I was trapped.

"Yes, Apollo and I are engaged." I answered.

I didn't recognize anyone in the room. The only people I sort of knew had stayed on the main floor. I looked to the door praying for Apollo to walk in any second.

"He must have paid a lot for you." One of them laughed.

"Excuse you?" I asked.

"No way you just agreed to marry him. He's a fucking nightmare. Why don't you find a real man? I'd take really good care of you." The man on the right said, moving closer to me. The two men were now close enough I could smell the alcohol on their breath. One of them tried grabbing my hair over my shoulder.

I slapped his hand off of me, and tried to push my chair back so I could leave.

"Where do you think you're going?" One of them asked.

"I'm leaving. Let go of my arm." I spoke up as loud as I could.

"You aren't going anywhere bitch." The man on the left grabbed my wrist and dragged me out of my chair. He forced me to stand as he stood behind me.

"I want to know how much Apollo paid for you. I'll pay your daddy double what he did."

I struggled and fought as the man tightened his grip. I kicked, and screamed but no one came to help me.

"Get your fucking hands off me!"

I screamed and threw my hands, as the other men in the room did nothing but watch. It's like I was making no noise at all.

"Calm down, we're just having a little bit of fun." The other man replied, dragging his hand over my stomach. He tried to pull my dress up as I fought back harder. It didn't matter how hard I kicked back, the man wasn't letting go of me.

My body was giving up, and sending me into shock. I tried to fight back against the man that held me, but no matter how hard I fought against him he wouldn't let me go. The walls of the small room were quickly closing in, and I knew there was so escaping.

"Apollo!" I screamed at the top of my lungs. I knew he wouldn't hear me, but I prayed to God he was on his way back with Antonio.

"I told you to get your fucking hands off of me!"

That only made the men laugh. One of them broke the strap on my dress. The only thing holding my dress up was the man's hands wrapped around my chest.

"Where's Apollo now Eliana? He can't hear you."

One of my arms was free, so I reached for the table. The only thing I could grab was an ashtray. I swung it around knocking the old man in the face. He stumbled back, wiping ash out of his eyes.

"Fucking whore!" He shouted, ripping my dress and grabbing my arm.

I had no other options but to scream. I screamed until my lungs burned, and I clawed at the men with my nails. I had no idea Apollo was back in the room until I saw him ripping the men off of me. I was dropped back to the floor as Apollo grabbed one of the men by his collar. Antonio ran to help me stand as I watched Apollo punch the taller man to the ground. The man who held me, and ripped my dress, was now lying bloody on the ground. His face was unrecognizable.

Apollo punched, and punched refusing to let go of the man. I could have stopped him, but I didn't. I wanted Apollo to punch the man who attacked me until his skull caved in. I wanted to watch him choke on his own blood as he lay there on the cold floor. I watched Apollo beat the man half to death. Each punch was harder than the one before. Apollo's hand was split and bleeding, but it didn't stop him. No one in the room had the nerve to get in his way. Finally, Antonio held Apollo's arm back.

"Apollo." He spoke. "Get Eliana out of here, I'll deal with him."

Apollo looked back at me, his eyes black. He stood over the unconscious man, trying to catch his breath. He stood up, and threw his jacket over my shoulders. I held onto the jacket as Apollo guided me out of the bar.

It felt like I was stuck in a dream. The noise of the music and people were gone, and I could hardly feel the seat I was sitting on. It was dead silent. A small voice was shouting my name in the distance. I couldn't figure out where it was coming from until I felt someone grab my hand.

"Eliana." Apollo said, concern in his voice. "Can you hear me?"

I looked over and saw Apollo sitting next to me.

"Eliana..." He spoke quietly.

"I'm okay." I said. I didn't mean it, but I thought I should say something.

"I'm okay." I kept repeating, trying not to cry. "I'm okay. I'm okay."

I heard Apollo's voice again, "Pull over."

The car stopped on the side of the road.

"Get out." Apollo ordered. Isaac got out of the car, closed his door and stood off to the side of the road.

"Come here." Apollo said, pulling me into his arms.

"It's just us. No one else is here." He whispered.

I buried my head into Apollo's chest, and grabbed his shirt as tight as I could. I relaxed my jaw, and let the tears fall. I cried as Apollo held me. It was the first time I'd cried in a while. Everything I'd been bottling up finally came pouring out. Marrying Apollo, getting fired, someone trying to kill us, and now this. I didn't recognize this life I was living. How the hell did I end up here?

"I can't do this." I cried. "I can't keep living like this."

Apollo brushed my hair and rubbed my back, trying to calm me down.

"I know." He hushed. "I need you to try and breathe for me Eliana. Feel my chest rising, and match it."

I leaned into Apollo's chest and tried focusing on only his breathing. I had calmed down, but the tears didn't stop. Apollo continued to hold me.

"We can stay here until you're ready to go back to the house." Apollo said.

Apollo rocked me back and forth in his arms as I cried. He hushed and whispered in my ear helping me calm down.

"I'm so sorry." He whispered every few minutes.

Finally calming down, I became increasingly aware of how trapped I felt in the car. I needed to get out of here before I freaked out again.

"I want to go home."

Apollo knocked on his window, and Isaac drove us back to the house. Apollo helped me get to the room before Maria or Rio saw me. He went straight to the closet to grab me a shirt. My dress was almost completely torn which made changing easy. He held my hand for support as I stepped out of the dress. He pulled an old shirt over my head, and pulled my hair out from under it.

I tried doing this all by myself, but my body wouldn't move. I begged my legs to move, or my arms to reach out and grab Apollo, but my brain ignored me. I was trapped, unable to process the pain my body was in. Apollo walked me to bed and pulled the covers over me. I wasn't sure where he went but eventually he came back to bed.

When he crawled under the covers, he slid over to me. He

tried wrapping an arm around me, but I stopped him.

"I told you I'm fine."

"I know you're fine. Just let me hold you. Please." He said in my ear.

One of his arms was wrapped under my pillow, and the other one crossed over my chest. When I opened my eyes, I saw his hand wrapped up in bandages. His knuckles were swollen, and his hands were covered in dry blood.

"Apollo your hand..." I whispered.

"I'm okay. Don't worry about it."

Wrapped up in Apollo's arms I played with the loose fabric on his bandages. I know he was lying about the pain. It looked like it hurt. Seeing Apollo's hands made my heart ache. It felt like I was going to cry again, but I didn't have any tears left. I laid there in Apollo's arms trying to relax, and not think about what happened at the bar. By the time I calmed down again I had a headache.

Finally falling asleep, I hoped I didn't wake up in the morning.

Apollo

I could tell how much pain Eliana was in as she slept. I shouldn't have left her alone. It was all my fault. What those men tried to do to her, it's all because I left her. As soon as Eliana woke up we were leaving. She wanted to go home, and I didn't want her stuck in Italy any longer. Nothing good happens here.

I felt Eliana shift and turn in the middle of the night. She was now facing me, and resting on my chest. I moved my arm so she would be more comfortable as she slept. I brushed my finger over her nose and cheeks watching her sleep. All I could think about was how all of her pain was my fault.

I fell asleep holding Eliana as tight as I could. I woke up around six, and started making calls to get the plane ready. I talked to Rio, and he agreed it was time to leave. Maria would have someone pack Eliana's bags up when she woke for breakfast.

It was almost nine, and she was still asleep. I went into the room to check in on her. Opening the curtains to let in some sun, she woke up.

"Eliana, wake up. We're leaving."

She sat up quickly, "We're going back to New York?"

"Yes, as soon as you're ready."

Eliana was quick on her feet. She dressed quickly, and had a bag packed before I ended my phone call with Dane.

"They're still prepping the plane. Go eat some breakfast, and say goodbye to Maria." I told her.

I gave Alex a call so he could meet us at the airport. The room was packed when I came back from the hallway. Eliana was downstairs saying her goodbyes.

"Promise you'll call me when you land." Maria asked.

"I'll call you as soon as I get to the house." Eliana promised.

"I'm going to miss you two." Maria said, hugging Eliana. "I'll have to wait until the wedding to see you two again."

That brought a smile to Eliana. "You'll fly over for the wedding?"

"Of course, and if there's anything you need you let me know and I'll take care of it. Especially if I need to talk your mom out of something crazy." She smiled.

Maria walked over to me and gave me a big hug.

"If you let anything happen to her I'll kill you myself. Forget what Rio would try to do to you." She whispered.

After hugging Eliana Rio came over for a quick hug, "Try and get back home safe."

Eliana and I walked to the car with our bags and loaded up the back. Saying one final goodbye to Maria, Eliana stepped up into the SUV.

The two of us drove off towards the airplane. Eliana sat next to me, holding my hand. I had never seen her this vulnerable before. She's never opened up like this to me. I wanted to be happy she was starting to trust me, but I knew the only reason she was attached to me was because of last night.

We drove in silence not saying a word, but I gave her hand a squeeze every time she would zone out. I kept her focused on getting home. Rio's men unpacked our bags and took them to the plane, so the two of us could get into the plane and settle in.

Eliana avoided eye contact with me as she sat down across from me at the table. She hadn't said more than ten words all day. She was trapped in her head.

"Do you need something to drink? Or eat?" I asked.

"No." She whispered.

I didn't want her falling back into a depression like before we left, but now was not the time to force anything.

Eliana watched me work, and type away at my computer. Every time I looked back up at her, her eyes were glossed over and numb.

"I'm going to go lay down." She spoke, walking away.

I heard the bedroom door close, and Eliana lay down. I didn't see her again for a few hours. I was busy working with Dane over the phone when I heard her walk back to the table.

When I looked up at her I froze. This morning Eliana was wearing one of my sweatshirts, but now she was wearing only a t-shirt. I scanned her arms. They were covered with cuts and bruises. Handprints of the men who held her wrapped around her shoulders and forearms.

"El..."

"Don't." She said.

I did as she asked, and went quiet. I didn't say anything, but that didn't stop me from scanning her arms. On her shoulder blades, I saw the handprints of the man who held her, and cuts from the man who ripped her dress. The worst part wasn't the bruises. It was the cuts and breaks of her nails that showed how hard she was fighting back.

I shouldn't have left her. None of this would have happened if I stayed with her last night. I was just as mad at myself as I was with the men who hurt her.

I looked back up at a sleeping Eliana when I heard my phone ring. I left to take the call at the front of the plane.

"Antonio."

"Sir." He answered.

"What did you do with them?"

"We took them back to Rio's safe house. I'm here with them

now."

"Tell Charlie I want him to cut off their hands, and tell him to take his time. The longer they suffer the better. Call me back in a few hours and I'll give you more instructions." I spoke, trying not to lose my shit.

I couldn't be there to do what I wanted to do with them, but I knew Charlie would get the job done. The two of them were lucky I was flying back to the states. I walked back to Eliana's table, and moved my things to sit next to her. It woke her up.

She saw I was next to her, but she didn't seem to mind.

"Why don't you go back to sleep until we land?" I asked.

She nodded, leaning into me. She rested on my arm and fell back asleep. I don't know if it's because she was tired, or because of last night, but she was still fine with letting me be near her. I worked until we landed. Going to Italy was necessary, but it put me behind on other work I had. Dane did his best to stay on top of things, but I'm glad we're back.

Leaving the airport and driving back to the house, Eliana watched out the window. She watched the city, and the people rushing through it. Her eyes followed the bright colors, and noise until we were in our quiet neighborhood.

She turned back towards me when we pulled into the driveway.

"Please don't tell anyone about last night. I don't want anyone in my family finding out what happened to me. It would only cause problems. If you tell anyone I'll never forgive you."

"I promise, I won't tell a single soul."

As soon as we were through the front door she went back to her room. I lost her again. Who knows how long she was going to trap herself in there again before she let me help her.

Eliana slept for close to a whole day, and then the next morning she was working in the house like nothing happened. Even though she didn't need to, she spent all day cleaning every room in the house. After cleaning for two days, she started rearranging her room. She kept herself busy for three days.

I couldn't leave her, so I stayed at the house and worked. I don't think Eliana slept once after the first night. I was known for staying up late to work, but Eliana was up later than me. I would occasionally hear her moving furniture, or playing music from a random part of the house. I couldn't take it anymore. I had to put an end to it.

I stepped out of my office to look for Alex or Kim. I found the two of them in the basement.

"Alex."

"Yes Sir." He answered standing up from his table.

"When was the last time Eliana slept?"

"She hasn't, Sir. I've been helping her with the house when I can, but even when we offer to take a break she declines."

"Where is she now?"

"Last I checked she was working in a guest room."

"You and Kim can take the rest of the night off. I'll spend tonight with Eliana." I told the two of them.

I walked, and followed the noise of the music blasting and found Eliana organizing shelves in a room I forgot I had.

"Eliana!" I had to shout through the music.

She couldn't hear me and I didn't want to scare her, so I waited for her to turn around.

"Apollo..." She shouted when she finally turned around.

"Eliana, it's late. Let's go to bed."

"No, I have a few more things I need to take care of here." She argued.

"El... this isn't healthy." I pleaded. "You can't function on a few hours of sleep like this. Let's go back to your room."

"No." She said, now angry. She stormed past me and walked down the hallway.

"Eliana, I'm not in the mood for games. You need sleep."

"No." She repeated again.

Eliana grabbed a set of sheets from the hallway, and brought it back into the room.

I followed after her one more time.

"Eliana, stop for one minute. Please." I stepped in front of her, blocking the door.

"What?!" She said throwing the sheets onto the bed. It was one of the few times she'd ever raised her voice at me.

"You need sleep." I spoke slowly.

The anger in her voice disappearing, she spoke, "I can't."

I could see her jaw clench, and her chin shake.

"Why not?" I asked, already knowing why.

She held back tears.

"I can still see them. It's like they're standing in this room with me. I feel their hands on me no matter what I do. They won't leave."

My heart sank, and my stomach turned. I thought she'd feel better if she got some sleep, but sleep only brought more suffering.

"El." I whispered. "Come here."

She came over to me and leaned into my chest. I wrapped my arms around her, rubbing her back. She grabbed my shirt, with a tight grip.

"What can I do? Do you want me to sleep with you?"

"I don't think that's a good idea. I just can't be alone right now." She confessed.

"Alright." I said, letting go. "Come with me."

Eliana was trying to create boundaries now that we were back in New York, but I couldn't let her sleep alone. I took her to my office, and walked over to a cabinet near my desk. Eliana waited for me near the couch by my desk while I brought back a blanket.

"You can stay here with me. No point in us both being awake, but in separate rooms. Stay here until you feel comfortable enough to fall asleep. I'll be right over there the whole time."

"You won't leave?" She asked.

"I'll stay here in the office with you. I promise. I'll have to do some work, and I might make a few calls, but that could be a good distraction to help you fall asleep." I tried to convince.

Eliana moved a pillow, and took the blanket from me. She laid down, curling up her knees, and laying her arm under her pillow. She looked around the room a few times before closing her eyes.

I went back to my desk, and watched her move and fidget until she fell asleep. Once she was asleep she stayed asleep until the morning. Nothing I did bothered her. Every once in a while, I would check on her to make sure she wasn't having a nightmare.

Relieved to see her sleeping peacefully I went back to work. She was finally resting.

Eliana

Apollo typed away on his computer while I laid down. I wanted nothing more than to be sleeping in Apollo's bed together like in Italy, but I knew we couldn't. We had to get back to our normal life. We were struggling before we left for Italy, and I couldn't ignore the problems we had just because of our trip.

Apollo knew I wouldn't be comfortable in his bed but being here in his office was exactly what I needed. Only once during the night I woke up because of a nightmare, but Apollo's quiet typing reminded me I was back home. I was safe. It made it easier to fall back asleep, knowing he was here.

A few times when Apollo thought I was sleeping he came over to the couch. He would fix my blanket, or carefully move my hair out of my face. I tried really hard to pretend to be sleeping. I ignored the butterflies doing flips in my stomach when he came to check on me. I knew like his other acts of kindness, he was only being good to me because of his own personal guilt. This would end eventually, and the old Apollo would be back.

I woke up early in the morning, and saw Apollo sleeping at his desk. He stayed here the whole night, just like he promised. I walked over to his desk, shaking his shoulder.

"Apollo."

He woke up quickly, "What's wrong?"

"Nothing, it's morning. I'm going to go take a shower, and get dressed." I said.

Apollo rubbed his eyes, and pushed his hair back. He looked around his desk for his phone to check the time. Before I left his office, I folded his blanket back up.

"Thank you." I spoke quietly, hoping he could still hear me.

He nodded his head.

I left to go get ready for the day. I didn't have anything to do, but I would feel better after a shower.

I tried to shower quickly. I couldn't stomach seeing my bruises trying to heal. My skin was covered in patches of blue and yellow. Nothing was fading, and it only reminded me of Italy. I didn't need a reminder on my skin. That night kept playing through my head over, and over again. Screaming for Apollo, kicking and clawing, and feeling trapped in a stranger's grip. Apollo was waiting for me in the kitchen after my shower. He had that dumb look on his face again, like he was going to say something that would upset me.

I grabbed the coffee pot and poured myself a cup.

"I think you should go see someone about what happened." He spoke.

I turned, grabbing the sugar from the counter.

"Who?" I asked.

"I don't know. Somebody, anybody. I'm not asking you to talk to me or your family, but you need to talk to a professional. A doctor, therapist, I don't care. I can have somebody here at the house in a few hours."

"I don't want to talk about it with anyone. It's in the past, it's done, leave it alone."

Apollo stood up from his chair and walked over to me.

"You can't pretend like nothing happened Eliana."

"And you can't tell me how and when I deal with it. I get to decide when I'm ready to talk about it." I said, holding back my anger.

Apollo went to say something back, but he was interrupted by the doorbell.

"Who is that?" I asked.

"I don't know." He replied.

He looked back at me before leaving to get the door. Apollo came back to the kitchen with Nora. She held a big box full of fabrics, and binders.

"El!" She smiled. "Mom asked me to drop off some wedding stuff now that you two are back in town."

Apollo followed behind her confused.

"What did you bring me?"

"You two need to pick colors for the reception, and she brought her guest list." She said, setting the box down.

She helped herself to coffee and a Danish that was sitting on the counter, and sat down near Apollo's spot at the table.

"So, tell me everything. I'm dying to hear about Italy. Mikey hasn't taken me on a trip in years."

I sat down at the table, an anxious Apollo close behind.

"It was fine. We had a great time with Rio and Maria."

"A week with Maria, oh my God!" Nora laughed.

"Tell me about it." I sighed.

While we were talking Apollo shifted himself closer to me.

He rested his hand on my thigh and left it there while we chatted.

"And then we visited Lizzi's shop. Everything looks exactly the same." I told her.

"So, it was a good trip?" She asked.

"It was great to get out of New York." I lied, trying to focus on getting Nora out of here.

I couldn't keep pretending like everything was fine. Soon Nora was going to know something was up.

"Now that you're back from Italy you have to get ready for Mom. She is hell bent on getting this wedding planned."

Apollo squeezed my thigh when he heard 'wedding'.

"Once I get unpacked and settled in I'll stop by the house." I told her.

"Mom says I'm your matron of honor, so anything you need me for just call me. I remember how bad Mom was at my wedding."

Apollo interrupted the two of us when Nora started to go on another tangent.

"Nora, thank you for stopping by, but we have things to do today." He said.

Nora looked at Apollo then back at me.

"What could you possibly be doing? You got fired."

Shocked, I looked back at Apollo. There she was, there's the real Nora.

"Alright." Apollo said standing up. "Time to go."

Apollo led her to the front door and watched her leave. Annoyed, Nora got in her car and drove off. When the door closed I turned back to Apollo.

"You just kicked her out."

"She was starting to upset you." He replied.

I let out a small laugh. Apollo gave a smile.

"Come on, I'm going back to my office to get some work done. Why don't you come take a nap?"

That sounded like a great idea. It wasn't even noon, but I was ready for more sleep. I knew Apollo wasn't finished talking about Italy, but for now he dropped it.

Apollo stayed close to me for the next few days. Everywhere I went, he went. He had a hard time leaving me to go to work. I know what happened in Italy was hard for him too. He still felt terrible for leaving me alone in that room.

I didn't mind a clingy Apollo. I never had someone to lean on before. Without him I'd be trying to deal with things all by myself. Apollo never asked questions, and never needed an explanation. I could sleep in his office anytime I wanted, and he never minded when I needed someone to sit with.

He was more affectionate these past few days too. It felt like we were still in Italy. He held me while we sat and watched TV, he found ways to be near me when I slept in his office. Just like how I needed Apollo, he needed me. The only problem was that I got used to how sweet he was being to me. I couldn't shake the thought that once I was comfortable around him he would turn off his kindness.

Lucky for me he didn't bring up that night again even though he wanted to. It was beyond frustrating for him, but he gave me my space. I knew having Apollo with me at the house was too good to be true, and eventually he would have to go back to work. Dane started to stop by more and more, trying to get

Apollo to go back to work. Dane's visits always ended with him storming out, mad that Apollo was refusing to leave the house. I appreciated Apollo staying here with me, but I couldn't keep him from work any longer. I knew I was the only one who could convince him to go back.

I knocked on his office door and waited for a response.

"Eliana?"

I walked through the doors, sitting down near his desk.

"I know you're busy, but I wanted to thank you for being there for me these past few days."

"Did you come in just to tell me that?"

"No," I paused. "I think it's time you went back to work. Let's be realistic, as much as you want to stay here with me you have things to do."

"I don't care about any of that. I'll stay here as long as you need me to. I'm not ready to just leave you here alone."

"Apollo, we have to get back to our normal lives. You need to go back to work with Dane, and I need to get used to not having you around. I'll be okay. Alex is here, and I don't plan on going anywhere. It's time. I know you're losing business every day you stay here with me, and as much as I appreciate it I can't have you jeopardizing the company."

"I don't give a damn about the company." Apollo snapped.

"That's the problem. There's a lot going on with the families right now. You know I'm right." I said. "I think you should call Dane, and let him know you're back. No more working from your office."

"Promise you'll be okay here?" He asked.

"I promise."

"Okay, I'll call Dane." He finally agreed.

"Thank you."

"Come here." Apollo said.

I walked over to him, and sat down on his desk. He took my hands and held them in my lap.

"If you need me, for anything, I'll come back. I don't care what it is."

"I'll be fine, you're overthinking it." I told him. "Go call Dane. I'll finish my projects in the basement and you'll be back before you know it."

Apollo stood up and kissed my forehead. Surprised, I convinced him to go back to work with Dane I left his office to give him some space. I'd soon find out if I was ready to spend a few nights alone.

I kept busy until Apollo got back. After hours of Alex entertaining my wild projects, I was tired and ready for bed, but I couldn't fall asleep. Apollo's office felt eerily quiet without him. Around ten I heard his car pull into the garage. The first place he looked for me was his office. He sat down on the couch, lifting my legs up so he could sit next to me.

"How was it?" I asked.

"Terrible." He sighed. "Shit fell apart when we left."

"I'm sorry. You should have gone back sooner." I felt bad, knowing he'd been avoiding work because of me.

"Stop it. It's not your fault. Dane messing up distribution would have happened no matter what went down in Italy. I'll be gone all day tomorrow. I have to drive out to Chicago. I don't know when I'll be back."

"Is it safe for you to be traveling right now?" I asked.

"I don't really have a choice. I need to meet with the Irish and try to make things work between them. They don't want us distributing in their neighborhoods anymore. I don't know how to keep them happy, and they hate working with Dane."

"Okay." I said.

"That's it? Just okay?"

"Well if you say you need to go to Chicago, then you need to go. It's not like you'd stay here if I'd asked you to."

"You don't know that. If you needed me here I would try to make it work, and stay."

I looked at him and tried to search for the truth in his words. He was dead serious. He would put everything on hold for me. As much as I wanted him to stay I knew he needed to go. The look in his eyes told me he was waiting for permission to leave.

"Apollo, you need to go to Chicago. Take care of things there, and work things out with the Irish. I'll be fine here until you get back. I promise."

Apollo nodded in agreement, resting his head back and closing his eyes. Lying there I wondered if I really would be okay with Apollo gone.

Chapter Thirteen

Eliana

I made it almost the whole night alone in my bed. Apollo
was gone, and the house was quiet. I tried to pretend I wasn't
waiting for my phone to ring or the front door to open, but I'll
admit I was missing Apollo. I knew I couldn't sleep in Apollo's
office forever, and it was time for me to start living again, but it
didn't make sleeping alone any easier. As much as my heart
ached, creating some space from him was good for the both of
us. He sent me a text the night before, but other than that I
hadn't heard from him at all.

Kim and I were in the kitchen figuring out what to do with
all the wedding shit Nora dropped off. The wedding planning
was a good distraction. For just a few hours I forgot about the
past two weeks. My relatively good morning was ruined with one
phone call. I picked up my ringing phone and was surprised by
the caller.

"Mal?"

"Eliana, I'm sorry to bother you, but Margaret asked me to call. This is so awkward, but she needs you to come clean out your office."

"What?"

"I know, I know. I begged her not to make me call you, but she needs the space. She also needs you to bring back any paperwork you have related to the company or your cases."

"You've got to be fucking kidding me." I said.

"Is there a good time I can tell her you'll stop by tomorrow?"

"No." I answered, hanging up the phone.

What a fucking bitch. God, I can't go back there, not after how I left.

"Is everything okay?" Kim asked.

"I have to go back to my office and clean it out." I told her. I threw the napkins I was holding on the counter and stormed out of the kitchen.

I called Alex, "We're going back to the office tomorrow."

"Your office?"

"Yes. Have the car ready by noon."

Hanging up, I went back to work with Kim on wedding plans.

I didn't sleep at all last night. I tossed and turned in anticipation of having to go back to the office. My career was already over. Margaret didn't need to rub it in my face. Deciding to get this over with, I went to the living room to grab my case files, but they weren't there.

"Alex, where did my boxes go?"

A voice that wasn't Alex spoke up, "I already put them in the car."

Whipping around I saw Apollo standing in the doorway.

"What are you doing here?"

"I'm going with you to the office. I'm not letting you go there alone."

Another grin crossed my face. I didn't have to go alone, thank God.

"Let's go, the car's ready." He said.

It was just the two of us alone in the car as Apollo drove. He rested his hand on my thigh. The past few nights Apollo's touch was delicate and careful. Like he was trying to keep me safe, or close. But now, his grip was rough, intense. He squeezed my thigh as we drove. It was causing my heart to race. It was getting harder and harder to deny how bad I wanted him.

I didn't want the Apollo from Italy, the one who held me when I cried. I wanted the aggressive Apollo back. I wanted him to touch everywhere on my body, not just my thigh. Doing nice things for me, like going to the office, had me believing he cared for me. I'm sure the lust I had was all he felt too. At least with the mean Apollo I could picture the criminal things he'd do to me in the bedroom without getting attached to his acts of kindness.

Apollo sped into the parking lot, and helped me grab my boxes from the trunk. I took a few steps toward the front entrance before turning around and standing in front of Apollo.

"Wait." I said, dropping the boxes to the ground.

"What?"

"You need to look intimidating." I told him.

"Intimidating?"

"Like when we first met at the party. That irritated, hot, mean look you do."

"You think it's hot?" He asked, amused.

"You're missing the point. Where's your gun?" I asked, searching his chest for his gun.

"Whoa, El, stop. Last time you did that it did not end well." He said, stepping back, taking my hands from under his jacket.

"Let's just get this over with then." I said, rolling my eyes.

The two of us ignored the women who called after us at reception. We helped ourselves to an elevator, and waited patiently for our level.

Stepping out of the elevator together, the room went quiet. Everyone looked up from their computers to stare at me. Apollo didn't waste a second taking my boxes from me and dropping them off on a random intern's desk.

Hands now free he rested his hand on my lower back as we walked. I made my way to my old office, trying not to seem too eager to leave as soon as possible. Stepping into my office I felt like a stranger. I sighed trying to collect my things. A few personal documents, pictures of the family, and a few plants.

Apollo waited at my door, looking out over the office. He wasn't intimidated by the stares like I usually was. His glares silenced even the worst in the room. He looked so fucking hot right now. Not now Eliana, think about that later, focus.

I had almost finished packing up my office, when Margaret stopped by. Apollo wouldn't even let her through the door frame. She stood there looking over his shoulder trying to find me in the room.

"Apollo, nice seeing you again." She spoke.

He said nothing. He stood there looking over her head like she didn't exist. It made her angry. He slowly looked down, glaring at her. She took the hint, and stepped back immediately. I had everything I needed and was ready to leave.

Apollo took my bag from me, and linked my arm with his. I took a few folders from my bag and handed them to Margaret. It was everything she needed for the cases she stole from me.

I didn't give her the satisfaction of saying a word. She stood there, silent, as we walked away. While we waited for the elevator Apollo stood behind me, blocking the office. He waited for me to step into the elevator before walking in, then he held my hand as I pushed the button. I watched Apollo stare down Margaret as the doors closed.

It was over, I would never go back.

We kept our cool until we were back in the car.

"God, that was so amazing!" I smiled, hitting Apollo's arm.

He let out a laugh,

"That felt so good. Fuck her! Fuck you Margaret!" I screamed as we drove down the street.

I could see Apollo's smile from the corner of my eye. He kept his eyes focused on the road, but every once in a while, I could see him glance over. He looked happy for me, maybe even a hint of proud.

I wasn't planning on feeling better going back into the office, but Apollo going with me helped. I got closure, it felt like I might have a chance at a career still. Margaret looked nervous, almost like she regretted firing me.

Apollo was back home, but he had a lot of work to catch up on. He stayed in his office past dinner. I didn't bother him until later in the evening. He was behind on work ever since coming back to Italy, but despite how stressed he was he still made time for me. I only wished there was something I could do to help him with his work.

"Apollo?"

He looked up from his desk, closing his computer.

"Are you still working?" I asked.

"I'm wrapping up. There's only so much I can do tonight. I'll have to go back to Chicago tomorrow. I have a problem at a club."

"Do you want to talk about it?"

"No, I want to drink."

He stood up, and pulled a bottle from a shelf. He poured a drink for himself, and then for me. He sat down on the couch with me, leaving little space between the two of us.

"Are you feeling better?" He asked.

"Hmhmm." I took a big sip of my drink.

Apollo leaned back, dropping his head back on the couch. He let out a sigh, creasing his eyebrows.

"Why is this all so fucking hard?" He asked.

"I don't know." I said, laying down on his chest.

He wrapped his arm around my shoulder as we both laid there. The more I drank the more I realized just how close Apollo was sitting next to me. Things were different between the two of us. We didn't have the nerve to say how we were feeling to each other, so we had to communicate in other ways.

Apollo had his arm tight on my waist. Setting down his glass he turned on the couch. He rested his head near my shoulder.

"El..." He whispered.

"Apollo..." I answered.

"Have you thought about it at all?" He asked.

"Thought about what?"

"Italy, that kiss? I haven't been able to stop thinking about it." He confessed.

I was quiet.

He lifted his head up, now inches from me. He looked down at my lips, then back up to me. With his hand on my thigh, my body started to burn. I felt hot, and I was having a hard time controlling it.

"We can't." I said, putting my hand on his chest to try and create some distance.

"Why not?" He asked, leaving small kisses down my neck.

"Because this isn't real. What you're feeling right now is going to end, and when the spark does die we're going to regret everything." I admitted.

"I'm not going to regret this."

His kisses got sloppier, and less delicate. I had to close my eyes to focus.

"It won't last. We're too different."

Apollo sat back a little. He put one arm on my neck, pulling me close.

"You're wrong this time Eliana."

Finishing his sentence, he kissed me.

He deepened the kiss when I didn't pull away. He pushed my lips open with his tongue. Leaning into me he held me tight, not leaving any space between us. He only pulled back for a minute so he could grab my hips and pull me onto him. Sitting on his lap I straddled him. I slowly grinded on his lap, gliding across a hard bulge from his pants. His cock throbbed from under his dress pants.

His hands slid under my shirt, cupping my breasts. He would squeeze harder every time I moved on his lap. He was losing his patience. Everything in my body told me to keep going, to not stop and give in but I couldn't. My brain was screaming at me. I snapped back to reality.

"Apollo, stop."

Immediately Apollo's hand slid out from my shirt, and he sat back.

"We can't." I said one more time.

"You have no idea how crazy you drive me Eliana." He said. "When you're ready to admit to yourself that you want me, I'll be waiting."

I climbed off of Apollo, and left the office before I changed my mind. When I made it to my room Apollo caught up to me. He grabbed the back of my arm, turning me.

"Eliana." He said, getting close to me again. "You had the strength to leave my office, but I know you don't have the strength to resist touching yourself tonight. You have to release all this stress somehow, so tonight when you're playing with yourself I want you to imagine how good I could make you feel."

He lowered his hands, playing with my leggings, "I want you to picture me there in bed with you, playing with you, and kissing you until you can't take it anymore. The walls are thin Eliana, don't pretend like I can't hear you in the shower late at night whimpering my name. This time when you come I want you to think of me gripping your thighs tight, holding you down while I eat you out. And if it's not enough, and you need more, you know where I'll be."

I was unable to move as I watched him leave back to his room. After taking a few deep breaths I quickly walked into my room locking the door. Apollo was right. I was headed to the shower. He knew, he's heard it all. I couldn't turn the shower on now, he would know he knew me better than I knew myself.

I laid under my covers, quietly playing with my clit, and fingering myself to see how wet I felt. Just like he asked, I pictured it was Apollo and not me. I pictured his long fingers, pulsing in and out, his tongue swirling around causing me to twitch. When I was close I had to curl my toes, and clench my jaw. I wanted to shout his name out, but I knew he was listening. He couldn't know I finished thinking about him. I couldn't let him win the game.

I wanted to stay in my room all day, but if I did Apollo would know I was avoiding him. After our encounter last night, I had tried all sorts of distractions to keep myself from going to his room. As much as I wanted him, I wasn't going to give in. Ignoring the charm, and wittiness of Apollo, he was still just a man who always won. Since we were little I never once saw a time he was told no. I could see a look in his eyes that told me he thought it was only a matter of time before I caved, just like the rest of them. I wasn't even married to this man yet and somehow, I was already exhausted.

Apollo thought he was a king, a god even, and I wouldn't stop until I had him on his knees. Begging for me until his mind, body, and soul ached for me, and only me.

I was up early for breakfast before Apollo left for Chicago. The two of us sat and ate our breakfast, across from each other.

"Did you sleep okay last night?" Apollo asked, a grin on his face.

"Fine, thank you." I answered. "And you?"

"Lonely" He teased.

I did my best to ignore him, "How long will you be in Chicago?"

Apollo sat up in his chair, finally giving up.

"A few days. We had a change of plans." He spoke. "I'm having a harder time expanding than I hoped. A lot of people are pissed that Raff and I are taking over territory. I tried to warn him, but like his sister he's stubborn."

"Is it anything you can't handle? Are you guys changing your plans?" I asked.

"No, but I'll need to spend a lot of time there over the next few days. I need to make sure things settle. Will you be okay here? You can come with me if you want."

"I'll be fine, plus I have some stuff I need to do this week, so it's probably best if I stay."

"What are you doing?"

Taking a sip of my coffee I looked down, I wasn't sure I wanted to tell him. I was hoping he wouldn't ask. I had nothing to hide, but I wasn't sure I wanted him to know.

"I have an appointment." I said. "With a therapist I found."

Apollo paused, staring me down trying to figure me out.

"You found someone? Someone you trust?"

"What is there to trust? I reached out to Emma, and a friend of hers said she would work with me." I answered.

"What if I connected you with a few people I know?" He asked.

"I don't want anyone connected to you or the family. I need

a stranger."

"Okay, yeah whatever you think is best." He replied.

"Thank you, for helping, but this is something I need to do alone."

Apollo's phone rang, interrupting the conversation. I wanted to sit and talk longer with him, but I knew he had work to do.

"I have to go. I don't know when I'll be back. If you can't reach me while I'm gone try Dane. Alex will stay here like always."

Apollo stood up and walked towards me, out of habit. He paused when he realized what he was doing. He looked like he wanted to kiss me, but he didn't. He leaned down kissing my forehead and quickly left the room. I kind of wish he had kissed me, I wouldn't have pulled away.

I hadn't heard from Apollo since breakfast on Tuesday. I'm sure he was busy, and whatever he was doing he didn't have time to reply to texts or calls, so I didn't even bother. A few days after Apollo left I got a call from Emma who let me know Kelsey had gone crazy. Kelsey thought fostering kittens would be a brilliant idea, and not at all challenging. She completely ignored the fact that her and Emma worked full time, and had no time to be taking care of seven kittens.

I had spent the last few days chasing and cleaning after a house full of cats.

"Emma, I lost the black and white one again." I shouted from their guest room.

Emma and I were trying to take care of seven kittens only a few weeks old. Emma said it was easy when they were first born. They barely moved, and napped after eating. But now they were adventurous and didn't seem to ever take a break.

"Well, shit, I don't know what to do. Kelsey was supposed to be back with the gate by now." She yelled back.

Kelsey was put in charge of finding gates tight enough the kittens wouldn't crawl through, but she'd been gone too long.

While looking for the black and white kitten that looked like a little cow, I found his sister, Marshmallow. Her fur bright white, and fluffier than the rest.

"How did you get out?" I whispered to myself.

This was a great distraction from everything. Part of me wanted to stay with Emma and not go home. Hanging out with her made my life feel normal. No family drama, no Italy, and no Apollo trying to tempt me.

Finally, the front door opened.

"I found one!" Kelsey exclaimed. "I had to drive an hour, but the pet shop manager says the cats won't fit through the fencing."

Emma went straight for the box, unwrapping the fence and setting it up.

I held onto two small kittens one gray, and one almost all black, feeding them their bottles of milk.

Emma finished setting up and picked up the rest of the kittens. One by one she placed them on the blanket in the middle of the gated off part of the floor.

"Thank God." She sighed.

Emma went to walk away, but stopped when Kelsey let out a tired cry.

"Oh, fuck me!" Emma said, putting her hands on her hips.

Kelsey was right, the kittens were too big to slip through the cracks, but they were somehow smart enough to climb over the fencing. Three were making their escape with the littlest one behind them.

I couldn't help but laugh. I had to hide my smile when Emma looked over at me.

"How would you feel about taking some back to your house? Just hide them in a part of the house Apollo doesn't go in. He'll never have to know."

"No, no way. I'm busy enough as it is. This is your problem." I laughed.

"You're sleeping in the guest room with the kittens tonight." Emma told Kelsey.

"Where will El sleep? We can't make our guest sleep on the couch." Kelsey protested.

"I'm going home tonight. I can't stay here forever. I have things to do at home that I've been avoiding."

Kelsey walked over to me, grabbing my arm.

"You can't leave me alone with her El, she wants me dead." She whispered.

I looked around Kelsey's shoulder and found Emma glaring at Kelsey, plotting her murder.

I was saved by someone at the door.

Emma walked to get it, "Alex, just in time. Do you like cats?"

I shook Kelsey off of me, and ran to grab my bag from the hallway. Alex had great timing.

"I wish I could take them off your hands Ma'am, but I'm allergic." Alex spoke.

231

"Emma, stop trying to hand off these cats, we aren't taking them! Alex, what are you doing here, is everything okay?"

"Everything's great. Apollo is on his way home. I thought maybe you'd want to go home as well."

"Yes please." I smiled, leaving Emma at the door.

"I love you, but if I wake up tomorrow and find kittens on my front porch I will kill you, and that's a promise."

Emma gave me a hug, and kissed me on the cheek. I said goodbye to Kelsey, and walked to the car with Alex.

"Alex, do you know how Apollo's trip went?"

"It went well. He sounded happy on the phone, not too stressed. I don't know the specifics of the trip, but Dane would have told me if things went south."

"Good." I spoke, leaning back into the seat getting comfortable for the remainder of the drive.

Alex wasn't lying when he said Apollo was in a good mood. Apollo was practically bouncing off the walls when I came home. He was buzzing with excitement. I have never seen him this excited about anything before. When he saw me walking down the hallway he froze, standing still and giving me a big smile.

"How was Emma's?" He asked.

"It was fine. Unrelated, are you a dog or cat person?"

"Alex already warned me about the kittens, and my answer is no, nice try. Cats have a tendency to ruin expensive things, and my house is only made of expensive things."

"Damn..." I sighed.

I walked past Apollo towards my bedroom. I had a few bags from Emma's I needed to unpack. When I turned around to see if Apollo was still standing in the hallway I was surprised to find him standing right behind me. Our chests were close to touching when I turned around. He inched forward, leaning into me.

I was too nervous to look up at him, so I pretended he had no effect on me, and turned back to my room. Before I was a safe enough distance away from him, he grabbed my arm.

"I'd like to take you to dinner tonight."

"Just you and me?" I asked.

"Mhmm, just us two. Think you can be ready by seven?"

I looked at the clock in my room and pretended like I needed to do the math in my head. I would have gotten ready in seven minutes if he asked me to. I couldn't explain it, but I found myself missing Apollo the few days we were apart, and I would give anything to be around him right now.

Finally building the courage to look him in the eyes I gave him a nod and a smile.

"Perfect, can't wait." He said, grabbing his phone from his pocket and walking away.

I had gotten ready a little early, but I was waiting to go downstairs. Apollo hated being late, especially because of others, and tonight I was trying to knock him off his routine a little. He was always the calm and collected one. I wanted him to be just a little bit nervous waiting for me downstairs, maybe even a little frustrated. Deciding I'd tortured him enough I made my way downstairs.

There are certain things you learn about a person after living with them for a while. You figure out their favorite foods, when they go to bed, music they love or hate, or even a favorite color. I'd had my suspicions for a while now, but after walking into the living room I was one-hundred percent confident that red was

Apollo's favorite color. His chest sucked in a big breath of air, and his eyes scanned over my dress as I hurried over to the door.

He loved the way my hips swayed in tight dresses, that was already very clear to me, but it was tonight's reaction that told me I would need to add some more red to my closet.

I stopped at the door and turned back to Apollo. He snapped out of his daze, and turned the door handle, opening the front doors for me.

"After you babe..." He said only loud enough for the two of us to hear. His men watching guard at the door, oblivious to our conversation.

"Thank you." I whispered, feeling my scarlet lips twisting into a smile.

I didn't know how tonight would end, but I did know one thing. I was done closing a part of myself off to Apollo. He wanted me, and that's what he was going to get.

The car ride to the restaurant was suffocating. Apollo's eyes were filled with frustration every time he looked over at me. I shifted in my seat, lifting my left leg over my right, letting my dress rise a few inches up my thigh. His eyes glared down to my thigh. He tightened his grip on the steering wheel. I almost felt bad for him, before all my distractions he was having a pretty good day.

I finally broke the silence, "How was Chicago?"

"It was fine. Everything went to plan, and so far, no one's fucked anything up. Dane suggested I put a little bit of faith in

Raff and let him have this one. I hate the idea, but he was right. I have enough to worry about. Raff can take care of things for a while."

"And we all know what you'll do to him if he messes up, so we can sleep easy knowing he won't let that happen, right?" I asked, letting a small laugh slip.

"Exactly." He smiled. "It's been awhile since I've taken my anger out on someone, and it's starting to make me itch."

Apollo slowed down, pulling up to the curb of a small building that looked like it belonged in the 1920's. Pulling open his door and running around to my side, he raised the car door open for me. I held onto my seat as I stood up. When I was out of the car I leaned into Apollo, taking a step onto the curb. Before walking towards the restaurant, I leaned up close to Apollo.

"Fingers crossed I do something to piss you off tonight, and you take that anger out on me."

Releasing my hands from his forearm, I grabbed my purse from the car, leaning my hips into his dick. Standing up straight I gave him a wink and walked into the small Italian restaurant.

I walked up to the host table, and shined my biggest smile to the young host.

"Table for Costa." I told him.

The host, whose name tag read Sebastian, grabbed two menus and motioned his hand into the restaurant. His smile faded when he looked over me, I'm sure the scowl on Apollo's face was what scared him. He lowered his eyes, and led me to a table on a small balcony.

I took my seat first, letting Apollo pull my chair out. Sliding closer to the table I grabbed my menu from Sebastian. My hands lightly grabbing Sebastian's as I set the menu down in front of me.

"Thank you, Sebastian, you've been a big help." I smiled.

Apollo rolled his eyes, sitting down. I ignored him and watched Sebastian turn pink with blush.

"Let me know if there's anything else I can do for you this evening." Sebastian said.

"Oh, I will." I teased, staring Apollo down.

As soon as Sebastian left Apollo leaned back into his chair and spoke, "What the hell was that?"

"Nothing, I was just being nice to our cute host. Is that a crime?"

"No, a crime is what I'll do to poor Sebastian if you keep up the flirting with him. Stop fucking playing around Eliana."

"You're being delusional Apollo, I have no idea what you're talking about."

Apollo folded his napkin into his lap, and tried to pretend he wasn't upset. This was the first time I'd ever seen him lose his cool over some harmless flirting. It was clear he was jealous. Of course, he would never admit that's what he was feeling. He'd make an excuse like it was bad for our image, or he wanted me to behave in case someone was watching us, but I know it's because the thought of me with another man makes him nauseous.

He's not ready to admit it yet, but he doesn't need to. His tense shoulders, and twitching fingers tell me everything I need to know.

I stayed quiet as Apollo ordered some wine for us, I skimmed through the menu looking for something savory. I hadn't had a real meal in a few days. Apollo wouldn't be happy knowing I was skipping meals again, so I didn't plan on telling him.

I swirled my wine glass and took a small sip as Apollo finished pouring his glass.

"So, Eliana, how were things at the house while I was gone? Did you see that therapist?" He asked, nervously.

"I did, she was fine. It was only the first session, so we didn't talk about much, but I think it's going to be good for me to have someone unrelated to the family to talk to. Of course, I have Emma and Kelsey, but I needed someone other than friends to lean on."

"Good, that's really great El. I'm proud of you, for so many things, but mostly for getting help." He smiled.

I'm proud of you.

Those words rung in my head like a cathedral bell announcing Sunday mass. I don't think anyone's ever said those words to me and half meant it. The way those words rolled off of his tongue so casually, had me trying not to spiral.

I brushed off Apollo's words, and continued on with dinner. It was nice having Apollo back from Chicago. It seemed he missed my company as much as I missed his. I hardly noticed the sun setting, and the stars trying to sneak through the clouds and heavy light pollution. Time drifted away from the two of us. I was a few too many glasses of wine deep, and the longer I sat across the table from Apollo, the more I loathed the distance between us.

"God, I can't wait to get out of this dress." I said, tugging at the straps on my shoulder. The moving of my straps gave Apollo a little sneak peak of what was hiding underneath my dress.

"Christ, Eliana, we're in public. Can you please at least keep your dress on until we're in the car?"

"But being in public surrounded by all these strangers, that's half the fun baby." I teased.

"Eliana... don't."

"Or what? What would you do to me if I kept misbehaving, hypothetically of course?"

Apollo shifted in his seat, leaning closer to me, resting his arms on the table, "Well, hypothetically, I'd take you to the bathroom, press you up against the sink, rip your panties down, and fuck you so hard against the mirror you wouldn't be able to make it back to the car. You'd be begging me to carry you out of here-"

"I'm not wearing any panties..."

"What?"

"You said you'd rip my panties off me and fuck me, but I'm not wearing any. The only thing keeping you from fucking me raw is this dress, and it's starting to get more and more uncomfortable by the second."

"What the fuck has gotten into you tonight Eliana? Are you drunk? Did something happen when I was in Chicago?"

"Nothing happened, call it boredom, insanity maybe, but as a result let's just say I've been taking a lot of showers recently."

Apollo pulled his wallet out and threw a couple hundreds on the table.

"Get up, we're leaving."

"But I haven't had dessert yet."

"Now." He spoke dryly.

I threw my napkin on my plate and followed him to the car. Well, it took shorter than expected to break him.

Apollo didn't speak on the car ride back to the house. His breaths were slow and calm as he drove. He refused to look at me once we were back home. He tried to walk back to his room, but I stopped him.

"Where do you think you're going?"

"To bed, which is where you should be going as well."

"I'm not tired." I told him.

"Why are you doing this to me Eliana? Did I do something to piss you off? Did I break another one of your rules? You have no idea how bad I want you, and these little acts of deviance are driving me crazy. You were the one that walked away in my office last week, you decided you didn't want this. You made it very clear to me from the beginning that whatever connection there was between the two of us was never going to happen, so why do you continue to torture me?"

I stood in front of Apollo, speechless. I had no answers to his questions. I became hyper aware of my surroundings. The guards laughing in the kitchen, the lights flickering in his bedroom, the clock in his office down the hall. All of it pounded in my brain as I tried to process his confession.

"Eliana Mariani is finally at a loss for words, I must be dreaming." He mocked, before walking back to his room.

I silenced the screaming in my head as I chased after him for the second time tonight.

"Apollo, wait!"

He turned to face me.

"I didn't know that's how you really felt. I thought this was a game to you. I was afraid of losing, like I always have. I was terrified I was the only one who felt this way. When I try to fall asleep I can feel your arms around me, even when you're not there. I hear you in your office, when I know I'm all alone in this house. It's sick, I was given to you by my father and somehow against all my morals I'm falling in love with you. I was hoping you'd be evil, cruel to me, so that it would make hating you easier, but every day you treat me better than the day before. I thought you were the one fucked up in the brain, but it's me whose fucked up. Even after everything, I still long to stand by your side, and to comfort you when you're upset." I confessed.

"And falling in love with me, is that such a bad thing?" He asked.

I didn't say anything. We both knew my answer.

"Then let's make a promise, not to fall in love with each other, simple as that. You can continue hating me, I'll make it easy for you."

"Stop. Don't do that. You know that's not what I want."

"Then tell me what you want, Eliana. No games, no tricks, just the truth."

"I want you. I want all of you, even if in the morning you hate me again, and you go back to being the cold Apollo I met all those years ago."

"Are you being serious? Because I don't think I'll have the strength to walk away from you again. Don't tease me, Eliana. Do you want me?"

"Yes, I want you. Do you need me to write it out for you? I fucking want you." I yelled.

Apollo didn't wait a second longer. He walked towards me, grabbing my ass, lifting me off the floor and carrying me to his room. As soon as his door shut he kissed me like I'd been hoping he would all this time. He bit down on my bottom lip, teasing me with his tongue. I could hardly breathe. His hands were gripping my ass so tight I knew there'd be bruises tomorrow.

"I won't be gentle tonight El. I told you, I have too much anger in me to take this slow. If it's too much for you and you need me to stop, you have to say something. I've dreamt of this moment for a very long time, and I don't plan on holding back. I take what's mine and I don't apologize. Do you understand?"

I nodded my head yes.

"Words, Eliana."

"I understand."

"Good, now get on your knees." He ordered.

"You first."

Chapter Fourteen

Apollo

I was surprised by Eliana's sudden boldness, but I wasn't going to protest.

I tried to commit this moment to memory. How I held her, how she smiled at me, the way her hands rested on my chest. Her fingers played with the buttons on my shirt as I took a deep breath and soaked in her lilac and honey perfume. She smelled so sweet, and I couldn't wait any longer to take a taste. I knew if she ever left me I would be reminded of her every time I walked the streets in the springtime. I'd never be able to forget about the way I felt about her, right here at this moment.

I wanted to be better for her, but I knew I would forever fail. She was too good for me, so there was no point in trying to be good. I needed her and nothing was standing in my way. I warned her I wouldn't be gentle tonight, but I'm afraid she doesn't realize what that means. In every sense of the word

Eliana is mine, and it's time I prove that to her. There was no one else and there will be no one else.

I kissed her one more time before sliding her dress up towards her hips. Eliana was telling the truth tonight, the only thing she'd worn to the restaurant was this dress. God, I wasn't worthy. I had no right to call her mine.

I found myself on my knees moving my hands all over her legs. I traced up from her ankle, all the way to her hip. Eliana sighed every time I moved closer to her core. She was getting anxious. She grabbed my hair in her hands and begged.

"Apollo, please."

She wouldn't need to ask twice. As soon as I heard please I dipped my head lower and gave her thigh a soft kiss. I left a trail of marks all the way up to her folds. Teasing them with my fingers I continued to kiss her. I held the inside of her thigh with one hand as the other played inside her with two fingers. I stretched my tongue out leaving sloppy kisses on her clit.

El tried to dip her hips back, but I held onto her tight. She wasn't going anywhere. I was barely getting started. I kept the pacing of my sucking on her clit as she moaned. I was exactly where she wanted me to be. I was enjoying myself on the floor, but I knew she'd enjoy what I could do to her on the bed, so I quickly stood up and grabbed her hips.

Bouncing after being thrown on the bed I grabbed her ankles. I pulled her legs down and spread her thighs. She swirled her hips once she felt my new angle. I sucked and bit and kissed deeper into her. Her thighs were closing on my head, so I braced them back onto the bed.

"Don't move, or I'll stop." I warned her.

Immediately she froze, although I'm sure for her it was torture. Despite her desire to move she followed my instructions.

She didn't move an inch. I leaned away from her, so that I could look at her lying there breathless.

Her cheeks were red, and her chest rose with her trying to steady her breathing.

"Why'd you stop?"

"Just enjoying the show babe, you have no idea how fucking hard I am right now."

Eliana smiled, and rolled her head back, letting out a satisfied laugh.

Ready to finish pleasing her I laid back onto my stomach. I kept up the same rhythm that had Eliana moaning before I stopped. I knew she was close. I teased her a few times, pulling my fingers away, but after feeling the way her nails dug into my hair I finally gave her the release she was begging for.

"Fuck, Apollo."

The noises Eliana made had my cock throbbing in my boxers. Her body twitched at the touch of me, I knew she was still riding out her orgasm. Her voice echoed through my room, bouncing off the walls. I wasn't going to last much longer if I didn't get inside her.

Leaning off to the side of my bed I started to unbutton my shirt while Eliana took her dress off. When I looked back over at her I lost it. There Eliana was lying in my bed, completely naked. She draped an arm over her breasts, squeezing them with a smile. Her thighs rubbed together as she leaned on my pillow.

A fate worse than the seventh circle of hell was this memory of Eliana being taken from me.

I leaned my chest into hers as I kissed up her neck. She tilted to the side, giving me more access to her neck. I noticed Eliana was starting to get impatient, so I found her lips and kissed her. I

244

nipped at her lips and slid my tongue in when a gasp escaped. Her nails clawed at my back, and I could feel she was ready to take control for a little while, so I let her.

Eliana

I was wrapped around Apollo and holding him to me as close as I could, and it still wasn't enough. I needed more. I pushed Apollo's shoulders down and straddled him. I ran my hands through his hair, kissing him like I'd been imagining since Italy. He kissed me like he was afraid he was going to lose me if he let go for even a minute. Leaning back up I smiled down at Apollo.

I was ready to let go of all of the doubts I had about him, and us. I wanted him, and for tonight that was enough. I lifted my legs over Apollo so that I was sitting to his side. I leaned down to meet his lips, giving one more soft bite to his bottom lip before moving down closer to the end of the bed.

I was near Apollo's hips and I started to take off his boxers. He raised his hips, making it easier for me. Once his boxers were off I grabbed his bulge, stroking my hands down his shaft. Apollo sucked in a big gasp as I played with him and started to squeeze harder.

Before taking him in my mouth I softly traced my fingernails down his legs. Pausing when I felt the scars on his leg. I turned my head to see all the scars that covered his legs. This was the closest I'd ever been to his injuries. I could feel all the creases of his healed scar tissue. Small rivers of scars ran all the way down to his ankle. It looked like it went on forever.

Uncomfortable with my stares, Apollo started to move, and tried to leave the bed. I looked back over my shoulder at him. I held onto his hips and held him down.

"Don't."

Apollo was hesitant to sit there, so exposed, but he stayed still. I carefully ran my hands over his leg, leaning down to kiss the scars on his thigh. That caused Apollo to tense up. Kiss after kiss I showed every one of his scars the attention and love they'd never received. I started low near his knee and kissed my way up to his inner thigh. Close to his cock I grabbed it in my hands one more time and left a sloppy kiss on the tip.

I wanted him to know I didn't care about the scars, or his past, or what the future held for us. I wanted him to enjoy this moment just as much as I was enjoying it.

"Eliana..." He begged, shutting his eyes.

That was enough for me to know I could continue. I kissed and licked down from the tip to the base of his dick. After teasing him for a minute with kisses I finally took him fully in my mouth. I sucked until he hit the back of my throat. He barely fit and I struggled to catch a breath. I grabbed and twisted the rest of him that wasn't going to fit as I bobbed my head up and down.

Pulling away to take a breath I swirled his cock using my spit as lubricant. I picked up my pace and waited for him to calm down before I went back to sucking. Holding him in my grasp was enough for him to lose control. I could taste the precum that had leaked out while I was sucking him. When my sucking rhythms slowed down Apollo grabbed my hair and pushed me back down. He moved his hips so that he could thrust into me. I knew he was doing his best to be patient, but he was struggling.

I wanted to let him know I was fine with him taking back the control. I wanted to give myself to him completely. I didn't want him to hold back, and I knew he was trying to hold back because he didn't think I could handle it.

I let go of his dick and leaned over to where his head was resting on the pillows.

"Apollo, I want you to take whatever you want. Don't hold back. I'm yours."

Apollo looked into my eyes, trying to figure out if I was telling the truth. I'm not sure what he was afraid of, but I wasn't going anywhere. I gave him one more small nod letting him know it was okay.

Apollo quickly threw me onto my back and lifted my hands against the headboard. I wrapped my hands around the pillow that rested above my head.

"Are you sure?" He asked.

"Please, Apollo just fuck me already."

That was enough to set him loose. He grabbed my hips and brought them closer to him. He leaned over to the nightstand, but I stopped him.

"I'm on birth control. Please, I want to feel all of you tonight." I told him.

He nodded his head and came back to bed. He squared his hips up to mine and slowly pumped his dick a few times before teasing me and sliding it over my folds. His devilishly delicious smirk was back as he looked up at me. He knew I was losing my mind every time he stalled.

Finally, he slowly pushed his tip in. It took a while for me to adjust to his size. He stretched me even further when he started slowly sliding in.

"You're so fucking tight Eliana, so tight and wet for me." He groaned.

Apollo was so big I was afraid he'd rearrange my organs if he wasn't careful. I refrained from telling him to slow down though, because I was loving every minute of this. He picked up the pace and continued to thrust into me.

I lost control and moved my hands from above my head. Apollo quickly noticed and pulled them back up. He held my hands with one of his, and his other one rested over my cheeks. He held my jaw and leaned down to kiss me. Tightening his grip, I was trapped underneath him. His body weight leaned into me a little bit. He held my face in his hand forcing me to look right at him while he fucked me.

Kissing me, and twirling his tongue around my mouth, he spoke.

"Such a good girl Eliana, don't stop moving, keep rolling your hips for me. I want to hit every corner in this pussy."

I was losing my mind and struggling to stay focused. I rocked back and forth with Apollo and let him push harder into me. The only things that could be heard were our hips knocking into each other, and the moans I was failing to hold back any longer.

I tried to lean my head away from Apollo, but every time I did his grip only tightened. He lowered his hands so that they rested on my throat. As soon as his hands were pressed against my throat the butterflies in my stomach lit on fire and rose to my chest. I was already struggling holding back another orgasm, and with his hands pressing into me I didn't know how much longer I was going to last.

I'd been dreaming about what his hands could do for a while, and this was better than I'd imagined. His fingers wrapped all the way to the nape of my neck. He sent shivers down my spine as he fucked me. My legs started to shake, and Apollo could feel I was close. My walls were tightening around him.

"Not yet baby. I have so much more I want to do to you. Don't come until I give you permission. Understand?"

"Yes."

"Yes what?"

"Yes, Sir." I cried.

Apollo grinned, letting go of my hands and throat as he leaned off of me. He pushed one of my legs to the side, giving him more room to tease me. He kissed my calf and rested it on his shoulder, and his cock pushed in even deeper. At the new angle, I could feel myself twitching against him.

He didn't stay in that position for long. Eventually he lowered my leg so he could start playing with me again. He quickly found my clit and started circling with the same speed and rhythm as he was thrusting into me.

His fingers teased me with every stroke. I was going to snap, but just when I thought I was close to releasing, he changed his pressure and slowed down. I was entirely under his control. He was going to choose when I came. All I could do was watch as he pounded into me and played with me. The nerves in my leg and pussy were starting to burn, and ache.

Apollo knew I had reached my limit and was ready to let me finish. He picked up his thrusts, as his fingers continued to play. Soon I was spasming on Apollo's cock and twitching with every thrust. Apollo finished quickly after throwing his head back.

"Fuck..." He sighed, pulling out.

While Apollo dropped onto his back and laid next to me I could feel his cum falling out, and onto the bed. I tried closing my legs to catch the drops, but he stopped my legs. He dipped down, sticking his fingers in me, and twirling them around. He brought them to my mouth and squeezed my cheeks open.

"Swallow." He ordered, waiting for me to take his fingers in my mouth.

I had never done anything like this with another partner, but I was past the point of no return, and something in me was turned on when Apollo gave an order. I sucked his fingers and let his cum fall down my throat. He took his fingers out of his mouth, and gave me a kiss on my forehead, "You did so good, baby."

Rolling out of the bed he walked to the bathroom. He came back with a wet washcloth and cleaned in between my legs. Throwing the washcloth over to the hamper he pulled me into his arms. I calmed down in his arms, still reeling from what just happened.

I half thought after he slept with me he would try and leave, but he stayed and made sure I was comfortable as we tried to fall asleep. My adrenaline was still too high to fall asleep, so I just laid there as he played with my hair.

I laid in bed with Apollo, trying to fall asleep, but it was impossible. The last few hours were on constant replay in my head. My skin still tingled at the thought of his hands wrapped around me.

I looked up and tried to figure out if Apollo was asleep or not. His breathing was erratic, and his eyelids were fluttering.

"Apollo, I can't sleep, are you awake?"

Apollo quickly opened his eyes and turned to face me.

"I don't think I'll ever be able to fall asleep again if you keep spending the night in my room."

"Do you want to go get a drink?" I asked.

"Yes, please." Apollo said, throwing the covers off of the both of us.

At the foot of the bed Apollo tossed me his shirt and slipped on his boxers. He turned on the lights near his door, to avoid me tripping over our clothes and shoes from the night before. It still hadn't sunk in yet. Don't get me wrong I remember all of it, but none of it felt real.

Apollo slowly walked down to the kitchen pulling out the whiskey and the vodka from the top shelf. I found the glasses and met him in the living room.

Apollo poured our drinks, as we sat in silence. I tapped my nails against my glass and tried to focus on anything in the room that wasn't a shirtless Apollo. He didn't have as many tattoos as I imagined he would. His back had the angel of death holding a rosary, and his biceps were covered in a few, small Cosa Nostra tattoos. Other than that, there was more bare skin than inked skin. I thought maybe the reason I never saw him shirtless was because of the tattoos he hid, but now I know it was because of the scars on his chest and back.

Apollo had caught me staring, again. I let out a laugh, that was quiet at first, but grew louder with each breath. Pretty soon my stomach was cramping from the laughter, and I had to set my drink down.

"What's wrong?" Apollo asked, concern in his eyes.

"I can't believe we just did that." I laughed. "You- you were- and I was... oh my God, I can't believe I just slept with Apollo Costa. Half of Italy will be coming for my head when they find out I stole their bachelor from them."

A boyish grin formed on Apollo's face, "Well you better start believing it babe, because it won't be the last. And besides, to the outside world we're getting married. All the women in Italy have been cursing you since our engagement party."

"You're right, at least now I'm deserving of the nasty stares I've been getting."

"We better make it worth our while then." He teased me. "We have a lot of time to make up for."

I slapped his chest and rolled my eyes.

"What makes you think I want you to fuck me again?"

Apollo's smile faded, and his eyes lost their shine. He dropped his glass on the table and inched closer to me.

"Don't tease me Eliana. The only reason I'm not taking you over the back of this couch right now is because I know that pussy of yours needs some rest. I know tomorrow you'll be begging for more, like the good little slut you are."

Fuck... I shouldn't have found the way he spoke to me like that hot, but we both knew it turned me on when I had to close my thighs to try and ignore the friction between my legs. Apollo looked down at the hem of his shirt that barely covered me.

"You know, the last man that called me a slut died a very painful death." I told him.

"I'll be the last to call you that too, if I ever hear it from another man's mouth I'll skin him alive. Don't you worry about it."

We stared each other down again, unsure what the other would do before the two of us broke out into a fit of laughter again.

When the tears settled, and I had calmed down, Apollo asked me a question.

252

"Did you really think after I fucked you that I would go back to being cold and distant to you?"

"I was afraid of that, yes. I thought you were playing a game of chase, and you would grow tired of me. I know your reputation with women. I've leaned on you a lot these past few weeks, and I was selfish. I didn't want to lose you. I thought it was an act, one you played with other girls before me." I spoke sheepishly.

"There was no one before you Eliana, and there will be no one after you. You are one of a kind. Don't let my past scare you away." The sincerity in Apollo's voice told me he was telling the truth.

"Well if that's the case we should probably get to know each other a little bit better."

"We've known each other since we were six. How much more is there to learn?"

"A lot, now answer my questions and if I think you're telling me the truth you can ask me anything."

"Fine." He agreed.

"First question, how do you like to spend your birthday?"

"Alone." He answered, "Unfortunately, it rarely happens that way. For the past few years Juliette has thrown me these *surprise* parties."

"Do you miss living in Italy?"

"Yes and no. I enjoy the city, but I do see myself moving back to my hometown when I'm older. I won't be able to keep up with the fast pace of New York forever. You're welcome to join me if you like, permitting we're both alive long enough to experience retirement."

"Do you want kids then?"

"If you want them." He answered quickly. "If you're happy, I'm happy."

"So, you'd be fine if I didn't want kids, and there was no one to become the head of the family?" I asked in disbelief.

"Yes, so much of your life has been chosen for you, hopefully one day you see that it's your life to live, and no one can tell you otherwise."

I had suddenly forgotten all other questions. All I could do was grab Apollo by the chin and give him a soft kiss on his lips. He had no idea what that meant to me.

"What's your favorite color?" I asked.

"Red."

I knew it.

"When did you first know you might have feelings for me?"

"When I saw you driving away in my car, that you *borrowed*. No one had ever stolen from me and lived to tell the tale, but when you came back into your apartment the next morning you didn't look one bit remorseful." He smiled.

"Okay, last question. Are you afraid to take over for your father when the time comes for him to step down?"

"Yes, terrified."

That was all he said, and I didn't want to push for more.

"Is it my turn to ask the questions now?"

I nodded, folding my knees into my shirt, and leaning closer to him.

"Back in high school when we were working in the bakery that summer, you asked me to cover for you that one time so you could leave early. Where did you go?"

"Cara, you know my cousin who's been married and divorced twice now, well she had this boyfriend at the time who was performing at this bar in the city. She made me go with her because she thought no one would turn away a Mariani. I bought a cute little dress from the shop down the road while we waited for our ride. I had to change in the back of the taxi and do my makeup with a small mirror I took from Aunt Lizzi's purse." I confessed.

"No fucking way." Apollo scoffed.

"Was her boyfriend's band any good?"

"No, his band was shit. My ears were bleeding by the end of the night, and after the concert Cara caught him making out with a girl in the back of the bar. She cried the whole way home."

"And here I thought you snuck out to meet a boy."

"Sorry to disappoint." I shrugged.

"Alright next, who's your favorite sibling?"

"I can't answer that!"

"You have to, it's the rules." He smirked.

"Frankie," I admit, "but if you ever tell the other's I'll kill you." I threatened.

Apollo laughed, and finished off his drink, "What happens if I do something terrible, something horrible? How will I ever get you to forgive me?"

"Well, if it's a small mistake, get me rubies. If it's unforgivable, only emeralds will do. And then I'll know whatever you did was to protect our family. But you only get one chance at forgiveness. I won't spend my whole life chasing after your mistakes. You won't play me like you play your men, I deserve more. Call it emerald immunity if you will." I laughed.

Apollo didn't say anything. He only nodded his head, taking in my words. The look on his face told me he knew how serious I was. I wouldn't be one step behind him, picking up the pieces, my entire life.

"Okay, last question, do you miss being an attorney?"

"Of course." I answered, my jaw clenching. He knows how much I miss it, why is he even asking?

"I'm sorry I didn't mean to upset you, I just needed to know if you ever planned on going back."

"I want to. I just don't think I'm ready." I spoke, looking down at my drink.

"Eliana, look at me." He said, lifting up my chin.

"Don't let what happened between Margaret and Sterling stop you from working. You are so incredible when you are protecting the people you love and care for. I know you're hesitant to keep going, but I won't let anything, or anyone stop you this time. It's my fault you were fired, and I'll never forgive myself for putting you in that position. I will be here to support you and your career this time."

I once again had no words. A man I felt nothing for a few weeks ago, was knocking the wind out of my lungs, again. I never thought Apollo would be the only one left in my corner. I hadn't heard anything from my family in weeks, Raff and Frankie only called when they needed something, and Nora was too busy taking care of the kids. All of them knew what I was going through, and none of them cared.

Since getting fired the only one who showed up for me was Apollo. I thought it was because of the guilt, but the more he showed he cared the more I knew it was deeper than that. For the first time, I believed Apollo was going to do everything he could to stay by my side, and support me. Not just as an underboss, but as a partner.

My lungs hurt, and my chest tightened. I couldn't say much without tears forming. I let a small thank you fall from my lips.

"Don't thank me. I've done nothing to deserve it. I owe you my life Eliana, let me spend the rest of my life repaying you." He spoke, eyes focused on mine.

My heart fluttered, and my stomach twisted into knots. Apollo Costa, the man sitting across from me, was all mine.

Apollo

I could hear my phone ringing, but I didn't know where it was coming from. Quickly sitting up I found myself on the couch. Resting against my chest, Eliana slept. The drinks must have put us to sleep before we could make our way back to bed. One more time my phone started ringing. I could hear it echo through the house. I sat up to try and search for it before it woke Eliana.

I stretched my neck muscles as I walked back to the bedroom. I loved falling asleep with Eliana pressed against me, but the couch was not kind to my body. I found my phone under Eliana's dress in my suit pocket. Caller ID unknown.

"Hello." I answered.

"Christ, it took you long enough to pick up. We have shit to do, money to make Apollo."

"Who the fuck is this?"

"It's Dane. I'm calling from the warehouse. The warehouse you're supposed to be at so we can trade with the Irish. They are half an hour out. Raff got them to agree to meet somewhere other than Chicago for once."

"You were supposed to call when you confirmed a meeting with them."

"Who do you think has been calling you all night?" He asked.

"I wasn't near my phone last night, I had no idea you were even calling."

"Well hurry the fuck up please. We make this trade and we don't have to work with Dunne for a while. Everyone is already here waiting."

I hung up on Dane and grabbed a new suit, taking it with me to the bathroom. As much as I wanted to stay here with Eliana I needed this trade to go down. We would finally have the support we needed in Chicago, Raff could take over for me, and the Irish would be in debt for helping them with a small distribution problem they've been having.

Grabbing my keys, I debated whether or not to wake Eliana. I wanted her to rest, but I didn't want her to see me gone when she woke. I walked around the couch and ran a thumb over her cheek. When she felt me near her, her eyes opened and scanned over me kneeling in my suit.

"You're leaving." It wasn't a question, merely a statement.

"I wish I wasn't. Dane and I have something to settle with the Irish. It's time sensitive, and they need me there. I can't keep giving all my work to Raff."

"How long will you be gone?"

"Late afternoon if I'm lucky. I woke you up to say goodbye,

and to tell you that I'm not running. I didn't want you to see me gone, and not know what was going on. I need all the men I can get with me today, so only Alex will be here with you. He is at the gate watching over everything. Will you be okay with less guards than usual? This is your first time being so under protected."

"I'll be fine. I doubt I'll even notice the change in coverage. Plus, Alex is the only one of your men I can stand. It will be refreshing getting the house to myself. You take care of the Irish, and then hurry back to me. I'll be here waiting."

She kissed me slowly, raking her hands through my still damp hair.

"I promise, I won't be gone long."

I stood up to leave and left her resting on the couch. As I walked to the door Eliana sat up.

"And don't come back injured. I need you in perfect health for what I plan to do to you tonight." She ordered.

I shook a stupid smile off my face and left for the garage.

I made it to the warehouse before the Irish, and found all of my men sitting around the back waiting for the trucks to show up. They had no idea I had arrived yet. Dane sat on the hood of a car smoking a cigarette. He paid little attention to the conversation happening around him. One of my younger men spoke to his cousin.

"I just don't see why I had to get here before the sun was even up, and the boss gets to show up late to his own meeting."

"Don't let Dane hear you talking like that dumbass. You're the one who asked for this job. Stop complaining." I overheard Luis' cousin answer.

"Bullshit, he was probably knee deep in pussy and couldn't

be bothered to pick up his phone. Ever since that Mariani bitch he's been distracted. I would kill to find a bitch who was half as hot as Eliana. Too bad she's crazy. All the good fucks are. I heard from one of her brother's men that she's got a short fuse."

That last comment was enough for Dane to look up from his cigarette. He stopped what he was going to say when he saw me standing behind my men. A nervous smile formed on his face, as he tried to figure out what I was going to do next.

"A short fuse?" I asked, walking towards the group of men.

The color drained from Luis' face. His eyes dropped, and his shoulder sank. He knew he was a dead man.

"Sir I-"

"Does anyone else have anything to say about my fiancé?" I asked the crowd.

Eliana has received nothing but disrespect from my men since day one. I am tired of having these conversations with the men that work for me. It was time to make an example out of the boy who dared say those things about my Eliana.

Dane stepped up to take care of my problem for me, but this was personal. I wanted to be the one to pull the trigger. If we weren't waiting on a shipment, and the Irish, I would take my time with this one. Luis was lucky. His death would be far less painful than he deserved. Not wanting to lose my cool before Dunne showed up I quickly pulled the trigger. Luis' blood spattered against his cousin. His body dropped onto the dirt.

My men stood around me in silence, watching the blood drip into the dry dirt, turning it into mud.

"The next person to speak ill of my future wife will be thrown into the same grave as this bastard right here. Someone get this fucking pig out of my sight. I want him gone before

Dunne shows up for the gun trade."

Dane followed me into the warehouse as someone began to drag away Luis.

"I had a few of the guys check the inventory. All the guns and equipment that they asked for. I found them the guns the French couldn't get. Should we be concerned others are having issues getting shipments through the dock?" Dane asked.

"It's nothing we have to worry about. There are a few people in Massachusetts that owe me a favor. Our export restrictions are the least of my concerns."

Dane agreed, and left the room after getting a text. Shortly after, he followed Dunne and his men in to check out the product. I sighed, fixed my suit, and walked over to greet our new business partners. The sooner I took care of this the sooner I could get back to Eliana.

Dane was with me on the drive back. I wasn't going to let Luis' comments ruin the rest of my day. I should be celebrating. I just made a ton of fucking money, and El was waiting for me back at the house. Dane and a few of my men were invited back to my place for drinks. I had offered a promotion to a few of my men who I thought could handle things with Raff in Chicago. Now that we had Dunne's support we could move forward with our plans.

"Dare I ask why you were late this morning?" Dane asked.

"It's none of your business." I answered.

"I thought maybe Luis was shot for stepping out of line, but now I wonder what had you so distracted last night that you didn't hear my phone calls. I've kept my mouth shut because I know it's not my business, but I know things have changed between you two. Just make sure whatever has changed doesn't affect the family, and that you know what you're getting yourself into."

I peered over at Dane, annoyed at the smirk on his face.

"I'm taking care of it. Don't worry."

"Oh, I'm sure you are." He laughed. "I know you don't want to hear what I have to say, but be careful. Everyone else is too afraid to tell you the truth, but we all know what happens when you let a woman become a weakness."

"Eliana is not a weakness. She is an asset. To this family, to me, and to the men who serve me. Need I remind you of your place in my business Dane?" I asked, raising my voice.

"Of course not, my apologies."

We drove in silence for the rest of the ride. Dane had more he wanted to say, but he wouldn't try again tonight. He'd already crossed a line. Dane parked the car near the garage, slammed the car door shut, and stormed back into the house. I'm sure he would have more to say about how I've been spending my time, but tonight was a celebration and neither of us wanted to fight.

I respected Dane for his work and his support as my number two, but I didn't need him telling me the risks I faced with Eliana by my side. I know what others will think when they see I have actually fallen for her. It was fun when we were playing the game and the crowd, but everyday it's getting harder to hide the way I feel about her. Everyone can read it on my face, my priorities have changed. It's Eliana above anything else.

The deeper my feelings for her the more I put her life at risk. And I didn't need Dane reminding me of that every goddamn day.

Entering through the kitchen I found a confused Eliana.

"I told you to come home alive and safe. I didn't think I had to specify that I wanted you to come home alone."

"I know, I'm sorry." I apologized. "But we traded guns for protection with Dunne. The boys wanted to celebrate. It's their first big partnership, and it means I'm officially done spending time in Chicago. I'll be back here in New York full time with you."

"You're out? No more trips?" She asked, not believing me.

"I'm done. Unless the men in my office mess up big time then I don't have to worry about it anymore. I can get back to figuring out who's trying to hurt me, and how to work with Rio on some expansion back home."

"So, you'll be spending more time at the house." She smiled, walking around the kitchen island towards me.

"Hmhmm." I mumbled grabbing her by the waist. "I'm all yours."

Eliana grabbed my face, lowering it to hers. Our noses brushing against each other. I would have pulled her close to me and kissed her, but we were interrupted by Dane.

"Everyone is waiting in your office for you." He informed me, doing little to hide the annoyance on his face.

I turned back to Eliana, "I'm sorry."

"It's fine. It's work."

We both knew it wasn't fine. She will forever lie and say it is fine, and I will forever pretend to not see the hurt in her eyes. I wish she'd get angry at me and complain about work, but she knows how important this is to me. She'd never throw it in my face even though I deserved it.

I left her standing alone in the kitchen and thought of all the ways I could make it up to her after this meeting.

Chapter Fifteen

Eliana

I waited in the kitchen until I couldn't see Apollo's silhouette anymore. I turned to leave but stopped when I noticed Dane still in the kitchen.

"Can I help you with something?" I asked.

"I just wanted to say congratulations. It looks like things between you and Apollo are going good."

"I guess they are." I replied.

I wasn't in the mood to have this conversation right now, especially with someone like Dane. Before I could leave Dane stopped me in the hallway.

"I've worked with Apollo for almost a decade, Eliana. I grew up with him. I like to think of him as a brother."

"And?" I asked.

"And I've never seen Apollo miss a work call. In all those

years when I called he's always picked up before the fourth ring."

I kept quiet, giving Dane the chance to keep talking.

"Apollo does a really good job hiding his emotions, but he's not normal. There is no gray with Apollo. He gives his all to everything. His work, his family, and anyone who enters his life. It's why he's so good at his job. Until you there's never been anything else for Apollo to care about. He was only ever focused on work. I'm afraid of what's going to happen now that he also has you." Dane paused, giving me time to process.

"So, I'm a distraction?"

"You are." He admitted.

"A month ago I promised myself as a wife to Apollo in front of all our family. I promised to love and stand by his side, and now you're telling me that's a problem? Help me understand Dane, what the fuck am I supposed to do? I'm damned if I love him, damned if I don't."

"I'm not telling you to not love and enjoy your life with Apollo Eliana, I'm asking you not to make him choose."

"Choose?"

"Choose between the business, or you. I can see it in his eyes Eliana. He would jeopardize the only life he's ever known just to see you smile for a second. He would suffer in ruins if it meant his sacrifice spared you. It's fucking dangerous."

"You have nothing to worry about Dane. He and I both know the family comes first. It's why we work. We have an unspoken agreement between the two of us. I know him better than you might think."

I moved to Dane's right and started to walk past him to Apollo's room, when he spoke one more time.

"He killed one of his men for you tonight. He held a gun up

265

to Luis' head and pulled the trigger just for disrespecting you."

I stopped, frozen in my tracks. My legs refusing to move me any further from Dane's news.

"If Leonardo wasn't so afraid of him he'd be at risk of a trial for becoming judge and executioner to one of his own men. He's lucky nothing's happening to him this time. The family doesn't like when their men take matters into their own hands. They don't like a man they can't control."

"Apollo is free to make his own choices. I can tell you're upset about this whole situation with Luis, but it's none of your business. Did you think by cornering me in the kitchen and trying to intimidate me that I'd solve your problems for you? I understand you're worried for Apollo, but don't even for a second, tell me I don't care about him."

Dane laughed and rolled his eyes.

"Apollo is the only person to ever put me first, my entire life. I have been second to my siblings, and my family, and Dad's work since the day I was born. I know how much Apollo cares for me, and for once I'm going to indulge in that. Call me selfish, I don't care. You won't scare me away from Apollo. If I were you I would go back to Apollo's office before they notice you're missing. And the next time you have concerns about our relationship please do me a favor and keep it to yourself. We're going to be just fine."

I turned and left Dane in the kitchen. I wanted to talk to Apollo about Luis, but I could wait until his meeting was over. I wasn't going to hide my feelings just to appease the men in my life. Fuck that, I deserved more. I lost myself along the way a few years ago and became wrapped up with complacency. But Apollo has helped me to remember who I am, and what I deserve. I couldn't care less what anyone else is going to think, especially when it comes to our relationship.

Apollo came back to the room exactly an hour later. I heard his footsteps walking towards the bathroom, and heard him search for his things in the drawers. I must have zoned out while he was getting ready for bed because I didn't hear him come back into the bedroom.

I heard him calling my name from the foot of the bed.

"What's with you tonight? I've been calling your name for a while now."

"Nothing, I'm just in my head a little bit, I didn't hear you walk over."

"What's wrong?"

"I had a really interesting conversation with Dane after you two got home."

"What did he tell you?"

"He told me all about your evening."

"Eliana, I can explain."

"There's no need to actually. I've thought about it enough, and there's only one thing I'm upset about."

"And that is?"

"I wish I was there to see you put that bullet through Luis' eyes."

Apollo stared at me, trying to read my expressions but struggling.

"You're not mad? I just killed one of my men, the boss isn't going to be happy about this. I could get in trouble."

"I know I should be upset, disturbed even, but I'm not. I can't force myself to be angry at you when I should be thanking you. You promised me you wouldn't let your men treat me like shit, and so far, you've never disappointed. It's refreshing."

Apollo walked over to my side of the bed and pulled me up by my hands. He stood in front of me, staring into my eyes. His muscles relaxed, and he broke into a warm smile.

"I don't deserve you."

"I know." I smiled.

Apollo leaned down, kissing me on my forehead, kissing lower on my temple, then on my cheek, before kissing me on my lips.

He pulled back slowly, took a deep sigh and then leaned back in for a kiss. He braced me by supporting the back of my neck so I could lean into his kiss. He tried to slide his tongue past my lip, but before I could give him access to my mouth he pulled away.

He let out a disappointed sigh before leaning away. I opened my eyes, confused at the loss of touch.

"What's wrong?" I asked.

"You're too stressed, I can feel how tense your muscles are. We're going to have to do something to fix that."

Apollo grabbed my knees and threw my legs back onto the bed.

"Lay down on your back and don't move."

"Apollo-"

"That wasn't a request Eliana, do as I say." He ordered.

I tried to hide the smile that was forming as I rested my head back on the pillow, letting my hands rest flat by my sides.

Apollo stood at the foot of the bed staring down at me. He shook his head, "Too many clothes. Take off your shorts."

I slid my shorts off my hips and down to my ankles. Apollo was pleased to see me not wearing any underwear underneath my shorts.

"Don't move Eliana, focus on relaxing."

Apollo crawled onto the bed and positioned himself so that he was kneeling in front of me. He ran his hands over my legs, his fingers traced over the outside of my thighs, twirling around my hips. He grabbed onto my thighs, surely leaving a few marks. He started to move his hands to the inside of my thighs, as he opened up my legs giving him room to get comfortable. Before settling down so he could lay more on his stomach, he crawled up to kiss me.

"Tonight is all about you El. You have to tell me what you need from me. Use your words, even if it's hard to speak."

Apollo kissed my neck, leaving small love bites on my shoulder blade, down onto my breasts, continuing lower. He kissed and licked down past my stomach. He let out a satisfied groan before lowering even further.

"Apollo, please, stop the teasing. I can't wait any longer." I admitted.

"Say no more." He smiled against my skin.

Apollo slowly took two fingers and teased my folds. Before kissing my clit, he played with my entrance. Finally, he ran his tongue down my lips and gave a soft suck.

He licked up from the bottom of my lips to my clit. Once there he spun his tongue around in small circles. Every few seconds he would stop to suck and apply pressure right on the clit. He did that last night too. It was the perfect balance between circling, and sucking.

Apollo could tell I was enjoying what he was doing because

he paused.

"More of this?"

"Yes please, don't stop. More, like last night."

Apollo went back to circling and kissing. Now that I was starting to feel warmed up he inserted two of his fingers. His pointer finger and middle finger curled into my pussy. I could feel him move around as he continued to tease me.

The slower he moved his fingers the more my core started to ache. I could feel my stomach start to burn, and my hips tingle.

"Not yet Eliana, I'm just getting started." Apollo spoke, still between my thighs.

He looked up at me, wiping his lips with the back of his hand.

"Feeling better?" He asked.

"A little. Keep going."

"I like it when you boss me around." Apollo said.

I put my hands on his shoulders, and lowered him back down. If he wanted me to tell him what to do I would. I repositioned my hips so that I was a little bit raised. He cupped my ass wrapping his hands underneath my legs. With both hands being used to hold me all he could do was use his mouth. He dipped his tongue in and out of my pussy. Before long the ache in my stomach was back. I could feel my back tighten, and my clit started to throb. I think Apollo could feel me pulsing because he started sucking me just like I liked. He knew exactly how to control my body.

I had nothing to say because he was doing everything right. There were no words needed between us. I couldn't think for another second because something Apollo did with his tongue had me shaking. Finally, I let go, I let my orgasm ride out as

Apollo laid next to me. As soon as I thought I had the strength back in my legs I climbed off the bed and started to walk to the bathroom.

"Where do you think you're going?" He asked.

"To clean off, so we can go to sleep."

"Why would you clean up if we're about to start round two?"

"Round two?" I asked.

"I'm hardly tired, we're just getting started." Apollo said.

I turned back around to face the bed. No point in going to bed now, I might as well enjoy this while I can.

"For round two I want to try something new."

"Your wish is my command, El."

"I want you to stay laying down, just like that."

Apollo looked around the bed, and then at me. "Now what?"

I leaned one knee onto the bed, and crawled closer to Apollo's chest. I could see the confusion in his eyes, so I quickly moved my way up towards him. With my pussy almost to his face I leaned down closer to him.

"I want you to eat me out, while I ride your face. I want to set the pace." I explained.

He smiled up at me, and gripped my thighs. I positioned myself over him as I grabbed onto the headboard for support. While Apollo ate me out I circled my hips around, letting him kiss only what I wanted him to. I had full control. Every time Apollo leaned into me to get deeper I would slightly pull away.

It was driving him crazy. He only got as much as I would give him. I leaned into Apollo eventually and gave him everything he was begging for. I let go, and gave everything of myself to

Apollo. He saw all of me, and for the first time I was ready to let somebody in.

I ran my fingers through Apollo's hair trying to find something to grip on while he ate me out.

I tried to muffle a moan that was trying to escape, but Apollo didn't like that.

"There's no one in this house that can hear you El, let it out. I want to hear you scream. Don't stop until this cunt of yours is throbbing, and you're running out of breath."

My walls tightened when I felt Apollo's words vibrate against me.

"You like that? Does it feel good?" Apollo asked, his voice getting deeper, and the vibrations getting stronger.

I moved around rotating my hips in a circular motion trying to keep myself from coming too fast. Apollo took control for the first time this round and locked onto my thighs. He gripped so tight that there was no escape. I couldn't pull away this time. He was frustrated I was limiting him, and he was getting greedy.

He sucked, and twirled his tongue deep inside me, and groaned every time I twitched.

I was having a hard time controlling my movements. My body was controlling itself at this point. I had to adjust my legs just to remind myself I wasn't floating, and was actually on Apollo right now.

When I was close to finishing Apollo started talking again to help me finish.

"You're so wet for me tonight." He mumbled, causing me to shake.

"Are you going to come on my face now Eliana?" His words were muffled by my pussy but I could hear everything he was saying to me. It was enough to send me over the edge. The friction and his hums were too much all at once.

In less than a few minutes I was a shaking mess again. Apollo helped me off of him as I laid back down.

The two of us laid next to each other on the bed.

After a minute of silence, he looked over at me.

"Round three?" He asked.

I laughed and threw a pillow at his face.

"Are you trying to fucking kill me?" I cried.

Apollo gave me a big grin before sitting up and swinging his feet over the bed. He walked away and came back from the bathroom with a wet washcloth. He rubbed down my legs, and cleaned me up. Helping me into a pair of his shorts he laid my legs back under the covers. Kissing my forehead, he changed into a new shirt, and crawled into bed beside me.

"Sweet dreams Eliana, I'll be here in the morning in case you reconsider my offer." He spoke softly, twisting and playing with the ends of my hair around his fingers. Softly humming, and mumbling nonsense while I tried to fall asleep.

"Goodnight, Apollo." I whispered right before sleep found me.

Things between Apollo and I were going great for a while, but then he started to create some distance between us. We talked more after dealing with Dunne and his men, and he told me about his plans to take care of his uncle. I thought he was finally opening up to me about the business, but something changed last week. I would have been more concerned, but I was also busy with the wedding and work.

After talking it through with Apollo I realized that I wasn't ready to give up being an attorney. I wouldn't let Margaret keep me from my dream job. I hadn't talked to Apollo about going back to work, but I knew he would support me.

I had a few contacts left that I could reach out to. I knew if I needed it my Columbia contacts would help me out. The only thing I struggled with was deciding if I finally reached out to the other side of the attorney world. I promised I would only practice law and help those unrelated to my family business, but a lot has changed in the past year.

Now I am the same amount of involved in this life as my brothers are, or Apollo. I didn't know if I wanted to finally start working for the family. I'd have plenty of time to worry about who I wanted to work for, but before any of that I needed to start preparing for interviews, and finding someone who'd give me a shot again. I belong back in a courtroom, I deserve it.

I had been working for a few hours when I heard the front door open. I knew it was Apollo, and if he wanted to come and talk he could, but I was too busy to stop working. After a few minutes of silence, I heard his footsteps coming down the hallway. He opened the door to the spare office I had taken over, and found me sitting on the computer.

"What are you doing in here?" He asked.

"I'm working." I answered, not looking away from the screen.

Apollo walked over to me, and hugged me from behind. He looked over my shoulder at everything I was working on.

"These look like your old cases."

"They are. I think I'm ready to start working again. I thought about what you said, and I know that if I don't try to go back I'll regret it."

"Are you ready to try so soon after everything that's happened?" He asked.

"Now that I've decided to try again I can't wait another minute to start working. I need this to distract me and keep me focused. I'm going through old cases to find someone to work with, or at the very least build a new portfolio to bring to interviews. I have a few old friends that can get me in at their firm, but I need to think about my options."

"Wow." Apollo said, eyes wide trying to process everything.

"What's wrong? I thought you'd be happy for me."

"No, I am, this is great. It's just all happening very fast. Are you sure you don't want to take some more time to think over things and your options?"

"What options?" I asked.

"Who you want to work for, who would be a good boss to work with, where you want to work? All those important things?"

"Don't worry, I'm slowly figuring it out. I won't do anything without doing my research, but it feels good to be considering my options again."

Apollo pulled out his phone and started to type a message to somebody. He looked back up at me from his phone and gave me a nervous smile.

"Let me know if there's anything I can do to help you. I have some work to get done, but stop by my office if you need me."

Apollo walked out of my room quickly, and left me to wonder what his deflective behavior was all about. Every time I talked about going back to work he was supportive. Now that I was actually trying to get back out there he was acting weird. Was he just lying to me to make me feel better? I tried to push back the doubts and voices in my head that told me this was a mistake, and focus on a firm I could be happy working for. I also needed to try and keep this all a secret because Mom and Dad were not going to be happy when they find out I'm looking for a job again. I think they were both secretly happy when Margaret fired me. This time around I wasn't going to let anyone talk me out of going back to work, and doing what made me happy.

I worked through most of the weekend, and only stopped for food breaks. I had more energy lately than I did for the past month. I felt like me again. On Monday, I had a few calls from some firms offering me an interview, but I was unsure if I was going to actually show up. I was still nervous to put myself out there again.

Between Apollo's work and my work, we hadn't seen each other in a few days. We tried to sleep when we could, but it rarely matched up with each other's schedules. When I was laying down for the night, his phone was ringing, forcing him to get up. We spent one night together for a few hours, but the two of us were too tired to even talk. We enjoyed the quiet of each other's company. He was surprised to see me at the table eating breakfast early Thursday morning.

"Good morning, my love." He said, walking to his side of the table.

Nearly dropping my toast, I looked up at Apollo. I'm sure I heard him wrong.

My love.

That sweet nickname had me crossing my legs to lessen the ache between my thighs. By the looks of it, Apollo knew exactly the effect he had on me this morning.

"Good morning." I smiled, "What do you and Dane have planned for today?"

"We are busy with meetings all day, and then we're spending the day with Dad. He's making some moves in the warehouses, and I need to get filled in on everything that's been happening with him."

"Sounds tiring, when will I see you again?" I asked.

"I'm not sure. Maybe late tonight?" He answered.

Apollo grabbed a croissant and started to pick at it. He noticed my laptop out next to me and got curious.

"What is all this? What are you doing this week?"

"It's not important." I tried to deflect.

"Come on, tell me. It must be important if you've locked yourself up in your office all weekend. If it matters to you it matters to me."

I hesitated to tell him, but figured now was as good a time as any.

"I have a few interviews at a couple of private law firms this week, but I don't even know if I'll go. It seems like it's moving too fast. What should I do?" I asked.

"Well, maybe it is too soon. You don't want to rush anything. And I'd hate for you to make a selection and it be the wrong one and you regret it."

"Yeah, you might be right, but there's something in my brain telling me to do it even if I'm afraid. I feel like this is my chance to get it right this time. I'm really excited about this, and it's the first time I've felt good about something in a while."

"I know you're anxious to start working with clients again,

but you don't want to move too fast. What if you took a couple of weeks to really think this through?" He suggested.

"Wait a few weeks? How does that make sense? I've finally decided I'm ready and now you're telling me to wait? If I wait, who knows what opportunities I'll lose. I've already wasted too much time."

"I'm just trying to look out for you. I don't want you to get hurt again. It doesn't seem like you're ready."

"This is ridiculous. I thought you would support me, and now you're trying to talk me out of it before it even begins."

I stood up to leave the table. I had officially decided I'd be going to these interviews. Apollo telling me to wait only confirmed that I wanted, and needed this.

Screw him, he was wrong about waiting.

While getting dressed Apollo stopped by my room. He watched me put on my heels, and leaned against my door.

"So, you're really going? There's no talking you out of it?"

"Not unless you can give me a good reason why I shouldn't go. Aside from it being too early because I already know it's not. I won't get another chance like this again."

Apollo looked at me like he had something he wanted to say, but he bit his tongue. He was holding something back, but what, I didn't know.

"Is there something you'd like to tell me, Apollo? I like to think I can read you pretty well, and I know when you're keeping secrets from me."

"No, I have nothing to say. I'll be gone until late tonight again. Will I see you, or will you be gone all day?" He asked.

"I have a busy day full of interviews, don't wait up." I said, leaving him standing there alone in my room.

"Eliana-" He tried to shout after me.

"No, Apollo, no! I'm not having this conversation with you right now. I thought you of all people would be in my corner, and already you're backing out. Unless you can tell me what you're hiding from me we have nothing to talk about. I am doing this, even if it sucks and it is too soon. I don't want to be talked out of it right now."

I grabbed my bag, and waited for Alex in the car. I had a meeting with a professor who introduced me to Margaret. Charles knew about my family situation, and what it meant trying to find work.

Messing with the broken zipper on my work bag, I waited in the lobby of Charles' law firm. I hadn't thought maybe he wouldn't want me stopping by like this until it was too late, and I was sitting down next to his secretary's desk. A quiet worker in a cute purple tie called my name and guided me to Charles' office.

"Eliana." He smiled when I entered. He opened his arms for a hug as I walked to the office.

"It is so good to see you, I feel like we haven't spoken since your first day with Margaret."

I tensed in the hug at the mention of Margaret. Charles let go of me, and rested his arms on my shoulders.

"Forgive me, I'm sure it's still upsetting to think about her letting you go. My apologies."

"It's fine, now that I've had some time to think about it, I think it was the right thing. I'm ready for my next adventure."

"Which is why you're here to pay me another visit I suppose. Here to find another job?" He asked.

"I am trying to find a new place to work. I know with my background it will be difficult, but I'm hoping that with my past experience at the Women's Work someone will hire me. There has to be someone who doesn't mind hiring a Mariani."

"Well, a Mariani now, but soon to be Costa I hear. That changes things. If you think it was difficult finding a job when you got out of school, this time around will be different. After everything that happened everyone knows about your personal life. It's only going to get harder and harder to hide I'm afraid."

"You've always helped me out when I needed it, what can I do? I know it's going to be harder for me, especially after the wedding, but I'm not backing down this time."

"Well, if you really think you can handle the pressure I have a few firms that would consider you, but unfortunately I cannot give you my official recommendation. I hope you understand that I have to keep some professional distance between the two of us. I will always support you Eliana, but publicly there's only so much I can help. You were an amazing student Eliana; your tenacity and determination deserve more recognition. If you do start at another law firm you would be starting at the bottom again. You'd practically be an intern."

Charles was right. I wouldn't be starting in the courtroom again or working with clients. I would be going on coffee runs, and working with paralegals on case prep. It didn't matter how much experience I had, I would be starting over.

Charles walked over to his desk and pulled out a folder. He wrote a few things down, and then handed it to me.

"These people might be able to help if you decide this is what you want. I think you should take a few days to think about it. It's going to be a long journey getting back to where you were, but if anybody can do it, it's you."

I took the folder from Charles and slipped it into my briefcase.

"I can't tell you how much I appreciate this, and I promise from today on if we see each other I'll remember to keep my distance. I don't want to do anything that would jeopardize your firm, and the work you do. No one needs to go digging through your case history all because you were caught helping me." I told him.

"Thank you, Eliana, and good luck."

Charles was right, starting over at the beginning was not something I wanted to do. If I wanted to be working with clients again I would need to reach out to one of my uncles, and that wasn't going to happen.

I was sitting in the kitchen enjoying some wine when Apollo came home. He was surprised to see me still awake, and grabbed a glass for himself.

"Eliana, I need to talk with you about going back to work."

I tipped my wine glass towards him, giving him a chance to continue.

"I'm going to ask that you don't go back to work for someone else. I think you should wait a while and see what other options are out there. I know it's not what you want to hear, but it's what I believe. Now isn't the right time for you to be starting over."

Apollo looked up, and waited to see a reaction from me. I finished my wine and set down my glass in the sink.

I crossed my arms against my chest, and tried to find something nice to say. It was difficult, so I remained quiet.

"Can you please trust when I say there are better options out there for you, and going back to work for someone who knows your history is not the best idea?"

"I know that I'll be starting from the bottom again, and I know I'll be putting in a lot of overtime, but this is important to me. I need your support on this, no matter where I end up, I can't do this without you."

Apollo sighed, dropping his shoulders, and leaning against the counter.

"I met with an old professor today, and he told me how difficult it would be to start over, but I'm standing here telling you I'm willing to try. I never would have thought this was possible without your support, so why are you making it so difficult now? You made me believe I could do this again, and now you're backing out. I know I'll be running and getting coffee like an office bitch, and I'll be back in the records room until the sun rises the next morning, but I don't fucking care. It makes me happy."

"I know it makes you happy Eliana, but please listen to me, you deserve more. Don't rush into accepting a job just because you feel rushed. You're going to regret it. I will support you when the time is right, but there is a lot going on with the business right now, and I can't guarantee I can keep an eye on you at your new job and continue to run things smoothly. If you just give me some time I promise I'll explain everything. I just can't give you answers right now."

"I'm tired of putting my life on hold for other people, Apollo. I thought you knew that, and I thought you were done trying to tell me what I could and couldn't do in my professional career. Two weeks ago I had your full support, and now I don't. Make it make sense Apollo, please. I know you've been hiding something from me, and I'm starting to think it has something to do with me going back to work. Do you really not want me going back to work that bad?"

"I have so much I want to tell you, but I just can't right now. I'm sorry, believe me, I'm sorry. I'm tired of keeping secrets, but if you can hold on for a little while longer it will all be worth it."

I went to speak, and demand some answers, but his phone rang. He hesitated to pick it up, but of course he accepted the call before the fourth ring, and brought it to his ear. I could hear Dane yelling through the phone from across the room.

"I have to go." Apollo said, turning to leave.

"Of course." I scoffed.

"There's an emergency at Dad's house. One of his men lost a big shipment they were tracking. We aren't done talking about this Eliana. We'll talk more tonight, so don't do anything rash just to piss me off. Think about your options, and don't agree to any offers yet."

"Do you really have to leave right now? You can't stay and talk about this with me? You're going to leave and demand I don't make any *important* decisions without you?"

"Yes, that is what I'm asking of you right now." Apollo looked defeated.

I was angry, but I owed it to Apollo to talk it out with him. I would try to get as much sleep as I could before he came home.

I only got a few hours of sleep before my phone woke me up. I let my eyes adjust to the bright light of my screen and saw it was Apollo calling.

"Hello?"

"El, I'm going to send you an address. I need you to get there as soon as you can. I want you to come alone. Don't bring

Alex. Can you do that for me?" He asked.

"Apollo, what is going on? Did something happen?"

"Everything's fine, no one's hurt, but I need you to hurry." He explained.

"Okay, I'll call you when I get there." I replied, hanging up and finding some clothes to put on.

The ride to Apollo's address had me driving towards Apollo's main office near his warehouses. Aside from his office and his distribution center there wasn't a lot out here. Mainly a few neighborhoods, and some houses spread far apart so you weren't bothered by your neighbors. There was never any activity out here, so I had no idea why he needed me in this part of the city in the middle of the night.

Just like I promised I called Apollo when I pulled into the driveway of an abandoned house. I didn't see Apollo or any cars, and the lights of the house were turned off. I could only make out a porch, and piles of supplies like they had been left on the side of the house by a construction crew.

I called Apollo but he didn't pick up. I got out of my car and walked closer to the house. I could see more of the house now that I was out of the car. I wasn't about to walk into an abandoned house, but from what I could see from the half open front door it was under renovation.

I called out to Apollo one more time, "Apollo, where are you?"

"I'm right behind you." He answered, causing me to jump.

"Apollo what is this? Why am I here?"

"I needed you to see this place, to see that I believed in you." He answered.

"What are you talking about?"

284

"I wanted to wait until the house was finished, and a few more pieces were finalized, but you forced my hand. I had it all planned out. I was going to wait until every room, every little detail was finished, and then I was going to bring you out here for dinner."

"Apollo... I don't understand."

"I bought this for you El. It's all for you. I knew after we talked in Italy that you would one day be ready to go back to work, and I knew when that time came you were going to need an office. I found this place for sale on my way to work, and I knew it would make the perfect office for you."

Everything Apollo said during our fight started to sink in.

"You bought this place for me?" I asked, still in disbelief. I felt tears starting to form.

"You, of all people, should not be working for someone else for the rest of your career. You've always dreamed of opening your own firm. I'm simply speeding up the five-year plan. Why don't you go in and take a look around? Your office is past the kitchen on the right."

I followed Apollo through the door, and watched him find the electrical lamps in the corner to bring some light into the house. The hallways were stripped bare, and doors were missing, but at the end of the hall was a room that looked brand new. I opened the door and saw an office styled just like the one I'd been using at Apollo's house.

"This isn't real." I mumbled, trying to steady my breathing.

"Yes, it is, and I'm going to support you every step of the way."

I walked around my office, taking in every little detail. When I walked around to the back of my desk, I broke down in tears.

285

There on the wall of my office, was a painting of a young woman reading beside a lily pond. It was the piece of art I fell in love with when Apollo and I visited his museum in Italy. It reminded me of my summers in Italy before I grew up and knew the truth about my family. I must have admired that painting for hours in the museum before Apollo begged me to leave.

I can't believe he remembered.

I sat in my office chair and let the tears fall. Apollo gave me a few minutes to calm down before he kneeled down in front of me.

"I don't deserve you." I whispered into my hands.

Apollo ran his hand through my hair, guiding me through deep breaths.

"I doubted you, every time you left with Dane I assumed you were hiding something, and the whole time it was this."

"Shhh, my love, breathe." He spoke softly.

"It's me who doesn't deserve you. Give me a chance to show you how much you mean to me. I promise Eliana, that from today on you have nothing but my support."

"This is too much Apollo." I cried. "I'm not ready to open my own firm."

"Stop. If I didn't think it was possible I wouldn't have done all this. You can do this, you're ready. And if you need some extra help I will be there. You don't have to do this alone."

I wanted to thank him, kiss him, do something, but my body was still in shock. All I could do was stare back at Apollo who looked at me with so much love and admiration it made my heart ache. I brought my forehead to Apollo's and leaned into him. I closed my eyes, and took a deep breath.

"This is real? I'm not dreaming?" I asked one more time.

286

"This is real. You are very much awake right now."

"I'm so sorry. I doubted you, even when you've done nothing to deserve those doubts." I said.

"Don't apologize. I had to keep this a secret from you. I wasn't ready to share it with you just yet. I'm sorry it looked like I was avoiding you this week, but I was waiting on confirmation the house was yours before I showed it to you. Also, don't be mad at Dane for pulling me away every two minutes, I made him handle all the issues with our contractors."

"I have no words, Apollo. This is too much."

"It's going to take some getting used to, but in the meantime, I have one condition. I want you on retainer as my attorney to protect us and our family for as long as you plan on working. I've never seen a more dedicated attorney, and we all know how much you saved us with Sterling, so promise me once you get your firm running I'm your first client." He said.

I wiped the tears from my cheeks, and gave Apollo a big smile, "With you as a client I'll never have a boring day of work ever again, will I?"

"Never." He said, kissing me softly.

Apollo

Hiding this secret from Eliana was killing me. She knew as soon as I started hiding things from her that something was up, but she knew better than to ask. That's what was so hard about keeping secrets. She understood that there would be secrets in our relationship even though I didn't want there to be. It was a habit she'd learned from growing up in this world, and it hurt me to think I was treating her like the men in her life before me. Hopefully, this helped her open up and trust me when it came to the two of us.

It's not that I didn't want her going back to work, but she deserved more. She told me the first night we met she wanted to run her own firm. She shouldn't have to start all over in her career working for some asshole. She can do more for this city working for herself than she ever could working under somebody.

Eliana took a few more moments to calm down before she stood from her chair and walked around the house. She wrapped her arm around mine as we walked through the empty house. We walked together quietly enjoying each other's company.

Eliana stopped when she got to the stairs at the front of the house.

"I only had plans for the first floor of the house. I figured you could turn the basement or the second floor into emergency overnight rooms for clients, or for anyone that needed it. It could be half office, half safe house. Now that the secret is out you can start working with our contractor."

Eliana smiled as she walked up the steps dragging her arm up the stairway railing.

"I've done a lot of bad things in my life but supporting you and the women you help is a good start to giving back to the community I've hurt. Whatever resources you need in these next few months you have."

Eliana stopped at the top of the stairs and looked down at me. I stopped two steps below her, so that we were eye level.

"You're a good man Apollo. Even if no one has ever told you that before, or you don't believe it, you are good." She spoke.

I didn't believe what Eliana was saying, but the look in her eyes told me she seriously believed I was good. A man who deserves no redemption, is loved by a woman as kind as Eliana. She saw past all the bad I've done, and still decided to love me. She didn't care about who I was, but who she thought I could be.

My heart ached to be loved by her.

I gave Eliana a few more minutes to tour the house by herself. I waited in the living room while she took notes on the other rooms of the house. I could see the wheels in her brain already turning with ideas. The old El was back.

"Babe it's almost sunrise, I think I should get you back to the house."

Eliana yawned as she walked to the front of the house. She didn't want to leave, but she looked like she hadn't slept in a few days.

"As soon as Bryan is in his office I'll let you give him a call to stop by here again and start working on some projects. He is expecting a call from you soon to get started."

"Okay." She reluctantly agreed, still taking in every detail of the small house.

The only thing I had left to do was to give Eliana one of the spare keys to the front door. She looked at the key I had pulled out of my pocket, and hesitated grabbing it. I took her hand and opened her fingers up, setting the key in her palm.

"Let's go home. I'll drive you back and have someone come pick up your car in the morning."

Eliana was half asleep by the time I got the car started. I rested one hand on her thigh as we drove. My thumb drawing circles on her leg was putting her to sleep. She was trying to fight it, but she was zoning out watching the lights as they zoomed past her window.

When we pulled into the driveway she heard the turning of the gates and opened her eyes, pretending she wasn't asleep. I held her hand through the garage taking off her coat and dropping it on the back of the couch.

"Do you have more work to do, or can you come to bed?" She asked.

"I told Dane not to bother me for the rest of the night, and I'll be here in the morning when you wake up."

Eliana held my hand and led me to my room. She only let go of my hand to strip out of her clothes. She slid off her leggings but left my shirt she was wearing on. After changing she was tiredly looking for my hand again. One of the things I'd grown to love about Eliana was how needy she was when she was tired.

I'm not sure she realized she liked to keep me close to her, but the more exhausted she was the tighter she held me. Tonight must have been a long night for her because her grip on my hand was numbing. She didn't plan on letting me go. I managed to get my suit off in time for her to grab me to bed. Without saying a word, she rolled onto her side and leaned into my chest.

I brushed her hair off of her shoulders. Her eyes fluttered closed, and her skin rose with goosebumps when I twirled my fingers around her shoulder. My cold rings sent shivers down her spine. El moved her legs around mine, shifting a few times to get comfortable. I begged her in my mind to stop because if she kept moving I wasn't going to be able to let her rest tonight. I cursed myself for getting hard just by the thought of her thighs rubbing close to my groin.

After a few minutes of playing with her hair and listening to her calm breaths, I heard her whisper my name.

"I've been thinking about it, and I think this might just

work." She spoke.

"What might work?"

"Us." She admitted. "I thought the fates would have to be crazy to pair us together, but maybe they saw past the crazy. All my aunties say you're supposed to find your opposite. They say if you're intense to find someone calm, and vice versa, but we did the opposite. When I agreed to marry you, I thought we'd kill each other before the wedding."

"There's still time for that. Don't jinx it."

That caused Eliana to laugh. God, that was my favorite sound. Her warm laugh filled the room around me, burning my ears.

"I thought I'd either kill you in a fit of rage, or have to fake my death. Both options are tiring and a lot of work." She said.

I tensed at her words. I knew it was a joke, and she meant nothing by it, but my blood ran cold imagining Eliana leaving me. She thought she could run from me, but no matter where she ran I would find her. There was nowhere she could hide, and I hope she knew that.

"Don't even think about it." I threatened.

"A woman needs options, Apollo. I know you have back up plans too. Everyone in our world does. You'd be a fool to not have a Plan B."

"I had a Plan B long before I met you Eliana, but that's changed. Mine no longer works because there's no way I could run without you by my side. The night we met I started working on a new plan."

Eliana looked up at me, concern in her eyes. She looked frightened, not by me, but what I was capable of. She knew I would put her before anything else if my hand was forced.

"So, tell me, how did you plan on faking your death to get away from me."

"It's a secret." She smiled

"Spill it."

"No."

"Eliana..." I warned.

"Tell me yours and I'll tell you mine."

"Car accident, two corpses that look like us ready to be dropped on the scene whenever we need them, and a friend who owes me a flight to Chile. I hope you can adjust to the Andes lifestyle because it's always been a dream of mine. To unplug, and maybe run a small farm up there, it'd be quiet, peaceful."

"You want to drag me to the Andes?" She asked.

"Yes, and now you're the second person that knows of the Andes. I can only trust Dane to take care of anything if I have to leave. If something happens to me the only person I trust to help you is Dane. Dane is the only one I want you to go to if something happens to me, okay?"

"Okay." She answered, half asleep.

"Now you have to tell me your plan."

"Well, statistics say that when women kill themselves it's clean, controlled. I want to go out with a bang. I want it to be bloody, and so disorienting that small flaws in my plan aren't noticed. Grief is a great distraction. I don't know exactly what I would do, but I would wait until I had a few days to myself, then I'd find someone with my hair and body type and blow their brains out. My dad already thinks I'm crazy. He put me in an institution my senior year of college because I called him and threatened to slit my wrists when he asked me to come back and work for him. He left me there for a month and didn't talk to me until he picked me up."

Eliana froze when she realized what she'd just told me. Wanting her to continue, I rubbed my hands down her arms, trying to calm her down.

"On the car ride back to my apartment he told me he wouldn't show up to collect my body if I tried something like that again. He promised me he wouldn't let the family say goodbye to me or give me a proper burial. Mom would be more worried about what others would think of the family to notice it wasn't me, and the others aren't smart enough. I'm sure Raff would eventually come for the fake me and realize what had happened, but we both wanted to run when we were younger. I know he wouldn't say anything. He would bury a stranger in our family cemetery, and wait for me to reach out to him."

I was speechless. She'd thought about this a lot. The thought of seeing Eliana like that made me sick, and nausea wasn't something I felt often. Hearing her words, I wrapped my arm around her waist and pulled her closer to me.

"I'm not going to let anything like that happen to you." I promised her.

"I know." She said, burying her face into my chest.

"I need you to promise you won't leave me Eliana. I won't be able to handle it, knowing you're out there somewhere without me." Fuck, I sounded pathetic, but I couldn't picture the future without Eliana in it. Even if those years were spent with her driving me crazy, I couldn't do it alone.

"I won't leave you Apollo, even when I probably should."

I could tell Eliana was close to sleep, so I didn't say anything else. She let sleep take her, and finally her body relaxed in my arms. I wasn't sure if she was telling the truth or not. I had a feeling that Eliana would always be able to run away if she needed to. I knew Eliana would be fine without me, but every day I got to spend with her only proved I wouldn't survive a day without her by my side.

Chapter Sixteen

Eliana

I had been working nonstop all week. If I wasn't at the office working on rooms with Bryan I was at the house working on a plan to get my firm running. I needed to let a few old clients know I was back and working again, and I needed a number two. Finding someone who wanted to work with me was going to be a challenge. Maybe I could convince a cousin I liked to go to law school and wait for them to graduate. I wasn't big on trying to find new employees, but it would need to be done soon. There has to be someone I like enough to let them work for me and help me run the office.

Bryan was close to killing me, but I didn't give a shit. Apollo was paying him to make sure everything I needed for the house was taken care of. Anything I wanted I was going to get. No point in holding back.

I found Apollo getting ready for bed when I came home. I didn't even realize how late it was until I got home and saw dinner on the table, already cold.

I was in front of the mirror taking off my jewelry for a minute or two before Apollo saw me. He looked tired, drained from work. I've learned that the longer the days are for him the more he struggles walking on his bad leg. As he dried off and found a pair of pants I could see a small limp in his step. I never brought up his accident after Italy because I knew how much it upset him.

It was probably the first time a powerful man like Apollo had ever felt truly alone and vulnerable. He thought he was going to die in that car accident, and the men who did it are still trying to kill him. He won't be able to put it behind him until he catches who is after his title.

The zipper of my dress made enough noise to let Apollo know I was in the room. He looked up from his side of the room and gave me a smile through the mirror. He threw his towel down and walked towards me. He stopped me as I attempted to get my dress off the rest of the way.

His hands were warm, pressed against my back as he unzipped me. He let the dress fall and then left small kisses across my shoulders. Finding his way to the back of my neck he gave me one more kiss before inhaling deeply and wrapping his arms around my stomach.

"Long day at work?" I asked.

Apollo didn't answer me, only nodding to let me know it was a hard day.

"Anything I can help with?"

Apollo dropped his chin so that his head rested on my shoulder as he shook his head no. I held his arms that were still wrapped around my waist.

"Why don't we go to bed, and let it be tomorrow's problem?"

Apollo relaxed his arms and gave me a half smile before turning around.

Apollo wrapped an arm around me as I laid on my side watching the wind outside the window rustle the tree. I didn't want to go to bed without getting to hear his voice so I built up the courage to say something.

"Apollo what happened-"

"Not tonight Eliana, please. Tonight, I just want to hold you for a few hours before Dane inevitably calls me and takes me away from you. Be mad and call me selfish, but please for tonight all I can do is hold you."

"Okay." I whispered, moving so that I laid closer into his chest. In a few short minutes Apollo was asleep. His breathing deepened, and his arms relaxed from their grip. Tomorrow I would ask questions, but for tonight I let him sleep.

In the morning Apollo was gone, and the house was quiet. It meant he needed all the men he could get working with him. With only Alex and me at the house I could get some work done with little interruptions. I had less eyes on me in the house to move around freely.

After breakfast, I went back to bed until lunch. Finally forcing myself to get up and get something done I headed to my office. I emailed a few attorneys I used to work with that I remember hating Margaret, and I reached out to a few paralegals who would consider leaving the firm they were at now if they were paid enough. There was risk in hiring people who were un-loyal enough to leave their old jobs so quickly, but all that mattered was after they were mine they were loyal to me. I had the resources to keep them happy. After searching for a few hours, I started calling up old shelters, and homes to let them know I was back to helping women who came looking for help.

I still had a few contacts from when I worked under Margaret that would help me get connected to the city again. I needed everyone to know I was back, but it was too soon. I needed to soft launch the firm before causing chaos. Plus, I had yet to tell Mom or Dad yet. Once they found out I was working again I would never hear the end of it. They'd be happy to know that I was willing to work with family this time around. That might help with their opposition.

It was way past a normal time to eat dinner, and I knew Apollo wouldn't be home tonight, so I settled for some day-old pizza and a bubble path that turned me into a prune before calling it a night.

Early the next morning I heard knocking on Apollo's bedroom door. I didn't have any plans, so I was surprised to see an anxious looking Alex in the hallway when I opened the door.

"I'm sorry to wake you up, but we have a small problem Ma'am. I thought I should tell you before we tell Apollo. I was hoping you could fix the *problem* before I had to ruin his already shitty week."

"What happened Alex?"

"Well, I don't really know how to- it's just that it's a sensitive subject for some people and-"

"Spit it out, what happened?"

"I'm sure you're aware that the men I work with keep girlfriends? Some of Apollo's warehouse workers often find comfort in other women, women that aren't their wives. There are rumors that those other women were approached by someone who offered money to get any information on the business."

"Are you kidding me?"

"No, unfortunately, and now there are a few men worried about what might have been shared, and more importantly their wives finding out about the whole situation. I was hoping you'd be able to take care of it before Apollo came for half of his men."

"What do you expect me to do Alex? I don't run the warehouses, I have no authority over them."

"That's true, but I know you agreed to work for Apollo as his attorney and you still have a few connections that could help us figure out if anything important was spilled."

"If I'm going to help I need names. Names of the men, and more importantly names of the women they're sleeping with. Anyone. Girlfriends, one night stands, anyone they might have paid, and anyone they got close with at a bar. Can you get that information for me?"

"Yes, of course. I'll go get it right now." Alex turned to leave, but I stopped him.

"Alex, wait. You know I'll have to tell Apollo about this right? He needs to know. As soon as I get it taken care of we're going to his office and giving him names."

"I know, just please fix it first. Maybe he'll be more forgiving if it's you giving him the news."

Unbelievable. In all honesty, I shouldn't be surprised that my first job as Apollo's attorney I'm hunting down his men who couldn't keep their fucking dicks in their pants. I grabbed my laptop, a few burner phones from Apollo's office and met Alex in the garage.

By the time we left the estate Alex had a few names of people we needed to meet with. As if Apollo's men didn't already hate me enough, by the end of today they'd loathe me.

Alex drove to the warehouse so I could meet with the men who think their girlfriends made a deal. It was so secret that the men in this world struggled with fidelity. For generations wives have ignored the obvious signs of affairs because they knew what it meant to protect the family. There was an unspoken agreement that the family business came first. Wives were incredibly loyal, even to men who didn't deserve it. The problem with mistresses is that they didn't share any loyalty to the men they were sleeping with. Some men think they're smart and know how to keep a few girls on the side, but I've never met a wife who didn't know about the affairs.

I knew that I would soon be one of those wives. The ones that show up to the parties with their husbands, and leave the party without them. I was terrified that one day Apollo would only need me to hold his arm at dinners, and then leave me sleeping in that giant house alone. Nora, Mom, my cousins, they all shared one thing in common. They were really good at pretending their husbands didn't have a thing for young impressionable women. I was sixteen when I accidentally met Dad's girlfriend that he kept until I was in college. Nora knew that Mikey wasn't putting in extra hours at work. There was an unspoken rule; as long as the girlfriends didn't cause any problems, we all pretended they didn't exist.

This little situation was forcing me to consider the girlfriends Apollo had running around the city. Before Italy I wouldn't have blamed him. But now I felt petty, jealous even. He was mine, and I wasn't big on sharing. I wonder if he'd ever considered I would find someone to keep me happy during our marriage. I felt uneasy driving to the warehouse knowing I might be walking right into Apollo's past.

Two men were waiting for me in an old office when I got to the warehouse. They stopped their bickering when I entered the room. They looked at me then at Alex.

"Are you fucking kidding me? You brought her?" One of them asked.

"No, you've got to be fucking kidding me. Tell me, how many girls have you slept with in the past month? Do you even know which one is the rat? You have ten seconds to fix the attitude and start talking because against my better judgment I'm here to save your ass. Tell me everything, don't leave anything out and if I think you're lying I'm leaving this office and letting Apollo deal with the two of you." I said, dropping my bag on a desk and having a seat.

The shorter of the two men sat closest to me near the desk.

"I met this girl a couple of months ago, and we had a deal. I was helping her through school, and in return she was always available when I needed her. A few nights ago, she introduced me to a friend. Don't get me wrong it made for a great night, but I got a little carried away with the drinks. The next morning the girls were asking me questions, asking me to give them details about the things I told them the night before. I don't remember any of it. They were asking about Apollo, and the men I work with, even times that I made deliveries. As soon as they dropped Apollo's name I left, but I haven't been able to find them since."

"Jesus Christ." I sighed. "And you, what did you do?"

The man with a buzz cut only stared at me. His buddy had to hit him on the shoulder before he agreed to talk.

"I had this feeling this girl I was seeing, Maggie, was getting upset I wasn't *prioritizing* her. She kept asking me if I treated my wife the same way, and if I was sleeping with other women. The bitch got real clingy, so I dumped her. I told her she knew what this was, and that I couldn't give her more. She came to my house late at night drunk and started telling me she should have taken the deal. She said she would have made good money, but she thought she loved me so she ignored it. I didn't know what she was talking about at first, but then she said she had nothing to lose anymore, and she was going to talk."

"And what did you do?"

"I panicked. I lied to her and promised her if she gave me some time I would leave my wife. She thinks I'm meeting her upstate, but I just had to get her out of the house before she woke up the kids. I haven't been picking up her calls."

"Are there any others that could become a problem? Anyone you met at a bar, or through work?"

The two men shook their heads no.

"I don't believe you."

The two men looked at each other.

"You have five minutes to write down any names you remember, and all the places you met them, or met up with them."

While the men wrote down names I texted Christian. I needed to know if this was related to Sterling, or if someone else was trying to get information about Apollo.

After I had my lists I left the two men in the office, and I walked back to the car with Alex.

"I need you to take me to Apollo's office please, Alex."

"Right now?" He asked through the mirror.

"Yes, we can't keep this from him any longer. He needs to get men out looking for these girls, and I don't have the resources for that anymore."

Alex hesitated putting the car into drive, but eventually worked up the courage. I hoped that whatever Apollo was dealing with was sorted out because this was going to piss him off.

Waiting for the elevator to Apollo's office had me thinking about all the other women who stood here waiting just like me to visit Apollo. I knew most of Apollo's history with women, and it didn't make me feel any better about our arrangement.

I tried not to let my anger show, but the closer I walked to Apollo's office doors the more upset I became. I was an idiot for thinking I was the only one Apollo was sleeping with. I wanted to put a bullet in the brain of a girlfriend I didn't even know existed. If I did find out he's been with someone else since our engagement I was going to lose my mind.

I didn't give Apollo the courtesy of a knock as I stormed into his office. He was standing over the conference table working on some type of mapping system with a few of his men.

"Eliana?"

"I need to talk to you, Apollo, it's important. I'm afraid this can't wait."

Apollo's men looked up at him unsure what to do. He gave them a nod and waited for them to leave before walking back to his desk and leaning against it.

"What's wrong?"

I sat down in front of him pulling out the list of names.

"You'll never guess where I was this morning. I was lucky enough to spend it at the warehouse with some of your men."

"Why were you there without telling me first?" He asked, upset I would go there alone.

"Calm down, I'm not the one you should be mad at. A few of your men think there's someone paying off the women they're sleeping with for information. Turns out your men enjoy some casual pillow talk after sleeping with strangers."

"Are you fucking kidding me?"

"No, I went over to see what information I could get out of them, but they didn't have a lot to give. All I have are a few girlfriends, and some hook-ups. Probably not even real names, but it's a start. I need someone working on tracking these girls down. I already talked to Christian. He doesn't know of any pending cases against you other than the failed Sterling one, and I don't know who else would be doing this."

"If it was anyone else, but the police, they wouldn't need to go the girlfriend route to get information." Apollo said.

"One of your guys said that the two girls he slept with mentioned your name specifically. This isn't just about the company, this is about you."

Apollo threw a book that was sitting on his desk across the room, "Fuck!"

"What do you want me to do Apollo? Do you want me looking into the girls? I might be able to find something if I track them down through the clubs."

"No, I'm going to give this to Dane. I don't want you anywhere near this. It's not safe right now." He answered.

I tightened my jaw. Is it really not safe, or does he just not want me anywhere near the women we need to track down? I was back to doubting his loyalty to me, again.

"You can let Dane handle it, but I need to be there helping him. I can't have this coming back to hurt us if there's more women or someone has already given up information."

Apollo sighed, "I know, once he's tracked down anyone who might know anything I'll let you handle it. Are you sure there aren't any pending investigations against us?"

"If there are, it's not local. I'm afraid that if it's not someone wanting to hurt the family, and it's not Sterling, then it's the Feds. They're the only ones who could afford to pay off these girls, and work under the radar. I won't know anything about that for a few days, but I have Christian looking into it."

Apollo looked over the list his men wrote, and started sending a text to Dane. The longer I sat there the more anxious I became. All I could picture was Apollo fucking someone in this office, someone that wasn't me.

Apollo sent his text, and then looked back up at me.

"Dane says he'll stop by later and work on finding the girls. He's a little busy taking care of a problem with the Russians right now."

"Is it bad?" I asked.

"It's not great. They got a little greedy at a meeting we had a few days ago. They seem to think they're entitled to more territory than we're willing to give them in New York. Don't worry though, everything will be fixed by tomorrow. Dane has a few friends that are more than excited to remind the Russians of their place."

"Does that mean you'll be home soon?"

"I don't know. I need to be here in case something happens."

"Okay, well I don't want to keep you from whatever you were working on, so just have Dane give me a call when he gets back."

"I will, and the next time you go to the warehouse give me a heads up first. I don't want you down there alone." Apollo walked over to me and gave me a peck on the cheek.

I stood up and started to walk towards the door. I stopped with my hand on the door handle. I turned to see Apollo back at his desk working on the plans from earlier. I could have left and gone back to the car, but I didn't move. I needed to know that I was the only one. It might be pathetic, but I wouldn't be able to sleep in his house and in his bed until I knew for sure.

I locked the doors to his office and turned around. Apollo lifted his head when he heard the lock.

"I need to know if there are others."

"Excuse me?"

"You signed a contract and promised me there would be no one else while we were together. You might think you're invincible, and good at hiding, but I'd figure out the truth eventually. I can't continue to grow in this relationship with you if there have been others. I won't close my eyes to the affairs like the other wives do when they find out their husbands are sleeping with someone else."

"Eliana..." He sighed.

"Just tell me the truth." I almost shouted at him.

"No, there's no one. Not since before the engagement party, and I promise you there never will be anyone else. I don't know how else to convince you El, it's always been you. There isn't even time for somebody else because you flood my thoughts every minute of every day. I wake up wondering if you're okay, and if you slept well. I make sure there's enough of your favorite foods in the fridge for when I'm gone. When I'm at the office I do nothing but worry and have to talk myself out of calling you every hour. I have Alex sending me updates just to make sure you're being taken care of by my men. There is nothing else I'd rather be doing than worrying about you. I'd be a fool to go looking for someone else when everything I've ever wanted was standing right here in front of me."

Apollo barely finished his sentence before I was wrapped

around him, pulling him into a deep kiss. He was taken aback by my actions, but quickly held me tight. I pulled at his hair, harder than I probably should have as I deepened the kiss. Just as Apollo was tightening his grip on my ass I pulled away. With Apollo leaning against his desk I dropped to my knees.

I was going to be the last person he fucked in his office. I was going to make sure he wouldn't be able to work in his office without remembering every little thing we'd done in here.

I started to unzip his pants when he put his hands on my shoulder. Apollo sucked in a big breath as I dropped his belt to the floor. I cupped his dick through his boxers as I pulled them down. His dick was already hard and sprung out right in front of me.

I wasted no time slipping the whole thing in my mouth. I was a little impatient, and I couldn't wait any longer. I wanted him so deep inside of me he was hitting the back of my throat until I couldn't breathe. I stroked him with my free hand as I sucked on his cock. Apollo nearly folded when I pushed him deeper.

Slowly pulling out I licked up my spit. I looked up at Apollo as his eyes rolled into the back of his head. He grabbed as much of my hair as he could and held it in his fist. I stroked him with both my hands before sliding my tongue up and continuing to suck. I struggled to breathe through my nose as he rocked back and forth. I let him take control as I stroked the rest of him I couldn't fit in my mouth.

Apollo let go of my hair and leaned back. While I caught my breath, I twisted and pulled at his cock. He wiped my spit off of my chin and shoved a few fingers down my throat. His thumb played with my lips as I sucked on his fingers.

I stopped sucking Apollo's fingers and let him know I wanted to keep sucking. He smiled down at me as I opened my jaw wide enough to fit him. I started bobbing my head slow but picked up the pace to let him know he could start fucking my face again. Letting go of his dick I held onto his thighs. My nails dug into his skin as he pushed into me as far as he would go. I twirled my tongue around every time he leaned out, playing with him as he thrusted.

Apollo quickly pulled away, "I don't know how much longer I'm going to last, and you aren't leaving here until I fuck you against this desk Eliana. Lay down on your stomach."

I did as he instructed, and quickly threw my dress off before laying down on the cold desk. I thought he might try and play with me for a little bit first, but I needed his cock inside me now. I was already wet, and I couldn't wait any longer.

He teased me with his fingers, so I had to beg.

"Apollo, please, I can't wait."

Apollo must have been just as impatient because with no warning he thrusted into me. Unlike the last few times where he gave me time to adjust to his size, this time he grabbed my hips and started moving. I grabbed onto the edge of the desk to keep myself stable. He pushed into me as far as he could. I felt knots in my stomach as I adjusted to his pace.

His hands dug into my hips, "Fuck." He groaned.

I tried to hold back my moans with Apollo's men right outside the door. I let a few whimpers out as Apollo continued to thrust. It must have been too much for Apollo because he stopped, and the sensation of him inside me was gone. He took my arms in his hands and flipped me over.

"I want to see you and play with you while I fuck you like this baby." He said.

I laid on my back with my hands against the desk trying to

grab anything around me. Before sliding his dick back in, Apollo rubbed my clit, teasing me. I grabbed his wrist, trying to keep myself from coming too soon.

Apollo looked back up at me, and waited for the okay before sliding back in. This time he moved at a slower pace. He continued to stare as he lifted both my legs up. Knees bent he held my legs pressed against my sides as he moved.

"Apollo, I'm close, I can't-" I cried.

Keeping his exact pace Apollo let go of one of my legs and flicked his index finger back and forth against my clit applying more and more pressure the closer I was to finishing. I knew Apollo was close when he struggled to stay standing, and he dropped his head back onto his shoulders. He let out a groan as he pushed into me a little bit deeper.

After a few more strokes I was shaking as I waited for Apollo. His thumb found my clit and he rubbed it in circles as I bit my tongue to keep myself from screaming. I was shaking beneath Apollo as he grabbed my hips when his thrusts became sloppy. I rocked with his rhythm, our hips moving at the same time. He grabbed me by my neck and lifted me up as much as he could while he finished, biting and kissing my lips.

The two of us laid there catching our breaths, fully aware of the noise we must have been making. I prayed the walls were sound proof as I rode down my high. It took a few minutes before I was ready to walk again. Apollo helped me clean up and helped me with my dress as I leaned against the desk.

While standing to find my bag Apollo grabbed my arm, "Don't ever doubt again that there could be anyone else for me Eliana. I'll fuck you like that every night for the rest of my life if that's what if takes for you to believe me. The next time you find yourself doubting this, us, again I want you to let me know so I can remind you just how much you mean to me."

Apollo walked up behind me, and pulled my hair behind my neck, "Don't just nod Eliana, I need you to say it. I want to hear you say there's no one else."

"There's no one else." I whispered.

Apollo smiled and kissed me one more time before returning the dropped items back to his desk. I picked up my bag and did my best to fix my hair before I left his office. I unlocked his office doors and turned one final time before leaving.

"Goodbye Apollo."

"Always a pleasure when you visit Eliana, I'll be home as soon as I can."

"Relax, it's just dinner." Apollo said. He put his hand on my thigh and tried to calm down my nerves.

"Dinner with both of our families. Not to mention my parents still don't know I'm opening up the firm yet."

"I promise we're only staying for dinner. Mom only invited everyone over, so that we could talk about the rehearsal dinner and your family's guest list. Just make bird noises or give me a wink when you're ready to go home. Damn, we should have practiced a hand signal before coming here. Let's work on that when we go home. We could have a code for anything. Anyways, I have Dane on standby ready to fake an emergency."

"You really have Dane on standby?" I asked.

"I'm sure he's sitting in a bar somewhere tossing his phone back and forth just waiting for me to call and need him for something. He knows to keep tonight available in case we need him." Apollo said.

I let out a little laugh, "I don't think he likes me very much. Every time he has to work with me he lets out this disappointing sigh."

"He does that with everyone. He's not so bad once you get to know him I promise. As for him not liking you, don't worry too much about it. Dane doesn't like people that are impulsive and unpredictable. It stresses him out. He sticks to a certain routine and lifestyle. You kind of stressed him out when you shot Jason. You might be the only person he's afraid of."

"Ah, so he hates me because I'm reckless and unpredictable. Lovely."

"Like I said, don't take it personally. He gets mad at me every time I send him on errands for me with less than a day to make arrangements." Apollo explained.

"Maybe I should get him a gift to make amends. Do you think he likes charcuterie boards, maybe a fruit basket?"

"Yeah, I'm sure he'd love that." Apollo teased, pulling into the driveway.

I dropped the Dane conversation as we walked up to the house, but I made a mental note to find out what he liked. It took me a month to break Alex, but now we're best friends... sort of. It was only a matter of time before I broke Dane too.

Catalina's laughter could be heard from the kitchen as we entered the house. Either she'd started drinking early or my mother was in there sharing the latest gossip.

"Mama?" Apollo called out, taking my hand and leading me to the kitchen.

"Apollo, Eliana you made it! Everyone else is in the parlor

waiting to eat."

I looked at Apollo, and whispered in his ear, "We're literally two minutes late."

"If you're not here an hour early, you're considered late. I figured being the last to arrive was better than being trapped here all night."

I laughed and left Apollo in the kitchen as I went to look for Nora. I found her talking with Mikey and Frankie. I wonder how she convinced him to come to dinner tonight. Usually he only showed up for public appearances.

"El!" Frankie smiled, "Damn I owe Raff money. I thought you'd cancel for sure."

"Nice to see you too, asshole."

"Auntie El, I made a new friend at school. They just moved here from Montana! They say it's even colder there than it is here. Montana is a state, by the way. We learned about it when Sophie moved, and we got to meet her brothers and all their pets. Mom says I can invite her over for a playdate once she meets Sophie's mom." Isabella said.

"Wow, who knows maybe you two will be best friends and get to be in class with each other every year!" I told her.

"That would be amazing! She's also a dancer, but she's not as good as me. I try helping her with her spins, but all she does is fall. My dance teacher Miss. Alberta says I'm better than the junior company girls!"

"Well keep practicing and maybe you'll be ready to audition for the company by next year." I said.

Isabella went to say something else but became distracted by something Thomas shouted at Mikey across the room. It sounded like they were being bribed with candy after dinner if they were good. The two of them went to hang on Mikey's arm and drag him down until he eventually broke and promised a treat.

He was a shitty husband, and a douchebag, but at least he was a good dad. He did his best to show up for them, and support Nora with them when she needed him. It almost made me not hate him.

I knew Apollo would make an amazing dad, and I hoped he wasn't upset I didn't want a family. I hoped being an uncle to my nephews and nieces was enough because I don't think I'd ever be able to give him kids. I know he promised it was my decision, but he'd never tell me if that was something he'd ever considered. My heart ached to see Apollo as a dad, but I wouldn't ever be ready after everything that's happened.

I could hear footsteps running down the stairs, and I knew they belonged to Juliette after she tackled me from behind into a hug.

"You're here!" She squealed. "I have so much to tell you! Emily and I aren't talking right now, and I literally have no one to talk to. She's being a total bitch about Penn. She won't stop talking about all these girls in the incoming freshman group chats and won't stop acting like she's better than everybody. She literally doesn't even go there yet. We aren't even seniors and she's acting like she's moving this August. I'm waiting for her to apologize before we can start hanging out again. Plus, I've been so busy researching schools I want to go to that I'm too busy to worry about her college."

I tried to focus as Juliette rambled on about school and Emily. I hadn't talked to her in a while, but the last time I did she was narrowing down her choices of school. I'd convinced her to add some American schools to her list, but she was still dead set on Italy. I need to remind Apollo I promised to take her on a trip

313

before December.

Juliette finally took a break and I had a chance to say something. "Why don't we talk about it after dinner? I have so much to catch you up on too. I convinced Mom to let me bring you dress shopping. Make sure your calendar is free next Saturday because I think I might die if I don't have one person on my side at the boutique. I need you to balance out Mom and Nora."

"Yes of course! I've been saving dress ideas since you got engaged. I have an album saved of dresses that you have to try on. It's going to be impossible picking just one dress though. You're going to look amazing in everything. Would you consider an outfit change between the reception? That's really in right now. Some brides even change twice after the reception. I could totally organize the outfit changes, so that they work with the whole vibe of the wedding."

"Okay, slow down. Let's find one dress first before we commit to another. I haven't even processed that I'll be walking down the aisle in a few months. I don't know what will happen to my brain if I try to imagine reception outfit changes."

"Promise you'll look at all the photos and videos I've saved after dinner?"

"I promise, now let's go to the table before your mom yells at us for being in here." I told her.

Juliette ran to the dining room and sat across from me at the table. Isabella and Thomas sat between Nora and Mikey while Frankie and Raff sat across from Apollo and I. Mom and Catalina each took a seat next to their husbands. Apollo squeezed my hand as I sat down and grabbed for my napkin.

Dinner was served, and Catalina was busy sharing details of the wedding with Mom. We all listened, but the only people who cared were Mom and her. They didn't want anyone's opinion on

314

how to plan the wedding, they wanted everyone to agree with their vision. They're lucky I didn't care at all how this wedding turned out. Maybe if I had more energy I could fake excitement, but there was too much going on.

Nora nodded her head, and agreed with everything Mom said, and would look up to smile in my direction every once in a while. Sometimes her glances would shift over to Apollo. She gave me a smile that told me she knew about the two of us. I thought we were hiding the fact that we'd been getting along better, but I can't hide anything from Nora. She probably knew as soon as I walked into the house that Apollo and I were sleeping together.

She gave me a small wink when my cheeks got red and I whispered for her to cut it out. I'm sure she would call later in the week to get caught up on everything going on in my life. She was excited for this arrangement from the beginning. Even when I promised her this engagement was a life sentence, she knew it was only a matter of time before I caught feelings for Apollo.

I said nothing about my firm, and luckily no one else did. Apollo told Raff about the new office, but I don't think anyone else knew. I decided I would tell them some other time. I didn't want to ruin the dinner that was going surprisingly well.

"So, Eliana, are you ready for dress shopping next week?" Catalina asked.

"I can't wait! I have so many ideas and styles in my head I hope that we find something perfect for the wedding." I lied.

"Well, we won't stop searching until we find the perfect dress. I can promise you that. The shop we're going to is the best in the city. They've never failed helping a bride find her dress." Catalina assured me.

I gave her a warm smile and went back to eating my chicken.

I slowly zoned out when I heard Cristiano and Dad share news about work. Before I knew it, dinner was over, and plates were being taken from the table as dessert was set in front of us.

Someone sat a small plate in front of me and handed me a dessert fork. I almost lost my breath as I stared down at the dessert before me.

Chocolate cake, fudge dripping down its side.

Apollo must have had the same thought I did because we both snapped our heads to look at each other. The first time Apollo kissed me flashed through my head. The taste of whiskey on his tongue as he licked off the fudge from my lips. The way my stomach tightened when he grabbed my wrist and pulled me closer onto his lap. It caused me to tighten my legs, as I forced the events from that night out of my head.

Looking back down at the cake the two of us let out a laugh. Apollo held his fist up to his face trying to hide his laughter, and I had to drop my head to hide my smile. Everyone at the table looked up at us.

"Is something wrong?" Catalina asked.

"No, of course not. Chocolate cake is my favorite, I'm just a little surprised it's our dessert for tonight." I answered. I cleared my throat and bit the inside of my cheek to stop smiling.

Everyone at the table looked at the two of us like we were crazy. Eventually they lost interest and started eating their dessert. When no one else was looking Apollo leaned down and whispered in my ear.

"You know what your little moans did to me the last time you ate this dessert Eliana. Be a good girl and keep those moans to yourself until we get home. Do you understand?"

I put a piece of cake in my mouth and quickly nodded my

head yes. I hoped that my hair was hiding how red my face was. It felt like it was on fire, and I knew it wasn't because of the wine I'd had at dinner.

I quickly ate my dessert and sat quietly while Frankie and Apollo talked about their time in Italy. Dinner was catching up to me, and I was starting to feel a little tired. Excusing myself from the table I went searching for Juliette. Before I found her, I was stopped in the hallway by Cristiano.

"I'd like to have a word with you if you don't mind Eliana. Do you have a minute to meet me in my office?"

"Of course, let me go grab Apollo and I'll be right there."

"No, I'd prefer if Apollo wasn't a part of this conversation. I'd like to speak with you alone. Please, follow me."

Cristiano guided me through the long halls of his house, the sound of everyone else fading the further we walked. I hadn't spoken to Cristiano since our engagement party. I wanted nothing to do with him, and frankly I didn't trust him enough to be alone with him.

"Can I get you something to drink Eliana?"

"No, thank you." I said sitting down on a couch near his bar cart. I watched him pour himself a drink and then sit down across from me.

"It's come to my attention that you've offered Juliette a girl's trip to Italy. A year ago, I had to remind Juliette that going overseas for school wasn't a safe option. Especially for a major like art history. It crushed her when I told her no, but it was a decision I had to make. Now I'm hearing that thanks to your words she's looking into it again."

"It wasn't my intention to cross any boundaries."

"I wasn't finished." He interrupted. "Now that you've gotten

317

her excited about Italy I once again have to play the bad guy. She'll never blame you for getting her hopes up, and I'll be the one ruining her dreams once again. I want to remind you of your place in this family Eliana. Juliette is young, and not fully aware of the family she is a part of. Do not make this harder for her than it has to be."

"With all due respect Sir, I think you're making a mistake by not giving her a chance to experience Italy."

"That is none of your business. Your role in this family is to marry Apollo and keep up appearances. It is not your job to tell me how to parent my own child. If I want Juliette to stay in the States and get a real degree then that's what she will do. Your dad made the mistake of letting you choose where you wanted to go to school and look at where it got you."

"I'm sure I don't know what you mean." I said, shocked he had the nerve to speak to me like that.

"I'm not going to sit here and take advice from a girl who got pregnant before her first semester of finals." He snapped.

I had no words. How the fuck did Cristiano know about that? Does Apollo know?

"I'm not sure what you've been told, but it's absolutely none of your fucking business."

I stood up from the couch.

"I promise you, Cristiano, if you don't let Juliette make her own choices about her future then you are going to lose her forever. Physically you can keep her as close as you want, and you can lie and say it's for her own protection, but she won't survive. Juliette isn't like the rest of us. She is good and kind and sees the best in people. She deserves a chance at a normal life. If you say no to Italy everyday she wakes up she will loathe you for keeping her trapped in a life that's not hers. My father did the same to me, and it killed me. I lost myself after I left for college, trying to balance working for the family and going to school. I thought I could do both but look where it got me."

"Eliana, that's enough!" He shouted at me.

"No! There was no one looking out for me when I was Juliette's age, but I'll be damned if I let you ruin her the way my father ruined me. Every night I went to bed praying to god I didn't wake up in the morning. I thought that if I prayed hard enough like Mom taught me to then someone would show up to put me out of my misery. Take your anger out on me, cancel the engagement, hurt me, I don't care. Do whatever you want but give Juliette her life back. You're making excuses for yourself when you say Italy is too dangerous for her. If you're really as powerful as you say you are, then there's nothing you couldn't do to make her happy. You're just ignoring the fact that if she's in Italy you have no control over her anymore."

I paced around the room trying to create some distance between me and Cristiano.

"That's all this ever is about; control. That's what it was about when I made this deal with Dad, and that's what this is about now. Let her go Cristiano, before it's too late. You will lose her just like I lost myself, and you'll never get her back. Even after she's forgiven you for keeping her close to the family, her resentment towards you will never fade. The only thing that will make her happy is the hope that one day she'll be far away from this sick and vile world she was born into."

Cristiano said nothing. He only stared at me. I slowly walked back closer to him and the couch, hoping he was listening to what I was saying

"It won't be long before she sees Apollo and you for who you truly are, and when that day comes she will doubt everything you two have ever told her. She will doubt her entire existence, and if she doesn't feel like she can trust you she will run. Give her Italy, and she'll feel like she has a choice in this world. She'll think you respect her enough to make her own decisions, and maybe when she graduates she will feel like she still has a family to come home to."

Pausing to steady my breathing, I stared at Cristiano. My words settled and the room became quiet. I wanted to get out of there. I had to get out of there. I don't know where my courage to speak to Cristiano like that came from, but my adrenaline was wearing down and regret was sinking in.

I turned to leave before he could say anything back. I didn't want to hear what he had to say. I'm sure tomorrow I would regret standing up to Cristiano like that, but it had to be said. I couldn't let Juliette suffer the way I had to.

Running out of Cristiano's office I went looking for Apollo. I wanted him to take me home.

Apollo

Eliana was quiet on the car ride home. She sat with her body turned from me. I don't think she knew I was listening in on her argument with my dad, but I couldn't be sure. I went looking for her after dinner and couldn't find her. Eventually I heard her yelling inside Dad's office. I was seconds from opening the door and getting her out of there, but I wanted to know what they were arguing about.

I had no idea Juliette was still dreaming about going to

school in Italy. I thought she'd dropped it and moved on. I wasn't sure how I felt about Eliana helping her. I was about to open the office door and end the fighting when I heard Dad say something about a pregnancy. My hand dropped from the handle as I continued to listen. Eliana pregnant? When, with who? How did I not know?

I can't believe I had no idea Eliana was pregnant her freshman year. I mean, I saw her at the Christmas party, and no one mentioned anything. Did she have the baby? Did she give it up? Who the fuck was going to tell me about Eliana's baby?

I was doing my best to stay calm on the car drive home to avoid Eliana finding out I was eavesdropping on her conversation with my father. I didn't want to get into an argument with her until we were back at the house. Eliana said nothing the entire drive back. She looked out the window and picked at her nails.

Back at the house I followed behind her to the room. Neither of us said anything. I watched her pull her hair into a bun and head to the bathroom. Before turning on the shower she turned back towards me and took her necklace off.

"You know, don't you?" She asked.

It was time to come clean, "I overheard you two yelling in his office when I was looking for you."

"And you heard everything?" She asked.

I nodded my head yes.

"Fuck." She said, grabbing a towel from the bathroom and leaving the room. She left the bedroom and started walking back to her old room. The one she stayed at when she first got here.

"Eliana, we have to talk about this. I need to know what happened. You can't just casually announce you were pregnant and not expect me to have any questions."

She ignored me. She walked into her room and started to close the door on me.

"Damn it Eliana, talk to me!" I shouted.

She flinched, her shoulders dropped, and she stepped away from me.

"No." She yelled back at me.

"Eliana, I need to know if you had a fucking kid with someone else, and I'm just now finding out about it."

"No, I didn't! I never got the fucking chance, okay? There was no baby! Are you happy now?" She yelled.

I stood there and watched her sit down.

"I got pregnant my freshman year and when the guy who got me pregnant found out he ran to tell Dad. He knew we had money, and he thought he could use the baby as some type of leverage. A week before I went to a clinic to talk about an abortion my dad asked me to stop by the house. When I got there, he was waiting for me in his office with our family doctor. He said nothing, just watched as the doctor handed me some pills. I was only a few weeks, and the doctor lied and said I wouldn't feel anything. He said I would go home and bleed less than a period and that would be the end of it. But when I went home I laid on my bathroom floor and bled for three days straight as I waited for the cramping to stop."

I searched behind me for something to lean against, trying to process what Eliana was saying to me.

"My dad told me no daughter of his was going to raise a bastard out of wedlock. It was that night I knew what his plans for me were. I was just a pawn in his fucking game. He made the mistake of letting Nora marry her high school sweetheart. He was saving me for when he needed a favor, or he needed to use me as collateral. I knew eventually he would find someone for me to marry, and a baby would ruin any leverage he had."

I wanted to hold her, comfort her somehow, but my body wouldn't move. I was frozen as I watched Eliana cry and sulk into her small frame. She looked broken, like she was reliving her worst memory, and she probably was. She was all alone when it happened. She had no one there to hold her, or cry with her. I couldn't sit and watch her cry alone now. I don't care if she wanted me a thousand miles away, I was going to hold her.

I stood up from the dresser I was leaning against and went to sit next to her. When I put my arm around her shoulders she let out a sob she must have been holding for a long time.

"I didn't even want the baby, but just like everything else he's taken from me he took away my choice to get rid of it. I was already going to talk with a doctor, and I know he knew that. He had men following me everywhere I went. He asked me to come to his office because he wanted to humiliate me. He needed me to know he knew, and that I was nothing but a disappointment. I didn't plan on having a baby but seeing the fear in my dad's eyes when I was in his office almost had me considering it. I wanted him to tell me everything was going to be okay, and that I was still his little girl, but I realized he never cared for me like he did Nora. He was going to keep me around and use me when he felt his power slipping away." She cried.

I pulled her into my lap and gave her a few minutes to let everything out. After calming down a few minutes later she held onto my bicep, holding me tight.

I knew nothing I could say would make her feel better, so I kept quiet. Soon her crying stopped.

"I can't give you kids Apollo. It will ruin me." She spoke.

"I know." I whispered, kissing her forehead. "I know."

Sliding an arm under her legs I pulled her up with me. I walked her over to the bed and laid her down. She rolled under the covers and hugged one of her pillows. I laid down next to her and rubbed her back while she fell asleep.

After I was sure she was asleep, I quietly left her room. Shutting her bedroom door, I pulled out my phone to call Dane.

"Hello?"

"I need anything you can find on the Mariani's family doctor. You have five minutes." I said, hanging up the phone.

Dane called back before I even made it to my car.

"Stephen Marshall. He lives an hour south of the city. Wife died a year ago, he lives alone. Retired, gave the family practice to his son. He doesn't work for the Mariani's anymore, but they still make a few large payments every year to his account. Address is already being sent to your phone."

"Anything else I need to know?"

"No, but Apollo, what are you planning on doing? Do you need a doctor? Because I can call Eric for you if you need someone. I can be at your house in twenty minutes if you need me to go somewhere with you."

"It's none of your fucking business what I'm doing. I have to go." I said, hanging up.

The drive to Marshall's house was a short one. It took less than an hour to get from my house to his driveway. He's lucky I only had an hour to decide what I wanted to do to him.

Ringing his doorbell, I waited for him to answer. An old man, with receding gray hair answered the door. His glasses rested low on his nose, and he turned the porch light on to see who was standing at his front door. He knew as soon as the light flickered on who I was.

He took a step back trying to close the door, but I stepped my foot out, stopping his efforts.

"You, why are you here?"

I stepped into his house and closed the door behind me. Grabbing Marshall to the living room I sat him down in a chair.

"You hurt Eliana."

"Please, whatever you think I did I promise I can explain."

"I don't want an explanation. I want you to suffer just as much as she did that night. I want you to bleed out on this floor, cold and alone until I finally show you mercy and put a bullet through your fucking head. I want you to know exactly how she felt that night, how scared she must have felt." I explained.

I rolled up my sleeves, and pulled my gun from behind my back, "Now, get on your fucking knees."

Eliana

He left me. As soon as he thought I was asleep he left me alone in a room I'd hated from my very first day here. A room I couldn't sleep in alone. Maybe this was too much for him. He didn't sign on for all of this. Everything in my past was enough to send him running. He couldn't even sleep next to me anymore.

I waited and waited to hear his car pull up, but it never did. I watched the stars disappear and the sun rise. Finally giving up that he was going to come back I woke up and watched for his car out of the balcony window. The gates eventually opened, and his car came into view. I heard the garage door open and close, and I waited in my room until I heard him go to his. I stood by my door and listened to the shower turn on. Quietly making my way through the hallway I opened his bedroom door. Scattered all over the floor were the clothes he was wearing the night before. Every single inch of fabric was covered in blood.

Some of it was dry, but a few stains were wet enough to leave marks on his floors. Before I had time to look around his room for more clues as to where he was, the shower turned off. I quickly closed the door shut and went down to the kitchen.

Grabbing my phone, I ran back to my room. There was only one person I thought to call.

"Eliana it's five in the morning, what are you and Apollo on? Don't you two sleep?" Dane asked.

"Dane, stop talking. I need you to tell me where Apollo was last night, and you can never let him know I asked. Please, I don't have a lot of time."

"Eliana, I'm not sure Apollo wants me to tell you. Why can't you ask him?"

"I just can't, he wouldn't tell me even if I asked. Please Dane, I am begging you. I need to know. Please."

Dane let out a sigh, "I don't know why, but I think it had something to do with your old family doctor. He wouldn't tell me why he needed a doctor that wasn't Eric, and then he hung up on me before I could get any answers."

"He asked for information about Dr. Marshall?" I asked, gripping the phone as Dane spoke.

"Yeah, and then I didn't hear from him for a few hours. He called me a few minutes ago and asked me to send a few men to the address I gave him for the doctor. I have someone driving out there now."

I wanted to know more, but I could hear Apollo walking towards my room. I thanked Dane and threw my phone into one of my dresser drawers. I crawled back under the covers just as Apollo was opening my door.

I listened as he walked over to the bed and felt the bed dip as he crawled in next to me. His fresh shampoo hit me as he leaned in to give me a kiss on my cheek. I fluttered my eyes, pretending to still be asleep. He took a deep breath as he curled his arms around my waist.

As I laid there next to Apollo I thought about everything Dane had told me.

Marshall, he killed Marshall. He didn't leave me; he went to try and make things right the only way he knew how. Marshall became the fourth man in my life to hurt me, and to die at the hands of Apollo.

As I lay there in Apollo's arm there was a sick feeling in the pit of my stomach that told me Marshall wouldn't be the last.

Chapter Seventeen

Eliana

We never talked about that night again. I never asked Apollo where he went, and he never asked for more details. The next morning, we went on with our lives like nothing had happened. I went back to working on the office, and Apollo was busy trying to run a few big shipments for Rio, and his men back in Italy.

It was almost nine in the evening and I was waiting to meet with a few of Apollo's men at the warehouse. Dane had tracked down a few more women that were paid off. I needed to have a talk with his men and remind them of the confidentiality of their jobs. I had some paperwork I wanted to grab from his office, and then hopefully I could go home.

"I hate it here." I sighed, sitting at a desk on the second floor of the warehouse with Alex.

"It's not so bad. Only downside is how cold it gets in the winter time." Alex answered.

"I can think of one more thing that's worse than how cold it gets during the winter."

"Yeah, and what's that?" He asked.

"The men that work here."

"Hilarious." Alex sighed, but not before standing up to greet Apollo. He waited behind me while Apollo entered the room.

"Sorry to keep you waiting, my love, but I ran into an old friend." Apollo said, leaning down to give me a quick kiss.

"Is this *old friend*, really a friend or someone we need to be worried about?" I asked.

"Just a friend, and someone who isn't smart enough to cause any harm."

"Then, let's get this over with please, so I can go home. I spent all day at the office and I need a long shower to get all this dirt and grime off of me. We finally started in the basement today, and I'm not sure I'll ever stop feeling itchy after what I found down there."

"After you." Apollo spoke, turning to the door.

Apollo led me down the stairs to a small break room where a few of his men were waiting for us. It was interesting to see how much their demeanor changed when it wasn't just me in the room yelling at them. They actually dropped their heads when Apollo entered.

I went to sit down across the room, so that I could take notes when a loud crash from the main floor rang out. One of Apollo's men ran into the break room screaming for Apollo.

Two cars had driven through the loading docks and were crashing into everything in their path. Stopping just a few yards from where Apollo and I were, the windows rolled down, and the passengers lifted out guns.

"Eliana!" Apollo yelled, trying to find me in all the smoke and debris. I had no time to find him as I fell to the floor covering my head. I laid under a table, frozen with my eyes pinched shut. I tried to block out the screaming and gunshots that never seemed to end. After a few minutes of chaos, a body laid on top of me.

The cars' tires spun out as they left the warehouse, and I waited for it to go quiet before lifting my head up. I looked around the room and found a few of Apollo's men shot, lying on the floor bleeding out. Alex was no longer in the room, but I could hear him yelling with Dane outside where the cars had been.

Apollo's voice calling my name pulled me back to what was going on in the main floor. He sat next to me and waited for me to look up at him.

"El, we have to go. I have to get you out of here."

"I can't- I can't move." I told him, panic setting in.

"Are you hurt somewhere?" Apollo asked, searching for any blood on me.

"No, but what was that? Who were those people? Why did they come here? Who... what if... I can't feel my legs. I think I should probably just stay here where it's safe." I stuttered.

"Eliana, look at me, only me." Apollo spoke softly. "I need to get you back to the house. I'll explain everything once we get there, but I need you to stand up so we can go. Do you think you can do that?"

"But we can't just leave them lying there. They're going to die. You have to do something. Tell Dane to help them. They're going to die. Look, he can't breathe. Let me help him please." I begged as Apollo tried to walk me past the men who lied next to my feet on the floor. One of Apollo's drivers laid on the floor choking on his own blood. The other was only shot in his leg and was conscious enough to know what was going on around him.

"Stop! I don't give a shit about my men right now Eliana. All I care about is getting you back to the house. Please just take my hand and let me get you out of here." Apollo yelled.

I didn't argue any more as Apollo carried me towards the back of the warehouse. Alex was waiting for the two of us in a different SUV than the one we drove here in.

Apollo helped me into the back seat first, and then slid in next to me. He closed the door and ordered Alex to start driving. As we drove away I looked back at the destroyed warehouse. I watched broken concrete fall off the walls and roll onto the street. Men were carrying the injured out of the building. Only a few were still standing.

Apollo tried to grab my hand, but I pulled away. I didn't want him trying to comfort me right now, lying to me and telling me everything was going to be okay. He was hiding something from me, and whatever it was almost got the two of us killed.

Alex made sure the house was safe before taking the two of us back there. I didn't love the idea of going there right now, but it was the safest place for the two of us. Dane called Apollo on the drive home and gave him an update on the warehouse. I couldn't hear what he was saying through the phone, and Apollo never spoke. He only listened to what Dane had to say. Apollo felt me staring and looked over at me.

His face changed from anger to guilt as he looked at me. He scanned me up and down checking one more time to make sure I had no injuries. I'm sure someone would be by later to make sure I was really okay. He wasn't going to believe me even if I said it a hundred times.

My hands were still shaking from the adrenaline, and my

brain was scrambled. I was trying to process the attack, and Apollo's men lying helpless on the floor next to me. It could have been me that was hit, but for some reason I made it out alive.

Apollo walked up behind me and tried to calm me down, but his touch alone made me want to vomit.

"Get the fuck away from me Apollo. I don't want to be anywhere near you right now. You should have let me stay and help those men. I could have done something."

"My only concern was getting you out of there before something else happened. My men knew what they signed up for the day they joined the family. There will always be losses in the business Eliana, and I need to know that you can handle that."

I glared at Apollo, trying not to throw the vase on the kitchen island at him.

"Don't treat me like a child Apollo. If you had given me two minutes I could have helped. I could have stopped the bleeding or gotten them to someone who could help them!"

"That's two minutes that I didn't have! Every second counts when I'm with you Eliana. Someone is trying to kill me, and they're willing to use you to get to me. What would have happened if something happened to you, or me today?"

I had no answer to his question. I didn't want to imagine something happening to Apollo. He was there too. It could have been him.

"How could I live knowing the reason you died is because I didn't get you out of danger fast enough? It would send me to the fucking grave." Apollo yelled.

Apollo and I stood across from each other in the kitchen. Neither of us moving. Like clockwork, Dane calling Apollo interrupted our fight.

Apollo sighed and walked towards me.

"I have to go and figure out what happened. Until I know more please don't leave the house. Alex will be here just in case someone comes after the house. We'll talk about this when I get back. Do not go back to the warehouse, and don't try to play the hero. Stay here where I know you're safe."

I'm sure under different circumstances I would have been able to come up with a witty remark or reply to him leaving me alone in the house again, but my nerves were shot. I had nothing to say to him, so instead I watched him leave the house to go fix things with Dane.

I needed something to take the edge off, so I grabbed some Vodka from the cellar and went to run a bath. There was nothing for me to do tonight but wait for Apollo to come back with some answers.

After relaxing my muscles in the bath, I returned to Apollo's bedroom to try and get some sleep. I thought I'd never calm down enough for sleep to find me, but somewhere around three I finally drifted off.

When I woke up I wasn't alone in the room. I could see a figure sitting on one of the chairs near the front wall of the bedroom. Apollo sat with a glass in hand as he turned the drink in small circles.

I sat up in bed and went to turn on the lamp.

"Don't." He spoke.

I froze and dropped my hand back down.

"I'm too much of a pussy to tell you this to your face. If you turn on that light I won't be able to do it."

"Tell me what?" I asked, my stomach knotting.

333

"I'm leaving." He whispered.

Throwing off the covers I walked over to where he was sitting. He set his drink down on the table next to his chair and stood up so that his back was facing me.

"A few days ago, my dad told the family he was planning on retiring. He said that after our wedding I would take over the Costa business, and he would step down. Word must have gotten out to my uncle of his plans, and that's what caused the attack on the warehouse. This fight with Giovanni and my uncle has gone on for too long. I thought maybe if I ignored their threats they would grow tired and give up, but it's only adding fuel to the fire."

"So, stay and take care of Giovanni here. You don't have to leave."

"This isn't your problem to fix. I know if I stayed you would want to help, and you would support me with anything I needed. I can't ask you to do that. I won't put you in any more danger."

"You aren't asking. I'm offering. I told you we were in this together now. You don't get to just leave because you're scared." I spoke, anger in my voice.

"Eliana, please don't make this harder than it has to be. Let me go and take care of Giovanni before he comes for anyone else I care for. It won't be just the two of us that get hurt. I need some time and distance to figure out a way to put an end to their attacks."

"You're making a mistake. As soon as you leave you're going to realize what a terrible idea this is. You can't do this on your own." I told him.

Apollo wasn't listening to what I had to say. He had already made up his mind. He was going to leave me, and everything we've built all because he was scared.

334

"I asked Alex and Dane to look after you while I'm gone. If you need anything I want you to call them. They'll know what to do if something happens." He said, turning to face me.

Apollo grabbed his jacket from the back of the chair and walked out of the bedroom. I followed him down to the living room, hoping, praying he'd turn around and change his mind.

"You're a liar and a fucking coward do you know that?" I yelled at him. "That night you surprised me with my office. You told me you couldn't picture running without me by your side. Was that just a lie you told me to get me to trust you? If you leave right now I promise you I won't be here when you get back. I don't care if it takes a week or a year. I'm not going to sit and wait all alone in your fucking house waiting for you to decide to want me again."

"You know I meant what I said that night, but this is different. I have to take care of the war my uncle wants to start, and I can't have you anywhere near it. I'm doing this for you Eliana. Believe me, everything I do is for you."

"Don't fucking leave me Apollo, please."

Apollo came up and wrapped his arms around me. He pulled my head into his chest and held me there as tight as he could. I wanted to wrap my arms around him, but I didn't want him to know that even if he left I would still miss him. I couldn't let him know how much I needed him.

"Goodbye Eliana." He whispered.

Before he let go of me he leaned back, looking one more time into my eyes.

"Eliana, I lo-" He stuttered, shutting his mouth before he made the mistake of finishing that sentence.

Once more he spoke, "I'm going to miss you."

335

As I watched him leave through the front door I silently begged for him to turn around one more time. I thought that maybe, just maybe, if he looked back he wouldn't have the strength to leave. But he never turned around, and he never looked back. I watched him drive away from the house, and this time I didn't know when I would ever get to see him again.

I told Apollo I wouldn't be here when he got back, but we both knew that was a lie.

I hadn't left his office in three days. Alex brought up food, and some more blankets so I could sleep on the couch.

On the fourth day, the doorbell rang. I let Alex answer it and knew if it was someone important he'd come and get me.

The doors to the office opened, and the last person I thought would ever pay me a visit walked in.

"How are you feeling?" Nora asked, setting down her coat and purse.

"I feel great, thanks for asking."

"Raff told me what happened. I came to check in on you. Everyone is worried about you."

I sat on the couch and avoided turning to face her. I knew if I saw the pity in her eyes I would cry. I didn't want her to know I was upset over something like Apollo leaving. This wasn't part of the plan. Nora sat down next to me and moved so that I could rest my head on her shoulder. I tightened the blanket around me and accepted the kind gesture.

336

"You know, if you need to cry and let it out I promise I won't tell anyone. It's okay to be upset, especially with the way he just left. You've always been there for me. When I got married to Mikey, when I had Thomas and Isabella, you've always been by my side when I needed you. Let me be here for you."

Hearing those words was all it took for the tears to start falling. I didn't cry like I thought I would. Instead the tears just sort of fell out and rolled down my cheeks. After I was sure Nora's shoulder was soaked, I sat up.

"I can't believe he left me."

"I know. None of us can. Cristiano and Dad are furious. They haven't been able to find him, and they're worried what he's going to do now that he's officially gone rogue. Raff said some men came looking for him at Dad's office the other day. Everyone is worried about what he might do."

"Is it pathetic that even after everything he's done I still worry about him?" I asked.

"No, that's not pathetic, that's just love El. Your brain tells you one thing, and your heart tells you another. All it means is that you care deeply for him and getting over those feelings takes time."

I nodded my head in agreement as I listened to Nora's advice. I hated to admit it, but she was right. After I had calmed down, and Nora and I talked for a little bit longer she decided to stay for dinner.

I was putting away the dishes when Nora came back from the office to grab her purse.

"I was talking to Dad and we were both hoping you would come home. Just for right now at least, until Apollo comes back. We don't want you here alone in case something happens."

"You're kidding right?"

"Please consider it Eliana. I told you we're all worried about you here without anyone looking out for you."

"I'm not alone, I have Alex and Dane."

"Come on, you know that's not what I mean. You should be with your family right now. Sitting here waiting for him to return isn't healthy."

"I'm not leaving, and if I did I wouldn't go home. I would find somewhere, anywhere else to live before I went back to Mom and Dad's. Tell them thanks for the concern, but I'm okay."

Nora sighed, but she wasn't going to fight me on it anymore. She gave me a hug goodbye and was gone without another word. I promised her I would call if I needed anything to ease her worry and concern.

Nora was gone, and I was alone with my thoughts again. I let my feet take me back to Apollo's office for the rest of the night.

As I laid in Apollo's office I thought about all the times I've slept in here since coming back from Italy. From the very beginning Apollo was always there for me. No words, just us.

I thought that's what was so special about what we had. We didn't have to say anything to know exactly what the other person was thinking. That's what made me feel like such an idiot right now. I had no idea he had plans of eventually leaving to take care of Giovanni. I thought that anything he did to fix his cousin's problem he would talk to me about. I have no idea how long he'd been dealing with this without me. That's what hurt the most. He was ready to leave that night. His mind was made up, and his plan didn't include me. He was able to walk away without even looking back.

I promised myself if I ever got the chance to see Apollo

again I would be the one to walk away. As soon as I was sure he was safe, and not in harm's way I would be the one to say goodbye.

Aside from Nora dropping off a few meals every once in a while, no one else stopped to see me. I'd heard from Nora just how upset Mom was. She was blaming me for Apollo leaving. Nobody but immediate family knew the real reason for Apollo leaving. Everyone was enjoying gossiping about my engagement, and whether or not there would even be a wedding.

I sent Mom's calls to voicemail because I didn't have the energy to get yelled at. She was going to tell me I had to stop hiding in the halls of Apollo's house like a Victorian ghost and start making appearances at events again. She wanted everyone in her circle to believe my life was fine, and everything with me and Apollo was being taken care of.

Each day I became more and more angry with the fact that I wasn't worth a single phone call. I know he was communicating with Dane somehow, but I was someone not worth reaching out to. All I wanted was a text that let me know he was still alive.

By the second week I was moving on from anger and resentment and working towards acceptance. Acceptance that Apollo wasn't coming back, and it was time for me to get on with my life. I cleaned up Apollo's office and started packing up my old room. I had a few boxes of clothes and work papers shipped to Frankie's in case I built up the courage to leave Apollo's house. I thought maybe in a few days I would be ready to finally leave.

My uninterrupted hide out at Apollo's was ruined by a surprise visit from Dad and Raff in the middle of the night on Wednesday.

I woke up to banging on the front door, and Raff yelling for me to wake up. Alex opened the door for them and did his best to keep them in the living room, but they found me in my room after pushing past Alex.

"Wake up Eliana, we're taking you home. It's not safe here anymore. Grab a bag, and let's go." Dad ordered, switching on the lights.

"Hold on, stop. What are you two doing here?" I asked, trying to grab my stuff back from Raff who was already packing for me.

"We're taking you back home. We don't want you here in case Michael and Giovanni try to retaliate and hurt you."

"Retaliate for what? What happened?" I asked.

"Apollo killed his Uncle Michael's number two. He slit his throat and left him on Michael's porch. Everyone is out looking for Apollo right now. There's a reward if they can bring him to Leonardo alive. I'm not going to have you sitting here in his house for anyone to come and hurt you. Everyone knows if they want to get Apollo to come out of hiding they need to get to you. I'm not taking any chances." Dad explained.

"Slow down, Apollo killed one of my Michael's men? How do we know it was him?"

"Apollo went to Leonardo and tried to bring evidence proving it was Giovanni and Michael causing the attacks on the Costa's. Leonardo told Apollo he had no evidence to send Michael to a trial, and that he needed more if he was going to offer his help. It must have pissed off Apollo because the next night Apollo dropped a dead Dante at the house."

"Shit." I whispered. What the fuck has Apollo gotten himself into?

"You have five minutes to get downstairs with a bag. I don't want to be here when Leonardo comes looking for Apollo." Dad said, leaving my room.

I had so many questions, but I knew it wasn't the time to ask them. I grabbed some clothes, and my phone and met Raff downstairs. Dad was already in the car on the phone with someone. It sounded like an angry Cristiano, but I couldn't tell from just the yelling.

Alex and Dane ran out of the house and to the car to try and stop me, but Raff got in their way. I wonder if Dane would let Apollo know I left the next time he talked to him. Would he be upset, or would he understand? What if he comes home and I'm not there anymore?

Dad pulled away as soon as Raff got into his seat.

I sat in the back of the car and turned my phone on. I thought maybe after everything that had happened Apollo would have tried calling or texting, but there was nothing. I fell asleep on the ride back to the house. I woke up when I felt the gravel of the driveway underneath the car. All the lights were on in the house which meant Mom was awake and waiting for us to come back.

I found her pacing the living room dressed in her robe. As soon as she saw me she said a quick prayer and ran to give me a hug.

"Eliana, I thought something had happened to you. After what Apollo did your father said they were going to come after you next. What if something happened to you in that house, and we had no idea because you wouldn't let us help you?" She cried.

"I don't want you leaving this house until Leonardo finds Apollo, and you aren't in danger anymore." Dad said, bringing in my bag.

"What is Leonardo going to do to Apollo if he finds him?" I

asked.

I was afraid of the answer, but I needed to know. Dane warned me that Leonardo didn't like his men stepping out of line. He was already hard to control, and now Leonardo had lost him again.

"I'm not sure. It depends on if Leonardo can look past Apollo killing Dante, and if he still considers him an asset. Leonardo doesn't keep men who break the rules Eliana. Best case scenario Apollo turns himself in and apologizes. Maybe then he'll be forgiven." Dad explained.

Fuck. They're going to kill him.

Seventeen days.

No one had heard or seen from Apollo in seventeen days. I called Dane a few days ago, but even he hadn't heard anything. After killing Dante, he just disappeared.

I pushed around the oatmeal in my bowl. Every morning Mom woke me up at seven sharp to eat breakfast with her. She said it was important to start the day with a healthy meal. She said I needed my energy, and that worrying was causing me to look sickly.

I let the cinnamon and nutmeg oatmeal drip from my spoon as I wondered what Apollo was doing right now.

Maybe he was alive, and he made it to the Andes like he'd always dreamed. Maybe he was hiding in some alpaca farm waiting for the right time to show his cowardly face again.

I left out a laugh, thinking about how I was probably the only one in the world that could track him down, and I didn't even have the strength to start looking.

"What's so funny?" Mom asked.

"Nothing, I'm just thinking about alpacas."

"Hmm." She mumbled.

Since moving back home Mom was convinced I'd lost my mind. I know she talked about me to her priest. Her precious Eliana had gone crazy from a broken heart.

Taking a sip of my orange juice I saw Raff walk into the dining room.

"Any news?" I asked.

"Not about Apollo, but I need you to go get dressed. We have a guest." He said.

"Who?" I asked, getting my hopes up.

"Leonardo." Raff answered. His eyes shifted, and his hands rubbed together. He looked nervous.

"Leonardo is here? In our house?" I asked.

"Yes, and he's waiting to speak with you in Dad's office. Go change quickly. Dad doesn't want you to keep him waiting."

I looked over at Mom who gave me a nod to leave the table. She knew how important a visit from Leonardo was. I'd never met him before. I had only heard stories from Raff and Apollo. He was king of kings. It was Leonardo's word against all other families. He was the glue that held the organization together. If Dad hadn't met him once I would have believed he wasn't even real.

I quickly slipped on a sage green dress and combed through my hair. I pulled it into a low bun as I ran back down the stairs to

Dad's office. Four men were waiting outside of the office, hands resting on the guns hiding under their jackets.

I knocked and waited for Dad to come and open up the door. Inside his office standing near the bookshelf was the tallest man I'd ever met in my life. He towered over everyone in the room. His suit was freshly pressed and looked like it was made from only the finest of fabric. His pepper gray hair was gelled back tight, and he played with the rings on his fingers. One of them being his family's crest. The one that let everyone know he was in charge.

I didn't know what to do or who to look at. Was I even allowed to look him in the eye? Was that against the rules? Do I wait for him to speak to me? Why was he here to see me?

"Eliana, it's a pleasure to finally meet you." Leonardo finally spoke. His accent thick, rolling off of his tongue. I could tell by the way he spoke that he had probably been born and raised in Northern Italy.

"Likewise." I responded, waiting for further instruction.

"I'm sure you know why I'm here. There are a lot of people out looking for Apollo right now and I was hoping as his fiancé you'd be able to help me."

"I'm sorry to disappoint, but I have no idea where he is. I haven't seen him in almost three weeks. He got spooked after the attack on the warehouse and left me to go try and fix things on his own."

"Is that so?" Leonardo asked. "He hasn't tried to reach out to you, not even once?"

"No." I admitted.

"You are aware of the crimes he's committed, yes Eliana?"

"Yes."

"And you know the consequences for committing a crime towards another family without my permission?"

"Yes."

"Then you'll understand my urgency in finding Apollo before he does something else just as reckless as the first crime. Something I won't be able to forgive easily."

"I wish I could help you believe me; I do. He left me and asked me not to get involved, so I left his house, and now I'm stuck here. Living with my parents and trying to pick up the pieces of a failed engagement."

Leonardo sat down at Dad's desk. He looked me up and down for just a minute too long before he spoke again, "How can I be sure you're telling me the truth?"

"What do I have to gain from lying? My fiancé left me six weeks before our wedding with no warning, no invitation to join him, and no plan to return. I know how badly you want to find Apollo and trust me when I say that I want to find him twice as much. If I had any information to give you I would have given it to you already. I have nothing to hide."

Leonardo decided to believe my words and nodded to his men standing behind me. They left the office and waited for him to gather his things.

"If you find him, or he reaches out to you I need to be the first person you tell. Do you understand Miss Mariani?"

"Yes." I replied, one more time.

"I will come for you, and your entire family if you lie to me. A missing Apollo will be the least of your worries. I'm sure I don't have to remind you and your father how important loyalty is. I'll be in touch Eliana." He said.

Raff walked Leonardo back to his car and came back to the

office once he was gone.

I sat on the couch and tried to calm down. That was the first time I've ever looked into a man's eyes and saw nothing but darkness. There was no life or soul behind his eyes. The way he looked at me was enough to make me pass out. For the first time since he'd left I'm glad Apollo hadn't told me where he was because I wouldn't have been able to keep it a secret from Leonardo. He would've broken me before lunch.

I wanted to hide away in my childhood bedroom and pretend like my life wasn't one never ending nightmare, but I had things to do. A week after Leonardo's surprise visit I gave Alex a call.

"Alex, I need you to come pick me up. I have a meeting with Bryan at the office in an hour."

"You want me to take you to the office? Right now?" Alex asked. Skepticism flowing through his questions towards me.

"I'm going crazy locked away in my parents' house. I need an escape for a few hours. I want to start getting back into my normal routine. How long am I expected to wait for Apollo?" I asked him.

"If you're worried about someone coming after me to get to Apollo then just bring Dane along with you. Between the three of us I'm sure we can survive an hour or two." I convinced.

"We'll be there in thirty minutes." He sighed.

I hung up the phone and started thinking of ways I could get Dad to let me leave the house. Maybe I could just tell Raff and leave, and then beg for forgiveness later. Maybe I could convince him it was a way to test the waters and see if there were any real threats. After getting dressed I decided I didn't need their permission. I was only staying at their house and not Apollo's because I knew how worried they were about Giovanni.

I grabbed my bag and walked right through the living room. I shouted for anyone to hear me that I was going to be out for a few hours, and then I waited for Dane down the street. There's no way he was getting through our security without Dad sending him packing.

Dane was not excited to be going on this errand with Alex and me, but he didn't have a choice. He promised Apollo to look out for me while he was gone. He rolled his eyes when I asked Alex to stop for a coffee along the way, but he stopped his complaining when I bought a dozen of the almond croissants I knew he liked.

I worked with Bryan in the basement for a few hours, and then worked in my office trying to get everything figured out, so I could start interviewing a few potential applicants. I thought about waiting until Apollo was back because it felt weird working on plans without him, but he was the one that left. I had real clients and women that I could be helping, and Apollo would be upset to learn he got in the way of me helping them.

Alex and Dane hung out in the backyard for most of the time that I was there. Every few minutes they did a sweep of the neighborhood and house, but for the most part it was quiet.

When I was exhausted, and ready for dinner I let Alex take me home. Both Alex and Dane said nothing about Apollo, so I had no choice, but to bring it up.

"Is he doing okay?" I asked.

"I don't know who you're talking about." Dane lied.

"Apollo, is Apollo doing okay? Has he told you when he's coming back?"

Silence. Neither of them said anything. I doubt Alex knew anything, but Dane definitely did. He was the only one that Apollo trusted.

"Can you at least tell me if he's alive?"

Again, silence. I couldn't even get a read on Alex. Usually his left eye twitches when he's hiding something, but today he gave nothing away. I pulled up to the house, irritated that they were unwilling to give me any clue as to how he was doing. I went to slam the door shut and storm back up to the house when Dane got out of the car and grabbed my hand.

"Let me walk you to the door, it's the least I can do."

I wanted to refuse, but Dad would feel better knowing I wasn't out alone all day.

When we made it to the front doors, just before I walked in he leaned down and whispered in my ear, "He's okay."

That was all he said before turning and walking back to the car and driving off with Alex.

He's okay.

I repeated that to myself for the rest of the night.

He's okay.

Apollo

I watched Eliana as she slept. I had been stalling for as long as I could because I couldn't imagine what it would be like to leave her, but I was running out of time. After the warehouses Dane and I both knew it was now or never.

I wanted to take her with me, but she was safer under the protection of her family. The less she knew the better. I knew they would come for her, and if they thought she was hiding anything they would break her. She must have sensed I was in the room because she woke up. I was sick to my stomach trying to figure out how I was going to tell her I was leaving. She didn't deserve this.

My heart shattered watching her eyes drop when she realized I was leaving and she wasn't coming with me. It was a slap in the face to see someone I loved so much look at me with so much disgust. She had no idea what I'd found out the past week. Giovanni was done trying to take me out and was starting to find ways to hurt Eliana. He knew it was the only way he was going to get a reaction out of me. I needed to create some distance between my cousin, and Eliana.

Walking to the car I dropped my head. I loved her, and planned on telling her, but I was a fucking coward. I couldn't say three little words. I deserved all the suffering I would feel being away from Eliana. I only hoped when this was all over she could still forgive me.

I had been tracking down anyone that Michael or Giovanni had ever paid off to do a job for them. They were dirty, and they were cheap. They hired anybody that was willing to cut corners. It was easy finding the men who worked for them, and all the men said the same thing. They said they reached out to Dante when they needed a job. I got a few confessions out of the men I met and saved some bank statements in case I needed them.

I only wanted to talk to Dante. I didn't plan on him coming at me with a knife. He must have known how close I was to being able to prove Giovanni was the one trying to kill me. It was an accident. I grabbed the knife from Dante and started swinging. He had cut my right arm, and I only had enough strength in my left for a few more hits. I knew I hit something important when the blood started spurting.

I drove him back to Michael's house and hoped he knew his gift was from me. I wanted him to panic. If his guard was down he was eventually going to make a mistake. I hadn't called Dane in a couple of weeks in case they were listening. I was on my way to Italy when he reached out to me again. I needed to find the men that chased down Eliana and me. Once I had something to prove Giovanni planned that hit then I could bring everything back to Leonardo.

My call with Dane was short as I waited for my plane. He barely finished filling me in on all that Leonardo was doing to find me before I interrupted him.

"How is she doing?" I asked.

He sighed before answering, "Not great. We took her back to work this week. It seems to be a good distraction for her."

"Is she still mad?"

"Every day just a little bit more, unfortunately. She asked about you the other day. She was upset I couldn't tell her anything, but she understands. After her meeting with Leonardo she's a little paranoid about anything related to you."

"Wait, she met with Leonardo?" I asked.

"He thought she might know where you were."

"Did he hurt her? If you let anything happen to her I'll drive back right now and fucking murder you."

"He didn't hurt her. He only stopped by her dad's house to meet with her and scare her a little bit. He knew that she had no valuable information. Don't worry about Eliana. She's safe with us. You need to focus on Italy and coming back before Leonardo finds you."

Worry about Eliana was all I ever did. I wouldn't sleep until this was all over, and I was able to hold her again.

"I have to go." I told him. I was going to be late to board my plane.

I hadn't seen Eliana in twenty-four days. Six more, and I will have been gone for a whole month. I wonder if she's given up the hope I'll ever come back.

Unable to think about anything other than Eliana on my flight, I decided to get some sleep. I should have been up, planning what I'd do when I landed, but there was no escaping worrying about Eliana. Walking down the landing tunnel and into the airport I was met with an empty arrival gate. There was no one. No workers, no passengers, and no one waiting to pick anybody up. Before I could drop my bag and run, two men grabbed me from behind.

"I told you I would find you Apollo. You should have known better than to run." I heard Leonardo say from somewhere in the distance.

How did he find me? I made sure there was no trace of me all the way to the airport. He shouldn't have been able to find me. I needed to get out of here. I needed proof Giovanni ordered the hit. I was so close to proving everything and getting rid of Michael and Gio for good.

I tried to throw myself out of the grip the two men had me in, but I wasn't going anywhere. The last thing I saw before everything went black was Leonardo walking closer to me and handing one of his men my backpack.

I woke up tied to a chair in a cement room. There were no windows, and nothing but the chair I was sitting on bolted to the floor. I was a good twelve feet from the small door in front of me. My body was stiff, and my muscles felt like soup. I assumed they'd taken me back to America because whatever they gave me was strong and knocked me out for a while. I was tied down in metal chains that pressed against two fresh cuts on my wrists. I relaxed my hands letting them fall. I couldn't work my way out of the chains without them burning the open wounds. I let out a small laugh. I taught Leonardo that trick the first job he let me work with him. It guarantees your prisoner isn't going to waste their time trying to escape.

After what felt like an hour Leonardo entered the dark room. As soon as the door closed a light turned on.

"You're not an easy person to find." He said.

"Then how did you find me?" I asked.

"Now Apollo, you know better than to ask me that. I can't go revealing all my tricks." He laughed.

"I know what you're thinking Leonardo, and you're all wrong. Dante's death was an accident, and I was on my way to prove Giovanni is the one who put the hit on me. You wouldn't believe me. I had to find a way to make you see."

"All I see is a man who is afraid of taking over for his father, so he's projecting his fears onto his cousin. You've never gotten along with Giovanni, but I hoped you could get past the little pissing game you two have been playing since you were young. Michael and his family have been nothing but loyal to me since the beginning."

"Leonardo, you know me. I wouldn't put myself or my family in danger if I didn't think the threat was absolutely necessary. He crossed the line coming after my family."

"By family do you mean Eliana?" He asked.

My whole body tightened at the mention of her name. I

hated the way her name rolled off of his tongue.

"I would go hunting down my own cousin too if it meant making a beautiful young woman like that happy. You sure tried your best to protect her, but unfortunately it wasn't enough. You left her here alone to fend for herself."

"What happened to Eliana?" I asked, trying to snap my hands free of the chains I was in. I wanted to bash Leonardo's head into the fucking wall.

"That's a story for another day maybe. All I can say now is that she'll be the one to pay for the mistakes you've made."

I thrashed against the chair, kicking my feet, knocking my shoulders back. Everything I did was a failed attempt. No matter how bad I needed to get out and find Eliana I was stuck, and Leonardo knew that was the cruelest of punishments.

No one came back into the room for what I think was three days. When Leonardo did come back he brought a few of his men with him. They all took turns beating me until I was unconscious. When I woke up they started over again. I knew this was only the beginning. Leonardo would grow tired of torturing me, and when he did he was going to give me over to Michael. Not even my father could stop this. I had to repent for my sins.

I had no energy left. I tried to save my energy for the next time someone paid me a visit, and I needed to stay awake. I let my head drop and I tried to control my breathing.

Right on schedule the door opened, and for a second I thought I must be going crazy. A familiar scent filled the room. Hints of lilac and honey, the perfume Eliana used to wear. The one that had me hooked on her from the first night we danced.

With what little energy I had left I let out a laugh. How cruel my mind to play tricks on me when I was trapped in this room unable to find El.

A pair of footsteps that I didn't recognize started walking towards me.

Finally, the person spoke, "It's impolite to ignore a woman when she walks into a room Apollo. I thought you had better manners than that."

Eliana.

Chapter Eighteen

Eliana

It was Sunday dinner. My first one in a long time. All of us sat around the table, not knowing what to say to make the situation better. Frankie made small talk with Mikey, and Nora spoke every few minutes when telling the kids to keep their mouths closed while they ate.

Every time I took a sip of my wine Mom looked up from her plate and gave me a sad smile. It was the first family dinner I wasn't getting yelled at, and I hated it. I didn't want them treating me any differently just because of what was happening. Apollo had been gone a month. The past week he hadn't even been picking up Dane's call. Something was wrong, and I couldn't help him.

We were interrupted by one of Dad's men running into the dining room.

"They found him. Leonardo found him in Italy and brought

him back. He's at Leonardo's house right now." He told us.

My eyes shot to Dad's. He knew exactly what I planned on doing.

"Eliana, no!"

"Dad, you can't keep me from going to see him. I don't care if it's Leonardo's house, I need to see that he's alive." I argued.

"It's too dangerous. Apollo has a debt to repay. I don't want you anywhere near Leonardo until he's settled it."

I looked at Raff, and then back at Dad. My odds of getting past the front gates if I could get to my car before he had time to alert his men were pretty high. Dropping my napkin, I ran to the garage. I had nothing on my feet, and clothes that weren't meant for winter, but I didn't care. I needed to get out now or Dad was never letting me leave this house again.

I stole Dad's keys to his car and raced down the driveway. It didn't matter if they started to close the gate on me. I was getting out. I pushed down on the gas and I didn't relax until I was half a mile down the street. I knew I couldn't go to Leonardo's like this, and they weren't going to just let me walk in. I needed Dane.

I drove to Apollo's house and ran inside.

"Dane!" I yelled.

He came running from the basement gun in hand.

"Eliana?"

"I know Leonardo has Apollo. I need you to take me to see him."

"I can't do that Eliana. Cristiano told all of us we were not allowed at the house until Leonardo gives us permission."

"I don't care what Cristiano says, he already hates me. Take me to Leonardo's or I'll go by myself. If you don't come with me

I'll have to explain to Apollo you let me go to Leonardo's unprotected."

Dane's jaw ticked. He knew I was crazy enough to try and get into Leonardo's with or without his help.

"Go change while I get the car ready, and call Alex. I'm not going alone."

I ran to my room and found sweats and a jacket that I hadn't packed yet. I found an old pair of sneakers in the back of my closet, and then I ran back down to find Dane. The drive to Leonardo's was long and dark. There were no lights on the curved road, and if you didn't know exactly where to go you'd easily get lost. I knew now I wouldn't have made it to Leonardo's without Dane's help.

We were stopped by two SUV's full of men with guns before we even made it to the gate. They pulled the three of us out of our car and led us to their cars. They took us into the estate and drove us around the main house. Attached to the back of the house was a smaller, older building. It looked like an office, or dormitory for Leonardo's men.

We were pulled into the building by the men that grabbed us from the car. They threw us into the center of what I'm assuming was Leonardo's office and then left.

A few minutes later Leonardo appeared from a door behind his desk.

"I knew it was only a matter of time before I had visitors. I thought I told Cristiano no one was allowed to see Apollo until I was finished with him."

I looked over at Dane and Alex and saw their heads lowered.

Standing up I spoke, "Cristiano doesn't know I'm here. I forced Dane to bring me here. I take full responsibility for showing up unannounced like this. My apologies for interrupting your evening, but I just need to see that Apollo is alive, and then I'll leave."

"This is a very foolish thing you've done coming down here Eliana. Why should I let you see Apollo? I don't owe you any favors, and I know your father would be disappointed to see you here."

There was one thing I knew about Leonardo that might work as leverage, but I was going to look like an idiot if I was wrong. I was hoping to confirm my suspicions before I told anyone about it, but this my only chance at getting to see Apollo one last time.

"Let me see Apollo or I'll tell all the families that you use their whores to keep tabs on them."

Dane snapped his head up. Shock on his face. He looked at me like I'd gone crazy.

Leonardo laughed, and he brought his hands to his chest like I'd just told him the funniest joke he'd ever heard.

"And how did you find that out?" He asked.

"I didn't. Well, not until right now. I only had a feeling the person paying off all those girls was you. I couldn't figure out why at first, but I think I know now."

"And what might that reason be?"

"Because you run your business on fear. My contact at the District Attorney's office told me there weren't any pending investigations, local or federal. When I asked around the clubs and spoke to the women you paid off they all said the same thing. They said the person who paid them off didn't really seem to care about the information. All they wanted them to do was drop a few names, and act like they were sharing secrets."

"Go on."

"It's the fastest way for you to find anyone who has something to hide. A guilty family member will try to take care of the problem before it gets back to you, but someone like Apollo who has nothing to hide will reach out to you as soon as they think there's a threat to the family. Now you know which families have secrets they want to be kept a secret even from you."

"I'm impressed, Eliana. I knew you'd figure it out. I almost called off my girls, but I wanted to see if you'd ever connect the pieces. Nikolas, take her to the basement, and bring Dane too. Let them see that the boy is still alive."

Dane and I were taken to the basement and left alone in a room full of TV's. One of the TV's on the far wall turned on and a bloody Apollo appeared on the screen. Leonardo met us in the room.

"See, he's still breathing like I promised. I can't deliver him to Michael dead otherwise I'd have a mutiny on my hands."

"Apollo." I whispered.

I touched the screen where he sat. I don't know if I felt better or worse seeing him half dead tied to a chair. This wouldn't have happened if he'd let me help.

"Promise me you won't kill him. You'll continue to let him work for you after Michael's finished with him."

Leonardo smiled at the idea. "I am loving this side of you Eliana. I wonder what Apollo would say if he heard you making deals with someone like me. I'm sure he'd be very upset."

"I don't care if he's upset I'm making a deal with you. I want him to live."

"Then he'll live."

I turned to Leonardo, "Thank you, that's all I needed to see."

"That's it? You don't want to go inside? He's been dying to see you." He teased.

"No, thank you. Dane, I'd like to go home now."

"Eliana..."

"Dane, take me home."

Leonardo led us to the front where our car was now parked. Alex leaned up against it talking to a few of Leonardo's men.

"Come back anytime Eliana. A mind as brilliant as yours is always welcome here." Leonardo offered.

I climbed into the car, and watched Dane drive us back to Apollo's house.

He looked over at me every few minutes to see if I'd changed my mind, but I wasn't going to. All that mattered was that for now he was alive.

Dane parked the car next to mine and waited for me to get out.

"You're really going to leave right now?" Alex asked.

"He left me. He was the one that walked away from all of this. I begged him to stay. He knew that if he left I wouldn't be here when he got back." I explained, tears threatening to fall.

"He didn't leave you Eliana, he was only trying to protect you!" Dane said.

I turned around, letting him continue.

"Apollo had been tracking Giovanni since you two got back from Italy. I'd been trying to convince him to go after him, but he told me he couldn't leave you. He said after everything you'd gone through during your trip he couldn't abandon you. After whatever happened between you two in Italy he put all of his Giovanni plans on hold. It wasn't until Giovanni started threatening you did Apollo decide to put an end to Giovanni and Michael. He knew it was only a matter of time before you got hurt again."

I bit my tongue as I listened to what Dane had to say. I couldn't go back.

"I was the one who told Apollo you couldn't be a part of the plan. I knew if Leonardo went looking for Apollo you'd be the first person he went to for information. Apollo agreed it was a risk letting you be a part of everything. I promise you Eliana he didn't want to leave. I told him he was running out of time, and if he didn't leave he was going to lose you. Don't be mad at Apollo, be mad at me."

"Is this true?" I asked Alex. He only nodded his head.

"The only thing that kept him going this past month was getting to come back to you Eliana. He asked about you every time I called. Sometimes I think he called with fake information just so he had an excuse to ask about you. I know he's sitting in that room right now, and instead of worrying about himself he's worrying about you."

I stood at my car holding the door handle. I had to get out of here.

"Before you go I have something to give you. Alex, don't let her leave until I get back."

Dane ran into the house and left Alex to guard me. Dane came back a few minutes later carrying a box.

"Before Apollo left he told me to hold on to this, and to give it to you if you tried to leave. He said you would know what it meant when you saw it. He always planned on coming back to you Eliana. He said if something went wrong and he couldn't give you this in person I had to make sure you got it. He told me if you still wanted to leave after seeing what's in the box then he would let you go."

I hesitated taking the box from Dane. He held it out further, waiting for me to grab it. Putting my keys in my pocket I took the box from Dane. I opened the box slowly and let the tears I was holding back fall.

Inside the box, pinned against a velvet backing were a pair of emerald earrings. A simple square cut of the finest emeralds I'd ever seen. They were rich in color and reflected off the moonlight.

"Damn it."

"What's wrong?"

The tears fell faster, and my cries turned into sobs. I held up the box so that they could see the earrings, "Emeralds... I have to forgive him."

Alex and Dane looked at each other, confused and missing the significance of the earrings. They didn't know that it was the only thing in the world that I couldn't walk away from. I had to go back.

"Dane, I need your phone. Now, please!"

Dane searched in his pockets for his phone, unlocking it before handing it to me. I scrolled through his contacts until I found the only person who could help Apollo.

It rang three times before he finally picked up, "Rio, it's Eliana. How fast can you get to New York?"

Apollo

I thought maybe I'd been hit too hard and I was seeing things.

"Eliana... what are you doing here?" I asked.

"I came to take you home Apollo."

"How?" I asked, still not completely convinced this wasn't a dream.

"I'll explain everything as soon as I can, but first we need to get you out of this room." She said.

A few of Leonardo's men came to unlock the chains on my feet and hands. Dane followed behind Leonardo's men and helped me to my feet. I leaned on Eliana as she helped me out of the room. Waiting for me in the hallway was Leonardo and Rio. Rio helped the three of us get to the car.

Alex was ready to drive us far away from Leonardo's estate. I was exhausted from the walk to the car, and I struggled to keep my eyes open. I had to lean my head against the back of the seat to keep myself from throwing up. The turns of the road must have caused me to pass out because I woke up in my own bed. When I opened my eyes again I was blinded by the lights on my ceilings and the cold feeling that I was alone and Eliana wasn't beside me anymore.

I tried to move, but the bandages on my waist limited the movement of my upper body.

"You're going to pop your stitches if you keep trying to escape like that." Eliana spoke.

I looked around the room trying to find where her voice was coming from. I found her leaning against the bathroom door frame, holding a few towels.

"Eliana."

"Apollo." She sighed, walking over to my side of the bed. She folded one of the towels in half and placed it under my back relieving the pressure of my broken ribs. With the other towel, she placed it underneath my left arm. I could see two cuts still open and bleeding. I knew what came next. I'm sure Eliana was hoping I was still passed out. These cuts needed to be cleaned and stitched back up before they got infected.

"Do you need something for the pain? A towel to bite down on?" She asked.

"No, just get it over with. I'll be fine."

Eliana looked at me unsure if she could continue, but I squeezed her hand to let her know it was okay. She took the disinfectant and irrigated one of my cuts as best she could. The burning eventually died down, and all I could feel was the throbbing of my sore muscles.

Carefully, but quickly she stitched up the wound making sure every stitch was secured before moving on to the next one. I laid my head back down onto the pillow unable to watch her work.

When she finished she wrapped my arm in bandages and removed the bloody towel from the bed. The whole time she cleaned up the mess of blood and bandages she refused to look at me.

I tried grabbing her arm, but she only pulled away.

"Eliana, how did you convince Leonardo to let me go?"

"I asked Rio for help. I called him a few days ago and asked him to verify all the attacks on the two of us. He came to meet with Leonardo and explained everything that happened in Italy. He also explained that he had been secretly tracking Giovanni's

364

movements the past few years, and it all added up to everything you tried to bring to Leonardo. Leonardo agreed to let you go, and to look into Michael's financials and any trades he has made under the table since your first accident." She explained.

"Why were you there tonight? Why did you come to get me?"

"I've been asking myself that question for the past few days. Why did I come and save you when you didn't deserve it?"

Making sure to avoid meeting my eyes, Eliana finished cleaning everything up and then started to walk away. She couldn't leave yet. I had so many questions. I should have been sent to Michael days ago. I shouldn't be here right now, and that means there's something she isn't telling me. I needed answers, but now was not the time to ask about them. I should just be happy I'm lying here with Eliana again. Nothing else besides that mattered.

"You aren't staying?"

"No..."

"Eliana-"

"Don't Eliana me." She snapped.

I tightened my jaw holding in a harsh breath, finally finding the strength to sit up on my elbows. Resting my back onto the headboard I reached out for her hand. She tried to pull away, but I wasn't planning on letting go anytime soon. I had only just gotten her back.

"What you did was fucking reckless." She told me.

"I know."

"And it almost got you killed." She added.

"I know."

"Then what were you thinking when you left?"

"I wasn't thinking. After the attack on the warehouse when I almost lost you all I saw was red. I should have taken care of Giovanni a long time ago, but I was stalling. I knew dealing with him meant having to leave you."

"You should have let me help you."

"I couldn't risk anything happening to you again because of me. You've already been hurt too many times because of me and my crazy fucking family. I promised myself after Italy nothing would ever happen to you again. I would rather you hate me forever than get hurt because of me. I'm sorry it looked like I was running away, but I will not apologize for leaving and trying to protect you. I am nothing without you Eliana. The thought of something happening to you makes me sick to my stomach."

I paused, giving Eliana a chance to process everything. She forgave me enough to come and save me, but maybe I was too late to save us.

"I should go. You need your rest." Eliana whispered.

"That's it? That's all you have to say to me? Do something, Eliana, anything! Yell at me, scream and tell me what an idiot I was, but don't leave. Please, don't leave right now."

Before Eliana had a chance to say anything, Dane walked into my room. Eliana took this opportunity to pull her hands away from me and walk to the door.

"I'll be back in a few hours with more medicine, and to check on your stitches. Try not to move too much in the meantime."

With that Eliana was gone. I was left alone in the room with Dane. While walking around the room I could tell Dane was just as mad at me as Eliana was. He dropped a few boxes down on my dresser harder than was necessary, and his sighs as he walked around my bedroom were nothing short of dramatic.

"Eliana, and now you? What did I do to piss you off?"

"You're a dumbass." He spoke. "You don't deserve to be here. I still can't believe it. You might just be the luckiest man alive."

"Please explain to me then how I am still alive. Because no one will give me any fucking answers. All I remember was Eliana finding me in Leonardo's basement and waking up to her angry, and not speaking to me."

"She saved you. That's what happened. She was ready to walk away from you forever in that basement, but as soon as I showed her those earrings she was on the phone with Rio in a heartbeat. She had him flying out here to save you faster than Alex and I could figure out her plan."

"You gave her the earrings?" I interrupted. "She was going to leave me?"

"After she made a deal with Leonardo to let you live, she was going to go back to her parents' house and leave. I thought I'd never see her again, so I grabbed that box you asked me to keep safe and told her everything about you not wanting to leave. She didn't sleep for three days once Rio got into town. She had all of his men tracking Giovanni and making a case to Leonardo that proved he hired men to attack you in Italy. Leonardo was impressed with Eliana the first night they met. I can promise you Leonardo will be working with her a lot more after everything that's happened."

"Since when did the two of them get so close? I thought I asked you to keep her away from him."

"She figured out Leonardo was behind the girl's trying to sell information. Leonardo was going to kill you after he gave you to

Michael. Eliana convinced him not to. You would have worked for Leonardo for the rest of your life, until he decided it was time for you to retire."

"Leonardo really believed everything Rio told him, and that's it? I'm free?"

"No, Eliana gave up collateral to take you home while Leonardo makes a decision about Giovanni. He gave you a week. Rio is staying at his house until they figure everything out."

"What did she give Leonardo that convinced him to let me go home?"

"No one knows. They spoke alone, and then next thing I know I'm dragging your ass out of the basement."

"Fuck." I sighed. "I need to see her."

"No, you don't. You need your rest. Leonardo expects you back at his house in four days. You'll be lucky if you're walking by then." Dane ordered.

"What if she tries to leave again?" I asked.

"If she was going to leave she would have left by now." He spoke honestly.

He was right. If she was going to leave me I'd still be chained to a chair in Leonardo's basement.

Dane looked at me like he had something to say but wasn't brave enough to speak the words. Deciding to speak he turned to me.

"Not that it's any of my business but give her some space. You asked the impossible of her these past few weeks, and it's going to take some time for her trust in you to come back. You have no idea how hard it was for her all this time. You left, and she was stuck picking up the pieces. She gave up thinking you'd ever come back. After everything you've been through, no matter

368

your reason, you left. If you ever hurt her like this again Apollo I won't do anything to stop her when she begs to leave. I barely had the strength to ask her to stay this time."

Dane turned on his feet and left my room as quickly as he'd entered. I was alone again, left to figure out what to do now. I killed Dante, I pissed off Leonardo, and worst of all I had hurt Eliana. I was stuck in my room unable to go after Eliana and beg for her forgiveness, and my fate with Leonardo was up in the air.

As I slipped away and let sleep take me, I heard my door open one more time, and quiet footsteps walk towards my bed. I begged my eyes to open up in hopes it was Eliana, but my body was betraying me. I was out before I had the chance to see for myself who had sat down next to me.

Eliana

He was home. Apollo was home.

That's all that mattered. At the very least he wasn't rotting in Leonardo's basement anymore. Maybe now I will be able to get some sleep. I would worry about the possibility that Leonardo was playing the both of us, but I was too exhausted to care.

Bringing Apollo home proved one thing. No matter how mad I was at him still, I wanted to forgive him. Every time I stepped into the same room as him I forgot all about the things I promised to do to him if he ever had the nerve to come home to me.

I promised myself I would be the one to leave him this time, and that I wouldn't let him make a fool of me like my family had always done before but seeing him again for the first time in a month was overwhelming. There was something holding me back from really leaving. I kept the emerald earrings in his office because it didn't feel right to wear them. They felt heavy, like they knew that to wear them meant I had forgiven him. I didn't want to forgive him, but Nora was right.

I loved Apollo, more than anything.

I waited in the hallway to see how long Dane would hang out in Apollo's room. I didn't want him to know I planned on spending another night with him to make sure he pulled through. I needed him to be asleep before I went back. When Apollo finally stopped moving around, and everything in his room went quiet I went back to check on him.

He slept with his covers thrown off, probably giving relief to the cuts and bruises on his abdomen that couldn't handle any type of pressure right now. The medicine I gave him would knock him out until the next morning. The next two days were going to be the worst. His body is going to give all of its energy to fighting off infections and keeping his organs from shutting down. There's no way to know for sure how much internal bleeding he has right now, and Dane doesn't trust anyone to come do a checkup.

This feeling in my stomach, the nausea I get staring down at a broken Apollo, is the reason I can't be in the same room with him yet. I want nothing more than to crawl into bed next to him and hold him as tight as I can. I'm pathetic, he left me, and I still long to be close to him.

The sun falling through the open window woke me up. I found myself in the chair holding Apollo's hand. Sometime in the night he started to have a night terror, and his body tensing isn't good for his muscles, so I did all I could to calm him down. I held his hand and waited for his body to calm and relax.

I let go and felt the cold, bitter morning air rush the hand that was holding Apollo. I wanted to stay next to him all day, but I didn't want him to see me in his room when he woke up. I slowly left his room and went back to mine. There wasn't a chance I would be able to go back to bed without Apollo, so I decided to get some work done. I had been balancing the firm and working with Rio this week and it was killing me. I needed a break, but I was behind and didn't have time to stop on-boarding with the firm. I needed people I could give some cases to, to relieve my workload.

A few hours of work later and my bedroom door was opened. Dane came in with some medicine and clothes that looked like Apollo's.

"He's awake and asking for you."

I debated whether or not to go see him right now. I decided to lie to myself and tell that disapproving voice in my head I was only going to his room to check on his injuries, and for no other reason.

Stopping at Apollo's door I paused, building the courage to walk in. As soon as I did Apollo sat up and put down the glass of water Dane had handed him.

"You're back." He spoke, sounding relieved.

"I came to see how you were feeling."

"I'm feeling good." He lied, "I think I'll be out of this bed and walking around by dinner."

Jesus, let's hope not. My only advantage is that he's stuck in a bed right now. Once he's walking he'll be able to find me anywhere in the house.

Pulling me from my thoughts, Apollo spoke. "Dane, would you give us a minute please."

Dane looked to me for confirmation that he should leave. These past few weeks had been hard for the both of us, but the relationship we had built with each other is something I will always be grateful for. I appreciated his silent support these past few days.

I gave him a nod, letting him know I would be okay.

Dane left, and I walked closer to inspect Apollo's stitches.

"How's your back doing?" I asked.

"Cut the bullshit Eliana. What am I doing here?"

"I don't know what you mean?"

"Why am I here? In my house, and not at Leonardo's. Dane told me everything. He says you have been making deals with Leonardo in exchange for favors for me. I need to know what you did."

"That's none of your business." I spoke flatly.

"Oh, come on, Eliana! I can't do this. I get it, you're mad, but I still deserve to know what is going on with you and Leonardo. Whatever deals you made with him affect the both of us. It's not safe for you to be working with him. You know how risky working with Leonardo is, and now you're wrapped up in the middle of this."

"And whose fault is that?" I shouted.

Apollo went quiet.

"Why was I at Leonardo's house to begin with? The only reason I ever had contact with him in the first place is because of you! He showed up at my house, asking questions about you and trying to intimidate me into giving you up. I was followed for weeks by his men everywhere I went. You knew leaving meant that I would be put on Leonardo's radar. The only person you're allowed to be mad at right now is you. I wouldn't be dealing with all of this shit with Leonardo and Rio if you hadn't left me."

Apollo shifted around before speaking again, trying to calm down.

"Look, Eliana, I'm sorry. You're right. I left you, and in return you had to deal with everything on your own, but I'm back now, and I can help you with whatever is going on with you. I promise I'm not going anywhere."

Lies, all he ever does is lie.

Tears were starting to form as I spoke again.

"You already promised that Apollo..."

"Promised what?"

"That you wouldn't leave me. You said you would never run without me by your side and I believed you. I thought we were in this together, and I would never have to be alone again. I still can't get over how easy it was for you to just walk away and leave me. After everything we've been through, you walked away and you didn't look back."

"Eliana, please..."

"No! You don't get to apologize and feel better for what you did to me, to our family! I trusted you, even after everyone told me not to! I let you break down my walls, and in return you ruined me. Leaving like you did and lying to me all this time hurt me more than any of the broken promises my dad used to tell me. At least when I was working with him I knew he was lying to me, and I could see the lies behind his words, but you... I believed you when you said you would always be by my side. I trusted you, and before we could even say our vows you broke the only promise I've ever believed in."

Standing as far away from him as I could I took a few deep breaths in before speaking one more time.

"You lost your right to have any say in my life, or the deals I made with Leonardo the day you left. You stopped being my partner that night you went looking for Gio. I saved you because I owed you that much, but that's all I can give. If you still care for me you will leave me alone, and let our arrangement continue to be a professional one."

Even though he shouldn't have, Apollo climbed out of the bed and tried to walk towards me.

"Don't."

"El..."

I took a step back, creating some distance between the two of us.

Apollo stopped at the end of the bed, barely stable and close to folding in pain.

"Is that really what you want?" He asked, standing.

"Yes."

For a minute, Apollo processed everything I'd just said.

"You're lying. I know you're mad, but that isn't what you want. I know you, Eliana. I know how hard it would be to walk away from this. I promise I'll give you your space but know that I'll be here waiting for as long as it takes. I would wait years just to be able to hold you one more time. However long you need to heal, I'll wait. I can't tell you how sorry I am, but you know I did what I did to protect you, and us. I couldn't see my own family hurt you the way they've been hurting me for years. I wouldn't have been able to live with myself if something happened to you."

Apollo's words had caused the tears to fall. I had to get out of there, away from him.

Leaving his room, I stopped in the hallway and let the stress of the past few days out. I let every emotion I'd felt since Apollo leaving pour out of me. As I made my way back to my room I thought that my tears would create just enough exhaustion that I would be able to sleep tonight. If I was lucky I would get a few hours of sleep before I had to be at work.

I tried to sleep, and not think about Apollo's new promise to me. He said he would wait, but I didn't trust him. He shouldn't have left in the first place, but there was no going back and changing the past. I still wanted Apollo, but until I knew exactly how he felt I needed to protect myself from him.

This was torture, Apollo is torture. Everywhere I escape to, I find him there. Every step I take he's two steps behind like a shadow. He promised space, but he's not giving very much. Every few hours he sends someone to invite me to lunch or dinner, and every time I have to decline.

He's trying to act like everything has gone back to normal. I need to get out of this house. I knew Apollo would say no to that, but I could probably get Dane on board. I found him walking back into the house carrying a cup of coffee. It was comical seeing someone like Dane holding one of those compostable coffee cups with flowers on the side. In the short while I'd known Dane I never knew him to be a coffee drinker.

Knowing now wasn't the time to interrogate him for information, I ignored the cup in his hand.

"Hey Dane, how's your day going?" I asked.

"No."

"You don't even know what I was going to ask." I complained.

"You can't leave the house. We're being watched by Leonardo. It's not safe to leave right now." He explained.

"I have to. I'm going crazy Dane."

"You're already crazy. A few more days in this house won't kill you. I'm sorry, but no."

"So, I'm not allowed to leave the house, but you're allowed to leave every time you get a craving for an Americano?"

"That's different."

"Sure." I said, rolling my eyes.

"If you're not going to let me leave, what am I supposed to do? Apollo is everywhere I look. Every time I turn a corner his sad little puppy eyes are looking at me as he limps away into the dark. It's depressing."

"You won't have to worry about him bothering you anymore. He's feeling well enough to get back to work. He'll be so overwhelmed with everything he's missed he won't have time to sulk." Dane explained.

"Good, I need a break. I'm running out of ways to avoid him."

"Why don't you head down to the gym and do some yoga or meditation? My sister says it's good for the soul." Dane said.

"You have a sister?"

"I have four."

"Ah."

"What?"

"Nothing, I've just spent months trying to figure you out, and there was always something missing, but now everything is starting to make sense."

"What's that supposed to mean?" Dane asked defensively.

"Nothing really. There's just a few more pieces to the Dane puzzle solved." I laughed.

Dane set down his coffee and furrowed his brow. Saving me from having this conversation Apollo walked into the basement. It was the first time in two days I was relieved to see him. He could save me from Dane.

"Apollo, did you know Dane has four sisters?" I asked.

"Yeah that's why he has all those control issues." Apollo teased.

I let out a quiet laugh, hiding my smile as Dane directed his irritation to Apollo.

"I prefer the two of you when you aren't talking to each other." Dane said, grabbing his things and leaving.

Apollo turned to me and smiled.

"You should have told me sooner about his sisters. That would have changed the way I tried to get on his good side. I thought he was a heartless man, not a tortured brother of four." I complained.

"I'm sorry. He doesn't like talking about them. I might be the only one other than you that knows about them. I'm surprised he told you, that must mean he's starting to trust you."

"Well, that's one good thing to come out of this situation then." I sighed.

"Yeah, I guess." Apollo replied.

Apollo waited to see if I would say anything else, or if I

would run away again. I looked at the door and made an excuse to leave.

"I have to go work out, maybe do some yoga." I said.

"Oh, yeah- of course."

"So, I'll just go then." I said, walking away.

"Will I see you for dinner tonight?" Apollo asked.

"I can't." I said, as I walked away, "I just... can't."

"Of course. No rush, I understand. Maybe another time." He spoke, hurt in his voice.

Leaving Apollo, I went to go find something to do before I truly lost it.

Dane was right, yoga did help a little. I didn't *heal my soul*, but it did give me a distraction for a few hours. Only problem is I'm hungry, and afraid of running into Apollo if I go to grab some food. I thought about waiting, but my stomach grumbling told me I needed food now.

I had almost made it to the kitchen without being seen when a voice carrying over from the dining hall stopped me. Juliette, she was here in the house. Probably seeing Apollo for the first time since he'd been back. She must have heard me walking because she ran into the hallway and ran towards me.

Grabbing me into one of her famous Juliette hugs she spun me around the hallway. I was sore from yoga and had no strength to keep her from guiding me to the dining room.

"I'm so glad you decided to join us. Apollo said I wasn't allowed to bother you, but I've been dying to see you!" She smiled as she prepared a plate for me at the table across from Apollo.

"Juliette, Eliana has other things to do, she might not want to sit with us for dinner."

Juliette dropped her smile and looked at me like I had killed her pet hamster. As much as I wanted to leave and be nowhere near Apollo I couldn't say no to Juliette.

"Actually, I finished my work out and realized how hungry I was, so I thought I'd pop in for some food really quick if that's alright." I smiled.

"Then sit, because I have so much to fill you two in on!" She exclaimed.

For the next hour Juliette didn't let Apollo or I get a single word in. Apparently, she worked things out with Emily, she was acing all of her classes, and she had even started to consider some new potential majors. Her new thing was botany. I'm sure her dad was going to love that and blame me for inspiring another unrealistic career. Hopefully her love of plants would fade and she would be back on track to picking a more realistic passion.

I had finished my food a long time ago, and wanted to leave, but there was no escape. Until Juliette had finished all her stories Apollo and I were stuck. Every time I looked over at Apollo he was doing his best to pretend he wasn't looking at me. He would shift in his seat, take a sip of his drink, or even throw a laugh back at Juliette to make her believe he was listening to what she was saying.

For a few minutes, here and there I forgot about everything that was going on, and tried to focus on just dinner. Eventually I would have to get used to this and be willing to spend more time with Apollo. If he continued to give me my space like he had tonight I think we would be okay.

Dessert had been brought out, and Juliette was exhausted from talking the whole time, even Apollo had started to doze off.

I could tell he was still in pain sitting at the table for this long of a time, but he endured the pain to spend just a few more minutes in Juliette's company. The way he loved her and supported her was something I would always be jealous of. At the end of the day, no matter what he had done, he was a good brother and a good son. Apollo was good, and it hurt to be reminded of that.

"Alright Jules, I have to go back to work. I'm sure Dane is waiting for me in my office." Apollo said.

"You're still working? Don't you think you should take a break? We go back to Leonardo's in a few days. You're barely walking." I said.

"I'm okay. I need to get back into my routine. My men struggled while I was away, and some things fell apart. I can't take any more time off."

"Apollo..." I sighed.

"I'm fine, Eliana, I promise." Apollo gave me a tired smile that I saw right through, but I didn't push him any further.

Juliette stood up to say goodbye to Apollo. All night long we hadn't talked about anything that had happened over the past month, but we all knew what was happening in a few days. Juliette gave her brother one more hug just in case it was the last time she saw him. Holding back her tears, she looked at me.

"I'll help you get cleaned up and then I'll head out." Juliette said, grabbing a few plates.

When I met her in the kitchen she was leaning against the counter and her head was dropped. I gave her a few minutes to process the evening. Looking up at me she waited for me to open my arms into a hug.

In a voice, so unrecognizable I almost didn't hear it, she spoke.

"Thank you. Thank you for saving him."

Holding her tighter I let my own tears fall.

"I know he doesn't deserve it after what he did to you, but I don't know what I would have done if I didn't get to say goodbye to him. He's all I've ever had." She cried.

"You're welcome." I whispered.

Letting go of me Juliette wiped away her tears and found her purse.

"I know what's happening on Friday. I heard Dad talking about it. I know how hard it was to come back for him. You did the right thing Eliana, I promise."

"How do you know that?"

"Because his whole life Apollo has always been alone. He's always put his family first before his own needs. Leaving you was wrong, but I think in some fucked up way he thought he was doing the right thing for you, his new family. He's a dumbass who thinks he's invincible, but in a moment of desperation he left to try and fix things the only way he knew how. He would do anything for you, I can still see the love he has for you every time he looks over to watch you smile."

"If he loved me he wouldn't have left." I said back to her.

"Eliana, he left *because* he loves you."

Taking that as her cue to leave, Juliette walked out of our house and drove back to her father's.

Her words echoed through my head as I walked back to my room. *He left because he loves you.*

I was too afraid to admit that Juliette was right, and that's why I was so angry. Walking to my room I saw that Apollo's office was empty. The lights were off and I didn't hear him working. Maybe the office would be a good place to try and get some sleep. It was the only place since he left that I was able to rest.

I walked in and looked around his office. Papers were left on the table, and his desk was a mess, but like before there was a blanket and a pillow waiting on the couch, just in case. I was about to lay down when I heard the door slide open. In walked a confused Apollo.

"Shit, sorry I didn't know you were in here."

I stumbled around the couch and tried to leave as fast as I could, "It's fine. I thought you were out with Dane. I just came to-"

"Sleep." He answered for me.

"Yeah."

Apollo walked to his desk keeping as much distance as he could from me. He sat down at his desk and watched to see what I would do next.

I started to leave his office, but he stopped me.

"Eliana, stay."

Apollo

Eliana stopped moving towards the door. I could see her contemplating staying. I know she wanted to, needed to. She hadn't slept a full night since I've been home. I hear her

382

wandering when she thinks I'm asleep. She's turned into a ghost, trapped in a house she can't escape. She needs this.

Finally, she turned around and walked to the couch. She didn't look up at me as she unfolded her blanket, but I could see a small smile on her face. Her trust in me was growing. She felt more relaxed at dinner, and now she's decided to spend the night in my office. She's finally done running away. All I had to do was show her how much I still loved her. I don't care how long it takes. I won't stop until she knows how worthy of love she is.

After Eliana laid down on the couch and closed her eyes I went to turn the lights off and hoped the light from my computer wouldn't keep her awake. In only a few minutes I could hear soft whispers coming from Eliana which let me know she had fallen asleep. Looking up every few minutes to make sure she was okay I sat and worked on some schedules for Dane.

Around eleven the front door slammed, and I could hear Dane trying to quiet an unwanted guest. Not wanting to wake Eliana I quickly left my office and closed the door. When I got down to the living room Dane was trying to hold back an angry Raff from running up the stairs.

"What the fuck is going on?" I asked.

"You son of a bitch!" Raff shouted at me, escaping Dane's hold and running towards me.

Before I had time to process what was happening Raff punched me in the face and was grabbing my shoulders back to hit me again. Dane barely caught his arm before he hit me again, surely knocking me out.

"What are you doing here Raff?" I asked again, trying to stay calm.

"It's all your fault!" He yelled.

"What's all my fault?" I asked.

"You fed her your pathetic lies, and convinced her you were better than us, and that's all it took for her to betray her own fucking family. I bet the whole thing was your idea."

"What are you talking about? I haven't told Eliana to do anything, let alone betray you or Marco."

"Bullshit. There's no way Eliana would give up her shares of the family on her own. She fought her whole life to keep them just to piss Dad off. The Eliana I know wouldn't have done that."

"What shares? What are you talking about?"

"You really don't know, do you?" Raff asked, stepping back and finally calming down.

I took a step towards him and waited for him to continue talking.

"The reason Leonardo let you go, it's because Eliana traded her shares of Dad's business for you. We all got an equal share when we were born. It ensured all of us had a say in the family business until one of us took over. Dad thought it would be safer keeping the business in the family. Only problem is, Eliana signed her shares over to Leonardo in exchange for your freedom."

"What?" I asked, shocked to find out that's the deal Eliana made with Leonardo. "She used her shares as collateral?"

"Fucking pathetic, isn't it? Every year since she was eighteen she's fought with Dad to keep her shares. Every time he tried to take them away from her and convince her to give them up she held onto them. She knew how important they were to Dad. It would have been easier to give them to me, or Frankie, and leave like she's always wanted, but for some reason she held onto them. Until now of course. Without any hesitation, she promised Leonardo a percent of the business if you don't show up to

Leonardo's on Friday."

"Why would she do that?" I asked, looking over at Dane. "How could you let her do that?"

"I had no idea!" Dane explained. "No one was in the room when they made that deal, not even Leonardo's men. She asked to meet with him alone. I just thought she traded information."

"Leonardo called Dad today and told us about what she's done. He says he's looking forward to you not showing up on Friday. If you don't show, the business my family has protected for generations will crumble all thanks to Eliana."

What was Eliana thinking giving up her shares for me? How could she know I would make it to Leonardo's on Friday? She risked losing her family for good just to save me.

Dane and Raff continued to argue as I tried to figure out what to do now.

"She's coming back with me. I don't trust her here." Raff shouted out again.

"Eliana isn't going anywhere right now. It's not safe to leave. She's safer here with us." Dane argued.

"I don't give a damn what you think about her safety. That wasn't a major concern when Apollo decided to leave her to go chase after his cousin. She's coming back with me, so she can fix this problem with Leonardo. Dad needs her home to make sure she doesn't do anything else to hurt the family."

I listened as Raff and Dane argue back and forth for another minute. Watching the two of them fight, I finally understood all of Eliana's frustration. It finally clicked.

Letting out a low laugh I watched Raff and Dane stop their fighting to figure out what I found so funny.

"It's all starting to make sense now. Eliana's whole life has been decided by her family, and for years she's said nothing even though every time her own father used her or lied to her for his own benefit it broke her. Then when she got older it was her own brother that started to make her decisions for her. After all, she trusted you just a little bit more than she trusted Marco. I know the only reason she said yes to marrying me was because you convinced her to. Eliana would be better off without you and your family, but for some reason she stayed. She could have left, should have left, but she's too loyal."

"You have no clue what our family has been through. Don't stand there and act like you have any idea what it's been like for Eliana." Raff interrupted.

"Oh, shut up Raff. Aren't you tired? Isn't it exhausting playing the victim? Can we all stop pretending you don't use Eliana for the benefit of the family any chance you get?" I asked, causing him to go quiet again.

"Eliana complained to me the minute we met how tired she was of being used by her family, and before I even had the chance to marry her I hurt her more than her family ever has. I'm a fucking idiot. I thought I was doing the right thing leaving her, but all I did was hurt her by forcing another decision onto her. She's been fighting for control of her own life for years, and I stole that from her when I left her alone to fix what I ruined."

Dane looked happy to see I was finally putting two and two together. Raff on the other hand was looking more upset.

"Wow, Apollo, that speech was beautiful, really it was, but if you're done I'd really appreciate it if someone could go get Eliana for me. She needs to start packing. I'm not letting her stay here any longer."

"No." I said.

"No?"

"There's only one person that gets to decide where Eliana wants to stay, and that person's not here in this room right now. You have no right walking into my house and making demands like this Raff. I've watched you and Marco use Eliana like a pawn in your fucking chess games her entire life, and I'm sick of it. Eliana deserves more than this, more than your pathetic fucking family." I spoke, walking closer to Raff.

"I thought I was doing the right thing by leaving to go fix my problems with Michael and Giovanni, but now that I'm back I can see how much I've hurt Eliana. Don't be angry at Eliana for what she did. The reason she gave up her shares and went through so much this month is because of me. I should still be locked in Leonardo's basement rotting for what I've done, but we all know if she had the chance to go back and change her mind Eliana would still give up those shares for me. So no, she won't be going back to your house no matter how much you yell and scream. I refuse to watch you continue to hurt and use the woman I love more than anything else in this world."

My words lingered in the air. Shocking everyone in the room, including myself. I hadn't meant to say that, but now that it was out I couldn't take it back.

"Jesus, there I said it. I love Eliana, and I'll be damned if I let you force her back to her father's house all because you're upset over a few shares. Because Eliana has the biggest heart of anyone I've ever met she put up with your bullshit all those years, but I'm not going to let it happen anymore. Eliana gets to decide what happens, and no one else."

"That's easy for you to say now, but you're only fighting me because Eliana is happy here. What happens when tomorrow it's you she wants to leave? Would you sit back and watch her leave if she wakes up and wants to come home?" Raff asked.

Honestly, I had no idea if I could do that. I wanted Eliana

here with me, but I was no better than Raff and Marco if I asked her to stay.

"If tomorrow Eliana decides she wants to leave me, no matter how much that would break me, I would help her pack her bags. All I want is for her to be happy, and if that's not with me anymore, then we will all support her. I will watch her drive away and know that I was the luckiest man in the world for getting to spend as much time as I did with her. Eliana deserves to be loved by a far greater man than me. She should run and start over somewhere none of us can find her. I have no right asking Eliana to trust me again, but I will spend my whole life begging for forgiveness should she decide to stay."

I had nothing left to say to Raff. He needed to leave before Eliana finds out he's here.

Pulling a gun from the back of my waist, raising it level to Raff's chest, I walked closer to him.

"It's time for you to leave Raffael. I don't want to see you here again without Eliana's permission. If you so much as step a foot onto our property I will tell my men to start shooting and not stop until they've hit something. Do you understand?"

Chapter Nineteen

Eliana

When Apollo was fourteen he killed for his father for the first time. After Italy Apollo told me all about it. He told me how nervous he felt pulling the trigger, and how he did his best hiding the tremor in his hand. His father ordered him to kill a man who had stolen money from them. Apollo never found out if that was the truth or not. The man never had a chance to plead his innocence. I will forever regret throwing Apollo's first kill in his face when I was angry at him.

When he found out Juliette was being bullied at school he made all his men walk with her to school. Juliette told me it was the most embarrassing week of her life, but the next Monday no one was mean to her anymore. The boys who bullied her ran away scared at the mere mention of Apollo's name.

On Cristiano and Catalina's thirtieth wedding anniversary an enemy of Cristiano's attempted an attack on the whole family while they were celebrating at one of their family restaurants. I never asked him, but the rumors were that Apollo spent the next four days torturing the men who tried to hurt Catalina. Raff said the longer he went without sleep the crazier he became. Catalina still refuses to celebrate anything not at the house.

Two days ago, Apollo held a gun to my brother's chest and forced him to leave our house because it was the first night I had slept in a month. Little did Apollo know I wasn't sleeping. I had crept out of his office right behind him, and I sat with my knees to my chest as he fought with Raff. I heard everything he said, down to the very last threat, and then I snuck back into Apollo's office. When he returned he sat next to me near the couch and played with my hair while I pretended to sleep.

"I'm sorry my love, I'm so sorry." He whispered, as he stroked my cheek. I'm not sure if it was exhaustion or delusion, but I'm almost certain I heard him say those words to me with tears stuck in his throat. I wanted to wake up and let him know I heard everything, but that would be a secret I took to the grave. He could never know I was sitting on the staircase, finally finding the strength to forgive him. That night I was ready to admit one thing to myself, I will forever love Apollo.

Apollo Costa was not a good man, but he was good to me.

He takes care of those he loves, and for some reason he has decided to love me.

Apollo and I were leaving in just a few minutes. It was time to return to Leonardo's. I honestly had no idea if Apollo would be returning back to the house with me or not. Everything I've sacrificed could all be for nothing. Everything I've lost would end with Apollo. Leonardo had too many cards up his sleeve. There was no predicting his next move. I only hoped he considered Apollo a bigger asset than Giovanni and Michael.

A voice I hadn't heard in a while surprised me at the door, "Eliana, they're waiting for you at the car." Alex spoke.

The house was quiet as I walked to the car. All of Apollo's men that had been staying with us were nowhere to be found. They had done their best to hide this past week, but even then, I had still seen them on occasion. Tonight however, the house was empty. They were preparing for the possibility Apollo did not return home with me.

Apollo stood waiting for me on my side of the car with the door open. He was dressed in a black suit and tie. He looked almost healed from the damage Leonardo's men had caused. The bruising on his face was almost gone, and the cuts were fading into scars. When he walked he was getting better at hiding his limp.

"You ready?" He asked as I walked over to him.

Nodding my head yes, I climbed into the car. To say yes out loud was a lie, so I kept quiet. My stomach was tied into knots, and I could feel my heartbeat in my throat. I almost considered staying home, but I knew Apollo needed me there.

A few minutes away from Leonardo's house I looked over at an anxious Apollo. His leg was shaking, and his fingers twitched in his lap. He was struggling to hide his nerves. It pained me to see him unraveling like that, so without saying anything I slid across the middle seat and placed my hand on his thigh. He turned from the window to see me sitting next to him. I could tell how surprised he was by my actions. Taking my hand from his leg he placed it in his hands. He held onto my hand as tight as he could as he played with my ring. Slowly his body relaxed, and he was able to focus on staying calm. I thought I was moving closer to him for his comfort, but I felt calmer sitting beside him. We both needed each other right now even if we couldn't say the words.

Looking over at me he gave me a small smile of appreciation. He didn't move an inch away from me until we were pulling into Leonardo's driveway. Looking more relaxed than when we left Apollo exited the car and walked over to open the door for me.

Walking up the stairs to the front door Apollo paused, "Eliana if-"

"No." I interrupted. "Don't do that Apollo. I don't want to hear it. We're going to be just fine. Okay?"

"Okay." He whispered, kissing my temple and walking up to knock on the door.

Almost a dozen of Leonardo's men were waiting to escort us to Leonardo's office. They all carried a handful of guns each, strapped to their waist or chest. This was Leonardo's way of reminding us he's the one in charge right now. The only way we walk out together is if Leonardo allows it.

We entered Leonardo's office alone. His men waiting in the hallway while we spoke. In the corner stood a tired Rio.

"Eliana, Apollo, I'm glad to see you two returning in good health. I worried about your state when you left Apollo. I'm sure you know your punishment was nothing personal, just business."

"Of course, Sir. I know how much trouble I've caused you and the families this past month." Apollo answered.

As Apollo and I walked closer into the room I noticed Apollo do his best to cover me. He walked in front of me putting as much distance as he could between me and Leonardo. I know he despised me being here with him today, but he had no chance arguing with me about coming. It was me who saved him in the first place.

Rio took a step forward out of the corner to join the two of us. His face gave no clue as to what Leonardo had decided. He showed no joy, no worry.

"Apollo, there's no easy way to say this, so let's cut to the chase. There are a lot of people who want you dead after what you did to your uncle. And I have to agree, what you did was reckless and dangerous. You killed one of his best men, and you went on a hunt to take someone from your own family down. It makes others worry what you would do to someone who isn't blood related." Leonardo spoke.

"If it weren't for Eliana there's a good chance you would already be dead. You make my life ten times harder than it ever needs to be Apollo. Maybe when I was younger it was exciting having someone like you to keep me entertained, but now that I'm old and looking to retire my excitement has turned to boredom. I lack patience with you these days Apollo, and I'm struggling to find a benefit to your work."

The longer Leonardo sat there, stalling, the more unsure about his decision I became. I knew Apollo being found guilty and Leonardo taking Michael's side was a real possibility, but I was in denial. I had convinced myself others needed Apollo as much as I needed him, but I was wrong. Leonardo could very well find a new enforcer to run jobs for him. One that wouldn't disobey his orders.

"Rio, do you know why I kept Apollo around for so long? Made all those exceptions for him even when he didn't deserve them?" Leonardo asked.

"Because he's lucky."

Leonardo smiled, "That's right. Because he's lucky. You were always worth the risk Apollo. Against my better judgment I gave you freedom to run, and this is how you chose to repay me. You started a war in my backyard, and now I have to clean up after you."

Apollo dropped his head, waiting to hear Leonardo had sided with Michael. It was over.

Interrupting Leonardo, there was a knock at the door.

"Come in." Leonardo said, standing up.

In walked two of Leonardo's men carrying a large tarp. They struggled with the corners as they set it down near Leonardo's feet. Standing up behind Apollo I waited to see what was laying on the floor. With a quick wave of his hand Leonardo ordered one of his men to lift the tarp over.

There was nothing that could have prepared either of us for what was laying on the floor in front of us. I felt my blood run cold and a hand grab my shoulder. Apollo tried to hide the look of shock on his face as he held onto me. The two of us struggled to hold back our mumbles of disgust as Apollo let out a string of curses. I swallowed the vomit threatening to rise up my throat.

The shock was wearing off, and I was ready to process what I was seeing, "Is that-"

"Michael? Yes, yes it is." Leonardo answered.

A rotting Michael laid still on the floor of Leonardo's office. His body already a few days into its decomposition. A single bullet wound in his forehead; his skin gray.

"Jesus Christ." Apollo mumbled.

A smiling Leonardo looked back up at the two of us, "Lucky... you've always been lucky Apollo."

Sitting back down at his desk Leonardo pulled a file out of

his desk drawer.

"Rio and I both agreed Michael needed to be taken care of. He was a threat to his own family, and we can't have that, can we?"

"What about Giovanni?" Apollo asked.

"Unfortunately, Giovanni had a chance to run before we could get to him. He must have known it was over for the two of them, and it was only a matter of time before we caught up to him."

"What about everything you said to me before all this? What happens now?" Apollo asked, still in shock.

"Now you go back to working jobs for me and your father, and things go back to normal. Unless, after everything that's happened, that's not what you want? Should I find someone else to fill in for you?" Leonardo asked.

Apollo shook his head no.

"It's no secret your father plans on retiring as soon as you two marry. There are a lot of people that doubt you will be able to run the family business without causing problems. I hope for your sake they are wrong because the next time you pull something like this I won't be as forgiving. You two will soon be the most powerful family that I've ever worked with and I can't have you continue to undermine me every time you feel wronged. This partnership won't work if you continue to put your own needs before your family. You two need to decide if you're ready for the responsibility."

Apollo and I looked at each other. Neither of us knew if we were ready to take over for Cristiano, but we didn't have a choice.

"It doesn't matter how good the two of you are at your jobs. You two are not invincible, and I will replace you if I have to. As for you Eliana, I'm looking forward to working with you. I want you to stay available. I'll reach out when I need you."

Apollo went to protest, but Rio shook his head no. Now was not the time to argue my involvement with Leonardo.

Taking that as his cue for us to leave Apollo grabbed my hand and led me out of the office.

"One more thing Apollo." Leonardo said, "Giovanni, he's yours to take care of. Consider it a wedding gift."

"Thank you, Sir." Apollo replied before stepping out into the hallway.

Nearly cutting off my circulation, Apollo held my hand as we walked back to the car. We stopped at the front doors to say goodbye to Rio.

"Go home and rest you two, I'll stop by in the morning."

I kissed Rio on the cheek and nodded a quick goodbye. Apollo patted Rio on the shoulder, and then took the stairs down to the car. We wasted no time driving away. The two of us sat in complete silence as Dane drove us back home. Apollo was a statue, frozen as he sat and questioned his own mortality. All of us expected a different outcome, but for some reason Leonardo gave him one more chance. A chance he didn't deserve.

I wanted to ask Leonardo why he sided with Apollo. I needed answers to calm my brain, but I wasn't going to get them. All that mattered right now was that Apollo was coming home.

I knew something was wrong as soon as Apollo got into the car behind me, and Dane started to drive off. We all pretended to not notice Dane wasn't driving home. He was driving out to a part of the city that none of us had any part being in. I couldn't catch a fucking break. Apollo was hiding something from me again, and just like when he left the first time I was left feeling like an idiot.

I came back for him, and he still didn't have the decency to fill me in on his plans. I expected this from Apollo, but Dane was better than this. He knew what I went through when Apollo left. How could he lie to me again?

Dane couldn't even look me in the eyes. He looked past me through the mirror as he drove. After almost an hour of driving I didn't recognize the neighborhood we were in. I thought about making a plan to get out of the situation, but if this was their elaborate plot to kill me I wanted to see how long they thought they'd be able to pull it off. I always knew when I got engaged to Apollo it was a race to death or divorce.

Dane pulled into a small, empty parking lot, but kept the car running. Apollo left from his side of the car and started to walk around to my side. He made a phone call a few feet away from the car before walking over to my door.

Looking up at Dane I finally said something, "Dane, what the hell is going on?"

He said nothing, only looking out the front of the car. He held onto the steering wheel with a tight grip.

Finished with his phone call, Apollo held open my door for me. He walked in front of me to an abandoned car. This was how Apollo planned to leave me for the second time.

"Eliana-"

"You're leaving again, aren't you?" I interrupted.

Taking a step closer, Apollo pulled out a car key.

"No, I'm not." He paused, "But you are."

"Excuse me?"

"Dane and I made arrangements to help you run away. We aren't sure there will be a better chance than right now. Dane made a few different aliases for you, and Alex helped us pack up some of your things."

"You want me to leave?"

"No, God, no. That's the last thing I want, but this isn't about me. This is about doing what's best for you. I can't sit by and watch you torture yourself. This is your chance to start over."

For a second I almost considered Apollo's offer. I had always wanted to run, but I never had the guts to actually pack up and leave. Maybe I could have left before, but not now, not anymore.

"Apollo, stop. This is crazy. I'm not leaving."

"Yes, yes you are." He said. "You're going to leave tonight in that car and you're going to drive until you're sure none of us can find you. I can only cover for you for a day or two. Eventually your family will come looking for you. I need you to promise you'll go somewhere none of us can find you- including me."

"Including you?" I asked.

"Yes, especially me. As soon as you drive away from here I'm going to regret letting you go. It's only a matter of time before I break and I start convincing Dane to let me look for you."

Apollo handed me a small manila envelope.

"Inside you'll find a few passports, some American, some not. It's enough to get you started and will last you a few months. I had Dane set up a bank account that I have no control over. There will always be three million in there no matter how much you take out. Alex packed a few work things, and some clothes for you. Everything you'll need is in the trunk."

This can't be happening. Does he actually expect me to leave?

"I'd get a new car once you're in a different state just to be safe. In the glove box is a burner cell with one of Dane's numbers. Only use it in an emergency. I'll assume you're safe until you call that number."

"Why are you doing this to me? To us? I came back for you, I decided to stay." I asked, still in disbelief he wanted me to leave.

"Because more than anything in this world I want you to be happy, and you're not happy. I can see it in your eyes. Dane shouldn't have asked you to stay. My hand was forced and in return you were asked to do things for me that I never should have had to ask. I put you in danger the minute I left to go hunt down Giovanni. All of this is my fault. This is the only way I can think of to repay you."

"But I don't want to leave. I can't leave."

"You can and you will. You'll start over, and you'll move on."

"But I don't want to move on." I admitted.

"I'm no good for you Eliana. I can't give you what you need. I'm a bad man, and once I take over for my father my work will only get worse. I can't ask you to make the sacrifice of being my wife. It's too late to save me, but it's not too late to save you."

"Apollo." I cried. "I can't do this."

"Eliana, if you stay... I'll ruin you." He almost whispered. "I'll ruin you."

"For how long would I leave for?"

"For forever, El."

"But we promised to never leave each other."

"That was before I saw how much pain you were in Eliana. I had no idea how much you were hurting. You deserve so much more than you've been given in this life. I want you to finally put yourself first. Not your family, not work, not me, but you."

Apollo walked closer to me when he saw I wasn't taking the keys and envelope from his hands. He took my left hand and gave me the two items. Wrapping his arms around me one last time he held me as close to his chest as he could. After a minute of silence, he kissed the top of my head and leaned back. He looked at me like it would be the last time he would ever see me. Wiping away a few tears I didn't even know were falling he kissed my cheek.

"Apollo, I can't do this." I cried into his chest.

"Yes, you can my love, you are stronger than anyone I've ever met. If anyone can do this, it's you."

"But Apollo I- I love-" I started to say but was interrupted with a kiss.

"If you say those words to me right now El, I won't let you leave."

I tried to hold onto Apollo for a little longer, but he let go of me, and took a step back.

"Good luck." He smiled, tears in his eyes.

Before I had a chance to respond he started walking back to the car.

"Apollo!" I yelled.

Nothing, he didn't even look back.

"Apollo!" I screamed a little bit louder.

He pretended not to hear me until he was back in the car

with Dane. Before I could catch up to them he drove away.

If I was the one leaving this time, then why did it hurt like the first time Apollo left me?

Apollo

I wanted to go with her. I wanted to be the one driving the car somewhere far away, but it was safer for her to go alone. They wouldn't let me run again. I made that mistake chasing down Giovanni and Michael already. The farther away from me she got, the safer she was.

"You're doing the right thing." Dane said, as he drove us home.

"It doesn't make saying goodbye to her any easier."

I knew for a while now that the best way to protect Eliana was to let her go. If I asked her to stay she would, but we both know she'd spend the rest of her life dreaming of freedom.

Pulling into the garage I left Dane at the car. I found my way to my office and poured myself a drink. I had a lot of work to do, but I didn't have the energy for it. Now that Leonardo had sided with me and not Michael I could focus on taking over for Dad. Giovanni was still missing, so I made plans to have Dane start looking for him. I'm almost positive he is headed back to Italy if he isn't already there. That's where he feels the safest, and that's where I know he'll run to because of the coward he is.

Soon I would need to figure out a way to tell Eliana's family that she was gone. I'm not sure if I can tell them the truth, or if I'll need to make up a lie to protect her. After using her shares as collateral I'm sure Marco won't try very hard to find her. He would cut his losses and continue running the family. I'm more worried about Raff. I know he would do anything to find her if he thinks I've done something to harm her. It would be best to tell him the truth, so he doesn't waste his time searching for her.

Tomorrow I would catch up on work, but tonight, all I could do was drink. For at least tonight I would try and forget Eliana. Drinking wasn't going to bring her back, or make any of this hurt any less, but it would help me forget for just a few hours.

I stood from my desk, grabbed my now empty glass and started walking to the bar cart. Before I had finished pouring another drink, one of my office doors crashed open, nearly breaking it off of its hinge.

"You're a fucking idiot."

Turning my head, I thought my mind was playing tricks on me.

"Eliana?"

"You think you get to just leave me in an empty parking lot and drive away?"

"Eliana, what are you doing here? You were supposed to leave- "

"Shut up. I've heard enough from you tonight. It's my turn to speak." She said, throwing her purse against the couch, and walking over to me.

"You really think after everything we've been through that I would be able to just walk away from us? You have no idea how hard I had to fight to keep you alive, to keep you breathing. If I wanted to leave you I would have left that night Dane showed

402

me those earrings. I didn't stay out of obligation to you or my family. I stayed because I fell in love with you, and there's nothing that could happen between us that would make me stop loving you."

"Stop Eliana. Don't do this. You're going to regret it."

"Do I need to say it again? Were you not paying attention? I love you Apollo. Against my better judgment, I fucking love you."

"Stop it!" I shouted.

"Why?" She screamed back.

"Because it doesn't matter how much you love me, or how in love with you I am. I can't give you what you need Eliana, and I'll forever feel like an ass asking you to give up the things you love all because you chose to stay!"

"You're not forcing me to stay Apollo, you're not even asking me to stay. I decided a long time ago that I can't leave you. I hated myself the first night you came home from Leonardo's. I couldn't even look at myself in a mirror because I couldn't admit to myself I needed you just as much as you needed me. I couldn't believe in just a few months you've shown me a love greater than I've ever received in my entire life. I'm the one undeserving of your love Apollo. You couldn't possibly ruin me."

Setting my glass down, I leaned down on the bar cart and dropped my head.

"You're wrong Eliana. Eventually I will hurt you. It's only a matter of time."

Walking over to me and placing her hands on my back she spoke again, "I'm not going anywhere Apollo. No matter what happens after we get married, or what happens after you take over for your father. I know you're worried that soon you'll turn into him. You're afraid once you're Don you won't recognize yourself anymore, but I'm not going to let that happen. I'm going to stay by your side for all of it. And when it gets too much for you I promise I'll still be there, holding your hand. All I ask in return is that you don't push me away."

"I don't deserve you El. I never will."

"I know." I could hear her smile as she answered me.

Silence filled the room as I thought about everything Eliana had just confessed. I wanted her to run, get as far away from me as she could, but it was pointless. She had decided we were meant for each other, and that meant there was no fate in any heaven that could tear us apart from each other. Eliana chose me.

Turning around to face her I grabbed her waist and pulled her close to me.

"If you knew you loved me and you weren't going to leave why were you so distant after bringing me back from Leonardo's?" I asked.

"Because I was afraid after bringing you home, and helping you recover you'd decide to leave me again. I felt foolish taking care of you, knowing you would leave as soon as you could, to finish your business with Giovanni. I promised you I would be gone if you ever returned to me, and instead I did everything I could to save you. It's pathetic."

"I had no idea me leaving would be so terrible for you, I swear. I thought I was doing the right thing leaving to keep you safe. I never should have left you here all alone. I don't know how I'll ever make it up to you."

"Just promise me one thing." She asked.

"Anything."

"The next time you decide to run, take me with you." She

smiled.

Nodding my head, I smiled.

"I love you." I whispered.

"One more time, I didn't quite hear you." She teased.

Leaning down into her ear I whispered, "I love you Eliana. I love you. I love you. I love you."

Leaning her head back and closing her eyes I knew what she wanted next.

Running my lips delicately down from her ear to her neck, I started to leave small kisses. Each time I kissed down her neck over to her cheek I could feel Eliana start to relax. I hadn't held her this close since before I left. I forgot how intoxicating she was. How quickly all other senses were dulled when I held her.

Eliana wasted no time dragging her fingers through my hair as she held onto me. I didn't have to ask her to jump as I grabbed her ass, she just knew. Finding my lips Eliana deepened our kiss. She leaned into me, and bit softly on my bottom lip, begging me to let her in.

When our tongues connected I could hear a soft moan leave her lips. I wasn't going to last much longer if she continued to moan like that as she kissed me. Changing my plans of sitting her down on the couch in my office I carried her across the hall to my room.

Throwing her on the bed I watched as a surprised Eliana looked up at me. I thought I'd lost Eliana forever, but now that she was back I would spend the rest of my life showing her how much she meant to me.

Eliana

Lying there on Apollo's bed I knew I made the right decision. My heart raced as he looked down at me. His eyes scanned over my body as he unbuttoned his shirt. It's like he couldn't decide what he wanted to do to me first. Finally making a decision he pulled my ankles and sent me to the edge of the bed. He teased me by running his hands over my thighs and legs. He left kisses over my thigh as he played with my panties. Sliding them to the side he finally touched me where I needed him to. He slid his middle finger down my core as he stared up at me.

I had played with myself a few times since he'd left, but nothing came close to how Apollo's fingers felt. He ran circles over my clit as he kissed closer and closer to my center. Unable to stand the teasing I started to close my legs. It was already too much for me.

Stopping what he was doing, Apollo spoke, "Try to close your legs like that again Eliana and I'll tie your ankles to the bedposts. Do you understand?"

"Yes."

Looking up at me, eyebrows raised Apollo sat there refusing to touch me.

"Yes, Sir." I replied one more time.

Spreading my legs as wide as I could I gave Apollo the room to kiss and tease me as he pleased. I could tell how much he missed this. He was going to take his sweet time, even though it was killing me.

He entered two fingers in me as he sucked on my folds. I started to shake, as he pumped in and out of me slowly. I couldn't handle his pace, so he slowed down. That only tortured me more. I wanted him to fuck me hard and fast. As much as I appreciated him being delicate, I'd missed how rough he could be. Grinding my hips against his face I tried to hint I needed more. Sitting back Apollo grinned at me.

"Tell me exactly what you want, Eliana."

"I want you to fuck me Apollo, and I don't want you to go gentle. Please."

"Are you sure?" He asked.

"Yes."

Flipping me over by my knees Apollo brought my hips up in the air. Wasting no time Apollo slid his dick over my pussy getting it wet.

In just a few short seconds Apollo pounded into me. I sucked in a deep breath as he pumped into me. Apollo usually spent a few minutes letting me adjust to his size. This time I had no time to prepare. He was hitting deep into me as he fucked me. Pushing my head down into the bed Apollo kept my ass high in the air. My knees barely touched the bed. Apollo held me exactly as he wanted me. Arching my back to let him know I had adjusted to his size and was ready for more Apollo grabbed me by my hair. He kept my hips close to him as he pulled me to his chest. Letting go of my hair and wrapping his hand around my neck Apollo kissed up and down my shoulders. He sucked, and left bite marks all over my back. I struggled to focus on one thing at a time. His lips burned on my skin as his cock drove deeper into me with every stroke.

I was struggling to keep my eyes from blurring as he fucked me. Dropping his head onto his shoulder's Apollo started to slow down. I thought he was close to finishing, but I was wrong when he spun me around.

"I need to see you, your eyes Eliana."

Grabbing both of my hands and placing them above the pillow he kissed me and pulled at my lips as he slowly reentered.

I rolled my eyes back as he started pumping one more time.

"Focus, Eliana, let me see how good I make you feel." He ordered.

Locking eyes with Apollo I bit my lip as he started to go faster. He knew I would keep my hands above my head, so he brought down his hand to play with my clit while he fucked me.

He circled me with the same pace as his dick. Every time he pulled out he made sure to apply more pressure to my core. I could feel myself start to shake.

"You're holding back El, I can feel it. I'm not going anywhere, and we're far from over. Let it go baby, I won't stop I promise."

Listening to Apollo I started to relax and let my first orgasm go. Apollo didn't change a damn thing. He continued to fuck me as I shook underneath him. After I came down from my high I almost asked him to stop. I was throbbing from the release, and thought I was going to explode. Eventually my pussy was ready for him to continue. It didn't take long for the buzzing to stop in my head, and to be reminded of Apollo above me.

Breaking the rules and moving my hands I found Apollo's neck and brought him down to me. I kissed him and teased him with my tongue as he continued to move.

Needing a change of pace, I held onto Apollo's shoulders and pushed him to his side. It felt cold feeling him not inside of me anymore, but I quickly fixed that by straddling him, and sitting back down on his cock.

Apollo's core tightened as I adjusted onto him. It took me

almost a minute to fully take him in. I had to brace myself with my knees. Once I was sure I could move without breaking I started to bounce up and down. At first, I could barely move, but soon I was riding Apollo as fast as I could. I rolled my hips in a circle which was supposed to feel good for Apollo but was driving me crazy. I thought I'd come again riding his dick. Bracing myself on his chest I let Apollo play with my tits. He rolled my left breast as he teased the nipple. He laid back and watched me start to unfold for the second time. I was starting to get sloppy and Apollo was jealous.

"I'm going to come again Apollo." I cried.

"Not without me you aren't."

Taking control of my hips Apollo started to raise his hips to meet mine. He pounded into me from below as his grip on me tightened. I knew he was close when his fingers started to relax, and his head rolled back. I took back over for him, rolling and circling with his rhythm. Soon I started to shake, at the same time I felt him come inside me.

Dropping to his chest I laid there and tried to catch my breath.

Apollo slid out of me and pulled my hair out of my face. After a minute or two I could feel his cum sliding down my thigh. I tried to get off of him to go clean up, but that wasn't part of Apollo's plan.

"I just got you back El, you aren't leaving me for a long time. We're just getting started. You can go to the shower to get cleaned up, but you're fucking crazy if you think I'm not joining you." He said, carrying me to the bathroom.

Chapter Twenty

Apollo

Eliana chose to stay. We both knew there would be days the family came first, and one day soon I would hurt her again, but she still stayed. Leonardo is right, I am lucky. I don't deserve a woman like Eliana. I deserve nothing but suffering, and instead I've been given the chance to love someone like her.

The next few weeks were a blur. I barely saw Eliana, barely slept, and had missed one too many dinners. Eliana said nothing when I came home late because she knew how bad I needed to find Giovanni. I didn't like knowing he was out there somewhere. I needed him found before he tried to hurt Eliana again.

Eliana went back to work as soon as she could. I don't know how she balanced opening up her firm and planning a wedding with both our moms, but she hadn't complained once. In the morning, she took care of her firm, and in the evening, she spent most of her time picking table arrangements, and bridesmaids dresses with Nora.

I needed this fucking wedding to be over with. I wanted to be able to call Eliana my wife, and I needed things between the families to go back to normal. After Eliana and I were married I would take over for Dad and everyone would soon forget my issues with Michael and Giovanni. The rumors that spread while I was missing were starting to hurt the business. Leonardo clearing my name helped, but until I was back to work full time I was going to get push back from other families. I hoped for Eliana's sake that no one tried anything at the wedding.

I was pulled from my thoughts to see Eliana standing at my door.

"You're back early."

"I think Mom could tell I was close to breaking down, so she let me go for the night. If I stayed any longer she knew one of us would be planning a funeral."

"That bad huh?" I asked.

Eliana rolled her eyes and sulked all the way over to my desk. Sitting down on it, I laid my hands on her thighs, glad to have her back home. It'd been a few days since I'd seen her, and even longer since we'd had any time for just the two of us. There was tension in the air both of us had been struggling to ignore.

Taking my hands in hers Eliana gave me her most charming smile. The one she saved for when she wanted something.

"What are the odds I can convince you to not go to work tomorrow?" She asked.

"You know I want to El, but I still can't find Giovanni, and you know I want him found before the wedding. If there's anyone that would try something it's him."

"Please, Apollo? We have the rehearsal dinner tomorrow,

and then after that it's going to be non-stop wedding events. I just want to spend one day with you before things get even crazier. You already have all your men working the wedding, and you have Dane trying to find Giovanni. I need you this week, and I promise all this work will still be here after the wedding. It's not going anywhere."

Looking down at the files sitting on my desk, I considered what Eliana was asking of me. She was right. I did have extra protection for all wedding events until our honeymoon, and everything I wanted to get done could wait.

"Okay." I smiled, pulling her down into a kiss, "No more work."

"Promise?"

"Promise."

Eliana wrapped her arms around my shoulders and closed her eyes as she rested her forehead on mine. She did that sometimes after a long day. I don't think I'll ever get tired of how clingy she is when she comes home from work. It made missing her throughout the day worth it just to have her home.

"Have you had dinner?"

Eyes still closed, Eliana shook her head no.

"Well that just won't do, my love. What do you want for dinner tonight?"

"Maybe we could skip dinner and start with dessert?" She smiled.

Before I could agree to that delicious request I was interrupted by a phone call.

Eliana groaned and dropped her hands from my shoulders. As soon as I saw who was calling I wanted to throw my phone against a wall and carry Eliana back to our bedroom, but I knew I had to answer. Dane might have answers on Gio. Eliana gave me a look that told me not to pick up the phone, but I had to answer it.

"You have terrible timing." I answered, walking away from the desk.

I didn't want Eliana to hear what Dane had to say in case I didn't like what he had to tell me. I walked around to the window and leaned against the back of one of my cigar chairs.

I looked behind me and saw an irritated Eliana looking towards the door. I mouthed sorry to her and continued to let Dane update me on his trip to Italy.

The next time I turned around to check in on Eliana I nearly dropped dead from a heart attack.

There Eliana was on my desk, playing with herself as she waited for me to get off the phone. I knew there was no redemption for a man like me, so why did Eliana feel a little bit too much like heaven? Eliana touching herself, trying to hold back moans almost sent me to my knees.

"Eliana..." I mouthed, warning her.

"What?" She whispered, continuing her teasing.

I knew why she was doing this. She wanted to punish me for picking up the phone in the first place. It'd been a few days since I'd gotten to taste her and it was killing me.

Not caring about Dane's updates anymore I threw my phone onto the nearest counter and walked back over to the desk. Just as I was about to tear Eliana's shirt off and start playing with her breasts she held a hand out against my chest.

Pushing me away from her Eliana jumped off my desk and walked out of my office like nothing happened. Following her to her closest I waited to see how upset she really was.

After she slid out of her skirt I watched her grab for one of my shirts. Walking past me like I was a ghost she entered the kitchen and started to make something for dinner. She cut and chopped her veggies for dinner like I was the one on the chopping block. *Shit.*

"My love..." I tried whispering in her ear from behind her, but she was too fast. She rolled away from my touch and went to fill a pot with water at the sink.

I sat at the kitchen counter and gave her some space.

"It was Dane giving me an update, I had to answer." I explained.

"Of course. I understand." She smiled.

I'm fucked. I'll be lucky if I survive dinner.

Eliana gave me the silent treatment all through dinner and into the night. Before she went to bed she paraded around the bedroom in nothing but one of my shirts. After breakfast Eliana was taking full advantage of my men still being gone and not working at the house until after the wedding. She wore nothing but a pair of my boxers and a tank top that covered absolutely nothing. I had never seen Eliana wake up before noon on one of her days off, but of course today she joined me in the gym before the sun was even up. Her joining me for my workout was my biggest clue she's madder about the phone call than I originally thought. I know for a fact she only runs when she's being chased, and even then when working out is life or death, she still finds time to complain about it. I had to bite my tongue every time she bent down in those tight leggings of hers during her squat set. Slowly, but surely, Eliana was trying to kill me.

The rules to her little game were simple. I wasn't allowed to touch her, but she was allowed to be as touchy and flirty as she wanted. After lunch, she found me watching TV in the living room and cuddled right into my lap, leaning back into my chest. As soon as I dropped my arms to her waist she slid off like I had done something wrong.

Hours later, I was now sitting near her vanity watching her get ready. I may not be able to touch her, but If I ever miss a chance to watch her get ready it will be because I'm six feet under, and rotting. I could sit and watch her for hours. The way her nose scrunched as she concentrated applying her makeup, or the way she sighed when she couldn't get her hair to fall the way she wanted it to. I considered picking up painting because there was no photo that did her justice. They all missed the way her eyes glistened when she smiled, or the way her cheeks blushed when she was excited. I could never get tired of Eliana.

Eliana messed her with earrings as I stepped closer to her and sat near the bed. She looked back at me through her mirror.

"Can I help you?" She asked.

"No." I smiled. "Please, continue."

Walking to her closet I waited for her return. She walked back into the room, slipping her dress over her breasts, as she struggled with the zipper. Her dress hung low on her chest and was tight on her waist. Its heavy blush colored fabric flowed as she walked over to me revealing a long slit on her left thigh.

Seeing Eliana in that dress had me thinking of ways I could kill Dane for calling last night. It wasn't his fault I picked up, but my frustrations needed an outlet.

Eliana held her dress up by her waist and turned back towards her vanity.

"Will you help me zip this up please?" She asked.

Abso-fucking-lutely.

I placed one hand low on her back, keeping the zipper down as I carefully zipped the rest of the dress up. I hesitated with the last few inches of the zipper because it was my first time holding her in over a day. I was craving just a taste of her. I wanted to rip this dress off and make her late to dinner, but the odds of that happening were next to none.

Eliana slowly turned to face me and looked me dead in the eyes. She fixed my tie as she looked down to my lips. I knew punishing me was also punishing her. She wanted me just as bad as I wanted her. Her cheeks were flushed, and her heart was racing. She could distance herself from me, but she couldn't hide her body's reaction to being near me.

Snapping back to reality Eliana took her hands off my tie and walked over to the door of the bedroom.

"We should leave now, or we'll be late." She said.

"Right, let's go." I said.

I followed Eliana to the car and held the door open for her. She dipped low into her seat, fixing her dress as I walked to the driver's seat. As I put the car in drive and slowly pulled out into the neighborhood Eliana fidgeted with the slit in her dress. No matter how she sat she couldn't get it to sit right on her thigh. It rode up almost to her hips. She struggled to sit with her leg straight or crossed. I nearly crashed the car looking over at her every time she tried to fix her dress.

Unlike at the house she was too distracted with her dress to notice what she was doing to me. I wanted those legs of her wrapped around me as she screamed my name. I wanted to dig my hands into her thighs as I ate her out and watched her squirm. She had no idea what those legs did to me. My pants were tightening every second she messed with her dress.

Locking the doors just as Eliana tried to get out of the car I threw my seatbelt off and reached over to grab her shoulders. Eliana fell back into her seat, staring at me with shock.

"I can't take much more of your little games Eliana. Pretty soon I'm going to snap and you'll regret teasing me like this. If we weren't already late I'd throw you over my lap and fuck you as I watched that slit in your dress ride up higher and higher on your legs. I know sooner or later you'll break, and be begging for this cock, and when you do I won't be gentle."

Stunned, and unable to stutter out any words, Eliana messed with her dress one more time. I took her wrist in my hands and held it up, "Tease me with those legs of yours one more time and I'll rip this dress off of you starting at that fucking slit, do you understand?"

Eliana nodded her head yes, still silent.

"Good, let's go. I'm sure everyone is waiting for us to arrive."

I walked over to Eliana's side of the car and helped her out. She held onto my hand tight, obviously turned on by my words, but doing her best to ignore how bad she wanted me.

It was time to start playing dirty, just like Eliana. She'd be begging me to fuck her by the end of tonight, that was a promise.

Eliana

I hadn't had a sip to drink all night, but I didn't need it. Apollo's touch was intoxicating. Every time he ran his fingers down my back, or traced circles on my leg during dinner I struggled to hide my excitement. I was supposed to be the one

417

teasing him, watching him suffer, but instead I was miserable. I hadn't given in to Apollo since his phone call, and I was at my limit. I needed him, and he knew it. The way he stared at me told me everything I needed to know. I had pissed him off, and sooner or later he was going to get his revenge.

I was barely paying attention to Nora's speech. I couldn't focus with Apollo's firm grip on my thigh. My blood pulsed beneath his touch. I got goosebumps when he'd let go, and the silk table cloth would fall back onto my exposed skin. I couldn't think with Apollo sitting so close to me. I needed dinner to be over before I slipped up.

Apollo put his hand back on my thigh, letting me know Nora's speech was almost over. I lifted my glass to raise a toast to the happy couple.

As the room went back to finishing their dinner and visiting with family, Apollo leaned down to whisper in my ear.

"Are you doing okay, my love? You look a little tense."

"I'm fine." I lied.

"Is there anything I can do to help?"

"I'm just a little overwhelmed with how many guests are here. I'll feel better once dinner's over."

Apollo sat back in his chair and continued a small conversation with one of his men across the table from him. I scanned around the room looking at everyone Mom felt the need to invite. She invited all the cousins and extended family on both sides, friends she'd known forever and Dad and Cristiano invited as many of their men as they could. Apollo, of course, had a lot of his men here, and the rest were my friends.

A guest I wasn't planning on being here caught my eye. At one of the last tables in the room sat an old friend, Carter. I quickly stood up to go talk to him but was stopped by Apollo.

He held onto my arm, "Where are you going?"

"I have to go say hello to a guest." I spoke, removing his hand from mine and walking away.

When I looked back I saw an irritated Apollo sitting at the table. He followed my every move. I could see how upset he was that I'd left him alone at the table with our whole family.

Walking up to Carter I pulled him towards the dessert table.

"What are you doing here?" I asked.

"I got done with the job earlier than expected, and I wanted to stop by to see when you needed your gift dropped off."

"You're four days early." I spoke.

"I know, but the job took less time than I thought it was going to take. I can still hold the package for you until you're ready, but I thought you'd want it earlier." He said.

"I thought I was clear. I don't need it until after the wedding. I'll send you the address and details of where I want you to drop it off, but until then Apollo can't know about any of this."

I looked behind me and saw Apollo start to walk over to Carter and me. I needed Carter gone before Apollo had a chance to ask questions.

I dragged Carter to the hallway, "You need to leave, now. It will ruin the surprise."

"Okay, okay, I'm going. Don't forget to call with specifics." Carter left just as Apollo found me in the hallway.

"Who was that?" He asked.

"An old friend who's helping me out with a favor."

I tried to be as casual as I could. I worked so hard for this surprise for Apollo. I couldn't ruin it now.

"What favor?"

"I can't tell you that." I teased, walking away.

"Eliana..."

"Do you trust me, Apollo?"

"Of course, I do."

"Then you'll just have to trust you'll know about the favor when it's the right time."

Apollo rolled his eyes before walking back to the dining room.

Apollo was giving a bit too much attitude considering I was still technically mad at him. Seeing him upset over not getting answers about Carter I knew I was doing the right thing keeping the one thing he really wanted away from him. Any chance of forgiving him soon was long gone.

For the rest of the night I made Apollo miserable. We both went our separate ways after dinner, thanking all the guests for coming tonight. Every time we thought we'd catch a break another cousin would come to say hi.

Every time I looked for Apollo in the room he was already staring. When I knew Apollo was watching me I messed with his head. Whether I fixed my dress, or raised my leg through its slit, the grip on his drink would tighten, or his jaw would flex. I could see his patience running thin. If he could he'd pick me up and carry me out of here. I'm not sure if we'd even make it to the car before he'd start fucking me. As much as I wanted that to happen, I had to stay focused. I pretended to be oblivious to my actions for hours. Every time I made eye contact I smiled at an annoyed Apollo.

An hour later, Emma found me near the bar.

"You look like you need a drink."

"I can't."

"Why not?"

"Apollo and I are fighting and if I drink I won't be strong enough to resist him. Drunk Eliana thinks he's dreamy."

"Fighting about what?" She asked.

"His priorities."

"Ah." She smiled.

"Don't give me that face." I warned.

"One drink wouldn't hurt and you know it. Champagne is basically water."

"Fuck it, you're right. It's my rehearsal dinner. I should be allowed to drink if I want, fight or no fight."

"That's my girl."

Taking a glass from the bar I walked around the room enjoying Emma's company. We talked about the wedding and everything that's happened the last few months. It was nice having her here with me. My only wedding request was that Emma was one of my bridesmaids. I knew Mom wasn't happy having someone not from one of the families involved, but I needed her.

While making rounds I lost track of the drinks I'd picked up and the night was starting to look more bubbly. Making a mental note to make the drink in my hand my last I ran into Juliette.

"Eliana!" She cheered. "Can you believe it? We're almost sisters!"

"No, I really can't believe it!" I answered. "It doesn't feel real."

"Look, I know you and Apollo are busy tonight, but I just wanted to say thanks." She smiled.

"Thanks for what?"

"For convincing Dad to let me go to Italy. He says he's taking me out there this summer to tour a few schools and visit Lizzi. He says I'll be staying with her and working when I'm there. He said if I'm going to school for something like art history he wants me working and staying close to family."

I had no idea Cristiano finally agreed to Juliette going to school in Italy. I thought after our argument it would be a done deal, and she'd never leave the states. The only way I could imagine him changing his mind is if Apollo said something.

Knowing that if I tried to say something I might just start crying I pulled Juliette into a big hug. I held her close to me as I pictured her all grown up exploring Italy on her own. I knew Apollo had done this for me just as much as he had done it for her. He knew how much hurt I'd faced in the past, and how important it was for me to give Juliette a chance at a better life.

Thanks to Apollo she would never know what it would feel like having a father rip away a dream. No matter how small or silly Italy seems to others Juliette and I both know how important it is to her.

She just wants to feel normal in this world we were born into. Maybe it was the champagne or what Juliette had just told me, but I was struggling to stay mad at Apollo.

I said goodbye to Juliette and went looking for Apollo. I found him talking to one of his men. He excused himself when I walked over and followed me back to the table.

I stopped and turned to face him before I sat down.

"I just talked to Juliette about Italy." I said.

"What did she have to say about Italy?" He asked.

"She said your dad finally agreed to her going to school there. He's even going to take her to Lizzi's this summer."

"Good for her." He said.

"Did you know Cristiano finally agreed to her going to school over there?"

"No, I had no idea. I mean, we talked about it a few times, but this is the first I'm hearing about it." He lied, trying to play it off.

"Really?" I asked.

"Yeah, I had no idea."

Apollo couldn't meet my eyes. He was an incredible liar to everyone, but me. He refused to look directly at me when he was lying. He knew how much this all meant to me, and still if Juliette hadn't said something I would have had no idea he'd done this for her. My heart hurt, ached really. How the hell was I going to be able to stay mad at him?

Grabbing Apollo by the neck I brought him to my lips. I gave him a quick kiss before leaning him away from me. I would have kissed him for longer, but I didn't need him knowing I was forgiving him.

Smiling as he leaned back, Apollo ran his hands through his hair.

"How many drinks have you had tonight Eliana?" He asked.

"One or two." I lied, "Why?"

"Because you only smile like that when you're looking to commit murder, or drunk. I'm just trying to figure out what Eliana I'm dealing with."

"Lucky for you, you're dealing with drunk Eliana. So far there isn't anyone who's pissed me off enough tonight to want to kill." I laughed.

"Then we should probably get you home before that changes."

"Probably." I agreed.

"I'll go let our parents know we're leaving. Go wait for me near the stairs." He ordered.

I did as he asked and concentrated on walking towards the front of the house. Leaning against the staircase I waited for Apollo. While I was waiting, the flower vases and statues in my parent's foyer were starting to spin. That last drink might have been a mistake. Soon I felt a touch on my shoulder. Looking up I saw a concerned Apollo looking down at me.

"One or two drinks huh?" He asked.

"I was never good at math."

"Let's get you home, my love." He said, wrapping his arm around my waist.

Apollo helped to make sure I didn't hit my head getting into the car, and then quickly closed the door. I struggled to get comfortable in my seat. I couldn't find the seatbelt, and I felt trapped sitting in Apollo's tiny car. As soon as Apollo pulled out of the driveway I rolled my window down. I needed something to cool down the heat in my cheeks. I could feel Apollo keeping a close eye on everything I did. He looked away from the road to me every few seconds to make sure I was okay.

Feeling better, I leaned back into the car. Shifting so that I had a better view of Apollo I leaned onto the middle console of the car. Apollo looked right at me as I stared at him.

"What's wrong?" He asked.

"Nothing. Just watching."

Leaning over to touch Apollo's face I ran my finger across the small scar by his ear.

"How did you get this?" I asked.

"Bar fight." Apollo's jaw tightened as I touched his face, exploring with my fingers.

I ran my hand down his neck and found another scar where the first button on his suit was.

"And this one?"

"I don't remember." He lied.

"Yes, you do."

"Training with my father gone wrong."

Dragging my hand down his chest I struggled to pull my hand away. My hand explored further and further down his shirt. Soon I was near his belt buckle. Apollo shifted in his seat and let out a small cough.

"Eliana..."

"What?"

"I warned you what would happen if you continued to play this game. Are you sure you want to continue?"

Knowing I wasn't ready just yet I quickly removed my hand from Apollo's lap.

The rest of the drive home was quiet. I didn't wait for Apollo to turn off the car before I was attempting to climb out of it. I was through the garage and the kitchen in under a minute. I wanted more than anything to get out of this dress and go to bed.

I had no idea Apollo was behind me until I heard the bedroom door close. When I turned around I saw Apollo leaned against the door.

I almost considered walking over to him to make sure he was okay when he finally spoke.

"I warned you Eliana. Didn't I tell you what would happen if you continued to tease me?" He asked.

"Yes."

"And did you listen?"

"No." I whispered.

Apollo slowly turned around, undid his belt, and threw it across the room. Unbuttoning his shirt, he walked over to me.

"Take off that fucking dress and get on the bed."

I could have left the room, or tried to argue, but I didn't. Just like he asked I let my dress fall to the floor, and I walked over to the bed.

I sat on the edge of the bed and waited for Apollo. He walked over to me and stood in between my legs. He towered over me as he grabbed my chin and squeezed.

"You have no idea what you do to me Eliana, it's cruel. I'm going to fuck you so hard tonight you'll forget why you were angry in the first place. I tried my hardest to be patient with you El, but I'm not letting you run away this time."

Pulling my chin up he leaned down to softly kiss me. He licked my lips, teasing me with his tongue. When I tried to lean into his kiss he pulled away.

"Go lay down."

I crawled onto the bed and laid down with my head on one of my pillows. While Apollo finished taking his clothes off I pulled at my lingerie I was wearing.

"Don't even think about it. Don't move." He snapped.

I dropped my hands and waited as still as I could on the bed.

Apollo pulled my two breasts out and started to suck them. His head dipped lowed as he played with each breast, taking turns to leave equal marks on either one. While he sucked on my left breast he played with my right.

"I missed this so fucking much." He spoke, muffled by my tits.

While Apollo sucked and played with me I ran my fingers through his hair. He'd barely just begun and already I was feeling knots in my stomach. I have no idea how I managed to survive this long without his touch.

Leaning back to face me Apollo ran his hands through my hair and pushed my loose hairs out of my eyes. Pulling my hair behind my back and gripping my neck he started leaving sloppy kisses down my neck.

I tried to take over, and guide Apollo where I wanted him to kiss, but he quickly took back control. I tried to bring my hands down to Apollo's waist, but he stopped me.

Pulling away from me Apollo leaned off of the bed and started to walk away.

"Where are you going?" I asked, sitting up on my elbows.

"I have to grab something. I'll be right back, don't move a muscle Eliana."

Staying exactly where I was I waited for Apollo to come back. When he did I almost lost the breath in my lungs.

"Where did you find that?" I asked.

"In that little black box, you hide in your closet. I found it when I moved you into the house. You're lucky I was the one who found the box, and not one of my men." He said.

Holding out his hand I had a better view of the little pink vibrator Apollo had taken from my closet.

Apollo came closer, sitting back down on the bed. He sat next to me and laid my vibrator on my stomach.

"How- What are you-"

"If it's not already obvious I'm going to make sure you never keep this fucking pussy of yours from me again. I'm going to fuck you with this vibrator, and then when you're ready to tap out I'm going to fuck you with my dick and remind you why these games of yours aren't appreciated."

"Apollo..." I barely whispered, in shock at Apollo's short temper.

"I warned you Eliana. I told you I wouldn't be forgiving. Now, lay down and put your arms at your side."

Following his directions, I laid down on my back and stared at the ceiling. Apollo clicked on my vibrator to the second setting and started teasing me. He ran it along my arm, then my stomach, tracing it along my thighs as he followed the vibrations with delicate kisses.

We'd barely just begun and I was already soaked. Turning it up another level, sooner than I was anticipating I reacted to the touch of the vibrator on my inner thigh.

"You have no idea how long I've been waiting to use this on you Eliana. And don't even get me started on the other toys you have in that little box of yours. Soon, I'll get the chance to use all of them."

For a few more minutes Apollo teased me, barely running the vibrator in-between my legs.

"Do you want me to fuck you with this Eliana?" He asked.

"Yes, please."

Smiling, Apollo pulled away. He dropped the vibrator on the bed and grabbed my legs underneath my knees. He spread my legs open and dropped so that he was lying on his stomach.

Surprised to see him drop the vibrator I looked up at him, confused.

"I want to play with that just as much as you do El, but first I need to taste you."

Wasting no time Apollo spread my folds with his tongue and started kissing and licking all over. He ran his tongue from as low as he could all the way up to the clit. Once he found my favorite spot he started to spin circles. He knew he was hitting the right spot because his grip on my legs tightened. Keeping me from being able to move. I was held down by Apollo as he ate me out. Showing no mercy, Apollo increased pressure on my sensitive clit. He must have been able to tell I was close because he stopped.

"It's your turn Eliana. I want to watch. You're going to play with yourself just like you used to do alone in the shower." He said.

Handing me the vibrator Apollo leaned back and watched.

I'd never been so quick to follow a direction before, but something about the way Apollo looked at me had me forgetting how to act. I wanted to see what would happen next, so I took the vibrator and turned it on.

Before I'd only had images of Apollo in my head when I played with myself, but tonight I had Apollo staring back at me as he rubbed the bulge in his boxers. I was losing it as I watched his head drop onto his shoulders, eyes rolling back in ecstasy. It was only me who turned him on this much, and I was excited to see if I could make him angry again.

Stopping the vibrator and setting it down I watched as Apollo turned his gaze back up to my eyes.

"I didn't give you permission to stop Eliana." He warned.

"And?"

"And you're going to regret that."

Pulling my legs down closer to him Apollo grabbed the vibrator and lifted my knees onto his shoulders. Apollo turned the vibrator up to its highest setting and placed it inside me. While he fucked me with my own vibrator he applied as much pressure as he could on my clit, sucking and kissing all over me.

In minutes, I was twisting and turning in our bed, trying to hold back my orgasm. I couldn't think straight. One minute I was focused on Apollo's tongue, the next I was shaking from the vibrator. I've never made it this long playing with my vibrator before on this setting. Apollo knew I was close because my legs began to twitch, but still he continued.

"Not yet." He mumbled, not removing his tongue from my clit.

Losing control over my own body I felt my muscles relax and my body melt into the bed as I came. I was spasming under Apollo's touch.

My orgasm didn't slow him down at all. He applied the same pressure as before and sped up his pumping of the vibrator. I didn't have time to ease the throbbing of my first orgasm before my second one hit me.

"Fuck, Apollo, I can't- I'm going to-" I moaned.

Apollo pulled out the vibrator and stuck his tongue as deep as he could.

"Come Eliana, don't hold anything back." He ordered.

Grabbing his shoulder, I cried as I released for a second time. My thighs were numb, and I could barely feel Apollo as he continued his long, slow, kisses.

Knowing I needed a few minutes to recover Apollo sat back. He watched and waited to make sure I was alright after my last orgasm. I could see it in his eyes that he wanted to go all night. We were nowhere near done.

After my breathing returned to normal, and my legs relaxed Apollo laid down close to me.

"You're not the only one who got off in the shower Eliana. Almost every night when I heard you in your room all alone I had to go take a cold shower to calm down. Some nights I'd picture you on your bed losing control just like you did right now. Other times I'd picture you in the shower, and all I could think about was how bad I wanted to be in that shower with you." He said.

"What did you think about while showering?" I asked.

"I'd picture you on your knees, smiling up at me, ready to take my whole dick in your mouth." He confessed.

"You like it when I suck your dick?" I asked, moving on the bed so that I was now the one sitting near the foot of the bed.

Before he could respond I pulled his boxers off and had started licking up and down his dick.

"Like this?"

Apollo took a deep breath, chest rising. I was impatient tonight. I couldn't spend as much time as I wanted teasing Apollo with kisses, because I wanted to see him unravel the deeper he fucked my mouth.

Sliding him down my throat as far as he would fit I played with his balls. Gagging, but not releasing him I felt him run his fingers through my hair.

"Fuck, El."

Sucking tighter and tighter as I bounced my head up and down I started to twist up and down his shaft. Barely breathing I had to take a break to get some air. While I was trying to recover Apollo dragged his fingers over my mouth cleaning off my spit. He grabbed my jaw and brought me up to his lips to give me a deep kiss.

"Keep going." He whispered.

I repositioned my hips so I could dip lower while on my knees as I sucked him. This time I gave a little bit more attention to his head as I rubbed him back and forth. After only a few more minutes of Apollo thrusting his hips up to deep throat me he pulled me off of him.

I was flipped onto my back as Apollo reached for the vibrator again.

"If you keep sucking me like that El I'll come before I get the chance to fuck this bad attitude out of you."

I smiled up at Apollo. I watched his every move as he spread my legs, reaching under my hips to set himself closer to me.

"Use our safe word if you need it."

With no other warning Apollo slid his entire dick into me. The sensation was overwhelming and I grabbed his forearms letting him know I needed him to start thrusting.

Apollo's fingers gripped tight onto my hips leaving marks as he fucked me. I was still sensitive from earlier, so every time Apollo slid in, my nerves were begging for a break. Grabbing the vibrator Apollo pressed it against my clit. The vibrations paired with Apollo's dick were sending me over the edge. I knew I was close to a third orgasm already, and we'd only just begun.

"Keep clenching around my cock like that Eliana and I'm not going to last much longer." Apollo moaned.

"I can't help it Apollo, I'm close."

"You aren't allowed to come yet El, I want you to beg for it."

"What?" I asked.

"I wasn't lying when I said I wanted you to fucking beg for it. You thought you could keep this from me and I wouldn't be upset. How many times do I have to tell you you're mine? I won't be as kind the next time you find the courage to keep me from you again."

"Apollo- please."

"Please what?"

"I want you to fuck me as hard as you can until I come again, please."

Leaning down, Apollo softly kissed my lips.

"Have you learned your lesson, my love?"

"Yes." I cried.

Apollo's sinister smile returned as he thrusted harder than before and turned up the vibrator to another level.

"Let go, El, relax." He soothed.

Letting my body relax and listening to Apollo I let orgasm number three take over my body. My walls tightening around Apollo as I convulsed sent him over the edge with me. After I'd come, he dropped the vibrator and grabbed my hips one more time to give him more control as he came. Apollo started to slow down, and his eyes closed as he cursed out my name.

Lying down next to me Apollo watched as I calmed down from my orgasm. He ran his fingers through my hair and left small kisses along my neck.

"Do you need me to bring you anything?" He asked.

"I think I need a shower."

"That sounds like an amazing idea."

"An actual shower Apollo." I laughed.

Sighing Apollo stood up, "I'll go get the water warm."

Leaving to go start the shower I waited for Apollo to come back.

"Do you need me to carry you?" He teased.

"You're kidding, right? I'll be lucky if I'm walking by the wedding." I laughed.

Apollo slid his arm under my legs and I wrapped my arms around his shoulders.

"This was great practice for our wedding night. Now I know why they call it a rehearsal dinner." He smiled.

"Oh God." I sighed, falling into his chest.

Chapter Twenty-One

Eliana

"Let's go!" Nora shouted at me from the other side of the door as I stood in front of the mirror. "You can't be late to your own wedding Eliana."

I knew she was right, and I knew I had to go before our guests started to whisper and guess why there was a delay in the ceremony, but I was stuck.

I couldn't pull myself away from the mirror. I was staring back at a woman I didn't recognize. She stood before me in a white dress, flowers in hand, and I couldn't find a single freckle or feature that looked like mine.

Maybe it was the dress, or the guests waiting in the other room, but something was wrong. It felt like I was in a dream, trying to run or scream, but being unable to. This isn't what I want. I didn't want Nora running around chasing after her kids, or Mom complaining about every little thing that hadn't gone wrong yet. I didn't want to hear from my father how excited he was to finally be walking me down the aisle. I didn't want to walk into a room full of strangers who were secretly praying for my downfall.

I promised a younger Eliana I was never going to get married and now here I was. It didn't mean I wasn't excited to be marrying Apollo, it just felt different. I could lie and tell myself it was nerves, but I knew why I was struggling. Years ago, fighting with Dad I promised I'd never marry. I warned him he'd lose me as a daughter if he used me and handed me off to the highest bidder. Now, here I was. Even though Apollo is my future, a future Dad isn't a part of, he still wins.

I let the intrusive thoughts win, as I struggled to stay calm.

What if someone is here to hurt Apollo or me? What if Apollo isn't there waiting for me at the altar? What if this is a mistake? What if-

"Wow." A voice interrupted from behind me.

Looking through the mirror, I saw Apollo staring back at me.

"Apollo, you can't be here! You aren't supposed to see me before the wedding. It's bad luck."

"You are so beautiful." He smiled, stepping closer to me, ignoring my attempts to create distance between us.

Turning around I tried to step closer to the mirror to stop him from walking over to me.

"Apollo..."

"You should know by now I don't believe in luck, my love."

"But still. If my mother sees you, she'll shoot you herself." I tried to reason.

"I'll take my chances." He spoke.

Apollo grabbed my wrist and pulled me close to him.

"I know I'm not supposed to be here, but I needed to see you." He confessed.

Suddenly, the terrible feeling in my chest started to disappear. The longer I stared into Apollo's eyes, the more I remembered what I was doing here in this church. I'd almost forgotten why I was standing in front of this mirror, in the priest's dressing room. It wasn't for my family, or for anyone else. It was for Apollo.

I dropped my head and rested it onto Apollo's chest as I let out a sigh.

"Something's wrong." He spoke. It wasn't a question. He knew I was upset.

"Before you showed up I was having a moment."

Apollo pulled my shoulders back to look at me again, "A moment?"

"It all felt wrong. I was trying to build up enough courage and force myself to leave this room."

"You were having second thoughts?" He asked.

"No, I just have this bad feeling that I can't shake."

"Did something happen?"

"No, it's stupid I don't want to say."

"Eliana..."

"It's my dad."

"Your dad did something to upset you?" He asked, shoulders tensing.

"No, he didn't do anything. I just- I don't want to give him the satisfaction of getting to walk me down the aisle. He doesn't deserve that moment with me. He's the reason for all this pain, and now in front of everyone he gets to look like a good dad." I confessed.

Apollo let my words sink in, saying nothing for a moment. Finally, after a minute of just staring down at me he held my hands in his.

"If you don't want him walking you down the aisle then he won't walk down with you."

Letting out a laugh I rolled my eyes.

"I'm not kidding Eliana. You don't have to do anything you don't want to do."

"And how do you suggest I tell my dad he won't be walking me down the aisle?" I asked.

"You don't need to explain your decision to him. It's our wedding."

I leaned my head away from Apollo's chest, looking back towards the door. Again, I got lost in my own thoughts. Could I really walk without my dad making a scene?

"Eliana, look at me." Apollo spoke, eyes staring straight at me. "I'll walk down with you."

"You want to walk down with me?" I asked.

"It would be an honor, my love."

Considering Apollo's offer I imagined walking down the aisle with him instead. Why couldn't I walk down with Apollo? He's right, it's our wedding.

"Okay, yeah, let's do it." I agreed.

"Okay." He smiled, leaning in for a kiss.

"Are you ready? Do you need another minute?" He asked.

"No, I'm ready."

Grabbing my hand and walking out of the room Apollo led us down the narrow church hallway. I had to let go of Apollo's hand to hold onto his arm as I struggled to keep up with him. He was so excited to walk with me he forgot for a moment I was in heels and a dress. I smiled up at him as he paused in front of the sanctuary doors.

438

The two of us ignored the yelling from both our families as we walked past them. The yelling faded behind us as the organs began to play. It mattered less who was standing in the pews as Apollo and I walked in. Half way down the aisle I started to turn my head to see if Dad had calmed down, or if he was still upset.

Apollo looked down, and squeezed my hand, "Don't look. This is our moment. No one gets to ruin this."

Looking up at him I smiled, trying to commit this moment to memory.

Finally, making it to Dane and Nora, Apollo kissed my cheek. I gave my flowers to Nora, and Apollo shook Dane's hand as we took our places in front of everyone. Just before Father Francis started the ceremony with a prayer, both of our parents found their seats. I don't remember if I even bothered to look and see if they were mad. I knew they wouldn't make a scene in front of all our guests.

As Father spoke on, I prayed for time to slow down. I kept my focus on Apollo. There was an unspoken irony to Apollo and I standing in a church together. I'm a little surprised Apollo didn't burst in flames the minute we walked in together. It was clear Apollo also found our wedding humorous as I watched him hold back a smile. He squeezed my hand every time Father Francis gave us a disappointed glare for messing up the ceremony.

The room went quiet and Father Francis gave me a small nod. It was time for the vows. Taking in a deep breath I focused on Apollo, and only Apollo.

"It is a gift to be loved by you Apollo. You made a world that once felt so isolating, and forbidding, feel like home. I wish I could go back in time and tell a young Eliana that the Apollo she got stuck working with in the bakery would soon bring her so much comfort. That he would stand beside her and hold her hand through all the painful nights. That he would show her the true meaning of patience, and self-love. To show her a kindness

439

that she never thought she deserved. I admire how hard you fight to protect those that you love, and I promise to spend the rest of my life protecting you. I promise to love you and stand by your side even when it feels like we're standing alone."

Apollo bit his cheek and gave the back of my hand a soft kiss after I had given him his ring. Time unfortunately ticked on, and soon Apollo was grabbing my waist to pull me into a kiss.

I barely remember what happened next. Together we walked down the aisle one more time, hand in hand. The church cheered for us newlyweds as we ran down the stairs into the back of a car. Dane had somehow made it to the car before us and was ready to take us away. Looking out the window of the car I watched as Mom cried, and Raff waved goodbye. It was over. Apollo and I were finally married.

Apollo did his best to keep me smiling during family photos, and soon we were leaving to go to the reception. Before we entered the reception we both took a minute to ourselves. We sat on a bench near the ballroom and sat in silence as we listened to the rush of the kitchen, the laughs of guests, and the clinking of wine glasses.

Apollo played with the rings on my fingers as we sat. He played with the band attached to the first ring he ever gave me. For the first time since our engagement, I knew the rings I wore meant something to the both of us. They were from a man who loved me unconditionally.

Walking in together one final time, we entered the main hall. Cheers from the families echoed across the room as we walked to our table. We had less than a minute to sit and eat before guests were coming to pay their respects. Like it or not, everyone knew it was Apollo and me who would be taking over the Costa business. Many came to the wedding to show support for Apollo, and his father's retirement.

"I have a few people I need to thank for coming tonight. Will you be okay?" Apollo whispered in my ear, placing his hand on my thigh.

"I'll be fine." I smiled.

The night carried on. Our guests were happy, dinner was delicious, and Mom had little left to complain about. I spent most of the night dancing with Juliette, and Nora. I had little time to enjoy my own reception with all the family members that wanted to offer their blessings. Apollo was just as busy entertaining our guests for most of the night. We both knew this wedding was more for his father and their business than anything else. I knew soon it would be just the two of us, and we'd have time to enjoy each other's company. Until then I drank champagne, ate a few too many pieces of cake, and enjoyed one last party with Nora, Frankie and Raff. We danced and laughed just like we used to when we were younger. It felt like the goodbye the four of us had been looking for all these years.

Towards the end of the night Maria found her way to my table. She sat next to me and offered her congratulations.

"Thank you for coming tonight Maria, it means the world to Apollo and me. We can't thank you and Rio enough for your support."

"Please, we're family. You call us anytime, and we'll be there."

"Maybe the next time we visit our trip won't be cut short, like last time." I said.

"And maybe next time you and Apollo won't feel like you have to lie to us." Maria replied.

"I'm sorry?" I asked.

"Oh, don't worry, I'm not upset. Rio and I knew the minute you stepped out of your car you two weren't thrilled about the engagement. We knew because we were there once. Young, arranged to be married, and trying to make your family happy."

"If you knew why didn't you say anything?" I asked.

"We enjoyed seeing Apollo well, dare I say, frazzled." She laughed.

"I could tell you two weren't in love yet, but Rio and I both knew that was changing. You needed more time to get to know Apollo, but he was already falling for you. He watched your every move, careful to not upset you. It was quite cute."

"Was it that obvious?" I asked.

"Eliana, he nearly had a heart attack anytime he had a chance to hold you or be near you. He was anxious and on edge, he just didn't know why. He thought it was because he was back in Italy, but it would take an idiot not to notice it's because he was in Italy with you."

"This is so embarrassing." I sighed, sinking in my seat.

Maria just laughed and looked around for Apollo.

"Look there, do you see Apollo?" She asked, pointing.

"Yes." I answered.

"That's real love. The way his eyes warm when he finds you in a room, the way his shoulders drop and relax when you smile. There isn't a woman alive who is lucky enough to be admired like that by anyone." She said.

Feeling my cheeks turn red I smiled and watched Apollo give me a reassuring wink as he ignored the men trying to have a conversation with him. Maria pulled me back to reality by grabbing my hand.

"I can't thank you enough Eliana. It was you, and you alone who saved Apollo. I'll forever be in your debt. I love that boy like a son. I can't imagine this world without him." She spoke, patting my hand and walking away.

Almost as soon as Maria left my table Apollo came back.

"What were you talking to Maria about?" He asked.

"Nothing important." I lied.

Apollo continued to stand near our table instead of having a seat. He looked around towards the dance floor, resting his shaking hands in his pockets.

"Apollo?"

"Mhmm?" He asked, not even looking back at me.

"You doing okay? We can leave if you're tired and need a break. I know you've been busy with guests all day. I'm sure no one would notice if we snuck out."

"We can't leave yet." He spoke quickly.

"Why not?"

"We just can't."

I hoped for a better answer than that, but Apollo was too preoccupied to continue bothering. Instead of waiting for Apollo to explain why he was acting so weird I tried to follow where he was looking. From where I was sitting it looked like he was waiting for something to happen near the band. After a minute, I saw the violinist give a quick nod to Apollo. Shaking his shoulders out and looking back at me he bit his lip trying to hide his smile.

"Apollo, what's going on?" I asked.

Before he could answer, a familiar melody sung through the room. I knew in the first three notes what song was being played. It was the same song from the night of our engagement party. I looked towards the dance floor and saw guests start to head back to their table. When I looked back at Apollo he was holding out his hand.

"Would you like to dance, Mrs. Costa?"

Chapter Twenty-Two

Apollo

I've always hated when someone called me lucky. They only ever used that word when I had cheated death. I wasn't lucky when I was born a Costa, I wasn't lucky when I learned I was the heir to my father's empire, or when I drowned myself in alcohol so a doctor could pull another bullet out of my torso. People only called me lucky when they were glad they weren't me.

In all my life I'd never felt lucky, but all that changed when I found Eliana standing there in front of the mirror. I didn't deserve her, but still the universe gave me permission to love her. I don't know how long I will get to spend loving Eliana, so for now I will cherish the minutes, hours, days we get together.

Eliana begged me to leave as soon as she saw me standing behind her, but I was stuck. There was no way in hell I could leave her now that I'd gotten to see her in that dress. The way it hugged her curves, her back exposed. There was no one more beautiful, and tonight I finally got to call her mine.

When Eliana gets nervous she never knows what to do with her hands. Back in the room she was fidgeting and picking at every little piece of fabric on her dress. Now that we were walking down the aisle together I gave her my hands so that she could calm down.

As the doors to the church opened she held onto me tight like she was afraid I'd let go of her, but every step we took together she became more and more relaxed. Soon she barely held onto my suit as we walked. The farther away we walked from her family the better she felt. I would have walked a thousand miles with her by my side if she'd asked me to. She almost turned around, but I stopped her before she could.

"Don't look. This is our moment. No one gets to ruin this." I spoke softly to her.

Eliana smiled up at me and washed away all the fears I had that she was regretting staying. She had been promising me for days she was sure she wanted to stay, but there was a small voice in my head that told me she'd leave one day. I knew for sure that voice of doubt was wrong because I'd never seen Eliana smile brighter than this moment. She always paused, taking a moment to relax her face before smiling, but right now I was seeing her real smile. I hope the dozen photographers we hired today captured this smile, because I'm not sure when I'll get to see it again. This smile wasn't forced or posed; it was just... her. As the priest started mass I thought of ways to make Eliana smile like that again.

I thought holding Eliana's hand would calm my nerves during my vows, but it only made it worse. Everyone in this room, me included, knew I didn't deserve someone like Eliana. Against everyone's better judgment she chose me.

"You once told me we would never last because relationships only work if you find your opposite. I could never figure out why you thought that because for all the bad that I am you are double the good. I hate that you see a version of me when you look in the mirror because all I see is warmth, kindness, and redemption when I look at you. I know it's hard for the two of us to forget how we began but starting today I want you to only think about our future and our end."

Eliana let a few tears slip as she squeezed my hand. Fuck, Eliana looking into my eyes sent my stomach twisting in to a million knots I'll never be able to untie.

Father had barely finished announcing we were husband and wife when I grabbed her and pulled her into a kiss. Cheers erupted from all of our guests as Eliana and I ran out of the church together. I trusted Dane to bring our car around before a crowd gathered outside. Once we were in the back of the car, everything went quiet. All the distractions and noise from the wedding were gone.

"Oh God." Eliana sighed, resting her head onto my shoulder.

"It's over, El." I said.

"It's over." She repeated, letting out a deep breath.

"Now all we have to do is survive the reception and keep everyone from killing each other." I joked.

"Piece of cake." She smiled.

As soon as we arrived at the reception Eliana and I were pulled into different directions. We both knew there were a lot of people I needed to speak with and thank for attending the wedding. Our wedding was the biggest reunion of all of the families in decades. I'd been meeting with business partners and distant relatives for hours. I did my best to stay focused, but I was exhausted.

My favorite part of the evening was knowing that no matter where I traveled, or who I talked to, Eliana was keeping a close eye on me. When I left for the back patio she coincidentally walked to the bar to give herself a better view of the outside. When I was sitting near a table with guests she found her way back to our table. We spent little time together throughout the night, but it was enough to know she was near.

Dinner was over, cake had been cut, and guests were using our wedding as an excuse to party. Eliana and I might be the only two sober people here. I went looking for Eliana and found her talking with Maria. I watched as the two of them laughed and said their goodbyes. I waited until Maria was walking back to Rio before I went over to El.

"What were you talking about to Maria?" I asked.

"Nothing important."

I knew that had to be a lie because Eliana's cheeks were rosy like she was blushing from embarrassment. Maria must have been giving her a hard time about me. Maybe one day I'll convince her to tell me what the two of them shared, but right now we had somewhere to be.

I'd been planning a small surprise for her for weeks with the band, and I was struggling to hide it any longer. She knew right away something was up, and thought I was ready to leave. I did my best to avoid eye contact with her, or else I would have given everything away.

Before Eliana could figure out what I was hiding I heard our song playing, and guests start to slowly leave the dance floor. I turned around and held my hand out for Eliana.

"Would you like to dance, Mrs. Costa?"

Eliana took my hand and let me lead her to the dance floor, just like the night of our engagement.

. . .

"Apollo..." Eliana paused, searching around the room for answers.

As the lights dimmed, and the band continued to play it finally felt like Eliana and I were alone. Gone were our guests and our family that had kept us apart all day.

"This is our song." Eliana smiled. "I can't believe you remembered."

"I remember everything about that night, my love."

"Everything?"

"Of course. You made quite the first impression storming into your dad's office like that. You were so pissed." I laughed.

"I was mad because you looked at me like you knew I was going to show up. It's like you were expecting me."

"I might have made a bet with Dane that you would show up." I confessed.

Eliana hit my chest, continuing to follow my lead as we danced.

"How did you know I'd show?" She asked.

"I hadn't spoken to you in years, and we never really were that close, but there was one thing I knew about you. No matter what, you always put your family first. Your whole life you sacrificed everything for your parents and siblings. You supported Nora when she married Mikey even though you knew your dad could only lose one daughter, and that meant you would marry for the family business. Right around the time you decided to go to law school Raff and Frankie started working high risk jobs for your father. After graduating, you represented them, and kept them out of jail. You stood up to my father and supported Juliette when she needed it most, and you've always supported any decision I needed to make. That's just who you are. You always put the needs of those you love above your own. I knew you would agree to marry me even though it meant giving up the life you built for yourself."

Eliana held a hand up to my cheek, leaned up on her tiptoes, and kissed me.

"I love you." She whispered.

Kissing her back, I held onto her tighter.

"I remember everything about that night too. Remember your little whisper counts?" She asked.

"I have no idea what you're talking about." I lied.

"Oh come on Apollo, just admit it! You were counting the steps in your head."

"I admit nothing."

Continuing to tease me Eliana fixed her posture and took control of the dance. She mimicked my counting as she danced me around in circles.

"One, two, three- one, two, three-" She laughed.

"Alright." I said, picking her up, and spinning her around. Eliana finally gave up her teasing and leaned her head into my chest for the rest of the song. She leaned into me just like this that first night. I replayed that moment in my head on loop for months. I tried to fight the voice in my head that told me to protect her and keep her safe, but it was pointless. Holding her now I could finally admit to myself I cared for her from the beginning. I danced with Eliana until our song ended, and for a few more songs after that.

I tried to enjoy this moment with Eliana and forget about the rest of the evening, but I couldn't shake the feeling I was being watched by an unwelcome guest. Looking out into the crowd I found a familiar face. The same man that Eliana kicked out of our rehearsal dinner.

I never asked her about him, but I hadn't forgotten how rushed she was at getting him to leave. As if she could sense my irritation Eliana leaned away from my chest and stared in the same direction I was staring.

"Are you ready to tell me who that man is, Eliana?"

"I already told you, he's an old friend."

"And does your friend have a name?" I asked.

"Carter."

"What is he doing at our wedding?"

"I needed his help with your wedding gift." She said.

"What was so challenging about my gift that it required this friends' assistance."

"When you see what I got you, you'll understand."

So, that's how she was going to play this? All these secrets and riddles just for a silly wedding gift?

"When exactly do I get this secret gift?"

"Carter being here means everything is ready. All you need to do now is sneak us out of here without our mothers stopping us."

"That shouldn't be too hard."

"Good luck, I know for a fact my mom has three guys on every exit." She said.

Looking over Eliana's head I found a small hallway not being guarded.

"Go over to that door and wait for me in the hallway. If you don't see me in two minutes just start running."

Letting go of Eliana I went looking for Dane. I found him talking to someone I didn't know. She wasn't related to any of the families, otherwise I would have recognized her. She had to be one of Eliana's guests.

"Dane. I need a favor."

"I'm a little busy at the moment." He said, not looking away from his friend.

"Okay, let me rephrase. Dane, I need your help and as your boss you have thirty seconds to help or I'll show this friend of yours how easy it is to break a finger."

450

Rolling his eyes, Dane fixed his suit jacket and set down his drink.

"What do you want?"

"Distract my mom for a few minutes so El and I can sneak out without being spotted."

"Only you two would try to leave your own wedding before any of your guests." He laughed.

Dane held his hand out to his little friend.

"Have you met Catalina yet?" He asked.

"Not yet." She smiled.

"Well you're about to, so prepare yourself. Let's go, I'll need your help distracting her so they can get out of here."

As Dane made his way towards Mom a few of the men in charge of her protection stepped away from their posts to watch over Dane's new friend.

This was my moment to grab Eliana and get out of here before any of her men saw us. Walking as calmly as I could into the hallway I saw Eliana ready to run. Catching up to her I grabbed her hand and ran outside. I looked for our car and began to take my keys out of my pocket. Before I could unlock the car, Eliana tried to grab the keys from me.

"What are you doing?" I asked.

"I'm driving."

Laughing, I moved the keys away from Eliana, "No you're not."

"You don't know where we're going. Plus, it's my surprise." She tried to convince.

"There's no chance I let you drive one of my cars again."

"Grow up Apollo, I borrowed your car one time, and I didn't leave a single scratch."

"I'm driving." I said.

"Then you aren't getting your gift."

I stood there, considering my options.

"Thirty seconds Apollo. That's how long you have until my mom finds us out here."

Eliana always drove like she was being chased. It was nauseating.

"Twenty seconds."

On the other hand, I knew she was dead serious I wouldn't get my gift if she wasn't driving.

"Ten seconds."

Fuck it.

I tossed Eliana the keys and ran around to the other side of the car. While Eliana was fixing her dress to fit in the car I saw three of Marco's men running towards us.

"Eliana..." I warned.

Looking over at me, Eliana gave me another one of her big smiles.

"Hold on tight, babe."

Chapter Twenty-Three

Apollo

While Eliana drove, I dealt with our parents. They were mad at us for leaving before our proper send off. They should be thanking us for staying as long as we did. I wanted to drive away with Eliana as soon as we left the church.

"Are they calling again?" Eliana asked.

"They gave up calling. Mom started sending me incredibly vague, threatening texts on Dad's phone."

Giving up, and not wanting to ruin this moment I took both phones and turned them off. I left Eliana's phone in the glove box and put mine back in my pocket.

Looking down the road to see where Eliana might be taking me I saw a few of my warehouses on the left. Neither of us had been back here since the attack.

"What are we doing here El?"

"I needed a private place to leave your gift without anyone finding it."

Pulling up to the warehouse I started to get a little nervous. Eliana wouldn't kill me on our wedding night, would she?

"I'm not here to kill you Apollo. You can relax." She laughed. Great, she can read minds now.

Walking into an empty warehouse Eliana held my hand.

"I wanted to tell you about this sooner, but then I got so busy with the wedding. I almost forgot about it completely until I saw Carter at our rehearsal dinner. I thought there was no reason to tell you about it until after the wedding when you had time to deal with it."

"Eliana." I said, stopping her rambling.

"Just... promise you won't be mad." She said.

"I promise, now please just show me."

Letting go of my hand Eliana unlocked one of our office doors and turned on the lights. Eliana stepped to the right so that I could see what was inside the room.

"What the fuck did you do Eliana?"

"I found Giovanni."

Eliana waited for me to walk into the room. Once I did I could see my cousin tied to a chair, his face almost unrecognizable.

"Surprise."

Eliana looked at me and waited for me to process what I was seeing.

"Why?"

"I wanted him found before he could hurt us again."

"How?"

"A few days after we left Leonardo's I called Carter and asked for his help. He found him trying to get back into the states from Germany."

"That doesn't make sense. Dane said there were sightings of him all over Italy."

"Dane only thought that because Carter and I spread those rumors. We needed to flush him out of hiding. Carter asked around for him and started spreading news of him being in Italy. We weren't sure if he was really there, but we knew if he was then he would be forced to leave. After Carter spread the word Gio was looking for a place to lay low in Italy I tracked flights and trains out of Italy with someone that matched Gio's description."

"And then what? You found him walking the streets of Germany and convinced him to come back here with Carter?"

"Something like that." Eliana laughed. "By the way, you owe that pilot of yours a raise. He was alarmingly comfortable flying a few unregistered guests back and forth from Europe."

I had more questions, but my brain couldn't spit the words out. Standing there in front of Giovanni I tried to picture everything Eliana told me. Does she have any idea how much danger she put herself in tracking him down?

I looked over at Eliana and saw how nervous she looked. She knows what she did was dangerous. I didn't have to tell her.

"You're not mad?" She asked.

I ran my hands down her arm.

"No, I'm not mad. I'm definitely surprised, maybe even a little terrified of what my own wife is capable of, but I could never be mad."

"I knew you would be upset if you found out I'd gone looking for Giovanni on my own, so that's why I asked Carter for help. You don't have to worry about this being connected to us. Carter worked for my family for years and knows how important this is to me."

"Does anyone else besides Carter know he's here?" I asked.

"No one knows he's here, and no one is looking for him. After Leonardo killed Michael their whole family liquidated what they could and left back to Italy. I think Giovanni's sister is staying in New York to finish school but trust me when I say she won't miss him when he's gone."

Looking back over at Giovanni I tried to decide what to do next. I was so focused on trying to find him I hadn't considered what I would do to him once I found him. Giovanni sat with his head dropped, arms taped behind his back.

"Is he even alive?" I asked.

"Barely." She smiled.

I almost forgot how hot this side of Eliana was. Eliana stood next to me and gave me a quick kiss on the cheek before walking to the door.

"You're not staying?" I asked.

"Since the beginning this has been about you and Gio, and I think that's how it should end. I'll be waiting by the car. Plus, I would hate to ruin my dress. Do you have any idea how hard it is getting blood out of silk?"

While Eliana closed the door, I took my suit jacket off. I threw it onto a table that I'm sure Eliana had prepared. On it I found enough tools and knives to last me a while.

I wanted Gio awake so I slapped him a few times and lifted his chin up to the ceiling. That was enough to wake him up and cause him to start fighting against his restraints. He tried to free his hands but sat still when he saw it was me standing in front of him.

"Apollo."

"Giovanni."

"Long time no see." He laughed, coughing up blood.

I said nothing, only walking back to the table to grab a few screws and a drill.

"I have to admit, it took you longer to find me than I thought it would. I almost sent you a postcard." He said.

I ignored Gio's comments and that only pissed him off more. He continued to try and get a reaction out of me.

"How's Eliana doing?" He asked. "You're one lucky son of a bitch, Apollo."

Ripping off the tape behind Gio I brought his hands to the front of the chair. I took great pleasure drilling his left hand onto the arm rest. Gio let out a pattern of curse words. He watched as I slowly drilled a few screws into the back of his hand.

Taking in a few deep breaths he continued to irritate me, "I'm sure Eliana was one of the reasons it took you so long to find me. I'd never get anything done if I had a fiancé with an ass like that."

"She's not my fiancé anymore." I spoke, grabbing his right hand and continuing to drill.

"Fuck!" Gio hissed through his teeth.

"This is your last warning Gio, if I ever hear my wife's name leave your mouth again I'll cut your fucking tongue out."

Dropping the drill, I punched Gio a few times just to make sure my message was received. I tried not to let him get under my skin, but him mentioning Eliana pissed me off.

Gio's body began to shake as he let out a low laugh.

"What's so funny, Gio?"

"After everything we've been through I was expecting a better send off. I was hoping my obituary would say something a little bit more dignified than 'murdered in a warehouse'. This is fucking pathetic."

"You think I'm here to kill you?" I asked.

Now it was my turn to laugh. Walking back to the table I grabbed a hammer.

"After everything you did to me and my family you think I'm going to let you off that easy? No, no way in hell Gio. This is just the beginning. I've had a lot of time to decide what I would do to you, and now that I'm here standing in front of you I think I know what I want."

"You've decided to be the bigger man, and let me go?" He joked.

"Not quite. I want you to know exactly how I felt all these years. I want you to know what it felt like lying half dead on the streets of Italy after you ran my car off the road or watching the terror in Eliana's eyes as we ran from your men until her feet were cut and bloodied. After all that you still sent men to shoot up my warehouse. The only reason Eliana survived that attack was because the bodies of the men you shot fell on top of her. I want you to know what it felt like finding her buried under my men, paralyzed from the shock. You are a spineless, pathetic, coward who couldn't beat me, so you started hurting those closest to me. You are a fucking embarrassment."

Grabbing a hammer from the table I stood in front of Gio.

"Unlike you, I always play fair. I promise to spend the next few months paying back all of the pain you caused me and Eliana. There's no better place to start than the beginning. Your first attack was the car accident. It took a little bit longer than I thought it would to recover from that one. Doctor's spent the first few months betting whether I'd lose my leg."

Grabbing Gio's leg at the thigh, and straightening his leg out, I swung my hammer just below his knee. I tried to line the hammer up exactly where the plates in my own leg were. I swung my hammer until I was sure he couldn't feel his knee any more. Gio clenched his jaw, and did his best to hide the pain he was in.

"Do you know how many surgeries it took to get me walking again, Gio? Four. They cut into me and placed long plates where my bone should be."

Taking a knife from the table and setting the hammer down I walked back to Gio.

"The first two surgeries were to clean out the scar tissue that had built up while I was stuck in a bed unable to move my leg. They had to remove the scar tissue surrounding my knee before they could even start working on my leg."

Cutting deep into Gio's thigh I used the tip of the knife to scoop through Gio's muscle. Blood started gushing out quicker than I was expecting.

"After the second surgery, they could finally start to fix my tibia. Do you know where your tibia is Gio? It's right here."

Cutting down Gio's shin I dug deeper until I could see an inch or two of his own bone. I was having fun cutting into Gio, but I knew if I kept going he was going to bleed out.

"After they were all done, they stitched me up and said if they could get me walking again I would probably have permanent nerve damage in my leg for the rest of my life. Guess what, they were right. I would hate for you to lose feeling in your leg just like me, so I'll make sure to fix all this up before I leave."

Grabbing a small butane torch, I closed up all the cuts I had carved into Gio's leg. Cauterizing Gio's leg I watched him slip in and out of consciousness. There was little left I could do tonight. None of this would be any fun if he was unconscious. Slapping his cheek, I forced him to stay awake.

I was deciding where I wanted to keep Gio when I heard him mumble something under his breath.

"I would be saving my energy if I were you Gio."

Ignoring me, he repeated himself, "I won't be the last."

"The last what?" I asked.

"The last one who tries to ruin you. Kill me today, tomorrow, or even a year from now I don't care. I know soon everyone else will realize you're a fucking fraud. You hate me not because I wanted to kill you, but because I was the first person to almost succeed. You've handled threats before, but after the car accident you ran away like a coward."

Grabbing a knife, I pressed it to Gio's throat until I saw blood slowly roll down his neck.

"Do it." He said.

I was frozen, unable to move the knife any further. We both knew if I did push deeper that I was admitting he was right. I ran

459

away from Italy. For the first time in my life I felt mortal, and I left because I was in denial my own family wanted me dead.

"You're right Gio." I admitted, taking a few steps back. "I left Italy because I was stalling. I was trying to prevent a war between the two of us. Ever since we were little we were always fighting. I thought I was doing the right thing by giving you space to self-destruct. I was doing our family a favor ignoring your tantrums. I'll always regret not dealing with you sooner."

I walked behind Gio, so that he couldn't see me anymore. Cutting his shirt, I ran the blade across his back. He tensed his body and let out a quiet cry.

"At best you were a pest, a nuisance that I kept forgetting to terminate. I probably would have forgotten all about you and Michael, but then you made the mistake of hurting my family. You knew the only way to get a reaction out of me was to hurt Eliana. That's the difference between me and you. I'm a lot of things, but I'm not a cheat, and even backed into a corner I would have never done what you did. You failed to keep this war between you and me, and now you're going to pay the price."

I knew I was pushing my luck messing with Gio like this. Soon I would need Dane to pick him up and bring him to a doctor. I was serious when I told him I needed him healthy. He wasn't going anywhere soon.

"I considered showing you mercy, but now I'm certain you don't deserve it. There's a reason I was chosen to run our family business Gio, and unfortunately for you you're about to learn why. Not even the grim reaper himself will show up to save you when he sees what I've done."

I released the knife from Gio's back and waited for him to have a rebuttal, but the room went quiet. Only a quiet whimper left Gio's lips as he sat still. The quiet of the warehouse was soon interrupted by a soft echo of music coming from outside.

Every few seconds the music grew louder until it was vibrating the office walls. All I could picture was Eliana sitting bored in my car messing with my radio. The music playing from the car meant that Eliana would stay out there all night if she needed to. She knew how much this meant to me, but none of it was fair to her. I was an idiot if I let her sit out there all night, on our wedding night of all nights.

I looked over at Gio and saw him passed out. He wasn't waking up anytime soon. I could get Dane out here within the hour to take care of him. Now that I knew where he was there was no rush dealing with him.

Grabbing my jacket and calling Dane to come pick Gio up I walked back out to the car. I found Eliana reclined in the driver's seat looking through a car manual, music blasting.

"Apollo?" She said, surprised to see me so soon.

Stepping out of the car, she walked up to me. Before she could ask me why I was already leaving I grabbed her and pulled her into a kiss. I held her face in my hands and felt her immediately relax into my arms.

"Let's go home." I whispered, unable to pull away from her lips.

Chapter Twenty-Four

Apollo

"Apollo, you're staring again."

"I can't help it, El."

Rolling her eyes, Eliana let go of my hand and rolled down her window. Twisting her hair into a bun and knotting it in place I watched her enjoy the drive home. She rested her head on her hand as she watched the traffic drive by. I slowed down at every yellow light just so I would have longer to stare at her while I drove.

God, she was beautiful. I had to tighten my grip on the steering wheel to keep my hands from wandering. Unable to take this distance between us any more, I drove a little bit faster down our street. Pulling into the driveway, I parked just before the garage. I walked over to Eliana's side of the car before she had a chance to open the door.

Eliana took off towards the front door, but I stopped her before she got there.

"What do you think you're doing?" I asked.

"I'm going inside." She sassed.

Grabbing Eliana's waist and dropping a hand below her knees I lifted her into my arms. Letting out a surprised shout Eliana grabbed onto my shoulders.

"Apollo, put me down!"

"I can't do that, my love. It's bad luck walking in without you."

"Oh, so you believe in luck now?" She asked.

"I'll believe in whatever hell I have to believe in to get to hold you like this."

Walking into the living room with Eliana I refused to let her go.

"Apollo, you can let me down now." She said.

"If you want down it's going to cost you, Mrs. Costa."

"Oh, really?" She asked.

"Really."

Eliana rolled her eyes and hid her smile as she grabbed my face and pulled me into a kiss. She pushed me away when I tried to deepen the kiss, but there was no escaping. Eliana let a quiet moan escape as I bit down softly on her bottom lip. She quickly snapped back to reality and kicked her feet as she waited for me to let go.

"I love you, but I need to get out of this dress." She said.

Following behind her to the bedroom I stopped her every few steps to pull her back into a kiss. Grabbing her hips as she walked I made sure to stay close to her. She was finally mine, and I didn't plan on ever letting her out of my sight.

Sitting on the bed I watched Eliana take off her jewelry and drop it on her vanity. Tossing her shoes back into the closet, she turned to face me.

"Are you just going to stare, or are you going to help?" She asked.

Jumping to my feet I walked up behind her and found the zipper of her dress. Eliana's muscles tensed as I ran my fingers down her back. I slid the zipper as far as it would go and slipped the dress off of her shoulders. Leaving sloppy kisses on her shoulders, I could feel Eliana's head drop to her shoulders. The stress she had held onto all day was starting to dissolve. I continued to kiss her but turned her so that she was facing me. Her dress fell to the floor and I was left to admire her in nothing but her white, lace lingerie.

"Jesus, El." I whispered in her ear, "You are so fucking beautiful."

Kissing her ear and down her jaw, I felt her wrap her arms around my neck. She tightened her grip on my collar as I kissed down her neck.

Before I made it any lower we were interrupted by a knock at the front door.

"Who is that?" I asked.

"Emma." She said.

"Why is your best friend knocking on our door in the middle of the night?"

"Because I asked her to bring food. I didn't eat anything at the wedding, and then we went straight to the warehouse. I'm starving."

Eliana gave me a kiss on the cheek and then walked over to the closet.

"Go grab the food. I'll meet you downstairs after I get dressed." She said.

Who can blame Eliana for being hungry? I was starving too. The only difference is I was planning on eating something else tonight. Letting out a sigh I went to the porch and found a brown bag sitting on our doorstep. A small note was taped to the side. I brought the bag into the kitchen and walked over to the bottom of the stairs.

"How did she get past the front gate?" I shouted loud enough for El to hear.

"I gave her the pin a long time ago." She replied.

"Lovely." I mumbled.

Eliana came down the stairs wearing one of my t-shirts. She grabbed onto my shoulder as she turned the corner of the staircase.

"Don't worry. She knows she's only allowed to use it in case of emergencies."

"And this was an emergency?"

"She's the only one I can trust to get my order at Joe's right."

Eliana grabbed her sub from the bag and sat down on a barstool.

"Don't worry I had her pick you up something too. Emma has this superpower. She always gets a person's order right without having to ask. It's like a sixth sense of hers."

Grabbing my sub from the bag and unwrapping it I took a small bite. I was hesitant at first, but El was right. It was delicious. I tried to hide my smile, but Eliana could tell right away Emma got my order right.

"How does she do it?" I asked.

"I have no idea, I've never asked. I'd be a fool to question her gift."

Setting down her food Eliana grabbed the bag and pulled off the note.

"What does it say?"

"Cheers, bitch. You owe me." Eliana laughed.

The only other thing left in the bag was a cheap bottle of wine. Eliana took it out and started pouring herself a glass. She lifted the bottle towards me and tilted her head.

"No, thank you." I declined.

"I'll pour you a glass." She said, ignoring me.

Against my better judgment I took a sip of the wine. It was terrible, and I hardly had the stomach to finish my sip. I was going to spit it out, but Eliana was having too much fun watching me drink it.

"This is terrible." I admitted.

"I know, it's awful." She smiled.

"Then why did she buy it?"

"It's the cheapest bottle you can get from Joe's. My sophomore year of college Dad cut me off, and I was kicked out of my apartment. Emma let me stay on her couch and helped me get a job. On the Friday's I got paid we'd go to Joe's and share a sub and split a bottle. I know it's bad, but after a while it became a tradition. It became my way of thanking her for all she did to support me."

"Emma is one of the good ones." I said, "And if this is what you're craving after a day like today then who am I to stop you?"

I picked up my wine glass and waited for Eliana to raise hers, "Salute, my love."

Eliana clinked her drink to mine, and then finished what was left in her glass. The two of us drank our wine and quietly processed our day. The more Eliana drank the more her chair magically inched closer to mine. By the time she'd finished her food and emptied the bottle she was an inch from running into my own chair.

Eliana looked disappointed to see she'd finished the wine and went looking for more. While she found another bottle, I cleaned up our mess. I slid in our chairs and grabbed two glasses to bring with me to the living room. Eliana found me waiting for her on the couch.

Pouring us another glass, Eliana sat next to me and laid on my shoulder. We used to sit like this all the time when we got back from Italy. Back then we were both too afraid to admit our feelings for one another. I tried to build up the courage to tell her how I really felt, but I was afraid I'd lose her. It was enough for me to get to be near her, even if I didn't have the courage to tell her how I really felt. Eliana was my comfort, and I was hers.

For hours, we sat and talked about our day. Who showed up late to the wedding. Who our parents were mad at for showing up even though they weren't invited. Who drank too much at the reception. After spending the whole day apart, we were finally enjoying each other's company. Soon the bottles were empty again, and Eliana was starting to fall asleep.

I watched Eliana swirl her glass and watch her wine twist and drip. She sat her glass down and turned closer to me.

"Apollo."

"Eliana."

"You know I love you right?" She whispered.

"I know, trust me, I know."

"Do you believe in soulmates Apollo?" She asked.

"I'm starting to."

"There is no one else I'd rather spend life with Apollo, do you understand?" She asked.

"Yes." I smiled.

"I'm serious, Apollo. I won't lose you; I can't lose you."

"I'm not going anywhere, Eliana. I made the mistake of leaving already. I can't even imagine how much pain you were in when I left, but I promise you El, I never plan on leaving you like that again."

"Sometimes when I wake up in the morning, this feeling of dread hits me, and it feels like I'm back in my parents' house waiting for you to come home. Even in the mornings I can see you asleep next to me it feels like you're still gone and I have to find you."

"El..."

"Just listen, please." She said, putting a hand on my arm. "I wake up like that most mornings because I can tell you're struggling to come home. You're here physically, but mentally you're still running away from something. It's like you don't believe you're really back, and one day Leonardo will change his mind. I need to know the vows we made to each other today weren't empty promises. Promise me you'll try to come home, for real this time. I don't need any more apologies, or any feelings of guilt for leaving. All I need is you there beside me when I wake up."

"I promise." I said, pulling her onto my lap. "I'll be there every morning El, I promise."

Wrapping her arms around my waist Eliana relaxed in my arms. I sat there and played with her hair and tried to not to think about how much hurt I had caused her.

"I love you Eliana and I promise I'll always be right here." I told her, kissing her forehead.

Eliana relaxed in my arms, as I rocked her back and forth. After the day we had, Eliana began to fall asleep. I could feel her trying to fight it, but she was exhausted. Soon her hand dropped from my shoulder, and I knew I could walk up the stairs without waking her.

Careful not to wake her, I lifted her in my arms and took her up to bed. Laying her down on her pillow and fixing the covers I sat down next to her. I kept telling myself to go to bed myself, but I was unable to leave her. I was worried she would wake up and I wouldn't be there. Once I was sure she was in a deep sleep I walked around the bed and took off my suit. Throwing my clothes somewhere in the room I walked around to my side of the bed. Lying next to Eliana I wrapped my arm around her waist and pulled her towards me. Fixing the hair that had fallen over her eyes as she slept, I thought about what she'd told me downstairs.

She was right about me not being present. Ever since getting back from Leonardo I had felt like I was a step behind everyone, and I was forever running to catch up. I thought I was the only one who noticed, but of course she could feel it too.

All I've ever been good at is running away. I left Italy, I left my family, and I left Eliana. After the year I've had there's one thing I'm sure of. I'm done running.

Eliana deserved more. She deserved someone who would be there for her in the mornings, and someone who would be there to hold her at night. I would give everything up just to be the one she looks for in a busy crowd. No matter what happens after I take over for Dad, or when Eliana's work gets busier I know we'll still have each other. There is nothing and no one that could convince me to leave her again. Eliana was someone worth staying for.

After a few hours of trying to fall asleep I felt Eliana move. The sun coming through the windows was bothering her eyes. As she turned she positioned herself so that she could lay on my chest. She looked up to see I was still awake.

"Apollo?"

"Yes, my love."

"You aren't sleeping?"

"I got a few hours. Don't worry."

"You'll be here when I wake up right?"

"I'll be here." I said kissing her temple. "Go back to sleep, El."

Watching her fall back to sleep I tried not to move. Wrapping her arm around my torso, she held me close to make sure I wasn't going anywhere. I knew I'd never get a full night of sleep ever again because it was impossible closing my eyes when I had Eliana right next to me. I'll never forgive myself for leaving her, but I had forever to try and make it up to her. I'd start tomorrow by making sure I was right by her side when she woke up.

Fuck, I'm lucky

Epilogue

Six months later

Eliana

As Alex drove me home I made a mental note of all the things I had to do tomorrow. I was struggling to balance representing my clients and keeping the safe house project up and running. I knew soon I'd need someone to help coordinate with families, and get them to a more permanent location, but I hadn't found anybody I trusted enough. I had given my all to keeping my firm alive, and I had serious control issues. Jaqueline was an amazing partner to have, but she had clients of her own to worry about.

My mind ran at a thousand miles a minute while Alex and I waited in traffic. Most nights I let Alex pick where we go for dinner, but tonight all I wanted was to get home. Apollo was busy with meetings this week which meant I got the house all to myself. I loved sharing a house with him, but that doesn't mean I don't enjoy a girl's night every once in a while.

Giving up on making a plan for tomorrow I leaned my head back and closed my eyes for a few minutes. I was interrupted by Alex's phone.

"Hello." He answered. "Yes Sir, she's here in the car with me now. No Sir, we're about fifteen minutes out."

Opening one eye I saw Alex looking back at me through the mirror.

"I could, but you should really ask Mrs. Costa first, Sir. I know it's your car- yes, I know I work for you- but she's... of course, here she is."

Alex held his phone out to me, shaking it slightly. Every second I didn't take the phone Alex grew more and more nervous. I sat up and grabbed the phone.

"Apollo." I answered.

"Your phone sent me to voicemail."

"I turned it off when I left work. I was trying to unplug and enjoy my evening. I knew if you needed me you'd find a way to get a hold of me."

"You need two phones." He said, "One for work and your family, and one for when I need to reach you and you've gone into hiding."

"Who says I wasn't also trying to hide from you Apollo?" I teased.

"Hilarious, my love." He replied, less than amused.

"I'm sure you're not calling for fun, otherwise you wouldn't have bothered Alex. What's wrong?" I asked.

"Nothing's wrong, but what are the odds you could take a few days off of work?"

"When?"

"Right now? I was hoping Alex would take you to the plane instead of taking you home."

"You know how busy I am this week, Apollo. I have a dozen meetings tomorrow alone."

"I know, but it would mean a lot to me if you came to Italy with me." He said.

"Why Italy?"

"There's something I'd like to show you."

"I don't know-"

"Please Eliana? I'll explain everything when I see you, I promise."

All I could hear was static as Apollo waited to hear if I'd agree to go with him. I know it would be hard leaving for a few days, but this could be exactly what I needed to get over my control issues. It's time I start trusting my own employees to do what I hired them to do.

"Fine." I said.

"I knew you'd say yes. You'd miss me too much if you didn't come with." He said. "Tell Alex to meet us at Gate C, and don't worry about having nothing packed. I'll get you whatever you need when we land."

I hung up the phone and handed it back to Alex.

"Alex, we're going to the airport, Gate C."

Alex looked back at me, "But I thought we were having a girl's night tonight?"

"I know, but Apollo says it's important. Girl's night will have to wait."

Alex frowned and turned left at the next light. Apollo was waiting by his car when we pulled up. When he saw us, he grabbed a small bag from the trunk of his SUV and waited for me by the stairs. I grabbed my work bag and turned to Alex.

"If you drink any of the wine I bought before I get back I'll kill you." I told him.

I think I saw a small smile from Alex as he walked back to his side of the car.

Giving me a kiss on the cheek Apollo grabbed my bag and waited for me to walk up the plane stairs. Apollo asked the pilot to take off before I had even found my seat. We were moving before my seatbelt was fully clicked into place. As soon as we could walk around I stood up from my seat.

"Wake me up when we land." I told Apollo, walking to the bedroom.

I was fine not getting a girl's night, but I still needed a few hours to catch up on sleep.

As soon as we landed, Apollo woke me up and walked with me to the car. As he drove I could tell his mind was somewhere else. I didn't push for answers, and instead enjoyed the ride. Apollo left the city and drove us down the coast. I thought maybe we were going to visit Rio, but after a few unfamiliar turns I could tell we were heading in a different direction.

All that could be seen for miles were small farm houses, surrounded by acres of land and sheep. I can't remember ever visiting this place when we would come for family vacations. Apollo turned left into a driveway that seemed to go on forever. After almost a mile he pulled up to a modern ranch. Apollo drove right up to the front of the house and turned the car off.

Apollo looked out the window for a few seconds, and then turned to face me.

"I met with Leonardo today." He said.

There was only one reason Leonardo would need to meet with Apollo.

"Did your father-"

"He's done. He let Leonardo know he's ready to officially retire, and hand the business over to me."

"And?" I asked.

"And Leonardo gave me his blessing. He said there's no one else he wants to run the Costa family."

"That means..."

"It's all ours." He said.

"Holy Shit."

"I know." He said, grabbing my hand. "Are you ready for this?"

"Does it even matter if I'm not ready for this?" I asked.

"No, it doesn't. When we get back to the States Leonardo plans on letting the other families know I'll be taking over as Don. I know it's selfish, but I wanted one more trip just the two of us before everything changes."

I'd be lying if I said I was surprised. Retirement was all Cristiano could talk about. After the wedding Apollo was the one making the big decisions. Cristiano was only a figure at meetings.

"Are you ready for this?" I asked.

"I was hoping Dad would hold on for a little bit longer, but I know he's tired. I can't ask him to stay when I know all that he's been through." He said.

"How long until we have to go back?"

"A few days." He answered.

"Well, we don't have any time to waste." I said, opening the car door, and stepping onto the gravel.

Apollo followed after me and took my hand. He tried walking up to the front door, but something was holding him back.

"What's wrong?" I asked.

"I don't know if I can go in."

"Why not?"

"Because- because I haven't been back since-"

"Since the accident." I said, finishing his sentence for him.

"As soon as I could walk I ran away and never looked back. I promised myself I'd come back when I took care of Michael and Gio, but even then, I couldn't do it."

Wrapping a hand around Apollo's arm I took a small step forward.

"After everything that's happened it felt wrong, like I didn't deserve it." He said.

"Like you didn't deserve what, Apollo?"

"To come home."

Finding out Apollo was still struggling to make peace with everything that happened broke my heart. How could he still feel that way after everything he's been through? Why does he continue to blame himself for running away after his accident? He did what anyone would have done. He didn't run away. Apollo wouldn't have made it out of Italy alive if he didn't leave when he did. Gio would have made sure of that.

"Apollo, you need to stop blaming yourself for leaving. It was the right thing to do at the time. You were barely healed from the accident, and you didn't have nearly enough resources in Italy. It wasn't safe for you here."

"I know." He said.

"But?"

"But it's still hard coming back after all this time. There was a time when I didn't think I'd ever be able to come back."

"Hey, look at me." I said, standing in front of Apollo. "After everything we've been through you made it back. You won Apollo. Gio and Michael, they're gone, but you're still here. The only thing that matters now is that you're back. The only reason we're standing here today is because you were smart enough to leave when you did. I'll stand here all day with you if that's what you need, but don't for a second think you don't deserve to be back here."

Standing next to him one more time, I grabbed his hand. "Take as long as you need Apollo."

I went to give Apollo a little bit of space, but he squeezed my hand. Staying exactly where I was I waited for Apollo. After a few minutes, he took a few steps towards the front door. Following along beside him I watched him enter the pin and swing the door wide open. Taking a deep breath, Apollo stepped into the house. A few hallway lights flickered on as we stepped into the main living room.

From where I was standing it looked like the house of a man who tried to pack his whole life up in a hurry. Photos we left turned over on shelves, clothes were thrown on the floor, and there was a scattering of paperwork on the dining room table. I can't begin to imagine how this must feel for Apollo. Not wanting Apollo to see me and think I was upset I started to pick up the mess in the living room.

"What are you doing?" He asked.

"Well, we're only here for a few days. The faster we clean up, the faster we can start enjoying our little getaway. Why don't you go check on the kitchen, and I'll take care of things in here."

Apollo tried to say something, but nothing came out. Giving me a small nod Apollo walked towards the kitchen. Halfway down the hallway Apollo turned around, and leaned back into the living room.

"El..." He said.

"Yeah?"

"Thank you."

After our first day in Italy Apollo finally started to relax. The regret he felt faded, and he was actually starting to enjoy the trip. I found myself enjoying Apollo's house a little too much. I was afraid I wouldn't want to leave in a few days. It was so peaceful here. There weren't any neighbors for miles, and thanks to Apollo hiding my phone there was no one bothering me. I hadn't felt this caught up on sleep in years. If it were up to me I'd never leave Apollo's bed, but I was driving Apollo crazy. I always knew it was time to wake up when I heard music coming from the kitchen. That was Apollo's not so subtle way of telling me breakfast was ready, and if I didn't get there soon he'd finish all the coffee.

Apollo was dressed and reading a newspaper when I came into the kitchen. His coffee cup was already empty, but like always he would wait for me to get my first cup in before pouring his second. I'm not sure why that became a habit of his, but I didn't mind it.

Grabbing an orange, I sat on Apollo's lap and wrapped my arms around him. He dropped his newspaper and took my orange from me. While I left soft kisses along his jaw Apollo started to slowly peel the orange.

"Good morning."

"Morning." I mumbled.

"Did you sleep okay?"

"Mhmm." I answered, stuffing a few orange slices in my mouth. "Did I sleep in too late, or is there still a chance to make it to the farmers market?"

"If we leave right now we might make it." He said.

"Then what are we waiting for?" I asked. "There's nothing left in the fridge for dinner tonight."

"Go get dressed and I'll clean up breakfast." Apollo said, lifting me off his lap.

Taking the orange from Apollo, and my coffee from the table I walked back to Apollo's room to change. Slipping on a dress Apollo bought for me our first night here, I tried to get ready as fast as I could.

"El?"

"In here." I said from the bathroom.

"I can't find the keys."

"You threw them in the fruit bowl last night."

"Why?"

"You said you like to leave them there so you don't forget where they are the next morning." I laughed.

"Brilliant." He said, walking back to the kitchen.

I was close behind him, grabbing a hat from the closet before meeting him outside.

Apollo drove as fast as he could through the back roads, and butterfly hills. I held onto my hat making sure not to lose it before we made it into town. A few vendors were closing up their shops, but the majority of the booths were still open. Apollo led me down the cobble-stone street as we tried to decide what to have for dinner.

I grabbed a few lemons, and summer squash while Apollo grabbed a few tomatoes. As soon as I was sure Apollo wasn't looking I ran to the bakery across the street. It was almost noon, and they would be sold out of almost everything by now. I'd be lucky if I got a few fruit pastries.

I was watching Apollo through the store window when he turned around and found me gone. Before I could even worry that he'd be afraid he lost me he looked right at me through the window. There wasn't a doubt in his mind where I'd run off to.

Slowly shaking his head, I watched Apollo cross the street.

"You promised not to go without me this time." He complained, walking into the bakery.

"It was an emergency, Apollo. It's past noon."

"Are there any other emergencies I should know about before I get back to shopping?" He asked.

"This was the last one."

"Unbelievable." He muttered under his breath. "You think you know someone..."

After sneaking a few treats, I went searching for Apollo. I found him looking at wine.

"That bottle right there is the reason you couldn't find your keys this morning. Do you really think we need another one?"

"Only the best for dinner tonight, my love. It's our last night here."

"Oh." I replied. I knew we couldn't stay here forever, but I was surprised to hear we'd be leaving so soon.

"We're leaving tomorrow?" I asked.

"Leonardo plans to make his announcement the day after. I wish we had more time, but we don't."

"One bottle won't be enough then. Grab two." I said, walking over to Apollo.

"I think you're right." He smiled.

For an hour longer, I followed behind Apollo as he shopped and chatted with the locals. He looked happy here. It wasn't fair we had to leave. I'd give everything up to move here with Apollo, but I knew that was just a dream. Sooner or later we had to get back to our lives in America. Tomorrow everyone would know Apollo was taking over for his dad, and everything would be different. Apollo and I were lucky enough to enjoy these last few days together in Italy, alone.

Tomorrow everything changes, but one constant remains. No matter what happens, Apollo and I have each other.

Printed in Great Britain
by Amazon

28646447R00269